THE MANY DAUGHTERS
OF AFONG MOY

THE MANY DAUGHTERS OF AFONG MOY

A Novel

JAMIE FORD

THORNDIKE PRESS
A part of Gale, a Cengage Company

Copyright © 2022 by Jamie Ford.
Thorndike Press, a part of Gale, a Cengage Company.

ALL RIGHTS RESERVED
This book is a work of fiction. Any references to historical events, real people, or real places are used fictitiously. Other names, characters, places, and events are products of the author's imagination, and any resemblance to actual events or places or persons, living or dead, is entirely coincidental.
Thorndike Press® Large Print Core.
The text of this Large Print edition is unabridged.
Other aspects of the book may vary from the original edition.
Set in 16 pt. Plantin.

LIBRARY OF CONGRESS CIP DATA ON FILE.
CATALOGUING IN PUBLICATION FOR THIS BOOK
IS AVAILABLE FROM THE LIBRARY OF CONGRESS.

ISBN-13: 978-1-4328-9760-4 (hardcover alk. paper)

Published in 2022 by arrangement with Atria Books, a Division of Simon & Schuster, Inc.

Printed in Mexico
Print Number: 01   Print Year: 2022

*This book is for anyone
with a complicated origin story.
I feel you.*

"We all have some experience of a feeling, of what we are saying and doing having been said and done before, in a remote time — of our having been surrounded, dim ages ago, by the same faces, objects, and circumstances."

— CHARLES DICKENS

"As far back as I can remember I have unconsciously referred to the experiences of a previous state of existence."

— HENRY DAVID THOREAU

"I saw that."

— KARMA

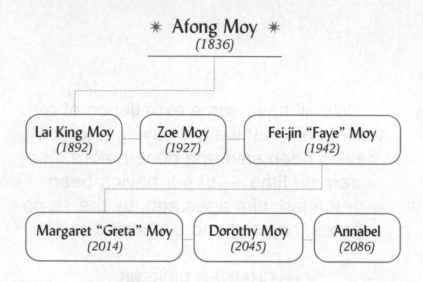

* Afong Moy *
(1836)

Lai King Moy
(1892)

Zoe Moy
(1927)

Fei-jin "Faye" Moy
(1942)

Margaret "Greta" Moy
(2014)

Dorothy Moy
(2045)

Annabel
(2086)

AUTHOR'S NOTE

My first concert was Van Halen in 1984
(yes, I'm of a certain vintage). I wedged my
scrawny fifteen-year-old self through the
tube-topped crowd, all the way to the bar-
ricade. Packed in like a sardine, I watched
David Lee Roth in leopard-print spandex
toss his bleached mane all over the stage of
the Seattle Center Coliseum. The evening
was hot, sweaty, redolent of weed, and so
loud that some days I swear my ears are still
ringing from "Ain't Talkin' 'bout Love."

So, imagine my surprise when decades later
my twelve-year-old son, Taylor, asked,
"Have you ever heard of this band called
Van Halen?" I'd never played any classic
rock for him (we listened to a lot of Radio
Disney in those days) and he somehow
bumped into the quartet on YouTube and
declared them *the best band ever.*

At least until he discovered Genesis. Not

the chapter in the Old Testament, but the prog-rock group fronted by Peter Gabriel and later Phil Collins. Genesis was another band I was into as a kid and within weeks my son anointed *this* group *the best band ever.*

At the time, I thought this was a strange and humorous parent/child coincidence. But years later, while reading about transgenerational epigenetic inheritance, I wondered if something else was going on. Something in the genes — or rather a lot of somethings — creating a genetic proclivity for a certain kind of jam. I mean, he inherited my hairline and my overbite, why not my questionable taste in music?

Epigenetics combined with the philosophical idea of Determinism made me wonder if free will is — if not an illusion — a bit of a mirage. That, in addition to the environment we grow up in, the contour and texture of our lives are shaped — in part — by some form of genetic predetermination.

One way to see this is with identical twins since they have identical genomes. Take the uncanny case of the Jim Twins. In 1940, they were separated at birth and put up for adoption, each finding new homes three weeks later. It would be nearly four decades before the brothers crossed paths and discovered some startling similarities. Both had a dog named Toy, both enjoyed woodworking, both married women named Linda, divorced, and then both married women named Betty. Both had sons, named James Alan and James Allan. Both were plagued with migraines. Both worked in law enforcement. Both vacationed on the same Florida beach. The list goes on . . .

Granted, not all identical twins have patterns of behavioral similarity, but when they do, it seems preternatural.

You see where I'm going with this?

The idea of epigenetic inheritance has long been embraced in many communities. Native Americans have talked about living with generational trauma for as long as I can remember and a hotly debated study of Holocaust survivors appears to show a higher percentage of PTSDs, depression, and anxiety in their children and grandchildren.

But the most captivating example was a study of laboratory mice that were exposed to a cherry blossom fragrance as the floor of their cage was electrified. (I'm so sorry, mice.) The mice were quickly conditioned to panic whenever they smelled that scent. But generations later, the descendants of those mice would have the same fear reaction to that smell. Even though they had never experienced that pain and discomfort in their own lifetimes.

They had inherited that trauma.

Take a moment and think about your own family, their joys and calamities. Do you see similarities? Do you see patterns of repetition? Rhythms of good and bad decision making? Cycles of struggle and triumph?

For purposes of fiction, I based this novel around an iconic woman who made front-page headlines in nearly every newspaper in the country, only to later disappear. I wanted to give her descendants, and an epigenetic legacy as broad and tragic as her own.

In 1834 that woman set her tiny, bound foot upon the dirty streets of New York City. She was — whether she wanted to be or not — the first Chinese woman to come to America. Identified in the press as Julia Foochee

Ching-Chang-king, Miss Ching-Chang-foo, and Miss Keo-O-Kwang King, she would eventually go by the name Afong Moy. Though most simply referred to her as *The Chinese Lady*.

Her early life in China is undocumented, but her middle years are a combination of fame and exploitation. Patrons paid fifty cents each to watch her perform in New York, Philadelphia, Richmond, Charleston, New Orleans, and Boston, and while on tour in Washington, DC, she traveled to the White House at the behest of President Andrew Jackson. Racehorses were named after her. Men wrote poems about her. The public was caught up in speculation about her prospects for marriage.

Her later years, however, involve P. T. Barnum, being discarded in favor of another, younger, Chinese performer, and eventually being relegated to a poorhouse in New Jersey, forever hobbled by her bound feet. In 1850, she vanished from the headlines forever and existed only in rumor: that she was touring Europe, that she finally returned home to China, that she had died on the street, homeless and alone.

When it comes to epigenetics, the transmission of trauma makes headlines because its manifest symptoms are more easily observed and reported. But the hopeless romantic in me couldn't help but wonder if other things are passed down genetically, like stratums of empathy, levels of limerence, and even the capacity (or incapacity) for love.

The more you think about it, if the genetic circuitry of trauma is intertwined with the genetic circuitry of wellness, together they form an intergenerational feedback loop. Where a parent's output is used as input for a child's future behavior. And while there is the latent possibility of cycles repeating themselves, if we understand who and where we came from, genetic destinies can be altered, hopefully for the better.

Or to put it in classic rock terms. If Van Halen's albums were generations, the first generation's songs were *"Ain't Talkin' 'bout Love,"* but six or seven generations later it was all "When It's Love," "Why Can't This Be Love," and "Love Walks In."

Don't get me started on "Jamie's Cryin'."

Act I

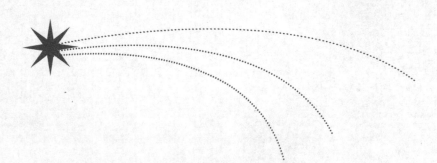

1
FAYE

(1942)

Faye Moy signed a contract stating that she would never marry. That's what the American Volunteer Group had required of all female recruits. Though as she sat in the bar of the Kunming Tennis Club, Faye thought that perhaps there should have been an exception made for older nurses. Not that she had any immediate prospects among the thirty young officers who made up the Flying Tigers. It was just that a notarized statement of marital exclusion seemed to hammer home the fact that she'd never been in love. She'd come close once, back in her village near Canton, amid the wilted lilies of her youth. Since then she'd felt many things for many people, but always more yearning than devotion, more appreciation than passion. There had even been an awkwardly arranged marriage proposal a lifetime ago, at the Tou Tou Koi

17

restaurant, where a dashing young man got down on one knee, with a ring, and too much pomade in his hair.

Wasted. That's what her father said when she turned him down. "Feijin? Why do you have to be this way? No one likes a stubborn girl."

She'd tried not to roll her eyes. "Why can't you call me Faye like everyone else?"

"Because I'm not everyone else. Look at you. You're not getting any younger. You should be happy someone still wants you at your age."

She'd been twenty-seven.

But as much as Faye had wanted to share her life with someone, to watch a sunset in the arms of somebody who wouldn't leave before sunrise, even then she knew that want was not the same as need. She'd refused to settle for convenience, or to abet her aching loneliness. She went to Lingnan University instead. She told herself that if she stopped looking, eventually the right person would come along.

That was decades ago.

Now she felt like the jigsaw puzzle of her life had long been completed, the picture looked whole, but there was one piece missing.

That's my heart, Faye thought, something

extra, unnecessary.

Now well into her fifties, Faye still couldn't forget how in nursing school, Chinese mothers used to point at her as she walked down the street in the evening. They'd turn to their daughters and say, "Don't be disobedient or you'll end up like her," or "That's what happens when you're too proud — too foolish. No one wants you." Faye would pretend she didn't hear. Then she'd run home and curl up in bed, crying herself to sleep. In the morning, she'd light a Chesterfield and stare at the tobacco-stained ceiling, aching inside, as tendrils of smoke drifted upward like unanswered prayers.

To her parents and those mothers on the street, Faye was *mei fan neoi zi.* Though she didn't feel like an old maid. Even after she arrived in Kunming, where she was twice the age of the American nurses who followed. On the bustling streets of Kunming, Faye was treated differently. Perhaps because she'd served longer and now hardly noticed the suffocating humidity of typhoon season. Or because she didn't scream when field rats crawled their way into her dresser and chewed the buttons off her clothing. Conceivably it was because she was fluent in English thanks to Lai King, her

American-born mother, and could quote poetry by Li Bai as well as Gertrude Stein and Oscar Wilde, yet also spend an entire afternoon playing canasta and whist while drinking tiger balms and not let the rum cocktails make her sick for days. Faye learned early on to avoid not only the whiskey the natives made, but especially the gin concocted by Jesuit missionaries.

"You want another?" Faye shook her glass tumbler.

Lois, the latest nursing recruit, a comely blonde from Topeka, looked back, bleary eyed. "Am I supposed to say yes? What is this, some kind of initiation?"

Faye noticed that Lois was slurring her words, so she peered over the recruit's shoulder and made eye contact with the bartender. Faye shook her head, almost imperceptibly so Lois wouldn't catch on, then nodded as the barkeep put his bottle away.

"I don't know why everyone around here drinks so much," Lois said, waving broadly at everyone in the club. "And why do they have to play such sad music?"

Faye listened to the jukebox as Frank Sinatra sang "I'll Never Smile Again." She thought about the flashes of light on the horizon each night, the peals of thunder.

Followed by the rumble of pony carts on cobbled streets in the morning and the wailing of widows as refugees flooded through the city's arched gates.

"It comes with the territory," Faye said as she worried about her parents, whom she hadn't heard from in two years.

She finished her drink, leaving only a mint leaf.

The mountains will protect us, Faye had been told when she first arrived, even after Shanghai, Nanking, and Hankow fell. Then word spread that the defenses around Chunking had collapsed and the wind began carrying the malodorous smell she'd learned to recognize as the fetor of burning bodies. Japanese bombers killed thousands of civilians in last week's raids, along with six American pilots. President Roosevelt, who had sent planes and men, publicly denied US involvement in the war between China and Japan. But after Pearl Harbor there was no need for the pretense, and now everyone in Kunming knew who the Americans were.

"I can't believe they made all the nurses swear we'd never marry," Lois said as an aviator walked by with eyes like Gary Cooper and a smile like Jin Yan.

Faye shook her head, grumbling, "They

21

should have made the men swear an oath as well." Faye felt invisible compared to Lois, who was so young and fetching and her periwinkle blouse so tight its buttons seemed ready to burst.

"Why would you want that? It would lessen our chances," Lois said. "But I guess at your age you could probably care less that the AVG is run like a seventh-grade church dance — after all, you must be close to retirement."

Faye cringed inside. She wished she'd cut Lois off two drinks ago.

"But for the rest of us girls, we're still in the game," Lois yammered. "You're so lucky. I always wondered what it would be like to live alone. To be able to choose how to spend my evenings and my days."

"I thought you had a boyfriend back home in . . . Kansas?" Faye asked.

Lois shrugged. "What if I do?"

Faye tilted her head and raised an eyebrow.

"Oh, please, don't Mother Hen me," Lois laughed. "We could all die over here at any moment. From bombs or malaria or sheer boredom."

Faye understood that all too well. Orders arrived like the tropical rains along the Burma Road — all at once, or not at all.

When the downpour of wounded came, the nurses gave up wearing white shoes because they were standing in so much blood. Those long days were followed by an idle stew of melancholy, lassitude, and homesickness.

Lois kept talking. "If I'd wanted to settle down I wouldn't have traveled halfway around the world to take this job. It's not paradise, but it's more exciting than watching the tumbleweed races back home. Besides, you only get one life, you know?"

Faye remembered feeling just as eager, years ago. Restless and weary of her parents' disappointment, she left her hospital job and sailed from Canton to Rangoon aboard the *Jagersfontein,* an ocean liner with a swimming pool and an orchestra. That's where she met and was hired by Dr. Gentry, a US army flight surgeon who was traveling with a group of pilots and aircraft mechanics. All of them with fake IDs in case they were stopped by the Japanese. Faye had been excited, but also nervous to join the Americans, especially when she heard the Japanese had issued an order to kill all Chinese doctors and nurses caught fleeing the occupied cities. Once she stepped off the ship, however, she felt at ease, as though the broken compass of her heart was now working. She traveled with Dr. Gentry's team on the Burma Road over the Himalayas to Yunnan Province. There her magnetic north led her on muddy roads, past water buffalo and roadside statues of the Buddha, toward something unknown, but oddly hopeful. Here in Kunming she almost felt complete, even as the world around her was on fire, falling to pieces.

"I thought you were gonna buy me another drink?" Lois said.

Faye cocked her head, eyes toward the ceiling.

"Fine," Lois said. "I'll go get one myself. Or maybe one of these handsome young fellas will come to my rescue . . ."

"Wait." Faye grabbed Lois's arm. "Do you hear that?"

"I don't hear a thing."

Faye watched as the bartender quickly unplugged the jukebox, which elicited a round of groans and complaints from drunken patrons. Their protests diminished, however, as one by one they heard the sound of a distant air raid siren.

"Oh God, not again." Lois knelt down, nearly tipping the table over in the process.

As pilots and crewmen began running for the door, Faye listened for the sound of explosions. Or the heavy thud of passive bombs filled with yellow wax and maggots designed to spread cholera. Instead, she heard the wail change into a long blaring tone.

"Let's go! Let's go!" Faye urged Lois, pulling her up and toward the exit. "That's the all clear. It means we're safe, but a plane is inbound."

Outside the club and into the street, villagers and merchants, beggars and monks all searched the late afternoon sky. Faye looked as well, hearing the all-too-familiar roar and sputter of a damaged P-40 engine — one of theirs. Then a shark-nosed fighter-plane sailed overhead, leaving a contrail of black oil smoke in its wake. The underbelly was painted sky blue with white stars, the colors of Nationalist China, but Faye knew the man trying to land the burning plane would be an American.

She sprinted in the direction of the new airstrip, a large clearing of land that used to be a sugarcane field, which sat beneath a slope of rolling hills covered in acacia trees. Lois stumbled behind, pausing and muttering as she removed her high heels.

As Faye ran she didn't feel her age or the alcohol, she felt needed.

When she arrived at the edge of the airstrip, out of breath, the smoking plane had swung around, dropped its landing gear, and was rapidly descending on an open runway.

Lois caught up and swayed next to her as a crowd of mechanics and pilots gathered, some praying, some cursing. Faye had seen this before, damaged planes making emergency landings anywhere they could, clipping treetops or crashing into nearby hangars. The last airman to attempt an emergency landing at Kunming died for his efforts, his body burned beyond recognition.

Faye took Lois's hand as the pilot shut off the engine on descent.

"It's going to be okay," Faye told Lois. Her words felt like a wish as the nose of the aircraft pitched upward to slow its silent approach. She watched the smoking plane glide above the ground for a breathless moment before its landing gear kissed the surface of the runway. The men around her erupted into cheers.

The plane was still smoking and the front of the fuselage was black with soot, the cockpit a web of broken glass. There were so many bullet holes, Faye wondered how the pilot had managed to survive, let alone land. When he threw back the canopy she saw his face, covered in blood. The young pilot climbed out, his flight suit slick with oil, and his wet boots squished on the runway as he limped toward them. Faye felt the crowd surge forward. She became a rock in a stream of people flowing past her, everyone laughing, cheering, until the cockpit burst into flames. The plane exploded, sending a billowing cloud of debris into the air that made a tinkling sound as hot metal rained down around them. The wounded pilot looked at her, dazed, as .30- and .50-caliber rounds from the plane's mounted guns began cooking off in the flames, shooting in all directions. The crowd dispersed in a frenzy, shouting, ducking, running. Faye heard the chirping sound of bullets piercing the air. She froze as the young man waved at her amid the mayhem, staggering in her direction. Faye could see his bloody, oil-soaked flight suit, the flammable grime that blackened his hands. She could smell the petroleum as he approached and could feel the heat of the burning wreckage. She watched in horror as the pilot tucked a crumpled cigarette into the corner of his mouth and fished out a Zippo lighter. Faye dashed toward the wounded stranger as Lois called her name, as men screamed, "Get down!"

She heard the pilot striking his lighter again and again and again, until a curl of fire flickered on the breeze, a wagging finger, orange and blue. Faye snatched his wrist and blew out the flame as the cigarette dangled from the pilot's mouth. His face lit up with a quivering smile as their eyes met. He looked like he was trying to fight through the pain, unsteady, his mouth moving as though he were about to speak.

Then he collapsed in her arms.

Faye felt the weight of his body, the warmth of his blood, the stickiness of oil on her skin as she held on tight, yelling for a stretcher.

For a nurse, Faye surprisingly hated the smell of ether. But Lois, who was still learning, seemed to relish the sickly sweet aroma. Faye caught a glimpse of the recruit's eyes and knew she was grinning from ear to ear beneath her surgical mask. Faye tried to remember if she was ever that enthusiastic during her own training. If she had been, seeing the cost of war, paid in the currency of young bodies, had tempered her zeal.

"That was quite a thing you did out there, Miss Moy," Dr. Gentry said, without looking up from the pilot's abdomen that had been cut open. Lois gently pulled back folds of muscle and soft tissue with a retractor while Faye handed the doctor a pair of forceps. "I heard all about it. You saved this man's life."

Faye always felt uncomfortable whenever someone called her *miss*, though it was only slightly less awkward than being called Mrs. Moy, leaving her to explain that she was unmarried. She watched as Dr. Gentry used the forceps to retrieve another bullet fragment from the man's gut. The doctor dropped it into a tin pan, pinging as it joined a growing collection of jagged metal.

"It was nothing," Faye said with a shrug. "You're the one saving his life, Doctor."

"She's being overly modest," Lois said. "There were bullets flying everywhere. You should have seen it, doc. We're all running and screaming, diving for cover. And here he comes, walking straight toward her, and she meets him halfway."

"I had my uniform on. He was in shock and saw a nurse."

"Okay, so he was limping like a dead man on his feet," Lois said. "But you — you just went right out there, calm as can be. What were you thinking?"

Faye paused. She remembered the blood that ran down the pilot's face. How he felt in her arms. That she didn't feel panicked or scared. "I wasn't thinking."

She handed the doctor a scalpel.

"Well, everyone's been talking," Dr. Gentry said as he kept working, searching for more fragments. "You saved this young man, giving me a chance to try to undo all the trouble he got himself into. Now he just has to make it through post-op. Either way, after what you did out there, I think it's only right that I recommend you for the Distinguished Service Medal. It's the best I can do for a civilian contractor. You deserve it. You did what needed to be done when everyone else ran. Just don't go rushing toward the bullets anymore. I need you here, on your feet, not on my table."

Faye nodded. She looked down at the pilot and realized she was holding his hand, which felt cold. The doctor had given him curare.

Faye wondered why the pilot landed here in Kunming. Someone figured out the call sign on what was left of his plane and looked him up. His name was John Garland and he'd flown out of Toungee, six hundred miles away. His squadron had completed a pursuit mission, but he'd been shot up badly. There were other airstrips readily available to make an emergency landing, but he found his way to Kunming. Maybe he couldn't find those other places. Or maybe he was delirious from the pain.

Whatever the reason, he was here. Even though he was unconscious, Faye couldn't help but brush aside a spit curl of hair from his brow with a surgical sponge.

Then Dr. Gentry dropped his forceps and scalpel in a pan with a clang and began wiping off his soaked gloves. "Let's close him up."

The sun was down and Faye sat in an airplane hangar that once a week was converted into a theater outfitted with charcoal heaters and a projector. There, members of the AVG gathered to watch one of three movies. Tonight's feature was *The Ghost Breakers.* With only three movies to choose from, everyone had seen it at least a dozen times. Some of the men had even memorized the words and would stand up front, pantomiming everything happening on-screen. Bob Hope and Paulette Goddard usually helped on nights like this, but Faye didn't feel like laughing.

Since her arrival she'd treated scores of young pilots and soldiers as well as locals — men, women, and children — some with severe burns, others riddled with bullets and shrapnel. She'd seen so much carnage, she simply regarded death as a byproduct of war. It was unavoidable and with it the feel-

31

ing of being perpetually detached.

That's how you keep from going mad, Faye thought as she tried to focus on the movie. *You simply can't let yourself care too much.*

"There you are," Lois whispered as she took an empty seat next to Faye and offered to share her popcorn, which was slightly burned from being cooked in a small coal-fired cannon that local street vendors used.

Faye politely declined. "How's the new pilot doing?"

"Hard to tell," Lois whispered. "Doc says he might be out for a day or two. Or he could come around as soon as the anesthesia wears off. Who knows?"

"Who's reading to him tonight?" As the senior nurse on staff, Faye encouraged the younger caregivers to read to the men in recovery. She believed that bedridden pilots needed the type of escape that could be found only in the latest novels by F. Scott Fitzgerald, Ernest Hemingway, or Agatha Christie that were occasionally included in Red Cross care packages. But Faye also added Chinese novels like *The Family* by Ba Jin for injured locals, as well as American classics by Charles Dickens and books of poetry, in translation — whatever she could find.

"No one," Lois said, blinking. "He's

sound asleep."

"We read to them anyway."

"Why?" Lois asked.

"Because it's comforting. Sometimes the men have nightmares, and if they stir, I don't want them waking up alone in such an unfamiliar place."

"But . . . it's movie night," Lois argued as she shoved a fistful of popcorn into her mouth, talking as she chewed. "Nurses need care too, you know. We don't even know if he's going to make it."

That's precisely why we do it, Faye thought as she stood up and walked out. Her silhouette graced the movie screen like a ghost with an hourglass figure, much to the delight of the men, who whistled and catcalled. Faye left Lois to be the object of their attention and walked back to the monastery that had been converted into a field hospital, when the one in the center of Kunming ran out of room. She found her way to the sanctuary, now crammed with twenty beds, occupied by a mix of Chinese officers, Americans, and civilians. She saw a handful of American nurses sitting bedside, quietly reading to their patients. Some read novels, some read comic books, while others read old newspapers from the United States with articles about scrap metal drives, the Yankees losing the World Series, and a movie called *Casablanca.*

Faye stopped at a vestibule that she had converted to a small library and pulled out a thick, leather-bound volume of poetry. She found John Garland unconscious, propped up slightly, the covers pulled across his chest, arms exposed. An IV bottle dangled from a tall wooden post, dripping fluids into a long rubber tube.

Faye sat down next to him. "You don't mind a little Edgar Allan Poe, do you?" She waited for a response and then said, "No? Okay, then we are in agreement, John Garland. Just make yourself comfortable. I'm Faye. We met out there on the runway, and as your nurse I must advise you that smoking is very bad for your health."

Faye was accustomed to the swagger of the cocksure American pilots, young and so eager to prove themselves. The braggadocio required to land that damaged plane, to walk away from the wreckage, bleeding. At twice the age of most of the pilots, she generally regarded the men as mischievous little brothers. Her feelings for them were always a mixture of admiration and annoyance. But there was something different about this one, a familiar feeling, like *Ci cang soeng sik* — waking from a dream —

34

though the Chinese version of déjà vu generally referred to two people who have met before.

As she opened the book, Faye thought she saw his eyes flutter.

She stared at the unconscious pilot, wondering if his movement was a figment of her imagination. She touched his cheek, the cleft of his chin, his chest, his arm. Then she opened the book in her lap, flipping through the pages, adjusting to the language. She began with "Eldorado," the tale of a gallant knight. She looked over at John Garland then moved on to "Spectacles," a comedy about love at first sight. Then she settled on "A Dream Within a Dream," a poem about the passage of time.

She read each page carefully, pausing, wondering, letting the words fill the air.

Lastly, she read the classic "Annabel Lee."

She held his hand as she read the poem of love and loss and a kingdom by the sea. She looked over at him, speaking the words from memory, first in Chinese and then in English. "But we loved with a love that was more than love . . ."

His hand squeezed hers, so tight she thought her fingers might break. Her pulse raced as his body jerked, racked with violent seizures that shook the army bed and brought the IV bottle crashing to the floor, shards of glass fanning out like rice thrown at a wedding. She watched his lips turn purple, then all color drained from his face and she knew he'd stopped breathing. Faye shouted for a doctor and tore her hands away from his grip. She tried to hold him down, keeping the spasms from ripping open his sutures, but she felt spreading warmth across his torso and knew that he was bleeding out. Another nurse hurried over to assist by holding his legs, keeping them from thrashing about while an orderly ran for help. Patients who were awake began shouting, screaming. As Faye applied pressure to the wound, she heard herself pleading, "Don't you do this, John Garland. Don't you dare leave." Then she loosened her grip as his whole body relaxed. As a long gurgling breath escaped his lips, his body seemed to deflate. His eyes opened, staring up at Faye, stormy pools of blue and gray.

An hour later, Faye took it upon herself to make the bed where the American had died in her arms. She changed the sheets and tucked in a freshly laundered wool blanket that smelled of lye. The broken glass had been swept, the old book returned to its place on a shelf. The only evidence of his

36

death was the lingering redness beneath her eyes from when she'd walked outside, sat on the stone steps, and broken down sobbing. Now she wondered why she cared so much and what she might have done differently.

"I'm still going to recommend you for that citation," Dr. Gentry said when he left the hospital and found her there. "Believe me, you earned it."

Faye didn't feel like she'd done anything special. She'd saved him only to watch him die hours later. Hardly an act that was medal-worthy. *Why am I even here?* She rubbed her forehead. *I should be back in Canton looking for my parents.*

When she walked back inside, Lois found her and offered a small cigar box. "I gathered up what little he had, his ID, a few personal effects."

Faye nodded solemnly and took the container with both hands.

Lois opened her mouth as though she were about to say something, then fell silent. She gave Faye a long hug and then left her alone.

Sitting on the nearest empty bed, Faye sighed and lifted the lid. She gently touched John Garland's dog tags. Then she sorted through a few notes, a faded flight map, a

37

New York subway token, a silver pocket watch, a blue flight pin with a gold bar, a half-empty pack of Camel cigarettes, and his lighter. There was also an old leather wallet. Faye hesitated. The pilot didn't have a wedding ring, but still, she expected to find a photo-booth snapshot of a stateside sweetheart, some Rita Hayworth–esque girl, all curves and dimples. Instead, she found well-worn photos of smiling siblings and grim-faced parents.

She took his pocket watch, which was old and tarnished, and held the heavy timepiece to her ear. The clockworks were silent. Idle. Dead. As she wound the stem, she felt tension and the spring-hinged cover popped open.

Faye dropped the box.

The room fell silent to her ears, all but the hum of a generator.

Inside the watch was a photo clipped from a newspaper.

The photo was of her, but she looked much younger, almost a teenager. She had no idea where or when the photo was taken. She'd never seen it before.

Faye felt light-headed; she turned the paper over.

Written on the back, in her handwriting, were the words *FIND ME*.

2
DOROTHY

(2045)

Dorothy Moy found herself in the beverage aisle of her neighborhood Safeway, watching two old Korean women fight over the last case of bottled water.

Couldn't you just share it? Dorothy wanted to ask. *Or take plastic jugs and go outside. This is Seattle, we're not exactly lacking for moisture these days.*

Then the lights flickered and the power went out.

Dorothy heard the collective gasps of dozens of last-minute shoppers, followed by worried cries for loved ones and affirmations of "I'm okay" from all around the darkened grocery store. She reached for the light of her phone as monsoon gusts from Tropical Storm Mizuchi made their presence felt, banging and flexing the sheets of plywood that protected the store's enormous front-facing windows. The sound died down to a rattle and the power snapped back on — along with the lights — which were now only half as bright, leaving the store looking pale and funerary, like a dimly lit basement.

Dorothy left the quarreling women behind. One had snatched the case of water in the brief amnesty caused by the momentary blackout, and they swore at each other in broken English amid the squeal of rusty shopping-cart wheels and the watery squelch of Dorothy's rain boots on wet linoleum.

She hurried through the aisles looking for powdered milk, duct tape, candles, anything that might be useful, but the shelves had already been stripped bare by locusts in duck shoes and Eddie Bauer raincoats. Gone were the canned goods and bottled beverages, the garbage bags and paper products, the diapers and formula. The produce section reduced to a few soft, overripe pumpkins and an enormous sixty-pound jackfruit that no one even knew what to do with.

Dorothy frowned as she passed a hoggish woman struggling to steer a shopping cart loaded with what appeared to be every bag of rice in the store. Then a man with bloodshot eyes wandered by, happily eating a strawberry Pop-Tart from an open box.

By the time Dorothy made it to a checkout line, twenty worried shoppers deep, all she'd been able to scavenge into her shopping bags were two cans of chopped clams, a jar of instant decaf, a package of tofu, extra firm, and three loaves of dark pumpernickel on clearance. Evidently urban Seattleites would rather starve or wait for the Red Cross to open a mobile kitchen than eat a loaf of stale bread labeled *Dark Pump.*

When Dorothy stepped outside, rain still poured from the October sky, which was now the color of a day-old bruise, black and blue and horrible to look at. The air felt warmer than when she'd gone in, muggier, pressing on her from all sides. In that blanket of humidity, she felt a whisper of déjà vu, a nudge, a jostle. Something to do with the weather, perhaps, a memory of her gap year in college, when she left Seattle, after a breakup and a breakdown, to spend a rainy winter in Myanmar. Like so many mishaps of her youth, the trip seemed like a good idea at the time.

As Dorothy looked for her partner, violent gusts of wind sent dead leaves, fast-food wrappers, and littered cigarette butts swirling into the air. The gusts nearly blew her into the loading zone where Louis said he'd wait, but their Tesla SUV was nowhere to be found. Neither was their five-year-old daughter, Annabel, who had been in the back seat. Dorothy frantically composed a text, chewing her lip, then realized there was no signal. Curtains of rain washed over the city, and she imagined cell towers being scraped off the tops of buildings like barnacles from a ship's hull.

He just left me. Something must have happened. He had to get Annabel home. Dorothy tried to convince herself, but she remembered how, when they were first dating, Louis used to drop her off at the entrance of restaurants and theaters. He'd leave to find parking wherever he could, often blocks away, then walk back through the downpour to join her. That seemed like a lifetime ago.

Dorothy found the nearest subway stop, but metal pylons blocked the entrance. She remembered that during Typhoon Ebisu, two hundred people — including forty-seven children — had drowned in the train tunnels while trying to evacuate the newly established flood zone. Since then meteorologists had stopped calling these new weather patterns *ARkStorms*. While technically correct, since they were cyclones hijacked by the arctic jet stream, that unfamiliar term had not elicited sufficient concern.

As pedestrians ran by, Dorothy looked up and down Western Avenue, which was quickly becoming more river than road. She felt sorry for motorists still stuck in traffic, idle as the salt water kept rising, a ticking clock to when they might have to abandon their electric cars, which floated surprisingly well. So well that during that previous storm, four years ago, dozens of extended-range vehicles — with passengers still inside — extended their range into the middle of Elliott Bay. Most were rescued by the Coast Guard the next day. An unlucky few were never found.

She tried not to worry as she flipped up the cowl of her jacket, wrapped her arms around her reusable shopping bags, and began the mile-and-a-half-long journey home.

As she walked, Dorothy saw flashes of lighting reflected in the steely glass of skyscrapers as businesspeople poured out, hastening past college students who were soaking wet in basketball shorts and Sounders hoodies. Dorothy smiled. She admired their joyful innocence, envious of their indifference as they took selfies, bracing against the elements. Then she stepped into a puddle that was hiding a deep pothole, tripping, falling, scraping her knee and flooding her boots.

She cursed amid the thunder.

In her frustration, Louis came to mind again. Being stood up by him or left behind was nothing new. In fact, to Dorothy, him leaving her to walk home in a torrential downpour was the cherry on top of the melting sundae of their six-year relationship.

She felt a strong hand on her arm.

When she looked up, she wasn't sure which was more depressing — how her heart raced for thinking it might be Louis, or how she knew it wouldn't be him even before she saw the tall police officer helping her to her feet.

"You know, I find it quicker to walk to where I'm going," he shouted above the sound of the rain. "Though they say swimming burns more calories." His smile was comforting even as the sky's underbelly lit up with electricity hiding somewhere within. "You know, you look somewhat familiar. Have we met before?"

No. Yes. Dorothy nodded, then shook her head. *Maybe.*

"I'm fine," she snapped as she pulled her arm away. "I don't know."

She felt like crying, and maybe she was, it was hard to tell. The last time she'd spoken to a police officer was June of last year. She had a bad fight with Louis and dissociated so badly that someone found her asleep a day later in an alley near Rainier Avenue. The police report said that she thought she was in Baltimore, a place she'd never been. Her shoes and socks were missing and she had no recollection of how she got there. Local newsfeeds about *Seattle's Missing Poet Laureate* were gentler than Bellevue College, which gave her a leave of absence for the last month of the semester. Then failed to renew her contract, citing budgetary concerns.

The officer picked up her bags and handed them to her. "Hey, tofu. My favorite. There's always room for tofu." He smiled again, trying to calm her down. "Look, I know it's a mess out here, but take your time, okay? It's just rain. God-awful buckets of rain. Some nasty wind. Maybe some scary lightning. But the worst of it won't make landfall until tomorrow. Until then just get to high ground and stay put, okay?"

Dorothy nodded again, sniffling, wiping her eyes and nose. She thanked him but barely heard herself. The rain now sounded like static on an old radio as heavy drops pounded the pavement, drowning out her voice, her occasional sob. She continued up the busy sidewalk past trash cans overflowing with the broken and tattered remnants of cheap, touristy, gift shop umbrellas. She wondered how Annabel was handling all of this.

When Dorothy thought about her daughter — scared of the lightning, the booming thunder, the howling wind — she stopped feeling abandoned, or angry, and instead felt like the worst mother in the world.

When she made it to the elevator of the Smith Tower, Dorothy was so wet — so completely drenched — the mirrored doors began steaming up as soon as they closed. She wiped the glass with her hand and saw her swollen eyes, red cheeks framed by watercolor streaks of mascara, strands of long black hair clinging to her face.

"Chinese women look ugly when they cry," Louis had teased, more than once, even though Dorothy didn't find it funny and her father had been mixed-race. "And what have you got to cry about, anyway? You were a little trust fund girl."

He never failed to mention the reason she had the money in the first place. She would dump it all into the sea to have her mother back, if only for a day.

Dorothy began to shiver. She was so sodden, she hoped he wouldn't notice or that the weather would distract him and he wouldn't care that she was having a moment. She didn't want to reenact old battles. Not tonight. She didn't want to reload the shooting gallery of her relationship, with him always taking aim, always keeping score, especially with the storm bearing down on them. She just wanted to hold Annabel and ride out the worst of it, like she'd done so often over the last few years, even on sunny days.

"Welcome home, Ms. Moy," the elevator said as it began the thirty-eight-floor journey to the executive apartment she shared with Louis. Dorothy stared into the mirror and practiced smiling. Louis sometimes spoke of her blue moods, her despondence, her pensiveness, as a convenient excuse for her not working enough, or a regrettable side effect of being a poet. He was too dismissive of her work to see that she was the most creative, the most productive, during these times.

"It's good to be home," Dorothy said to the elevator, whose simple reactive programming wouldn't care or even notice if she was lying. Or be bothered by her silence as she reflected on how strained her home life had become.

At first, dating Washington's poet laureate was an asset for Louis Green Analytics. Dorothy's esoteric ethos softened the sharp corners of his successful data-mining firm. But shortly after she'd lost her teaching job, she was asked to step down from her two-year term representing the state. Within a year, the qualitative value of their relationship began suffering because of the quantitative way Louis regarded her. In the beginning the tension was simple chiding, joking, teasing, like at the firm's annual holiday party, where Louis proclaimed, "Being a poet is a condition, not a profession," and everyone had a good laugh at her expense. But the jokes became arrows that pierced her in soft, vulnerable places, like her value as a woman or her ability to function as a mother. His words became hammers and everything she did looked like a nail.

"Are you certain you should be here, Ms. Moy?" the elevator asked.

For a moment Dorothy thought the lift had somehow read her mind.

"The National Weather Service predicts that Tropical Storm Mizuchi will make landfall near Ocean Shores at six forty-seven a.m., Pacific Standard Time, with a forty percent chance of continuing all the way up to British Columbia before slowing," the elevator said. "There are several evacuation routes I could recommend."

"Thank you," Dorothy replied. "I'll be okay."

She drew a deep breath and sighed, realizing her words were a wish and, like most wishes, if you say them out loud, you diminish their chances of ever coming true.

"Then have a pleasant night." The elevator chimed softly and the doors opened to her one-of-a-kind home, an airy loft tucked into the neoclassical pyramid atop what was once the tallest building west of the Mississippi. Dorothy stepped off the elevator and heard music, a remake of a remake of an old song called "Splendid Isolation."

A woman sang passionately, "Don't want to wake up with no one beside me, don't want to take up with nobody new, don't want nobody coming by without calling, don't want nothing to do with you . . ."

Dorothy saw Louis standing with his back to her, taking photos of the ornate Chihuly chandelier that dominated the center of their tapered ceiling. The chandelier was the size of a commercial freezer and looked like a giant sea anemone, with tendrils of red and orange glass. It looked gorgeous at sunrise but absolutely monstrous after dark.

Dorothy hated it.

"You're late," Louis said, without turning. "I was almost starting to worry." He didn't bother looking up from his phone as a drone the size of a hummingbird flitted about the chandelier. "You'll be happy to know that I've found a potential buyer for this thing. Now would you mind stepping to the left, babe? You're in the picture. I need to get these photos taken so I can get them sent off before we lose power."

Dorothy set her grocery bags down and stripped off her coat and scarf, then stepped out of her boots and peeled off her socks. She doffed the damp sweater that clung to her body, and her pants were soaked below the knees where her raincoat ended and bare denim began. Her cuffs dripped on the parquet flooring.

Through the apartment's windows — great triangles that matched the shape of the walls — the dark sky was a featureless void fulminated by flashes of lightning. The brief moments of luminosity revealed hail piling up on the sills.

Dorothy felt a touch of vertigo, but realized the movement was from the building gently swaying in the baleful winds. She immediately regretted letting Louis talk her into staying and waiting out the storm. He'd argued that the Smith Tower had been built

50

like a battleship. It was true the building had only suffered minimal damage during last year's typhoon season — the first time the rainy months of late summer in the Pacific Northwest had officially been called that. But nearby residences and businesses all had their windows blown out. Homes and offices were ravaged by wind and rain. Dorothy tried to calm herself by remembering there had been a precedent of safety, even if in all likelihood they would soon be atop a very tall building without a working elevator.

"Some idiot investment banker in Singapore offered ninety thousand in Bitcoin," Louis said with a derisive chuckle. The drone made the *click-whir* sound of a camera shutter as it took image after digital image. "Can you believe that?"

"Where's Annabel?" Dorothy asked.

Louis had once left their daughter in the parking garage, fast asleep in her booster seat. *She was sleeping so peacefully, I didn't want to wake her up.* Dorothy recalled his excuses. *I locked the car doors. Turned the monitor on.*

"She's fine, she's in her room playing some stupid game." Louis took another photograph, then put his phone away as the drone auto-landed atop a bookshelf. When he turned and saw Dorothy, his face looked as though the roulette wheel of his mind was still spinning, the gamble of their relationship unresolved, the ball of his opinion skittering between pockets of red and black, frustration and disappointment.

"Jeezus. What happened to you?" Louis walked over and kissed her on the forehead. He refrained from hugging her when he realized how wet and cold she was. "You look like you tripped and fell down a well and then the well went over Niagara Falls," Louis said, teasing, but his worried eyes, his body language, seemed to be groaning, *Great, it's happening again, isn't it?*

"I walked home," Dorothy said, sniffling. "Sixteen blocks."

"Why on earth would you walk home in this weather? Why didn't you just take the subway like I told you? I sent you a text. Let me guess, you forgot to charge your phone again . . ."

Dorothy ignored him and scuffed off to check on Annabel.

Dorothy peeked into her daughter's bedroom and saw her, still in her little yellow raincoat, sitting in front of a wide touchscreen, engrossed in an immersive program designed to teach art and Spanish at the same time.

On the monitor, an avatar in an embroidered dress bore a striking resemblance to Frida Kahlo, complete with rouged cheeks, a unibrow, and bougainvillea in her hair. She looked serious as she touched her paintbrush to a palette covered in oils and said, *"El azul es mi color favorito."* She pointed to a canvas with her chin. *"¿Cuál es el tuyo?"*

"My favorite color is red," Annabel answered in the chirpy voice of a preschooler, hardly noticing the lightning and thunder outside her window, much to Dorothy's surprise and relief. The program offered faint outlines to trace or color, and Annabel chose a new template then set to painting on-screen with her finger, as a cannonade of hail pelted the windows, rattling across their slanted roof.

While relieved that her daughter was safe, Dorothy worried about both of their futures. Especially after she came home early from teaching a class two months ago and walked in on Louis imploring Annabel to eat her vegetables by saying, "Finish your peas. You don't want to grow up crazy like Mommy, do you? She hates peas."

He didn't apologize.

Instead he said he was joking, that he

needed to vent. But that unguarded moment confirmed Dorothy's worst fears: that she wasn't getting any better, that Louis had little patience for her erratic behavior, and that he too worried that her unresolved malady — borderline personality disorder, manic depression, anxiety, whatever mysterious misdiagnosed ailment that had plagued Dorothy for most of her life — might be passed down to their daughter. It didn't help matters that Annabel, while only half-Chinese, looked and acted so much like her mother. Annabel had the same stoic moments where she seemed lost in thought. The same restless creative yearnings as Dorothy. The same quiet yet stubborn rebellion, often in the face of reason or convention.

In the aftermath of that night, Dorothy felt hope slipping away. She thought through clouds of melancholy that if she wasn't around, perhaps she could somehow spare her daughter the same mental tribulations. That's when Dorothy began romanticizing what it would be like to climb over the railing of their balcony and plummet 462 feet to the city below, crashing through some rooftop in Pioneer Square. She spent hours, then days imagining herself printing out her favorite poems by Anne Sexton, cutting those lines of poetry into strips, and then falling backward. *My friend, my friend, my life has been a reference work in sin, and I was born confessing it.* She fantasized about staring up at the sky as she plummeted through the cool air, fistfuls of poetry drifting from her fingertips. *This is what poems are: with mercy for the greedy. They are the tongue's wrangle, the world's pottage, the rat's star.*

But then, Annabel.

As storm winds howled outside, Dorothy took a plush bath towel that was hanging from a bedpost. She dried her hair and wiped mascara from her cheeks as she watched her daughter draw. Even when Annabel strayed from the lesson plan, for instance, creating a bird when the program asked for a cactus flower, the digital art instructor clapped her hands and said, *"¡Excelente! Eres una gran artista."*

"Good job, Baby-bel," Dorothy added.

"Ah-ma!" Annabel shouted. She jumped up and ran into Dorothy's arms.

Dorothy smelled the familiar lilac shampoo in her daughter's hair, felt the softness of her warm cheeks as she kissed them again and again. As she held her daughter, Dorothy felt an updraft and downdraft of emotion at the same time, a swirling tornado of happiness and guilt. Happiness and elation from seeing Annabel's sweet, innocent face, and spiraling guilt and shame for having thought, even for a moment, that she could hurt herself and leave her daughter without a mother.

"Sit, Ah-ma, sit," Annabel pleaded, tugging her mother's arm with both hands. Then she tapped the screen and called up a gallery of drawings, swiping through them. "Look, Ah-ma. I drew them all for you."

"For me?" Dorothy asked as she tried to appraise the drawings one by one. "Slow down, Baby-bel." If a voice could smile, hers would be beaming with parental praise. "Are these all yours?" Dorothy couldn't help but notice how Annabel ignored all the tracing assignments and created her own artwork instead.

That's my girl.

Annabel nodded vigorously, the pride on her cherubic face mimicking that of her digital instructor. Then the program and Annabel both crossed their arms and said in unison, *"Un artista debe ser un inconformista."*

The program tipped her head in a moment of stern confirmation.

Dorothy caught herself nodding in return as though the program were a real person, the two of them quietly acknowledging Annabel's nonconformity. Dorothy remembered being forced to write metrical poetry in college and how she too refused to comply. The free-verse poems she wrote instead earned her a D from her professor, but were among the first Dorothy had ever published, many of which were still in print.

Besides, a lesson plan for toddlers is like a swimming plan for cats.

Annabel swiped back and forth through her drawings and Dorothy could see the faint guidelines of a house, a tree, a simple mountain with clouds — the images that children were supposed to follow — but Annabel's were different. She'd ignored the outlines and instead had drawn a face that looked like a monkey, a strange shape that looked like either a tobacco pipe or maybe a fat golf club, and a ship at sea.

"These are wonderful," Dorothy gushed. "I wish I could draw as well as you. At your age, I was finger-painting all the colors of the rainbow into a muddy mess."

"I remember their stories, too," Annabel said as her smile vanished.

"Really?" Dorothy flipped through the drawings, then pointed at two figures on the ship. "Who is this? Is this Mommy and Daddy?"

Annabel shook her head. "That's me. And a boy. A very sick boy."

Storyteller, indeed. Dorothy stared at the drawings. She looked at the strange shape, the one she couldn't quite figure out. "And what's this?"

Dorothy watched as her daughter pressed her palm to the screen, which flashed twice, allowing Annabel to continue working on the drawing.

"This is an unfinished *obra maestra,*" the program scolded in Spanglish. "You interrupted her before *mi estrella* could finish her masterpiece."

Dorothy ignored the program. She felt spellbound as she watched Annabel add two vertical triangles to her drawing, long and slender, top and bottom. As her daughter worked furiously, Dorothy was reminded of Samuel Taylor Coleridge and how he wrote his classic poem "Kubla Khan" in an opium-induced delirium, but his flow had been interrupted and the poem was never finished. Legend had it that Coleridge fell asleep atop a book called *Purchase His Pilgrimage,* a tome that chronicled his travel to faraway places. Dorothy felt in strange communion with Coleridge, especially since last month she'd exhausted the capacity of her longtime therapist, who recommended

Dorothy for some kind of new, bleeding-edge epigenetic treatment.

While Annabel continued drawing, Dorothy watched the golf-club pipe-thing transform into something else. Something familiar. Something she herself drew as a toddler, almost obsessively. So much that Dorothy's teacher had been concerned, thinking she had OCD or was somewhere on the autism spectrum. But that was years ago and Dorothy never kept those drawings, let alone shared them with Annabel.

"Ahhh," the program said. "Very nice. It's *un avión.*"

"It's not an airplane," Annabel said and pointed to the mouth and jagged teeth. "It's a sky tiger. Or maybe a flying shark."

Annabel added a figure of a man on top.

Dorothy froze, unblinking. The hair on the back of her neck stood on end, goose pimples rising on her forearms. "Who's the man riding the sky tiger?"

"Not a man. That's the boy."

"Boy?" Dorothy asked.

Annabel pointed. "That's the boy who's looking for me."

Before Dorothy could ask her daughter more questions, the lights flickered once, twice, and then the entire building went dark.

3
AFONG

(1836)

Afong waited backstage listening to the audience while her eyes adjusted to the darkness. As the first Chinese woman to set foot on American soil, she had grown accustomed to being stared at by people on the street and fawned over during one of the many intimate salons hosted by her new manager, Henry Hannington. But nothing could prepare her for three thousand people packed into the plush seating of the Baltimore Athenaeum for fifty cents apiece to see her in person and marvel at her tiny, bound feet.

Set foot is a strange phrase, Afong thought, as Mr. Hannington introduced her to the crowd and the red velvet curtains were drawn while a twelve-piece orchestra played in earnest. Afong felt the warmth of the gaslighting and could not help but stare blindly at the shapes of the audience beneath an enormous crystal chandelier that looked like an upside-down carousel made of ice and fire.

She straightened her back as the audience clapped, her tiny frame enveloped by the rosewood chair that had been made by craftsmen in Hoiping. The chair — which was more of a throne — sat atop a gilded riser, and her feet, in lotus shoes, rested on a matching footrest. The New York press had described her as cold and taciturn, "an antipode of the modern American woman," but her stoic appearance and lack of movement were beguiling to the gathering of Baltimoreans. In truth, she guarded her motions lest the weighted headpiece made of silver, inlaid with pearls and kingfisher feathers, topple from her head. That mishap happened only once, in Philadelphia, but she could still hear the clang of the metal, the laughter of the crowd, and the sound of a horsewhip cutting through the air. "If you ever embarrass me that way again," Mr. Hannington had said through clenched teeth, as he held the whip to her face.

When the orchestra stopped playing, Afong rose to her feet and carefully descended the steps. She shuffled downstage, balancing on the four-inch soles of the silken footwear she had made with her ah-ma on her fourteenth birthday.

Afong had been saving the bright red shoes, embroidered with flowers and song-birds in golden thread, to wear on her wedding day, but when she learned who her husband would be, whose household she would join, she hid them away.

For most of her childhood Afong thought that she must have been a horrible man in her previous life to have been reborn a woman. She must have been cruel, to be reborn powerless. She must have been greedy to come back as property. She must have been shiftless, to have had her feet bound in this life. She must have been vehement to have been forced to marry an old man whom she had never met, never seen, unable to forget the young man she cared for, dreamt about.

"Afong," her ah-ma called to her.

Afong walked carefully in her lotus shoes into her mother's room.

"I have news about your wedding." Her ah-ma pressed her lips together as though she did not want the words to escape, like horses that she could not rein in.

It was in these moments that Afong had learned to not show her distaste for her arranged marriage. To not wear her doubts about the old matchmaker who wore court necklaces strung with fat pearls, fingers of jade and gilt silver, gifts that everyone knew had been encouragements for her to favor the marital interests of the Yu family.

When Afong was younger she had heard stories of how the Yu were so powerful they could realign the stars. But in reality, the stars did not move for them. Celestial beings did not whisper in the matchmaker's ears. For if they did, they would have chastised her for taking bribes and upbraided her for placing Afong and her sisters in Yu homes as servants and concubines.

"Dei Yu is gone," her ah-ma said.

"Gone?"

"He was killed in a mudslide. They found his body two days ago."

Afong felt something inside that had not been there before: hope. But she held her breath. She remembered the same feeling when her *yin yin* had died two years earlier. During her vigil, Afong sat with her grandmother's body, and when she touched her arm her grandmother's eyes opened. Afong ran to the window and shouted for her ah-ma, who came running, but by the time she arrived the old woman's eyes had closed halfway and she continued to stare at the spot where Afong had been. That is when she learned that the dead never really leave.

Now as she listened, she pictured a funeral procession for Dei Yu. His wives wailing and rending their clothing, a tearful competition to see who could profess the most grief and curry favor with their mother-in-law. Yet she still feared him, still saw him reaching for her, snatching her wrist, grinding his yellow teeth.

Her ah-ma looked pale. "The wedding will proceed in two days, as planned."

Afong imagined her aa po's eyes, staring up at her, her lips moving, silently telling her to run. "But who will I marry?" Afong's voice trembled and her thoughts found their way into the arms of Yao Han, whom she had hoped to wed since she was eight, even though he was poor and his father had gambled away his meager inheritance. Yao Han had excelled in school and was chosen for the *wui si,* a version of the Imperial Exam taken by young, gifted students. It was a rare honor, despite his father who was now a bondservant in her family's orchard. Yao Han was gentle and wrote tales about their spirits meeting on the dot of a unicorn's horn. How if their hearts were gold they should fear no fire. He always said, "We have many lives, Afong, but this life begins when we realize we only have one."

"You will marry Dei Yu." Her ah-ma closed her eyes, as though seeing Afong's reaction was too much to bear. "Your father has already spent your bride price. You will be delivered and married as planned. Then you will enter the Yu home as a widow."

Afong opened her mouth but could not speak.

"Two days from now you will wear white instead of red," her ah-ma informed her. "I will use the time we have left to teach you how to mourn properly."

Her ah-ma spoke, but they both knew she did not need a lesson in grief.

She had been born a woman.

Afong sat in the red sedan chair that would carry her to the threshold of her new home and longed for her three older sisters. Each of them had their fates decided by the matchmaker, each left to become a member of someone else's household. They never left the homes of their new families, they were never seen again in public, and even if their parents died and they were allowed to attend their funerals, they would do so as strangers, members of another family, paying their respects.

When servants from the Yu household lifted her up, Afong looked down at her ah-ma through the stringed veil of the beaded headpiece that her mother had made for her. Her ah-ma did not cry. She did not say a word, but her eyes betrayed her. When Afong looked down at her father he merely looked away. In her fourteen years of this life, he had rarely spoken to her or to any of her sisters, except to yell, or complain that "daughters are as useful as rocks in soup." Afong knew that to him she was a living reminder of his failure to have a son. Living echoes of the laughter she heard from villagers, how they had called him *sa hok* behind his back. She could not comprehend why they called him a sand crane or why that was humorous, until Yao Han explained that male cranes sit on the female's nest. Then she understood.

When the Yu servants carried her away, there were no gongs or drums or firecrackers to mark the occasion, to scare away evil spirits. All Afong heard was the memory of her father yelling at her ah-ma, that she failed him, that her bride price had been used to obtain a second wife, one who might bear him a son. Her father was the eldest, but his younger brother had two heirs and would take over the family business.

Instead of a little boy running ahead of

the procession to symbolize the son Afong would soon be expected to give her husband, there was only an older woman in white.

She looked back and said, "I am second wife. First wife is in mourning. You will do everything I say. You will speak only when spoken to. If you are obedient and show proper respect, eventually we might forget how you brought death into our household."

Afong noticed the people on the street, men and women, farmers and officials, merchants and beggars alike, all had stopped what they were doing to silently watch them pass. That is when she noticed Yao Han, sitting on the thick branch of a willow, a tree that symbolized eternal life, but also eternal grief. He did not wave and she did not acknowledge his presence. Though her heart raced and she wanted to jump down from her chair. She wanted to run to him, but she could not. She did not know how. She could only shuffle on the shriveled flowers her feet had become.

As Afong looked over her shoulder, back toward her old home, there were no musicians following, no men and women of the Yu clan carrying signs and banners of boastful celebration. All she saw was her ah-ma, in the distance, on her knees, her mouth open, in so much pain that sound could not escape.

When Afong arrived at the gates of the Yu home, white banners of mourning hung from the outer walls and the trees. The entire household staff stood waiting on either side of the circular entrance. There was fabric stretched across the ground. She was no one of consequence, but even the Yu could not allow her feet to touch dirt upon entry.

Servants helped her from the sedan chair as second wife watched. They led Afong to a courtyard where an iron stove sat on the stone walkway. She could feel the heat, smell the burning wood. She stood in front of it, waiting, her dress blowing in the wind.

"A member of the Yu family will help you step over the flame, to cleanse you of bad luck before you enter their home," her ah-ma had told her.

Afong felt the woman's hand squeezing the back of her neck, long slender fingers, the legs of a spider. "Stop shaking," second wife snapped as a servant stoked the coals. With her other hand, she gripped Afong's elbow. "Grand Mother did not want you here. When tradition dictated that you join our family as a widow, she said you should be disfigured, burned, robbed of your beauty so you cannot seduce Dei Yu's brothers and cousins. She said you must remain virtuous so Dei Yu can properly deflower you someday in the spirit world."

She pushed and Afong stumbled forward, tripping over the stove, flame scorching the fringe of her dress, a river of smoke flowing up into the charcoal sky. For a moment, the warmth was Yao Han, her head on his chest, listening to his heartbeat quicken as he read poems that he had written for her. Then his words turned to ash and floated away.

"I changed Grand Mother's mind. I convinced her to send you far away, to America," second wife whispered in Afong's ear as she tried to stand. "I told her Dei Yu's spirit would rather have a beautiful whore than an ugly virgin." She caressed Afong's cheek. "Only time will tell what you become."

Afong found her mark upon the apron of the Baltimore stage as the chair was removed and unseen ropes were pulled. Great canopies of dyed silk draped down, flowing, spilling on either side, creating a giant proscenium of fabric. Then the black curtain behind the silk rose into the rafters, revealing a colorful, panoramic painting of the

Chinese countryside, complete with pagodas and cranes in flight.

As Afong began to sing "Mut Lei Faa," a song about the jasmine flower, the audience gasped as the scenery behind her started to move. The canvas, which was really many painted canvases sewn together, traveled by means of a clever mechanical cranking system, creating the illusion of motion as it scrolled from right to left. Afong sang and the images framed behind her gave way to cascading waterfalls in painted relief, to sharp mountains in winter, then villages with paddies of rice, and onward to a colorful facsimile of Canton harbor at sunset, with junks and fishing boats bobbing on the waves. When the harbor gave way to a scene of a flower garden, jasmine petals began to gently fall from the loft, like snowflakes, upon the stage and the rapt audience as well — red and pink, white and yellow — matching the colors of her embroidered silk tunic and pantalets.

The crowd cheered wildly as Afong sang the last bars in English, "Let me pick you with tender care, sweetness for all to share, jasmine fair, oh jasmine fair." She smiled but knew this moment of happiness was as fleeting and artificial as the painted scenery behind her. She knew later, as always, she

70

would spend the night alone, as she had for two long years, seven hundred and thirty days, ever since a dead man's family gave her to the men from New York who brought her to this country.

The curtains fell as the song ended, but the orchestra continued playing. Afong remained still, listening to applause as stagehands removed her headdress and handed her an ornate cane with an inlaid, mother-of-pearl handle. She did not need the cane to walk, but Mr. Hannington thought it looked more dramatic. When the curtains opened again, Afong walked from stage right to stage left then back again to center, careful not to slip on drifts of flower petals as the audience stood and raised their opera glasses to get a better look at her feet. She understood the morbid fascination. Whenever she met a woman whose whalebone corset had been cinched so tight the poor lady could hardly breathe, she felt the same way, wondering how they ate in such condition.

"For more than one thousand years, girls of the Celestial Kingdom have undergone this strange and ungodly ritual," Mr. Hannington bellowed. His tailcoat smelled of stale sweat, tobacco, and rye as he put one hand on her shoulder, squeezing while he

71

pointed at her shoes with the other. "Binding their feet in strips of cotton, tinged with herbs and soaked in animal blood, which constricts like a nest of serpents as it dries, a bondage which crushes their bones into the shape of a water flower as they lie helpless in their beds. All because a loathsome empress with a clubfoot grew tired of being different, being looked down upon by her own subjects, and thus she dictated that all women of that godless empire be crippled just so. I ask you decent people, what foul human could be so cruel to such a lovely creature?"

Afong stepped to the edge of the stage so theatergoers could get a closer look. She wondered if they would still think she was lovely if they saw her crying at night.

What would my mother think?

Afong displayed her bound feet and the audience chattered, in delight or disgust, awe or bewilderment; in the cacophony of voices it was hard to tell. Though a woman cried out, "God save that poor child," as a man in the back yelled, "Heathens, all of 'em!"

Even though she learned a fair amount of English during her travels in America, it took a while for Afong to understand that Mr. Hannington was what some considered a member of the shoddyocracy, a fabulist, prone to saying whatever would hold the audience spellbound. She had tried to explain that many years ago, a dancer named Precious Thing performed on the tip of her toes, like ballerinas in America. A noble prince, Li Yu, was so smitten with her performance that other women adopted the fashion. But her manager concocted his own fable.

"Don't get too high for your nut, girl," he had said as he chewed on a cigar while counting the night's receipts. "Your history is whatever I tell them. In America, a lie becomes the truth with sufficient repetition. I merely tell the crowd what they need to hear to be satisfied." He smiled. "Because every crowd has a silver lining."

To Afong, Mr. Hannington spoke in riddles and parables, like Confucius, if the great philosopher were drunk, greedy, and indolent.

"But the Chinese Lady does have her unique skills and refinements," her manager said to the audience, removing his top hat. "As you will soon see."

It was in this moment that Afong caught a glimpse that took her breath away, a young Chinese man waiting in the wings. She wanted to run to him, talk to him, she could

73

not stop staring. She heard that Mrs. Hannington had found a new interpreter, but Afong expected a bald old scholar with an abacus, a round belly, and gray hairs growing from his ears. Instead this fellow, perhaps in his late twenties, was remarkably handsome, though she was unsure if her heart was racing because of his looks or simply because she had not seen another Chinese person in months and those *had* been bald old men, merchants and importers. This young man, however, did not have a queue and wore a Western-style suit. He was buttoning his golden waistcoat, when he looked up and caught Afong's eye. He smiled and she looked away as she turned her attention back to tonight's patrons.

"But first I need two volunteers, hale and hearty, strapping gents with the most copious of appetites," Mr. Hannington said as he motioned to various men, encouraging them to join him onstage. "This will be dinner theater for two of you."

A pair of burly men, one in a fine wool suit, though its threadbare condition spoke of its age, and the other in workman's dungarees, stepped over the balustrade and alighted on the stage. Afong stepped back as the Chinese man brought forth a lacquered tray with three bowls of rice and three sets of ivory chopsticks.

"Nei uk kei mou mong gei nei," he whispered to Afong as he set down the tray.

She froze, unsure of what she had just heard: *That her family has not forgotten.* Afong pursed her lips as she stared at the man, bangs tilted as he leaned in. She could see his eyes, which revealed nothing more. Afong's heart asked a million silent questions, but he remained stoic as he performed his duties and left the stage.

Afong snapped to attention as Mr. Hannington took her cane and handed her a bowl and a pair of the utensils. He did the same for each man.

"If either of you strong and corpulent men can consume this small measure of rice using these peculiar sticks of the Orient faster than the Chinese Lady, I will give you . . ." The showman paused for effect. "Five hundred cash dollars!" He turned to the audience. "Do you want to see one of these men get rich here tonight?"

The crowd roared and the spectators in the back rose to their feet.

Afong looked at the rice in her bowl. Her hand was shaking and she felt light-headed at the possibility of hearing from her ahma, her family. That and she had not eaten all day, since Mr. Hannington had forbidden her from taking meals until her performance was done. Though that never stopped her managers from lavishly dining in her presence, enjoying lamb, ham soup, and salmon pie, while only allowing her to sip black tea and smoke an occasional cigarette, which was illegal, to stave off hunger.

"Commence!" Mr. Hannington shouted, and the men began fumbling with their chopsticks, trying to use them as a thin spoon, or stabbing their bowls of rice in vain.

The orchestra proceeded to play "Flight of the Bumblebee," which drove the crowd wild, laughing and heckling as one man kept dropping his utensils.

Chopsticks in hand, Afong began to feast on the rice with precision. As she ate, the audience cheered her on as though she were a trained seal bouncing a ball through a hoop in the circus of Pépin and Breschard. She knew that her life onstage, while loathsome in the company of the Hanningtons, was better than the life of a ghost bride. She had traveled so much that now the idea of being a housebound servant to the family of a dead husband — forever unseen and friendless — that life was now inconceivable. But she missed her ah-ma, her sisters, and still dreamt of Yao Han. She longed for the times he would meet her at the well and they would steal away together, lie in the cool grass, and share fresh lychee in season, savoring the sweetness.

"I will pray that you pass your tests," Afong had said, though she knew that meant he would be sent to an elite academy in a faraway prefect. But he would not spend the rest of his days in poverty, tending to another man's field. Yao Han would finally be able to pursue his art. At last, his words would have a canvas worthy of them.

"What if I don't want to leave?" Yao Han looked up at the streaming clouds, searching for the sun that had disappeared. "What if I want to stay?"

They both left those questions unanswered, holding hands and letting the fog of silence fill the valley between them. Neither needed reminding that her father, a salt merchant, would never let his daughter marry the son of a servant. Afong knew she could never ask her father for anything, let alone for him to change his mind. Her thoughts, her wishes, her presence in his life, carried the weight of thistledown in the wind.

"If I leave, I will come back for you," Yao Han said, but she heard resignation in his voice. His affirmation was more of an aspiration, filled more with doubt than belief.

"I will be right here," Afong had said as her bound feet began to ache.

Where would I go?

Now in America, a day did not pass that she did not imagine Yao Han returning to their village someday as a scholar, a magistrate, a merchant of words with provincial glory. But now she imagined that the boy who used to leave flowers on her windowsill would do so one last time and the flowers would wilt, dry up, and blow away.

Afong remembered the last words her ah-ma said to her. Her mother tried to pass on what little hope she had. "Women are born to lead lives of inconsistency." She tried not to cry as she held Afong's hands. "While it is our curse, it can also be our strength."

Afong finished her bowl and raised it high, exclaiming, *"Sik yeun!"* as one man began eating with his hands and the other threw rice at the heckling congregation.

When the show ended and the applause faded, Afong sat backstage on a wooden stool thinking about what the man in the golden waistcoat had said, daydreaming that one day she might be able to buy her freedom, and with that independence, passage back to China, to her village, to her family, to Yao Han.

Unfortunately, the Hanningtons paid her only two dollars and fifty cents per week, so she tried not to entertain such hopes. Whenever she had come close to saving up even a portion of the eighteen dollars needed for a third-class ticket on a steamship to Canton, they found ways to garnish her wages, leaving her with a handful of pennies. "Five dollars for your meals, for your transportation, for your lodging," Mr. Hannington would say, smiling benevolently as he went over a ledger that Afong could not read. "Ten dollars for our priceless stewardship and boundless support."

Tonight, that support would be escorting her to a boardinghouse.

"Only the bawdiest, most tawdry of women are seen on the streets without an escort," Mrs. Hannington reminded Afong. "You don't want people to think you're one of *those* girls." She held up a flask, drained the last of its contents, then laughed and slapped Afong on the knee as though someone had told a joke. "It's trouble enough that you're a foreigner, but with those silly feet of yours you couldn't even run away. You'd fall prey to the worst sort of people. I would know."

As she looked down at her lotus shoes, she remembered her quiet jealousy of beggar women with unbound feet on the streets of her village. They were the lowest of peasants, spending their days selling bundles of green kindling, but at least they could go where they wanted without hobbling like toothless old men.

Meanwhile, Afong was rarely allowed out in public.

"If the people out there on the avenues want to gawk at you, my little squab," Mrs. Hannington had once snorted as she rolled down the curtains of the carriage they were riding in, "they can buy a bloody ticket just like everyone else. Trust me, as a woman, you should never give away anything for free that men will gladly pay for."

Afong understood that her presence fascinated Americans, especially wealthy men. She was also aware that her name had appeared in scores of newspapers after President Andrew Jackson had asked to meet her when she arrived in Washington, DC, for a performance. She was impressed at how the *zung tung* had opened his emperor's home to the common people. There was even a 1,400-pound block of cheese in the front entrance hall. Afong found the taste, smell, and texture utterly disgusting, but her handlers at the time, Francis and Nathaniel Carnes, cousins who originally purchased her a year earlier along with a shipload of Chinese curiosities, seemed delighted and laughed heartily as they ate.

Then she and the cousins were ushered in to see the president. Afong had been worried about his well-being, after all, since she was told that someone tried to assassinate him while attending a funeral the week before. But as she timidly approached the man on her bound feet, he appeared to be a stout figure of good health. Though perhaps it was not really him, as he seemed lacking in grandeur, wearing a dark suit like most American men, and sat in a common chair, not a throne.

Afong had listened as Nathaniel Carnes did his best to translate their brief encounter. "I wish you the power to persuade your countrywomen to abandon the custom of cramping your feet," the president said, believing she was an ambassador or emissary of some kind. "It is in total opposition to nature's wiser regulations."

Afong listened to his words, nodding. She thought about the women in America. They had enormous, hideous feet. But they could also be outspoken, and in this upside-down world, the poorer they were, the louder they seemed. While she was limited in where she could travel, American women came and went as they pleased. There were even times when Afong thought she might be allowed that kind of freedom, but then the cousins lost everything in the Great Fire of New York and she lost hope once again.

Afong's stomach grumbled as she waited backstage, wondering what might be taking so long. The Hanningtons were cunning promoters and the evening had gone well. Perhaps they were booking a second night, or a matinee, or off celebrating. Maybe they forgot her altogether. Afong smiled at the wishful thought. She envisioned flying away from the theater like a bird from a cage, singing. Soaring back over the ocean through a cloudless sky. Finally going home.

Her smile faded when she heard a sputtering, popping sound from above as gaslights lit up the backstage gloom. The lamps were so bright that she had to squint and shade her eyes to see the man who was stepping through the curtains.

Her heart sped up as she thought about the handsome Chinese man in the golden waistcoat and what he might be able to share: news of home, the health of her ah-ma and sisters, if and when she might be able to return.

But another man stepped through. And another.

As her eyes adjusted to the light, Afong counted eight men, each in fine suits. Some in long coats, and two of them carried leather satchels. They all stared at her, intrigued and eager. Some stroked their beards as they whispered to one another.

"There she is, gentlemen, just as I told you," Mr. Hannington said as he stepped through and closed the curtain behind him. He turned and spoke to Afong. "We have some special visitors tonight. They would like an encore performance, so to speak."

Afong stepped back and bumped into someone.

"Don't be a prude, girl. These men are all doctors," Mrs. Hannington said from behind. "The finest in New England. And they all paid to see you."

Afong felt trapped, her heart now racing for other reasons entirely.

"May we?" a doctor asked Mr. Hannington, who merely nodded.

Mrs. Hannington took Afong's hand and led her back up onto the riser, where a stool had been placed. She sat as the doctor donned a pair of spectacles and opened his satchel to retrieve a host of brass instruments that he spread out on a folding tray. The fiery glow of the gaslights reflected on the surface of scalpels, probes, and calipers.

"We'll have to cut through her bandages," another doctor said as the men surrounded her. "But first she'll have to remove her queer footwear. And this costume altogether, if we're to do a proper physical examination."

Afong shook her head frantically, helplessly.

No man had ever seen her bare feet. Not even her own father. She had always been told that someday, if she were worthy, that privilege would belong to her husband.

She flinched as the men began to unbutton her shoes.

4
DOROTHY

(2045)

Dorothy removed Annabel's shoes and raincoat and gently wrapped her in a comforter that smelled flowery, like fresh linen. She held her daughter in the darkness, gently rocking, whispering, "It's just the wind, Baby-bel. We're safe. Nothing can hurt you. Ah-ma's right here." Even as she said those words Dorothy knew she was merely firing blunt arrows into the storm, hopeful platitudes from a mother's quiver of comforting phrases. She wished she could be certain. She wished she could spirit the two of them far away, someplace warm, sunny, and dry, someplace where the frailty of modern society wasn't put to the test each year by one-hundred-mile-per-hour winds.

"When's it fixed?" Annabel asked.

"I don't know, Baby-bel. I don't know, maybe tomorrow. Don't be scared."

Annabel leaned in and shook her head. "I'm not."

Dorothy considered this. "Of course, you're my brave girl."

To Dorothy, the building felt eerily quiet. No humming from monitors or appliances, the subtle murmuring of the HVAC units tasked with moving air throughout the circulatory system of a thirty-eight-story building were currently quiescent. This new canvas of silence was being painted over by violent swashes of wind, hail, and thunder, framed by Louis occasionally yelling from the living room.

"I thought I told you to pick up some spare batteries for the flashlight. I can't believe you forgot!" he shouted. "Wait. Never mind."

She heard him tripping over furniture and cursing as heavy rain lashed the windows and lightning coursed through the sky.

Dorothy remembered an old line of poetry from Rupi Kaur: *If people were rain, men would be drizzle, and women a hurricane.*

"Why's this happening?" Annabel asked.

"It's just a storm, Baby-bel. They happen once a year now, and that's why we live in this big strong building. We'll be just fine."

Annabel nodded as though that all made sense, or the tone of her mother's voice was convincing enough that it didn't matter what Dorothy said, but how she said it.

For a moment, she felt grateful they were far above the possible storm surge, the flooded streets, downed power lines, the perilous, flying debris. A fearsome gust of wind rattled the skylight windowpanes, and as the building swayed, Dorothy began mentally planning their escape to the stairwell if things got worse.

While Louis stumbled about the living room, Dorothy pondered Annabel's drawings and the uncanny similarities to her own. As a parent, she expected Annabel to grow up and, at some point, have the same alarming revelation that she too — in so many subtle and unsubtle ways — had become her mother. As an observant adult, Dorothy had witnessed how children inherited traits from their parents, a receding hairline, a jawline, a tolerance or intolerance of spicy foods. She also understood that every child ends up an amalgam of genetics and modeled behavior, nature and nurture — at least to a certain point. Her enthusiastic friends were often beguiled by how their offspring shared similar tastes with their parents, or had the same claustrophobia, or fear of heights. To Dorothy, these observations had the same gravity and validity as the predictive power of a fortune cookie. More wishful thinking than science. An aspirational concurrence. An example of that reasoning in mathematical terms would look like this: imagination + a desire for the world to make sense = a society that thinks dogs always look like their owners.

But Annabel's airplane drawing was an unsettling coincidence, something Dorothy endeavored to sort out in the light of day after the storm passed.

As the wind howled, Dorothy remembered how warm and welcome the rain had been during her time in Myanmar, back when she was a nervous, angry, twitching twenty-something. She'd arrived at the tail end of monsoon season. She'd felt compelled to visit and become what Kipling called "a neater, sweeter maiden, in a cleaner, greener land." She thought the Burma rains would be baptismal, restorative. That she'd return with answers to questions she didn't even know she had.

But all she brought back was malaria.

Louis walked in wearing a headlamp that gave him the appearance of a cyclopean coal miner. "This is all I could find. Plenty of batteries though."

Dorothy chewed her lip. She wanted to yell. She wanted to argue that they should have done what more sensible people had done and left the city, moved to someplace inland, like Wenatchee, or maybe Yakima. That they didn't need to be here. But a part of her felt comfortable in the storm. Happy that he was wrong.

Louis held up one of the loaves of bread Dorothy found at the store. "Why on earth would you bring home stale pumpernickel? Especially with a typhoon bearing down. We never eat this. You should have bought sour-dough."

This isn't even a real typhoon, Dorothy thought. *This is what — a post-tropical storm? The season isn't over and there are other cyclones out there spinning, careening into one another, and here we sit.* She imagined the South Pacific as a giant pachinko machine with lights and bumpers, bells clanging, chaotic. "Things could get worse."

Louis opened his mouth to speak, then hesitated. He looked at her as though he wasn't sure if she was talking about the bread, the storm, or their relationship.

As though on cue, a howitzer boomed from the roof, a crack of thunder so loud they all ducked down to the floor, crouching, covering their heads in a reaction that was a collective nod to some latent primal programming.

"Too loud," Annabel said.

"We should move away from the windows." Dorothy hoisted her daughter to her hip. "As far as possible. Let's you and I sleep in the living room tonight, Baby-bel. It'll be like we're going camping."

Sometime in the night Dorothy opened her eyes. She touched the empty space next to her where Annabel had been. The blankets were still warm. Dorothy sat up, unsure of the time because her phone died and the electricity still had not come back on, rendering the wall clocks and the timepieces in the kitchen useless.

Louis was sound asleep, lightly snoring on the far side of their sectional sofa. He'd taken a sedative to get through the storm, but Dorothy passed on that idea. She didn't want to be medicating her parental responsibilities for a few hours of sleep.

Dorothy looked around, searching the dark forest of silhouettes their furnishings had become. "Annabel," she whispered as she looked toward the guest bath, then back in the direction of her daughter's room.

In the calm, Dorothy heard echoes of thunder rolling in the distance. Everything was quieter now, the wind reduced to an occasional light whistle, the rain and hail had stopped. The air was warm and stagnant, almost musty. She reasoned that they must have passed through the eyewall of the storm and were now in the center, an oasis of calm, with the bulk of the tempest now swirling all around them. She knew that as the storm rolled over the contours of the land it would lose its power.

The worst could be over. Just more rain, and Seattle was built to handle rain.

Then lightning flashed and she saw Annabel.

She was still wearing the footie pajamas Dorothy found for her. Her hair still in pigtails. Annabel was standing on the cushion of a window seat in the living room, a reading nook Dorothy had custom-built that offered a breathtaking view. Annabel stood in the darkness looking out over the city and the roiling black waters of Elliot Bay. As electricity discharged inside distant clouds, Dorothy could see her again, hands on the cold glass, staring up into the darkness, waiting.

5
GRETA

(2014)

Greta Moy stared up at the enormous projection screens that flanked the elevated podium of the Westin Hotel's Grand Ballroom. As the nominees were announced, one by one, she tried to look calm, wishing she had checked to make sure there wasn't lip stain on her teeth or pineapple curry on her blouse. She held her breath through the presenter's dramatic pause, filled with the beating of her anxious heart. Then she heard her name called and a roar of applause as her nervous, wide-eyed expression — thirty feet wide and twenty feet high — was splashed on the monitors for all to see.

"The award for GeekWire's App of the Year goes to Syren!" The emcee held up a statuette of a fat robot with a bow tie and welcomed her to the stage.

Greta felt her cheeks redden as "Crazy Little Thing Called Love" by Queen boomed throughout the event space. En route to collect her award, she shook hands with smiling people she didn't know, received hugs and air kisses from colleagues she did but whose names were momentarily lost in the fog of pride and embarrassment, modesty and astonishment as two thousand people — the beating heart of Seattle's tech community — cheered, politely clapped, or offered forced grins that were more smirk than smile. A handful of attendees, including some of her coworkers, whispered to one another with knowing looks and conspicuously raised eyebrows.

Greta held up her award and posed for a photograph as she surveyed the crowd. She understood the gossip. After all, it wasn't every day that such an honor went to a dating app created by a young woman who's been notoriously single for as long as anyone could remember. But she also wondered how the audience would react if they found out that Syren, a feminist dating platform designed by women, for women, was funded almost exclusively by a man rumored to have paid off women who'd accused him of sexual assault. That's when Greta noticed Anjalee, the company's CFO and one of the founding partners, standing and clapping, pausing to raise a single finger to her lips.

■ ■ ■ ■

An hour later Greta's face was tired from having to smile so much and her pockets were filled with business cards — from potential employers, business reporters, or hopeful strangers looking to hook up the old-fashioned way — she really couldn't tell.

"Hey, so I heard this weird rumor that you're not going out with us tonight? What's that about?" Anjalee caught up to Greta as she waited in a coat-check line. "We're all going to Knee High. They have this fabulous new retro drink — I think you'd love it — it's called Absinthe Minded. You should let me buy you one, or two, or five. That way you'll be too hungover tomorrow to ask for a raise."

Greta winced. "I'm so sorry." She'd never been to the Knee High Stocking Company, one of Seattle's trendy speakeasies, and had always wanted to go. "I wish I could join everyone. I really do. But . . . I just can't." She traded a small plastic token for her coat. "Truth be told, I'd planned to sneak out early, after the winners were announced, because — and I kinda hate to admit this — I didn't think in a million years that I'd win. Also, my parents just got back from

Shanghai and I haven't seen them and I promised I'd stop by their place over on Beacon Hill and . . ." Greta looked down at her phone. "Oh God, I'm already two hours late. My mom made my favorite dessert, which takes all day to cook. If I stood them up now that would be the end of me. Rescue workers would find me buried under an avalanche of guilt."

"Why not just tell them you won a big award?" Anjalee smiled with Botoxed sincerity. "Or better yet, bring 'em along! I'd love to meet your family."

Greta envisioned her parents reluctantly showing up in matching knockoff Adidas track suits they'd haggled for at some stall in the Qipu Road Clothing Market. They'd shake their heads in disapproval and speak to her in Chinese as her coworkers ordered round after round of bougie, eighteen-dollar cocktails made with Strega and grapefruit bitters. Her parents had retired with a bit of money. Her dad even bought a new Honda last year, but on the way home he stopped at Walmart because there was a sale on toilet paper. The car was packed with bathroom tissue even before it had plates.

"Thank you. But — yeah — tonight's not good, but definitely next time." Greta remembered that her parents mentioned they had some papers for her to look at. She'd forgotten that detail since she assumed it was something to do with their will or a DNR, and she'd flatly avoided that morbid discussion, thinking that if she ignored it long enough they'd move on to her aunt or a cousin. How after all these years she'd somehow become the de facto responsible one was a mystery.

"Please, take this in my place." Greta smiled as she offered Anjalee the robot statuette. "Just make sure he has a designated driver."

"You sure?" Anjalee asked. "You did all the heavy lifting on the new dating app, that's why I wanted you up there collecting the award and all the glory. Maybe catch up to us later? I think there's going to be some utterly shameless karaoke involved."

Greta smiled an apology and buttoned her coat. "Sing some Sinatra for me."

Even before she walked through the front door, Greta could smell the red bean paste and the copious amounts of butter baked into her mother's nian gao.

"Hey! There's our Miss Margaret," her mother said from the kitchen as Greta walked in and took off her coat. "What happened to you? We'd almost given up."

"I'm sorry I'm so late, Ah-ma." Then Greta shouted, *"Emhou yi si ngo cidou!"* to her father, who was in the living room with the volume turned up too high on the television as he watched the Mariners' Willie Bloomquist strike out against a Yankees pitcher. "Dad! I had a work thing."

She gave her mother a big hug and offered to help with dessert, but the gao had already been cut into thin slices, dipped in egg, and was almost done being panfried, Cantonese-style, the way Greta liked it. She sat down at the dining room table as her father turned off the TV with a heavy sigh and a serious look on his face.

Greta noticed a folder of papers on the lazy Susan. "How was your vacation?"

"Gah! Shanghai's too big," her father said, shaking his head. "Construction cranes everywhere. But still worth it because we made a special detour."

"Really?" Greta looked at them both, worriedly appraising their weight loss or gain, their gait and general constitution. She'd known other retirees in the neighborhood who'd flown back to China for strange experimental medical procedures that always seemed to be a mixture of Western medicine, Chinese herbalism, and old-fashioned, dollar-driven quackery. Things like consulting a supposedly blind I Ching expert, or trying electric acupuncture on for size, or drinking tea made from powderized rhino horn and dried seahorses — stuff that generally wasn't covered by Medicare. Then she remembered her grandmother. Maybe they went back to Zou yi's old village?

"We did make a special trip — you know? Just for you." Her mother set a teapot on the table. Then a sizzling plate of sweet, fried gao, with the edges perfectly caramelized. She sat down and reached for the folder. "Now, before you say no, just hear us out. Remember, we're your parents. That means we care about you the most."

Greta didn't like where this conversation was headed.

"Look," she said. "If this is about giving me power of attorney . . ."

Her father said something to her mother in Chinese, so quickly that Greta didn't understand. But she noticed that the looks they exchanged betrayed a sense of worry. Or was it strange conviction? That's when she realized it was the same look they'd had when they fixed her up on a blind date at the Tai Tung restaurant with the son of a family friend, a dentist or a chiropractor or an accountant or something. He was purportedly rich and successful but looked like he'd gone bargain shopping for a toupee and had the personality of an artichoke.

Greta swore *never again.*

Her mother asked, "Have you heard of the Shanghai Marriage Market?"

Greta's mouth hung open.

"OH MY GOD, MOTHER! Please tell me you didn't . . ."

Her mother opened the folder, took out a file, and Greta saw an enlarged press photo from when she'd been hired at Syren, fifteen pounds ago, when her hair was longer and before she constantly had bags under her eyes from working seventy-hour weeks. There was her résumé too, both in English and Chinese, with an approximation of her salary. Also sheets that listed her grade point averages in high school and college, her measurements from bust to shoe size. Even her cat allergies were mentioned.

Greta covered her face with her hands and let out a horrified groan.

"It was quite illuminating," her father added. "They have a matchmaker . . ."

Greta wasn't listening.

Working at Syren, she'd seen the research from social scientists about the many ways couples were meeting in the twenty-first century. From the popularity of group dates in Japan, to pay-per-hour hotels in Argentina, even the fact that — much to her surprise — there really wasn't a word for *date* in the French language. But she'd been positively mortified to learn that a park in Shanghai had been taken over by well-meaning Chinese mothers and fathers who sat at folding tables beneath beach umbrellas, with large photos of their unmarried children on display. They passed out marriage résumés and networked with other parents who were equally desperate for grandchildren.

"Now, before you say no," her mother said as she took out a photo from another file and held it to her chest as though it were a closely guarded state secret.

Greta kept repeating, "No. No. No. No . . ."

"This is Sam. And he's from Seattle, but he's been living in Shanghai for five years. He teaches English and Sanshou — the Chinese boxing your father watches."

"He's quite good. His parents are very nice, we had lunch with them. Both doctors," her father added, tapping the table twice for emphasis.

"I'm. Not. A leftover woman!" Greta protested, knowing that was the hideous term for women in China who reached the ripe old age of twenty-seven without being married. She scrunched up her face and closed her eyes as though this were a bad dream or the premise for a reality TV show called *The Chinese Bachelor: Old Maid Edition.*

Greta opened her eyes and stared at the plate of warm mochi, realizing dessert was the bait and she'd fallen for it. "Ah-ma, I'm single because I haven't met the right person, okay? I work — constantly. And believe it or not, I'm happy." *Or at least okay,* Greta thought, *the next-door neighbor to the gated community of happiness. I'll find my way in there someday. Either that or I'll become the mayor of Okayville.*

Her mother showed her the photo. "We know how shy you can be. Just give him a chance, Margaret, who knows?" She said *who knows* with the smile and guile of a seasoned politician. "What do you have to lose? You might be surprised."

Greta shook her head. She hated it when her mother called her Margaret, and was about to remind her of that fact. Then she saw the photo and couldn't say a word.

The young man appeared to be mixed-race — Blasian — half-Asian, half-Black. About her age, which was a small relief, because the mechanics of all of this was uncomfortably reminiscent of picture

101

brides, a century earlier, who were generally married off to men twice their ages. However, this fellow didn't look like he'd have any trouble finding a wife, or a date, or a harem. To Greta's hormonal astonishment, he was distinctly handsome in a way that reminded her of classic poems from high school. *Come live with me and be my love, and we will all the pleasures prove.* She hated herself for having such a shallow reaction to a set of high cheekbones, a strong chin, and a welcoming smile. To the steely opalescence of his eyes, the curls of his long dark hair that reached his broad shoulders. There had to be a catch. Why was he single? Why were his parents trying to set him up? What crimes had he possibly committed? Greta searched for the asterisk, the fine print, the part that said *batteries not included, some assembly required, may be a choking hazard.*

"Well," her mother asked, "what do you think? He's very handsome."

Greta thought about the early planning meetings for the Syren app. How she fought to create a way for women to make the first move, to protect their identities and not become part of an online rotisserie of push-up bras and sorority smiles. Instead of hooking up with guys on a trash app like Tinder, whose mission statement, Greta thought, should have been *True love is just a dick pic away®*. Greta's all-nighters had been spent in a cubicle where she created an algorithm that let women self-select the inner workings of a person. By their clever answers to unique questions, their reactions to pop culture references, their fears, their hopes and aspirations. Their physicality was an afterthought, a validating proof of identity, but not a definition of that person. Looking at the photo in front of her, though, her entire body wanted to *swipe right.*

Then she thought of all the times she'd been disappointed by boys, by men, by men who acted like boys. "It doesn't matter what I think, he lives in . . ."

"Ballard." Her father shrugged. "A half hour away, depending on traffic."

"Wait, what?"

"He's in Seattle for one month, at least. And I think you would be good for each other. Don't be mad, but I told Sam he could pick you up for lunch tomorrow. I know you work every weekend, so I gave him your company's address."

"Ah-ma!" Greta felt herself dividing in two. Half of her was furious that her parents were playing matchmaker again, without her consent. The other half was upset that it was a week before her period and she felt bloated and she didn't have anything to wear. She brought the two sides back together and said, "Fine, but this is the last time."

She saw both of her parents smiling with relief. Then her mother handed over the file with the rest of Sam's biographical information. "You should read for yourself."

Greta reached for a piece of fried gao and took a bite. She tasted the crispy edge, the warm, chewy, glutinous middle. She stared at the file and sighed, briefly satisfied, but knowing that gao, like people, can look sweeter than it is.

6
DOROTHY

(2045)

Dorothy dropped Annabel off at preschool with a container of fried gao that her daughter could share at snack time. "Be good, Baby-bel." Dorothy snuck a piece and took a bite. It was still warm on the inside and chewy. "Your mommy makes the best, huh?"

Annabel nodded, took a nibble, and smiled. Then Dorothy gave her a hug and watched as an employee took Annabel's hand and led her back.

The school worker at the front desk, a young Japanese woman named Toshiko, said, "She's our favorite little artist, that one." She regarded Dorothy for a moment. "You know, Mrs. Moy, while I have you here, do you mind if I ask you if there have been any significant changes at home? Annabel's been acting a bit strangely since the last storm, and I've been meaning to check in with you or your husband."

"We're not married," Dorothy corrected. "And what do you mean by strange? Annabel can be a bit dreamy and distracted at times, but I think that's part of the job description of a five-year-old. Maybe even certain thirty-one-year-olds." Dorothy pointed at herself. She tried to joke, but she'd seen how restless her daughter had become lately and worried that Annabel might be picking up on the tension between Louis and her.

"Oh, I apologize. I should learn not to presume." Toshiko made a note on the front desk computer. "I know this time of year, with the nonstop rain, the flood warnings, it can all be pretty stressful for grown-ups — but for little ones, we see all kinds of unusual reactions, different ways of coping. What's been happening with your daughter, specifically, involves nap time. As you know, after lunch, we put out cots and each child stretches out with a small blanket from home. We then lead them through a short mindfulness exercise. I've been here for a while. I've definitely seen kids fight it. But those fifteen minutes of meditation have worked miracles, especially with the restless children. It's a simple way to work on their neuroplasticity. Before you know it they're out cold, drooling on their pillow, and when they wake up their focus has improved."

"Is Annabel drooling again? I'll have a talk with her."

"No, it's nothing like that. I'd love it if she were drooling, but the problem is, her focus has been acutely elsewhere. Last week it took an unusual turn."

"Really?" Dorothy asked. "Like, day-dreaming?"

Toshiko rubbed her temple, as though she didn't want to trouble Dorothy with this latest information when all the residents of Seattle were still trying to recover. "Last week, as the other kids had tucked in with their blankets and were focusing on their breathing, Annabel just lay there, staring up at the ceiling. When one of the teachers asked what was wrong . . . she didn't respond. She was unresponsive for several minutes. Her teacher thought she was teasing. After all, Annabel's medical history shows no previous signs of seizures or narcolepsy, but she is quite precocious. Then when she snapped out of her day-dream, or whatever it was, she began crying. We calmed her down and then she fell asleep, almost immediately, and when she woke up she didn't remember it. I thought that perhaps something was going on at home, or maybe she'd seen something online that upset her, or on the news. Things that we take for granted can often be quite upsetting to someone so young."

"Not that I know of," Dorothy said, embarrassed and concerned about her daughter's peculiar behavior. Worried that Louis would use Annabel acting out as another example of how Dorothy had failed as a mother. "Thank you, I'll look into it."

Dorothy tried to clear her head as she walked through the rainy corridors of downtown Seattle, which looked like a prizefighter's face after going twelve rounds for the title. Instead of black eyes and missing teeth, the weather-beaten buildings were missing windows and a few doors, leaving offices and storefronts as murky hollows. Most of the damage had been boarded up, though some had been left dark and vacant as local lumberyards were in short supply of everything.

She remembered stepping out of their building after the storm passed and being overwhelmed by the salty stench of damp seaweed. The rain had eased to a drizzle and the water had long since receded. The power had come back on, illuminating streets strewn with bull kelp, eelgrass, tubeworms, starfish, and the occasional dogfish that had been sucked up into the storm surge and marooned along the waterfront. The city seemed eerily quiet in the absence of moving cars, except for the sounds of seagulls and murders of crows noisily squabbling for feasting rights upon the small, bottom-dwelling sharks that lay rotting on the sidewalks.

Annabel seemed fine at the time, lost in her own imaginary world.

Today the avenues had been cleared just enough to be reclogged with bumper-to-bumper traffic and adorned with street musicians and buskers who reoccupied their usual corners. As Dorothy walked to the entrance of King Street Subway Station, she noticed the policeman who'd helped her on the night of the storm. A streetlight was being repaired, and he was directing traffic. She waved and he nodded, his arms in motion, though she wasn't sure if he recognized her or was just being cordial. Then he yelled, "Hey, how was the tofu?" much to the confusion of the other pedestrians.

Dorothy smiled and kept walking. A block away she turned and looked back, hoping to catch another glimpse, but he was gone.

When she got to the station, she passed a Buddhist monk who was playing a flute, badly. He looked lean and pale, with jaundiced eyes. Dorothy dropped money into his basket, wondering if he had hepatitis or was coming down with what the news was now calling "Emerald Fever." This particularly pernicious breed of leptospirosis caught the city off guard four years ago, but now most knew to avoid pools of standing water, stray animals, and anywhere mosquitos might breed. The monk nodded and played faster. Another monk, a woman, smiled and offered Dorothy a bracelet made of wooden beads. When she said, "No thank you," the woman frowned and handed Dorothy a thin, gold-colored medallion. She glanced down at the image of the Buddha, then groaned. The cheap medallions were the hallmark of fake Buddhists, panhandlers in saffron robes. Dorothy shrugged and put it in her coat pocket anyway.

On the subway, Dorothy felt a subtle change in the social fabric of the city. There were more smiles and eye contact than usual. Strangers joked about the storm or the smells or were generally more considerate in ways they hadn't been before. Even the Amazon workers looked happy.

That's the silver lining to disasters, natural or otherwise, Dorothy thought as she watched a group of young tech bros with job-stopper tattoos offer their seats to elderly passengers. *It strips away pretension and brings out the better nature of people.* Dorothy remembered reading about how Londoners missed the togetherness they felt during World War II, during the Blitz. That shared trauma revealed something that was already there, just below the surface.

"Excuse me, ma'am, is this seat taken?"

Dorothy stared out the window.

"Well then," a man said. "You either need a double cappuccino or you've become an expert in Zen and the art of subway meditation. How have you been!?"

Dorothy looked up and smiled when she saw it was one of her favorite cohorts from Bellevue College. A fresh-faced English professor who had been the closest thing to a best friend on campus. She shook her head. "Did you just call me ma'am?"

"There she is! My long-lost poetess," the man said as he gave her a hug and then sat down next to her. "It's been forever. You left campus without saying goodbye. You didn't respond to my texts or emails — and don't be afraid to be a ma'am, by the way — it commands authority and respect. Plus, it rhymes with glam, and Sam, and . . . Spam." The man smiled. "See, that's why I'm not a poet."

Dorothy laughed, then realized she hadn't done so in a very long time. She grimaced and sighed. "I didn't say goodbye to anyone because admin didn't renew my contract, which was a polite way of firing me. I just wanted to disappear. I'm sorry, Graham, I know I told your husband I'd come over for dinner . . ."

"That's okay," he said. "Clarke's cooking is still unspeakably dreadful, so you dodged a bullet there. But we did want to spend time with that sweet, talented daughter of yours. She needs some uncle love in her life. Though Clarke still thinks you missed an amazing opportunity by not naming her Toto."

"Just one word?" Dorothy laughed again. "Like Beyoncé?"

"That's all the great ones ever needed," he said. "How are you, Dot? Still with that special man of yours? Still living in that wild, art deco palace atop that scary old building? Still getting paid to break your own heart for a living?"

"Yes. Yes. And it turns out breaking one's heart doesn't pay what it used to."

He hugged her again. "Well, you have our sympathies for all three. If there's anything we can do to ease that trifecta of crazy, don't hesitate. Where you headed?"

Dorothy didn't feel up to sharing that she was starting a new form of treatment. "Nowhere special." She shrugged. "Just needed some me time, I guess."

As Graham talked, Dorothy realized how much she missed being on campus. How much she missed human contact. How much she missed socializing with other academics. She also realized that the main reason she got along with Graham so well was that he had assessed the dysfunction in her relationship the first time he met Louis. When Louis gave her a backhanded compliment at a faculty gathering, Graham left a note in Dorothy's office the following Monday that read: *When in doubt, kick him out. I don't care how gorgeous he is.*

Graham took her to lunch every week even though Louis would get jealous like a hormonal seventh-grade boy whenever she spent time with male colleagues, even in public places, even when only discussing lesson plans and syllabi, and even when those male colleagues were married to other men. In retrospect Louis's concerns seemed comical, utterly ridiculous, but at the time, no one was laughing and Dorothy was always too emotionally drained to argue. The one time she did try speaking to Louis about his concerns was after sex, the one love language they were still occasionally fluent in, yet in that relaxed, unguarded, afterglow moment, he merely said, "It's fine," as his phone lit up with messages from work, effectively putting an end to the conversation.

Dorothy missed her friend. Those lunches with Graham seemed a lifetime ago.

"Seriously," Graham continued. "I mean it, this is my stop, but text me when you're free and we'll plan a little playdate for you and that little Toto too!"

Dorothy watched him leave, watched the doors close behind him. That brief moment of kindness and understanding leaving with him. She wished she'd told him where she was going, what she was doing. He'd always been like an open door. Made her feel less trapped, less confined. In contrast, the soft blanket of gray flannel that passed for a Pacific Northwest sky had always made her feel stuck, made the city feel like a padded cell. The perpetual rain was isolating, the gloom suffocating to the point that there had been days when she felt numb and couldn't bring herself to get out of bed. As an angsty teen, her jokes about eating sadness for breakfast were fully appreciated only by her artsy peers, who teased that if she ever formed a heavy metal band, it would be called Melancholica. That if she ever had a perfume named after her it would be called Abandonment and come in a cracked bottle. Now, as an adult, her personal brand of perpetual disquiet was something she'd embraced as a poet. She danced to it on the page, but was wary that bad things might happen if and when the music ever stopped. That was the Faustian bargain she'd made regarding her mental health. That leaning into her sadness might give her work a certain vitality, but could also lead her down the one-way path traveled by Sylvia Plath, Virginia Woolf, Yukio Mishima, and Kurt Cobain. She rolled her eyes when Louis sarcastically pointed out that most of the books on her shelf were by people who had either been locked away, committed suicide, or both.

On the inside, though, she worried.

That's when on dark, rainy days — in moments between feeling low and not feeling anything at all — she worried about Annabel. Louis thought the idea of inherited trauma was a joke. A very expensive joke at best and a dangerous scam at worst, high-tech snake oil for desperate, gullible people. "Let me get this straight. They inject you with a virus that alters tissue in the brain," he'd argued, throwing up his hands. "And no one — not even the geneticists involved — know what the long-term side effects could be. So they basically charge you for being their lab rat — charge us thousands of dollars for something that's unproven, unsanctioned, and unsupported by the FDA because it's too *experimental.*" Dorothy hated the way Louis put words in air quotes almost as much as when he talked about money, especially since she'd allowed him to use what was left of her mother's estate to launch his business and lease their apartment.

Dorothy tried to explain how the entire field of epigenetics had blown up two decades earlier with an experiment at Emory University using *actual* lab rats. Researchers released a citrus spray while electrifying the floors of the animals' cages, habituating the rats to react in fear whenever they smelled that particular scent. Years later, researchers noticed that the offspring of those lab animals, three and four generations later, had the same fear reaction to citrus.

Louis shook his head. He tried not to roll his eyes but failed. "And of course, no insurance company will touch something so completely unknown."

"It's not completely unknown. It's just

unknown to you," Dorothy argued. "My therapist said I'm a perfect candidate for this kind of treatment."

"Why am I not even remotely surprised?"

"Why do you say that?"

"Because," he groaned. "You'd have to be out of your mind to hand over our money for something so breathtakingly foolish."

As the subway slowed for her stop in Ballard, Dorothy knew Louis would find fault in anything she tried, but especially this. The idea of treating trauma passed down from one generation to the next in humans was highly controversial, to say the least. Just the idea of historical trauma was argumentative, though the concept had been widely accepted in Native American communities for hundreds of years, or more recently, within groups descended from Holocaust survivors. Yet therapists and geneticists had been puzzled for decades, searching for evidence of what they called transgenerational epigenetic inheritance.

Dorothy didn't know what to expect, but she did know that whatever the process was, it wasn't even remotely approved by the American Medical Association.

Walking to her appointment, she found that the address she'd been given led to a small windowless building that appeared to have made it through the storm relatively unscathed. There was a simple sign on the door that read: *Epigenesis.* Dorothy felt nervous and remembered an old poem by Wendell Berry. Something about fearing for what a child's life may become. Then she quoted the great Southern poet as she opened the door. "I come into the peace of wild things."

7
ZOE

(1927)

Zoe Moy's ears were filled with the happy squeals of a child's laughter as a group of third graders chased a loping clumber spaniel around the base of an old English walnut tree. Above the fray, sitting on a thick branch in a green dress, her feet dangling, was Zoe's favorite teacher, Mrs. Bidwell, playing "The Wreckers Overture" on her violin.

Zoe stood perilously at the edge of the diving platform of the new swimming pool at Summerhill, the boarding school where she'd lived for the last eight years. She waved to her teacher, who smiled and nodded. When the song reached its crescendo, Zoe looked up at the rare, clear blue August sky, drew a deep breath, pinched her nose, and jumped, plummeting six meters. As she plunged into the cool water, she puffed out her cheeks and slowly released bubbling air from her lungs, allowing her to sink to the bottom, where she sat, legs crossed in a lotus position like the Hindu swamis she'd read about in World History class. She opened her eyes, appreciating the rays of light that sliced through the water, illuminating the churning legs of the boys and girls above her in the middle of the pool. The teenage girls wore only bloomers, the teenage boys, like their younger cohorts, wore nothing. Zoe winced at the whiteness of their posteriors, though she thought their shriveled boy parts looked cherubic, like the dangling participles of the Roman statuary that haunted the school's wild rose garden.

Zoe's heart raced and her lungs began to burn, so she pushed off from the bottom of the pool. She kicked until she broke through the surface as a bell was ringing and most of her classmates were busying themselves by toweling off, putting their clothes back on, though a few ignored the clanging and continued playing, splashing in the pool.

Having spent half of her lifetime at Summerhill, Zoe knew that the bell meant afternoon classes would begin. The academic classrooms, the woodworking studio, the art room, the music parlor would all have faculty ready to teach those who felt like learning, exploring, indulging their whims of curiosity. Those who didn't feel like attending class today could go back to their rooms, or read in the library, or play anywhere on school property. At Summerhill, play was encouraged and learning was allowed, the opposite of a traditional English boarding school.

Zoe squeezed water from her hair and toweled off. She put her shirt back on as she walked barefoot to where Mrs. Bidwell was packing her violin. "Did you see me?"

"That was a brave leap, Zou yi," Mrs. Bidwell said as she closed her case. "Even some of the older boys are afraid of jumping from such a precarious height."

Zoe smiled. Her teacher was the only person who ever called her by her Chinese name. She turned her tan body toward Mrs. Bidwell, as though her teacher were the afternoon sun and she a hopeful flower. "You really think I'm brave?"

"Fearless as they come," Mrs. Bidwell said. Then she smiled and Zoe marveled at her dimples, the soft cleft of her chin. Her eyes, pale blue, like moonstones. She watched, spellbound, as Mrs. Bidwell brushed a dark finger curl of hair from her brow. Zoe loved the way she wore her hair, in a daring shingle bob that framed her face, stylish and reminiscent of Josephine Baker.

Zoe glanced back at the diving platform and the pool, where two dragonflies chased each other above the rippled surface of the water. She caught her breath and contemplated climbing the ladder and jumping in all over again.

"Going to class today?" Mrs. Bidwell asked. "I wish you were still in mine, you know, but I'm teaching the littles this semester. They're lovely but so impetuous and dastardly creative when it comes to voting on how the class should be run."

Zoe turned back to the teacher, who was stepping into a pair of sandals.

"Maybe I could be your assistant?"

"That would be excellent, truly, I'd love to have you but I'm afraid my littles might vote to smother you in honey and make you lie down upon an anthill." Mrs. Bidwell winked. "For science, they'd say."

Zoe remembered being a little at Summerhill. How it took her almost until the tenth grade to fully appreciate the merits of every child having a vote on all matters related to their education. Now that equality made her feel safe, ensconced in a colorful autonomy that she couldn't imagine giving up at a stuffy, black-and-white school. Children who transferred to Summerhill from elsewhere shared stories of how they'd lived in fear, of the violent wrath of their teachers and the cruel hazing rituals of the older students. Though Zoe knew all too well that soon she'd graduate and be forced to join the real world, which, while pretending to be a democracy, was just a sexist illusion, a mirage of freedom. Even after British women had fought and won universal suffrage, Zoe was keenly aware that she still wouldn't be able to vote until she turned thirty, nearly twice her age, and then only if she were the head of a household or wedded to the head of a household. She couldn't imagine that life.

"I guess I'll just get dressed and head to the library," Zoe said.

Mrs. Bidwell walked back with her toward the main school building. "That seems to be your favorite hideaway these days. Still searching the Romantics for a kindred poet? I thought you'd found Mary Robinson. Her work is much better than Hemans's melancholy poems about women being kidnapped by Vikings or pirates, or how a lady can only be faultless in her moral conduct if she's married."

"I've read all of Robinson," Zoe said. "And *you're* married."

"Then let my faults be a cautionary tale." Mrs. Bidwell sighed as she curled her arm around Zoe's. "In any case you should be so kind as to call me Alyce from now on."

Zoe laughed, but inside she swooned.

Ever since she set foot in Mrs. Bidwell's class, she'd been smitten. Part of that admiration was surely because she'd only been teaching for a few years and was much younger than the other instructors. Or because Mrs. Bidwell knew how to drive a car. Perhaps because she had the audacity to postpone having children and talked liberally about the relief she felt after being fitted for a Dutch cap. But if you asked Zoe, she would have said it was because Mrs. Bidwell was who she imagined herself to be one day, minus her joyless husband, Stanley, who lived in town but traveled for most of the year as a surveyor for the Royal Cartographic Society. He was uptight and measured. If Mrs. Bidwell were a lioness, he was her cage. How she could be married to a dull man like that — any man really — Zoe never knew.

"Well then, Miss Alyce, I should be getting on to the library now."

Zoe thought that perhaps she'd reread the stories of the British author Sui Sin Far. Zoe was fascinated by the author, not only because she was Chinese like her, but because she wrote stories of daring and comfort, like "The Heart's Desire."

"And when you're there you should look into a poem called 'Ode to Aphrodite.' It's in a book of Greek poetry that I ordered from a store in Brighton and Hove. I left it at the desk, just for you. You have a poet's heart, Zoe. I thought you might enjoy a special gift from your former teacher."

Zoe beamed.

Alyce smiled. "It's like me. Mysterious and tragic."

When Zoe arrived at the library, she found Augustus Moss at the front desk, reading a book. He was her age, but shorter and slight of build, with a swoop of blond hair that tended to hang down, covering one eye, which made him look like a pubescent pirate. Despite his height, he was a grade ahead of her. He'd worked hard during the summer to pass his classmates, a fact he liked to remind people of.

"Hello, Augustus," Zoe said with as little emotion as possible. She'd learned not to engage him, lest she be drawn into some long, circular, philosophical argument. "Mrs. Bidwell left a book here for me. I'd like to pick it up, please."

"You know I hate that name," he said, without looking up from the book. "Why don't you call me Guto, like everyone else?"

Calling the boy by his Christian name was Zoe's one needling indulgence. She called him Augustus after reading the obituary of Charles Dickens's scandalous brother of the same name, who eloped to America with a mistress when his wife became blind. When Augustus Dickens died, his final postscript read: *He was competent enough, but addicted to intemperance to a degree that practically blighted his usefulness. What he might have become, if of correct habits, no one dared to predict.*

What Guto might become, Zoe didn't dare to predict either. But whatever it was, she was certain it would be a bitter brew of malevolence, heartlessness, and guile.

"I don't know. You just seem more like an Augustus to me," Zoe said with an innocent shrug. "Is my book of poetry hereabouts?"

Guto ignored her request. "Did you know that Aladdin was Chinese?" He lifted the book so she could see the title, *One Thousand and One Nights.* "It says here, 'He was born to a poor tailor in the capital of one of China's vast and wealthy kingdoms.' I never knew that China even had wealthy kingdoms. The world is a queer thing, I suppose."

I knew that, Zoe thought, *and so does he.*

126

"My book, please?"

Guto frowned as he closed the book and set it aside. Beneath it was a smaller, newer hardback, which he opened and pretended to read. He nonchalantly licked his thumb and turned the page. "Oh, this one?"

Zoe read the title. *Sappho* by T. G. Tucker. She stepped closer. In Mrs. Bidwell's class, their book of classic Greek poetry listed Sappho in the table of contents, but when you turned to her section of the book the pages were blank.

"That's in tribute," Mrs. Bidwell had said. "Because we know so little about her. She was the greatest poet of her time. Regarded as the Tenth Muse. But now most of her poetry has been lost. All that remain are bits of crumbling paper. Ah, but those bits — those bits — will take your breath away."

Zoe had been intrigued ever since. "That's mine. Please give it to me."

Guto scratched the inside of his right nostril and then used that finger to turn another page. "This is quite humorous, this book, I took a hard look at it. Did you know this Sappho woman was married to a man named Kerkos?"

"I would if you'd let me read it."

"It says here her husband's name was a joke. Kerkos translates to Dick Allcock.

That she wasn't really married and her make-believe husband lived on the Isle of Man."

Zoe felt herself blushing.

Or was it furious anger that colored her cheeks?

"This is quite the book." Guto looked up above the margins, smiling. "Apparently the author had some irregular habits when it came to — shall we say — desires of the flesh." His eyes traced the curves of Zoe's young body, from chin to toes, then back again, lingering on her youthful, womanly features.

He closed the book and rested it on the counter, his hands crossed atop of it. "I'll give it to you if you give me a kiss." Guto smiled.

Zoe felt her skin crawl.

She tried not to show her revulsion, knowing it would make this even harder. She looked at his face, his pitted, acne-scarred cheeks, the whiff of hair beneath his nose, his earnest attempt to grow a mustache.

Zoe did the split-second calculus in her head, weighing the derivative of their lips touching for a brief second versus the function of him giving her the book. The differential, she hoped, would be him leaving her alone for the rest of the week.

If I just give him what he wants, he'll go away.

"Fine," Zoe said. She leaned forward, tilting her head.

Guto smiled as she closed her eyes.

She felt his lips for a moment, cold and rough. Then she felt a hand on the back of her head as he pressed harder, parting her lips with his sluglike tongue, his mouth wide as she felt his breath through his nose on her face. She whipped her hand up to knock his away with a loud smack. She stepped back, wiping her lips with the fabric of her shirt, then realized he was looking at her bare midriff and stopped. She wanted to spit on the ground but held back. She felt a rush or fear and anger and confusion.

Guto smiled. Then he pushed the book forward until it dropped from the counter, tumbling to the wooden floor where it landed with its pages spread open.

"Enjoy," he said as he licked his lips.

Zoe knelt and collected the book and what was left of her dignity.

On Sunday, the entire student body regrouped in the dining hall — kids of all ages — from the littles, with their bare feet, restless energy, and uncombed hair, to those who would graduate this year. The faculty

129

gathered as well, along with the janitor, the school cook, and the groundskeeper, all former students. Zoe smiled at Mrs. Bidwell, thinking of the book and how she'd read it every day since. Her teacher smiled and nodded at her before taking a seat. Lastly the headmaster, A. S. Neill, meerschaum pipe dangling from his mouth, waded through the crowd of children sitting on the floor, the chairs, the tables. Some of the students lay in each other's arms, in couples and small groups, more platonic than romantic.

Zoe imagined for a moment that this gathering was a tribunal, a legal body gathered to convict Guto of his social crimes before banishment. But as she caught his eye and he blew a kiss from across the room, she knew that was not the case.

The headmaster sat down and everyone quieted, even the littles, though they fidgeted and whispered to each other.

"As you know, our weekly general meeting is more important to me than all the textbooks in the world." He spoke softly so that everyone had to lean in, his Scottish accent on full display. "This is where we set rules, address grievances, and come together as a community. Each of you has one vote, simple, precious, and powerful, as do I. Together we will make collective decisions, and for a time, live with those decisions, because the best way to learn, in my opinion, is through trial and error. No error is a failure, it is an opportunity. Now, before we set sail and chart our course for the week, would anyone like to share with the rest of us?"

Zoe listened as two boys recited poetry they had written. A young girl with a viola played a suite of sonatas by Brahms. Then a group of littles performed a variation of "Snow White" by the Brothers Grimm. An elaborate skit about Snow White learning to sword fight and then challenging and defeating the Huntsman in a duel, much to the delight of all the animals in the forest. The older children passed out enormous bowls of popcorn to be shared as everyone watched, laughed, and finally cheered.

The headmaster gave the skit a standing ovation, offering copious praise, then he remained standing as he drew a slip of paper from his waistcoat. "I do have one advisement, before we address rules and such. The advisement involves swearing."

"Fuck, I knew it," one of the older girls said and everyone laughed.

"Yes, that's it," the headmaster said. "I would advise for the benefit of all that when you go to the village of Leiston, you try to

131

limit your swearing. While we know swearing can be cathartic, used in a response to pain, or emphatic as one of our students just demonstrated, the people in the village find it socially offensive. And as we want to be good neighbors, I advise you to extend them that courtesy."

Zoe and the rest of the student body nodded along in agreement. Here at school they could swear, try cigarettes, lark about the forest instead of going to class, break bedtime as long as they weren't keeping others awake. They could even swim without the burden of clothing, which had been unanimously voted for by the students, but in town they would behave in a manner that didn't arouse concern or intervention.

"Now, this quarter we will be studying one of my favorite topics of discussion" — the headmaster removed his pipe and coughed — "government."

A few of the older boys booed.

The headmaster continued, "I don't necessarily disagree with you lads. As a school, we aspire to be a functional, benevolent democracy. If this were Parliament, we would be neither the House of Lords nor the House of Commons; we would be the house of the people. But a few of the faculty members have suggested that we operate the school with a different form of governance. An object lesson writ large, if you will. We will do so for one week." The headmaster bit down on his pipe and smiled. "And we shall see how we do. Now what form of governmental theory should we explore?"

One of the older girls suggested Trotskyism. One of the little boys waved his hand in the air and asked if he could be a king. One of the older boys teasingly suggested patriarchy and was promptly booed by the girls.

One of the teachers even suggested anarchism. "I think it would be interesting if we dissolved the school as the state and observed what formed in its absence."

Mrs. Bidwell said, "The villagers already think that's how we operate." The other teachers laughed. "I'm not sure we want to validate those erroneous assumptions."

"What about fascism?" a boy named Theo suggested. He was tall and handsome, charismatic and charming. The rest of the group recoiled, though, as if he'd opened a bag of cobras and dumped them on the floor, leaving them to slither between students' legs, biting them, poisoning anyone within striking distance.

"What about that?" the headmaster said.

"Did you see how you all had a visceral reaction to Theo's idea? Perhaps that's one we should vote on if we all feel so strongly. Perhaps that's one worth studying under a microscope to see what contagions lurk within, so we can inoculate ourselves from that type of infection in a society."

Ultimately, the school as a collective group chose three ideologies to bring to a vote: social democracy, meritocracy, and fascism. Zoe looked on as the headmaster called for a vote by a simple show of hands. Teachers would tally the votes.

"Who votes for social democracy?" the headmaster asked.

Zoe raised her hand along with a few of the other students, mostly girls, and a majority of the faculty, including Mrs. Bidwell.

Zoe wanted to stand up to lobby for more support.

"Who votes for a meritocracy?"

As Zoe expected, the students who excelled at traditional academia all raised their hands. They were a frighteningly small minority. They all looked disappointed. They all understood math and probability. They should have known what was coming.

"And lastly who votes for" — the headmaster sighed — "fascism?"

Most of the older boys raised their hands, along with the girls who were good at sports or the most attractive. Zoe wasn't sure if they fully understood what they were voting for, or did so merely as an act of rebellion, like smoking. They were saying, *Look, I can do something dangerous and no one can stop me.* Zoe observed that the littles were easily led. They saw the number of hands rise and went along with the social inertia, following suit. Even a few of the teachers voted for fascism. The rebellious teachers who she knew would always favor the dark horse in a race or a wild card in the deck.

The headmaster raised his arm, pipe in hand. "I, too, would like to see where this train of fascism is going. Though I suspect it is traveling headlong into another locomotive altogether. But we shall see, won't we?"

Those who voted for an authoritarian regime all kept their hands raised high. Two of the teachers stood and performed the act of counting, but Zoe knew who had won and who had lost. She saw Guto smiling at her, his arm raised high. She remembered his sour breath, his porcine tongue, his grip on the back of her head. She wanted to be enraged, she wanted to stand and accuse him, but instead she chewed her lip, overcome with emotion. She tried to think of other things as she stared back at him so she would not cry. The Pythagorean theorem, hummingbirds, the words of the poet Ezra Pound — "Speak against the tyranny of the unimaginative."

The headmaster stood up and clapped his hands. "Well done. Well done. Those of the majority party — or those newly willing supplicants — you may gather elsewhere to select your own leaders, and your rules by which the rest of us will live for a week." The class waited as Theo stood and led his followers out of the room.

Zoe looked across the room to Mrs. Bidwell. Her teacher smiled and nodded, her eyes hopeful as though she were silently saying, *It's okay, we'll get through this.*

"Tomorrow at sunrise," the headmaster said, "we will be living under fascist rule. Let us hope we all earn passing marks."

That night, after most everyone had gone to bed, Zoe took a blanket, some stationery, and the book Mrs. Bidwell had given her and went outside into the warm, humid summer evening. She sat in her nightshirt atop an old picnic table in a small glade where there were so many glowworms it was hard to tell where the earth ended and the starry sky began. As the full moon rose

136

above the trees, she opened the book and read, inhaling lines of poetry along with the fragrance of wisteria in full bloom.

Inspired, she licked the tip of her pencil and used the words of the Greek poetess to compose a note to her teacher, whom she struggled to think of as Alyce. However, on paper, Zoe found her courage. *Dear Alyce.* Zoe's heart raced as she wrote the name. *Again love, the limb-loosener, rattles me, bittersweet, irresistible.* She added, *If only I could reach you, a sweet apple turning red, high on the tip of the topmost branches, forgotten by pickers. But my tongue is frozen in silence and instantly a delicate flame runs beneath my skin.* Zoe clutched the paper to her chest, her pounding heart. Then she finished with *Someone will remember us in the future. But for now, I sleep alone.*

Zoe carefully folded the letter, slipped it into an envelope, and sealed it. She looked in the direction of the school and Mrs. Bidwell's classroom, when she saw a figure walking toward her in the moonlight. She carried a brass lantern with a candle inside. Even in the twilight Zoe recognized the green dress swaying in the breeze.

Zoe froze, not knowing whether to run, hide, or spontaneously combust.

"Fancy finding you out here," Mrs.

Bidwell said. "Everything okay?"

Zoe slipped the letter inside the book, almost dropping it. Then she held the book up and hoped the night was dark enough to conceal how much she was blushing.

"Ah," Mrs. Bidwell said. "I brought a candle, but you brought the torch. May I join you?" Zoe nodded as her teacher sat down next to her. Zoe offered part of her blanket, which Mrs. Bidwell used to cover her bare legs.

"What are you doing out here?" Zoe asked. "Don't you live in town?"

Mrs. Bidwell nodded. "This is what happens, Zoe, when you're an old spinster like me with no one to go home to. You start to collect cats by the dozen, or ghost about, stringing violets at night." She tied off the open end of a garland and draped the flowers around Zoe's neck. "There, now you look a proper goddess. You'll make all the other pagans jealous."

The flowers were painfully soft. Zoe felt her heart beating amid the chirping chorus of field crickets. "You're hardly a spinster."

To Zoe her teacher looked as though she belonged on the campus of the University of Suffolk. She still had the youthful bearing of an undergrad. It pained Zoe to think of Mrs. Bidwell living alone while her husband was off traveling the world.

I wrote you something. Zoe said the words in her mind but couldn't bring herself to say them out loud.

Her teacher sighed.

To Zoe, Mrs. Bidwell seemed equal parts happy and sad. Victorious and defeated. Brave but frightened. Surrounded by students, but perpetually alone. She turned and for a moment, Zoe thought a dam might burst between them, words pouring forth, creating a whirlpool of sentiment, drowning them both in honest confession.

"How do you like the book?" Mrs. Bidwell asked.

"It's breathtaking." Zoe shook her head. "I can't thank you enough."

"Seeing you out here, sitting under the stars on a night like this, book in your lap, this is what teachers live for," Mrs. Bidwell said. "What I live for, anyway."

Zoe thought about the note she'd written.

"Do you hear that?" Mrs. Bidwell said as she closed her eyes. She turned toward Zoe, eyes still closed, whispering, "That's a nightingale."

Zoe leaned in.

She'd kissed many boys. From the chasing, giggling, kiss game she'd played as a little, to the awkward, chapped-lip, teeth-bumping exchanges with boys her own age. But until this moment she'd never understood the fuss and why other girls seemed so preoccupied with the act. Now she understood why Shakespeare wrote so many sonnets. She understood why Mr. Darcy closed his book and watched Elizabeth walk about the room. She understood what *crossing the Rubicon* really meant, because here she was, close enough to smell perfume, to feel the warmth of quickened breath.

Her teacher opened her eyes and said, "It's getting late."

Mrs. Bidwell patted Zoe's hand.

Zoe turned hers up and their hands clasped, fingers laced, her teacher's thumb brushing the back of Zoe's hand. They both looked down curiously, appraisingly, as if their bodies had acted on their own.

Then Mrs. Bidwell let go and said, "Good night, Zou yi."

"Good night, Alyce," Zoe sighed.

As Mrs. Bidwell left, Zoe walked back to her cottage. When she reached her door, she turned, not wanting to go inside, not wanting her feelings to evaporate back in the noisy world of housemates and homework. She stood still, breathing in the cool night air, searching the darkness as it began to rain.

8
FAYE

(1942)

Faye was nearly out of breath as she ran to the hospital through a torrent of rain. She heard a jeep, gears grinding, blaring its horn in the distance amid the thunder. Not the thunder that comes from a formation of bombers or Japanese artillery, but the kind that heralds the arrival of monsoon season. Sharp cracking explosions, followed by the sound of gargantuan trees falling in a deep forest, a booming so loud she could feel it on the soft soles of her oxfords. Echoing like timpani, part of the seasonal symphony of water dripping from metal roofs, quickened steps on sodden boardwalks, the rhythmic thrumming of rain on puddles that grow and swell until they become estuaries that spill into muddy streams, flowing through the streets of Kunming.

Faye arrived at the hospital beneath sprites of red lightning as Lois was still laying on

141

the horn, blaring her presence to those inside. The jeep she was driving was occupied by an injured family from a nearby village. A father in the front passenger seat, mother and daughter in the back, their legs blackened and cinched with tourniquets where their feet were mangled or missing, their blood-soaked clothing in tatters.

For a moment Faye was frozen, speechless, a statue weathering the storm. She wasn't thinking about John Garland or the photo he'd left behind, because she couldn't take her eyes off the mother and daughter. The carnage of war contrasted how tender they looked with their eyes closed, their bodies together, the mother's limp arms still wrapped around her broken child as the rain washed over them. The sight awakened a longing Faye had tried for years to ignore, the desire for a child. It haunted her the way she'd seen amputees try to scratch an itch from a part of them that was no longer there.

"What happened?" Faye asked, even though she'd been in Kunming long enough to recognize the various types of war wounds. She'd accumulated a mental encyclopedia of bloodshed and suspected that she'd find this family's horrific injuries filed under *L*.

"A neighbor said the girl was playing and chased her dog into a field full of land mines," Lois said, her voice shaking. "Her mother and father got injured trying to rescue her. I heard that the dog came through without a scratch, though."

Faye touched the pale neck of the father, who was slumped against the door. Even in the sultry air, his body temperature was far below that of the warm, tropical downpour.

"He's gone," Lois said, sniffling, wiping the rain from her eyes. The crushing humidity turned Lois's curly blond hair into a wet mop that clung to her cheeks. "I lost him on the way." She draped her nurse's cape over the face of the dead man.

Faye blasted the horn again until orderlies came rushing out. They called for stretchers, shouting in English and Chinese, and carried what was left of the mother and daughter inside the hospital.

After surgery and her final rounds for the day, Faye sat once again in the bar of the Kunming Tennis Club, nursing her third drink. Her surgical mask, still tied around her neck, hung loosely below her chin as she stared at the photo of her younger self. She sighed and finished her drink as a song crooned from the juke box. "I go around wanting you. And yet I can't imagine that you want me too."

The front door opened and closed, and Faye heard the rain, felt a gust of monsoon air. She heard footsteps that grew closer and then stopped next to her.

"I thought I might find you here," Lois said as she placed two bowls, two sets of chopsticks on the table. She sat down and then slid one of each over to Faye. "I'll be honest — I don't like how much I'm getting used to this."

Faye held her bowl and mixed the rice noodles with the tofu pudding and pickled vegetables. "The *dau faa min*?" Faye asked. "I think it's quite good."

Lois sighed. "You know that's not what I meant."

Faye nodded and took a small bite of the flat noodles and creamy tofu, which tasted rich and savory, topped with fresh mint, chives, and chrysanthemum. It felt like the food, so reminiscent of her mother's cooking, was healing her from the inside out, showing her that good things could still come out of this ailing land, salted with so many tears.

"How have you made it this long?" Lois asked.

Faye shook her head. "I don't know." She

tucked the photo into her breast pocket. The photo with her words: *FIND ME.* None of this made sense.

Maybe I'm losing my mind. But if I am, how would I even know?

Faye thought about the survivors of the Canton Uprising, fifteen years ago. How the Red Guard was crushed and how many of the wounded had healed physically, but remained shell-shocked, benumbed with facial tics, shakiness, sensitivity to light and sound. Many of them lost weight and died or later took their own lives.

The lights flickered as thunder rattled the windowpanes.

"I thought we could save them," Lois said, shaking her head, staring down at the bowl of noodles that she hadn't touched. "I used to think we could save everyone."

Faye nodded. She'd once been that hopeful. That naïve.

Then something caught her eye.

A shape. A figure. A man, passing by, walking in the rainstorm.

Faye watched him but he was already moving down the street, his back toward them. He wore an oil-stained pilot's uniform, now soaking wet. He walked briskly, but with a familiar limp. Faye hesitated for a moment, unsure of what just happened, what she'd seen, and then she leapt to her feet, shoved chairs out of the way, and scrambled to the nearest window. She wiped the condensation off with her sleeve and saw the man disappear into a crowd on the far side of the street.

"What are you doing?" Lois called out. "Are you okay?"

"He's alive . . . ," Faye said under her breath.

She left her coat and Lois behind and ran out the door, stepping off the boardwalk into a deep puddle that was as warm as the rain. She felt the water fill her shoes as she splashed her way across the street, past pack mules, a diesel freight truck in the process of being unloaded, and stray dogs that barked at whoever was near. She caught a glimpse of the man walking away from her as townspeople dashed into buildings and slipped beneath awnings to avoid the storm.

"Wait! It's me! Wait!" she called out, but her voice was lost in the downpour.

She kicked off her shoes before they were nearly consumed by the mud, and carried them as she ran, splashing in wet stockings that grew muddier with each step.

Faye brushed aside her wet hair, wiped her eyes as she caught a glimpse of the young pilot through the rain. He turned down an alley.

Faye's heart raced as she followed him around the corner.

He was gone.

She walked down the vacant alley that was lit by hanging oil lamps, the walls painted dark yellow. There was a stone footpath covered in mud that led to the street. Directly across the roadway was an ornate iron door beneath a stone arch, the entrance to a small building, a chapel that had recently been repurposed.

"Now I really am losing it," Faye whispered as she approached the door.

She reached into her pocket for the photo, but the image, printed on old newsprint, had been soaked, waterlogged. The wet square came apart at her touch. The more she tried to squeeze the water out, to keep it whole, the more it fell to pieces. She dropped to her knees in front of the chapel, trying to salvage the fragments of muddy paper.

"No, no, no, no, no . . ."

She felt hollow inside. Her strange hope disappeared and her heart ached as she realized the photo — all that was left of him — was now gone, and all that remained was longing and confusion. Unanswered questions. The sweet and terrible memory of catching him, holding him as he collapsed in her arms. How he made her feel whole again for the first time. Losing that piece of paper was like losing him all over again. She shook. She raged. She sobbed for what she'd lost and what she never had, letting out a cry that had been inside her body for decades.

Then she heard the sound of a heavy door opening on rusty hinges.

"Hello," a voice said in Chinese.

She looked up and saw a man standing beneath the stone arch. Faye recognized him as a Buddhist monk by his amber robe and crimson sash. She glanced back through the drizzle, down the alley, searching, wondering what happened.

He regarded her with concerned eyes, for her shoeless, bewildered state, covered in mud, soaking wet in the dark night. Then he recognized her nurse's uniform and switched to English, tinged with a heavy British accent, a by-product of the decades foreigners had spent trying to connect Burma and Yunnan Province with a colonial railway. "You're welcome to come in if you'd like? To pay your respects or just to get warm. The chapel has been repurposed as a place for the newly deceased, but there are extra sheets, blankets. You can dry off."

He stood aside, inviting her in. "Please."

She rose to her feet, stepped inside, dripping wet. The monk fetched her a blanket that she used to towel off and dry her hair. She wiped mud from her legs and tried desperately to remember the photo. In it she was young, smiling. But her expression was more than the blissful, unjaded naïveté of youth. She had the regal bearing of contentment, belonging. She looked satisfied in a way that'd she'd never felt whenever she viewed herself in a mirror. The photo was like a version of her that she'd always hoped for — daydreamed about while lying in her bed in nursing school, staring up at the ceiling — the life she'd always felt she was meant to live. A stark contrast to the heaviness she was resigned to when her eyes adjusted to the dimly lit room and neat rows of wooden tables appeared in front of her, each with a body covered by an old sheet. The monk was lighting sticks of incense placed in wooden holders near the head of each of the deceased. Near the feet were small ceramic teacups.

"I know this might be startling to most people," he said as he worked. "But since you're a nurse, I'm sure you understand the need for a temporary morgue."

Faye nodded, then stepped closer, surrounded by musky swirls of agarwood smoke, traditional incense that smelled like a forest of flowers and ripening fruit. As she walked between the tables she recognized the shapes of men and women and the tragic outlines of children beneath their thin shrouds of cotton.

Her heart felt heavy as she stopped next to the figure of a tall man. She sighed as she read his toe tag, then gently pulled back the sheet. She stared down at the pilot, studied every detail of his face, his cheekbones, his dark hair, the stubble on his chin, his eyes, which had been closed and sewn shut. Here too, she was afraid of the inevitability of forgetfulness. Then she touched his arm through the fabric. After seeing the pilot in the street, following him, a part of her expected John Garland's body to be warm. She'd hoped it would be, through some bizarre miracle. The same way he'd shown up in Kunming with a photograph of her that she'd never seen. That perhaps she'd somehow crossed into a place where the rules of life and death were only advisements, suggestions, allowing wishes the possibility of fulfillment. But now he was cool to her touch. What was once a body that she had briefly held in her arms had become a cadaver.

"Did you know him?" the monk asked, looking up from his work.

Faye stared at the man's body. "I . . . think I did."

"Then I'm sorry for your loss," the monk said. "And his."

"I'm sorry for showing up like this," she said as though this were a lucid dream, as she heard the distant murmur of airplane engines somewhere far above, fading away. "I thought I saw him, outside, in the rain. But . . ." She rubbed her weary eyes.

He looked at her appraisingly. "I don't know if it will bring comfort in your particular situation," the monk said, "but in my tradition, this is not the end of your friend's journey, or yours. All of this" — he motioned to a wall as though staring through a window that wasn't there, observing a world she couldn't see — "is a stepping-stone in a wide river that connects us all."

Faye nodded out of politeness, abiding a communal moment the way the living cling to each other at a funeral, more emotional necessity than understanding. Loose gears fitting together because their mismatched edges have been momentarily worn down by grief. "But," she asked more of herself than of anyone else in the room, "I barely knew him. How do I grieve for him?"

She watched the monk light his last stick of incense, blowing on the ember until it was bright red, glowing. He washed himself with the smoke, then looked down at the shrouded shape of a child beneath a sheet. "We don't have to grieve only those we know. Sometimes we grieve for that which was lost, that which was never allowed to be."

Faye pondered this as she walked around the pilot. She came here looking for answers but was forced to settle for repose. "May I ask what the cups are for?"

She'd been to funerals for aunts and uncles in Canton and Hoiping. As a child, she'd helped her mother light prayer sticks for her ancestors during each Lunar New Year's celebration, especially for her grandparents who died in San Francisco, long before she'd been born. She'd watch as her mother burned joss paper, spirit money to be spent by the dead. As a nurse, Faye had long since surrendered superstition to reason, given religion over to science. She had little faith in a hereafter, and if there was such a thing, she certainly didn't believe that a soul needed spiritual pocket money for celestial bribes. Though she patiently acknowledged that in anyone's family, traditions were important. That understanding where a loved one came from often eased the burden of letting them go to a place of such shadowed uncertainty. Even if that place, that final destination, was just an ossuary of memory in the minds of the survivors.

"I'm offering prayers of guidance," the monk said as he opened a jug of water and poured a little into each cup. "Blessings that those lost to us might be treated favorably by the goddess Meng Po, whose task is to ensure that souls of the departed do not remember their previous lives. She does this by offering trapped spirits a cup of her five-flavored tea of forgetfulness — *mai wan tong* — the waters of oblivion. That the soul will forget everything from this life, and all the lives before. That the slate will be clean when she accompanies them to a long bridge of mist that the soul must traverse to return to this world, where they can begin again at a different point in time without being weighed down by memories of family, of suffering, of wishes unfulfilled."

Faye had a vague recollection of this myth from childhood. She'd been taught in school that Meng Po was a version of Lady Meng Jiang, who Buddhists believed was so encumbered by grief from the death of her husband that she was unable to move on, to be reborn. Instead she dedicated herself to relieving the pain of others with a soup that would allow spirits to forget the misery and suffering of the material world, leaving them with only the karma they'd accumulated on their journey.

She looked down at the body of John Garland once again. She thought of how he looked at her on the runway, how he struggled to speak, how he felt in her arms.

"But . . . what if I don't want to forget?"

The monk looked up from filling a teacup. He furrowed his brow as though she'd offered a Zen koan, a riddle with no answer, like *What is the sound of one hand clapping? Or What was your original face before your mother and father were born?*

He finished pouring water into the last cup. "I'm afraid that only a truly enlightened being is able to bear the burden of universal knowledge, to share the memories of ancestors. All others . . ." He motioned to the bodies.

Faye watched as the monk bowed three times to the deceased and then collected his things. "It's clear that you're looking for something very important." He paused. "Perhaps you are searching in the branches for what only appears in the roots."

Faye pondered this for a moment. "That's not the Buddha, that's Rumi."

"So it is." The monk smiled and nodded. "And I think both of them would tell you to look deeper." He departed, gently closing the door behind him.

Faye sighed and covered John Garland's face once again.

She caressed the smoke, watching it slip through her hands.

Then she quietly took his cup away, setting it on a nearby shelf. She dabbed her forefinger into the water and touched her thumb as though wiping a tear. She moved to the other end of the table, near the pilot's burning prayer stick, waving her palm over it, feeling the exiguous warmth of the glowing, cherry-red ember. She pinched her wet thumb and finger around the ember, feeling a brief sizzle of pain. Then quiet relief as she let go, the aromatic burning extinguished. She leaned over, hesitated, and then kissed the pilot's cheek through the fabric, gently, softly, the way a downy feather settles on the surface of a still pond.

"Don't forget me."

9
LAI KING

(1892)

Lai King Moy sat like the Buddha atop a pyramid of empty shipping crates, her favorite place to be on a rare sunny spring day in San Francisco. From her lofty perch, she could see over the stone seawall of Chinatown's old, decrepit port, and also watch ships at newer piers on either side being unloaded with steam cranes that seemed magical compared to the old tread-wheels operated by Chinese stevedores. The shirtless men had long black braids, but their queues were wrapped around like headbands to keep from getting caught in the spokes of the giant wheels and being crushed like a walnut. Lai King watched another group of men drape ropes and nets from the bulwark of the SS *Australia.* The four-masted steamship arrived that morning, offloading travelers first, then luggage, mail, and package freight, before finally addressing its cargo.

Lai King held her breath in anticipation, leaning forward as British sailors wrenched open the doors of the main cargo hold. She felt a cool breeze coming from the vessel and pinched her nose when she smelled white vapor, pumped into the air by the new reefer ship. The aroma of drying seaweed gave way to something pungent, like the sharp smell of salts the local pharmacist once used to try to revive her elderly neighbor who had hit her head and fallen into a stupor.

"The belly of the ship is cold like winter."

Lai King jumped when she heard her father. She turned and found him standing behind her, watching the ship. He put a hand on her shoulder. "See, everything stays nice and cool, even when the sun is shining."

"I'm sorry, Ah-ba," Lai King apologized in plain English. "I know I'm supposed to be in school. I just wanted to come and see the ship. I promise I'll go tomorrow."

For a moment, Lai King thought she might be in trouble again. Her father's voice had startled her in the same way the iron bell at the Chinese school could snap her out of a wistful daydream. She heard the ship's horn again, reminding her of the many times she'd been late for class. Or absent altogether, like today, when she left her books and slate behind to see if the ship really was delivering a cargo of winter.

Her father hugged her tight. Then he took her hand. "That's okay, little one, I was curious too at your age. Let's watch this winter ship, but don't tell your mother."

Lai King thought her father was teasing when he'd said the ship was delivering a cargo of wintertime. That he was spinning a folk tale, like how a wicked old man died on the first day of December and that's why they ate red rice in winter, to scare away the man's spirit. Or the tale of Captain Stormalong, whose ship was so tall the masts had to be hinged to avoid catching the moon. That story seemed as unbelievable as when he once told her that a stranger found him as a baby, in some dirty alley, in a city far away. That his ah-ma was the most famous Chinese woman in America and when she died in childbirth, her spirit flew like a grasshopper sparrow, carrying him over the mountains to California, where he was raised by a mission home.

Lai King smiled and looked back at the ship, hoping to get a better view as seamen barked orders to the boss stevedore and his foremen. She watched the Chinese men climb the treadwheel, which hoisted a cargo net into the air laden with crates of bananas and pineapple. She'd secretly hoped that the wooden boxes might be covered in snow. But they looked as boring as the rice cake her mother had given her to eat for lunch. She unwrapped it and took a bite. She tasted rosewater, wishing the chewy rice had been flavored with brown sugar and fried in egg the way her father made it whenever he cooked. She offered him a bite, but her father smiled and shook his head.

Disappointed in both the ship and her lunch, she glumly watched a flock of herring gulls as she ate. The noisy seabirds were circling, swooping, darting, as they battled a fat crow intent on stealing a few of the cockles and clams that the gulls had scavenged and dropped from the sky, cracking them open on the seawall.

Then the birds scattered as the ship's horn blared.

She put her fingertips into her ears as the horn kept bellowing, sending gusts of steam skyward. She watched as the stevedores who had been unloading the ship, porting heavy burlap bags of coffee, halted their labors. Then she heard a sailor on the forecastle yelling, cursing. One of the Chinese foremen shouted, *"Aai yah!"* He implored whatever deity he worshipped as he took the red scarf from around his neck and retied it, covering his nose and mouth. He called out to the men who had stopped unloading the cargo, many of whom were backing away.

"I don't like this," her father said.

Lai King imagined that perhaps winter really was about to emerge from the belly of the ship, that the men were bundling up in preparation for a swirling blizzard, or would soon be dashing home to get heavy wool coats, mittens, and hats. She smiled eagerly as she pictured a frozen cargo net, dripping with icicles, lifting a snowy, cloud-covered mountain peak above the bulkheads. She'd been taught that white bears lived on top of the world. She pictured one of those great creatures climbing out of the hold with a salmon in its mouth, dropping the fish to announce his presence with a frightening roar.

But as the ship sounded its horn again and again, a few of the dockworkers pointed up to where a thin veil of black smoke floated out of one of the freighter's giant, funneled stacks. Lai King cocked her head as she watched two British sailors hastily lower the ship's ensign, the red duster of Great Britain. Then the men on the docks stepped back even farther as a broad sheet of yellow fabric was hoisted to the top of the foremast. The makeshift flag was plain, boring, unremarkable, yet as men on nearby piers saw it waving in the wind they too began shouting, pointing, panic in their voices.

"What does a yellow flag mean?" she asked.

A man aboard the ship, bald and round in the middle and wearing a leather apron, stepped out of a metal door with something dark on the end of a long pole. She squinted as she tried to see. The men on deck stepped back as the lump on the end began moving, writhing. The man shook the end of the pole over the edge of the ship, banging it until the lump fell. The dark shape wasn't one thing, it was three — enormous rats, hissing, their tails whipping wildly as they tumbled to the water below. Lai King gasped as the bodies of two men, loosely wrapped in sheets, were dragged topside.

She heard the word *stowaways* as she stared at their limp corpses.

"It means we need to go," her father snapped. "Right now."

She followed her father, scrambling down the stack of old crates, trying not to get slivers as the ship's horn sounded. When she looked back, more British sailors and Chinese workers emerged from belowdecks, this time amid smoke, followed by a mischief of rats that scurried in every direction. Men were hastily climbing the masts and rigging, or running for the gangway. Others threw themselves over the wooden taffrail and began furiously climbing down the cargo nets to escape.

"The yellow flag means something bad." Her father spoke in Cantonese as he took her hand. As a translator for the Kong Chow Association, he'd always encouraged Lai King to practice her English. But she also knew that whenever he was upset, he would revert to his mother tongue. *"Jau gam faai, dak gam faai!* Let's go. Let's go."

They ran through the pandemonium, his hand clasped over hers. She could barely keep up. As workers and sailors swarmed in all directions, she tripped over a loose board on the pier and fell, skinning her knees and tearing the hem of her dress.

She sniffled as a tear ran down her face. "What's going on?" She winced as she brushed bits of dirt and gravel from a bloody knee.

"We'll talk when we get home," her father said, picking her up.

Lai King had seen him this upset, talking this frantically, only once before, when he ran out into the darkness late one night and helped the other men in Chinatown put out a fire. He came home exhausted, blackened with soot, coughing but smiling, because the fire had claimed only one home and not the entire neighborhood.

As her father carried her down a darkened side street, the cobblestones seemed to light up as though the sun were coming out of hiding. Lai King looked skyward and saw that the long clotheslines that hung between the buildings, from the second, third, and fourth floors — fifty, sixty, maybe one hundred lines in all — were quickly being reeled back in by the residents on either side. Thousands of garments parted the sky like clouds of white cotton, dappled with pink, red, and yellow. Most of the laundry was dry and merely blew in the wind, while the rest dripped upon them like falling rain.

To Lai King it looked as though Chinatown was closing down early. Flower carts were being covered. Merchants hurried to bring all their barrels of fruits and vegetables inside. Windows were shuttered. She looked over her father's shoulder and watched officers from the Chinese Six Companies, in traditional riding jackets, directing people to their homes. Even the beggars had migrated elsewhere. Lai King saw a plump rat with a long pink tail scurry beneath the boardwalk. She shuddered and hugged her father's neck as she looked away.

At their tenement, he carried her up the stairs and into their one-room apartment.

"Zum mo liu?" Lai King's mother asked as she turned from their open window. "Is it another fire? Have the Knights of Labor come back?"

Lai King's father set her down. He stretched his back for a moment, catching his breath, then closed the window and drew the curtain.

"They found two stowaways. Both dead," her father whispered. *"Syu jik."*

Her mother paused for a moment as the news sank in. Then she knelt down and rolled up Lai King's sleeves, her pant legs, appraising her skin, her scraped knee. She touched the sides of Lai King's neck. She touched her own.

Lai King felt scared, sensing fear and worry in her parents, but she didn't understand. She didn't know what the *black death* was. She imagined a dark cloud covering all of Chinatown, bolts of lighting, striking down men, women, children in the street. She imagined the fallen people, lying in the gutters. Then she swallowed and recalled the words of Li Qingzhao. In school, Lai

164

King had been taught that in times of trouble *one should become a ghost hero,* as the poetess implored.

While her parents began to argue, Lai King sat at a small table and played with a bouquet of forget-me-nots that she'd picked the day before. She'd been told that the small, ocean-blue flowers smelled better in the evening, though she wasn't sure if that was true or another one of her father's stories.

"We can stay inside, keep the door locked," her mother pleaded. "We have enough food for a week — three if we skip meals. Besides, where would we go?"

Lai King's father peeked out the window. "The Chinese mission on Battery Street. They'll take us in. Long enough to kill all the rats and clean the ship."

Lai King pictured a horde of rats pouring down the gangway, flooding the streets, climbing up drainpipes, and infesting their home.

"Pack your things," her father said. "We're leaving."

Lai King heard bells ringing as she held her mother's hand and they ran from the heart of Chinatown, up the steep hill to the south. In Lai King's other hand, she carried the small bundle of flowers. As they fled it appeared that everyone who was Chinese had already retreated to their homes, their workingman's hotels, their alley apartments where families lived. The only people on the street were British sailors, longshoremen, and Western merchants with negroes readying their horses or loading wagons so they could leave with their wares. Lai King and her parents, suitcases in hand, followed a stream of people leaving Chinatown. Some of them cursed Lai King and her family, yelling and calling them names, but she'd been born two years before the Chinese Exclusion Act and had grown up learning to ignore certain words.

When they neared the boundary of Chinatown, they stepped out of the street and up onto the boardwalk as an open carriage rolled past in the opposite direction, pulled by a single bay horse. The sign on the carriage said *Bureau of Health.* Two men in white gowns rode inside, their heads covered in white hoods. Only their faces peeked through, forehead to chin. *"Gwai,"* Lai King whispered in awe. To her they looked like ghosts.

"We'll be safe at the mission," her father said to himself as much as to anyone else. "They won't let anything bad happen to us.

Then when this is all over, I can go back to work. Lai King can go back to school. It's going to be okay."

Lai King wondered how her classmates were doing, her friends and playmates. She imagined them locked inside their homes. She wished she were back in her apartment. She'd visited the mission home once and it felt like school.

"Maybe the outbreak is not so bad," her mother said as she looked over her shoulder. "The illness. Maybe it's just a few sick people, nothing more."

They rounded a corner and five police officers in dark uniforms blew their whistles, sharp and piercing. The men waved their truncheons as they ordered Lai King and her parents to turn back. Lai King thought the men looked regal in their custodial helmets, their gold buttons polished to a marvelous shine. But they all had white kerchiefs tied around their noses and mouths. Other men stretched ropes across the street, blocking all passage. A large wooden sign dangled from the top rope, rocking in the wind. Painted in red lettering was a word she didn't know: *QUARANTINE.*

Lai King watched, confused. She didn't understand, because dozens of English sailors were allowed to leave. As well as the white merchants and dockworkers, who slipped beneath the ropes, smiling and sighing with relief. That's when she realized that all the Chinese and Black people were forced to stay. As her mother began to cry, Lai King watched small petals drop from the forget-me-nots, drifting to the filthy pavement like *sing can.* Stardust, trampled underfoot.

10
DOROTHY

(2045)

The first thing Dorothy noticed about Epigenesis was that it didn't smell like a typical doctor's clinic. Instead of something cold and antiseptic, there was a hint of warmth, a fragrance, like scented candles, or the dusky notion of dried flowers.

The second thing was that there was no one else in the tiny waiting room, which was fine with her. She'd had her fill of awkward moments sitting in therapist's offices filled with old magazines and new faces. Everyone avoiding eye contact. Dorothy found that such close proximity to silent strangers always left her feeling naked and vulnerable, as though everyone were thinking, *I may have problems, I may need help, but at least I'm not her.* Meanwhile a bossa nova version of "Stairway to Heaven" would play on an office sound system, music so awkward, so sublime, she wondered if there wasn't a dedicated satellite radio channel called Therapy Nation.

The third thing she noticed was a Native woman who opened the glass panel of a reception desk. She smiled and asked Dorothy to sign in on a tablet and take a seat.

When she sat down, Dorothy thought about what her therapist had said when she'd recommended her for treatment. "I think you're a perfect candidate. Go with an open mind. Or don't. It doesn't matter. This methodology will open it for you."

Dorothy wasn't fond of riddles, so she'd Googled the place, but all she learned was that their process was based on experimental methods used to help restore the failing memories of those suffering from Alzheimer's disease. In tests at the University of Washington, Alzheimer's patients undergoing epigenetic treatment occasionally reported having memories they couldn't account for — artifacts, contrivances — recollections that weren't there before. Those seemingly random thoughts were dismissed as synaptic misfires. But over a ten-month period, researchers noticed that those extra memories were never in the present, nor abstract in the future, like lucid dreaming. They were always in the past and always before the lifetime of the individual patient.

Dorothy felt goose bumps on her arms, a tingling in her spine as she recalled reading that article and how they used the term: anamnesis. She hadn't thought about the concept of inherent knowledge since her college philosophy days. Then she chewed her lip as she remembered trying to explain Plato's theory of memory to Louis. That, combined with the speculative nature of the Alzheimer's report, only made her sound a bit unhinged, like a zealous convert. He regarded her as though she'd fallen in with the last holdout Scientologists in town, or was about to run away to some new minimalist ashram tucked into one of Seattle's tony bedroom communities, bent on giving up their worldly belongings for the prospect of enlightenment.

"There's a reason why this place is in some tiny office in Ballard," Louis argued. "And that reason is: they're charlatans. I hate to be the one to tell you, but if they're really, seriously what they claim to be, why aren't they in some biotech center with hundreds of scientists and billion-dollar budgets?"

Dorothy had no answer, just scars on her arms and a lifetime of suicidal ideation.

At first, Dorothy thought that perhaps the humble nature of the facility was designed to hide it from prying eyes, or to afford local celebrities and businesspeople a measure of discretion. There were no press releases and no online presence. The business model of Epigenesis appeared to be exclusively based on word of mouth. Those facts, mixed together and seasoned with Louis's doubts, created a recipe for suspicion. She only hoped that the secretive nature of this place was because of its treatment methods and not a way to fly below the radar of litigious clients who'd been cured of their bank accounts.

Another Native woman in a lab coat opened the door into the lobby and said, "Hi, I'm Dr. Shedhorn. You must be Dorothy Moy. The lab sent over a report on your blood work, and everything looks great. Come on back." Dorothy looked around, realizing there was another explanation. The doctor was indigenous and had the benefit of transitory sovereignty. Many tribes had given up their reservations in return for the right to claim any building or compound that they owned as an extension of their nation. This building was like a Native embassy. Unencumbered by the regulations of the mainstream medical community, Epigenesis was free to offer radical medical procedures.

"Welcome to my humble treatment center," Dr. Shedhorn said. "I'm not sure how much your therapist told you about what I do here, but my success rate is fairly robust. Eighty-two percent of my patients have been relieved of their depression, anxiety, debilitating phobias, even PTSDs — within six months. I've been over your files and your medical history, and I think I can help you a great deal."

Dorothy followed the doctor, admiring her thick hair that was tied up in a bun. The doctor led her to a windowless room with a chaise-type lounge, IV stand, pulse oximeter, and a sleep study monitor with a chest strap and surface electrodes.

"All I know is what I've read online," Dorothy replied, looking up at the ceiling, which was comprised of thousands of LED lights, honeycombed with arrays of fiber optics. "Something about Alzheimer's and lost memories. That and my partner keeps insisting that you inject everyone with a virus. The way he talks about it, one would think you were hastening the next global pandemic."

Dr. Shedhorn raised an eyebrow, then suggested that Dorothy get comfortable. "He's not wrong — I do use a live virus, but it's not quite so menacing."

173

Dorothy stretched out on the chaise, which was surprisingly warm and conformed to the shape of her body as a nurse joined them.

"As your therapist may have told you, I led a series of Alzheimer's trials that involved people with a genetic predilection for the disease," Dr. Shedhorn explained as the nurse put gel on the electrodes and gently affixed them to Dorothy's neck, face, and temple. The metal felt cold, like being dotted with an ice cube. "I had those subjects spend extensive mapping sessions inside an MRI machine, while I asked questions — who they are, where they were born, specific memories about marriage, family, and career — their happiest moments, their saddest. While they were asked to ruminate on those moments, the MRI was busy taking magnetic snapshots of their brain activity."

The doctor fit the chest strap across Dorothy's torso and slipped the pulse oximeter onto her forefinger. Dorothy listened and drew a deep breath.

"Take a first kiss, for example." Dr. Shedhorn smiled.

Dorothy remembered the first time she'd kissed Louis, or more aptly, when he kissed her on their first date, an awkward meeting at a bougie coffee shop that was also a feline adoption agency where dozens of rescue cats had the run of the place. Dorothy was allergic and sneezed immediately after their lips touched.

"As that kiss happens, the amygdala stores the emotions of that event. The occipital lobe stores the visual. While the cerebellum stores the physicality — the smell of perfume, the taste of lipstick, the warmth of skin, the sound of birds in the background."

Dorothy's nose seemed to itch.

"The MRI captures the thousands of areas in the brain that collectively fire at once to create that memory. We call that snapshot an engram. By cataloging engrams, I was attempting to create a rough backup of a subject's formative memories."

Dorothy thought of Annabel. How her daughter felt in her arms.

"A few years later, at the first sign of Alzheimer's, those subjects were injected with a benign virus designed to attach light-reactive proteins to the surface of neurons in the brain," Dr. Shedhorn explained as the nurse prepped Dorothy's wrist and asked her to relax as she inserted an IV stent into a vein and taped the tubing to her arm.

Dorothy grimaced as she felt the needle. She tried to focus on the doctor.

"Those proteins function like switches, triggered by light, turning the ion receptor channels of those areas of the brain on and off," Dr. Shedhorn said. "Then each subject is seated in front of an array of thousands of pinpoint lights — like the ones above you — designed to trigger those switches, firing the connected neurons to recreate the engrams previously captured by the MRI."

Dorothy furrowed her brow. "So . . . if an Alzheimer's patient struggles to recall something, like where they were born . . ."

"Then I trigger the saved engram of that place, creating a reproduction of that lost memory. The process is proximal," Dr. Shedhorn said, "but the mind does a nice job of connecting the pieces and recreates that moment, in effect replanting the memory."

Dorothy watched as the doctor entered a code into the keypad of a pharmacology cabinet, which chimed as it dispensed a small vial of milky, copper-colored liquid.

"But during clinical trials," Dr. Shedhorn continued as she shook the glass vial, "not only were my patients recovering lost memories, there were distortions, extra memories that couldn't be accounted for."

"Epigenetic memories," Dorothy said, remembering what she'd read.

Dr. Shedhorn nodded. "During the Alzheimer's treatments, a small percentage of memory breakage was expected. I discounted artifacts as missed engramatic connections due to cellular deterioration caused by age or injury. But when those extra memories were correlated with the patient's family history, I was stunned at the findings. For example, a patient named Cecilia, who had a fear of flying, developed new memories of airplane crashes. But the aircraft she described were of early twentieth-century vintage, large passenger planes with twin propeller-driven engines. Upon further investigation, I discovered that the patient's grandmother was one of three survivors of a plane crash in 1951, when a twin-engine DC-8 went down in a snowstorm near Bothell. Cecilia's parents rarely talked about that traumatic event. As humans, we seek to hide trauma. Even Hitler burned *All Quiet on the Western Front* because it remembered the horrors of war. In Cecilia's family, no one wanted to remember the plane crash, but her DNA remembered and she ended up with that phobia nonetheless."

Dorothy remembered Annabel's drawings. The boy and the airplane, her sky tiger. How her daughter's artwork was so similar to Dorothy's own at the same age.

"Cecilia's treatment had activated latent engrams — buried epigenetic memories — that were so traumatic they altered the methylation of her DNA at an early age, which affected her behavior and mental health. She had literally inherited her grandmother's trauma, didn't know it, and couldn't escape it. Theorists used to call this phenomenon morphic resonance, or they'd try to explain it through family constellation therapy. But what I do here is biological instead of philosophical."

Dorothy gazed up at the lights. Over the last two decades, she'd taken an alphabet soup of antidepressants, anti-anxiety meds, and drugs for seizures. She'd meditated, used mindfulness apps, explored Kundalini yoga, cryotherapy, somatic therapy, play therapy, group therapy, and music therapy, until her counselor's notes had become an orgy of acronyms as the PTSDs on her ACE score had been treated by EMDR, MFT, and ACT, but had become TAU. Nothing had helped.

Dr. Shedhorn nodded to the nurse, who then left the room. "Consciously or subconsciously, we're capable of remembering much more than we're aware of. The average person could never remember pi calculated to twenty thousand digits, yet there are stage actors who have memorized every line of *Hamlet,* which is more than forty thousand characters. Because memory uses the same areas of the brain as imagination, we remember stories more easily. Using your therapist's notes, your medical history, and genealogy, I map out the known or suspected trauma within generations of your family. Instead of treating DNA as a blueprint, I regard it as a scorecard." Dr. Shedhorn pushed the hypodermic needle through the top of the vial and drew ten milliliters of the fluid. "Then I use engrams from a shared database of tens of thousands of patients. By giving you the benign engrams of a place related to historical trauma, your brain will begin to process the buried epigenetic memories."

"And generations of skeletons come out of the closet," Dorothy said with equal parts wonder and trepidation. "I don't know about specific trauma, but my five-year-old daughter appears to be mirroring some of the same obsessions I had as a child."

"You share the same DNA," Dr. Shedhorn said, "and a toddler is at an age where they're forming their own memories and experiences, but not burdened by current events, so they remember more, for a while anyway. It's tragic that children lose that epigenetic insight — or echo — around the time they're learning to speak."

Hearing that explanation made Dorothy feel a little less crazy. "As the US poet laureate Anis Mojgani once said about toddlers: *They cannot be understood because they speak half English and half God.*"

"I like that." Dr. Shedhorn smiled again. "We'll proceed whenever you're ready." She held up the syringe. "Once I push this through the IV, your brain will become minimally light receptive in a few minutes, with deeper receptivity building over time. This first session is like dipping your toe in the shallow end of the memory pool."

Dr. Shedhorn paused. "Eventually you'll be ready for the deep end."

Dorothy thought about the possible merits and potential hazards of opening a Pandora's box of familial tragedy. The conceit of addressing the pain and sorrow of others in the past — the whole uncanny idea — gave her hope. But as Nietzsche argued, "Hope is the most evil of all evils because it prolongs man's torment."

As Dorothy nodded she felt a burning sensation in her arm that dissipated as it spread through her body. *What would Louis think? He might use this against me. He could*

*say it was another example of how unstable I
am. That he can't trust me around Annabel.*
He'd argued that before, on her twenty-
seventh birthday, when she'd been so depressed she couldn't leave their apartment
and hadn't showered for days.

"Wait. Stop, stop, stop."

"I'm sorry, Dorothy," Dr. Shedhorn said.
"Is there something wrong?"

"I don't want to do this anymore."

Dorothy removed the chest strap as the
lights in the ceiling came on. She squinted
beneath waves of colored fractals as she
stood up and tore the electrodes off. She
pulled the IV out, ripping tape from her skin
as she stumbled from the room.

"I'm sorry, I can't. I just can't."

Dr. Shedhorn was calling out to her as
Dorothy found her way back to the lobby,
then outside, to the world of traffic and
typhoon season, of distress and dislocation.
Dorothy thought about what she'd say when
she returned to her old therapist, defeated
and scared. *What could they do now?* Dorothy felt as though they'd been stitching up
her wounds for as long as she could remember. Perpetual triage on her emotional well-
being. She began to hyperventilate, noticing
that the air was warmer than when she'd
gone inside and it stopped raining. The city

smelled different too, more beer and urine than Seattle's normal bouquet of pine needles, evergreen trees, and low tide. She looked down at the cobblestone street and wondered if the tidal surge from last week's storm had somehow eroded the concrete, revealing what lay hidden underneath. She remembered that when the city tore up the streets in the International District to put in light rail, the engineers found old rails and brick avenues that had been used by street-cars a century earlier. Dorothy felt a wave of remembrance as she noticed horse-drawn carriages. Not the hansom cabs that worked the waterfront during the heart of the sum-mer tourist season, but surreys and wagon-ettes with teams of draft horses. There was even a polished hearse, pulled by black horses who shook their heads and flapped their ears, chasing away flies as they clip-clopped back toward the center of an old city that she no longer recognized. Dorothy froze when she saw the men and women coursing up and down the boardwalks dressed in vintage finery, the men in wool suits and derby hats, the women in flowing dresses with bouffant sleeves and tightly cinched bodices, who carried lace parasols as they strolled. The buildings that Dorothy walked past en route to Epigenesis had been replaced with stately row houses and brick colonials with gas-lighting. Through watery eyes she looked up at the sky, cloudy and raven, as coal smoke hung above the tree-tops like the dark silk lining of a coffin. Disoriented, she leaned against a cold brick wall, watching the strange world pass by. Then she noticed something moving in a dirty, garbage-strewn alley. A fat tomcat hissed and scurried away as she stepped into the narrow passageway, shadowed by clotheslines with drying garments that waved on the breeze like prayer flags.

In the alley, Dorothy smelled soap, fermenting malt, rotting garbage, discarded beef bones and offal from a butcher, mingled with the stench of human waste where chamber pots had been emptied. The alley smelled like poverty and desperation, fleetingly interrupted by the pleasing fragrance of vanilla-scented tobacco.

Dorothy heard sobbing as it began to rain.

When she looked, she found a young Chinese woman with bound feet sitting among the piles of garbage, leaning against the wall. She looked to be in her late teens, her hair dark and wet. Despite the Western dress she wore, a green frock that was tight around her pregnant belly, she was clearly Asian. As she held her knees and gritted her teeth, crying out, Dorothy realized that the woman's dress, her many layers of fabric and petticoats, were soaked with the ruddy ochre of blood. Next to her was a disheveled sack of her belongings and a tin cup.

Dorothy's heart raced as she shouted for help but was ignored by the men walking by. A few well-heeled ladies slowed and looked pityingly at the woman in the alley, then continued their strolling, moving swiftly to get out of the downpour.

When Dorothy turned back to the woman, a man was there, dirty and disheveled.

"Here, Dorothy, drink this, it'll help you wake up."

Dorothy heard a vaguely familiar voice and saw that the tin cup was now plastic. She picked it up. It was warm. She held it in her hands and felt as though she'd been sleeping, dreaming. The lights came back on and she realized she was still at Epigenesis, in the chaise, which was mechanically adjusting, gently easing her to a sitting position. The grid of lights faded and the smells of the alley and the sound of trotting horses vanished from her senses into a place of memory. She no longer felt cold, damp from the rain, and her mouth was dry. Her feet tingling as though they'd both fallen asleep. It would be a moment before she could stand, let alone walk.

"Welcome back. That wasn't so bad now, was it?" She heard the soothing voice of Dr. Shedhorn. "That's valerian root tea, it eases residual anxiety and wakes you up a bit. It would appear that this treatment method works quite well for you. Not that I'm too surprised. I've found that people who work in the arts have an easier time accessing old memories. I'll make a few neurochemical adjustments, then next week we'll go deep."

Dorothy blinked as she looked around the room. "I'm . . . confused."

"That's a common side effect. As trauma is revisited it takes a while to reconcile memory with present reality, which sometimes causes disorientation. Like waking up from a dream and you're unsure where the subconscious ends and the real world begins."

"But . . . I saw a young woman . . . a girl. She was pregnant. I think she was dying. There was a homeless man. Blood everywhere. She was in terrible pain." Dorothy tried to remember, but her recollection of the woman in the alley began to blur. "Who was she? She seemed so familiar." Dorothy sipped her tea. She felt tingling as the hairs on the back of her neck began to stand on end. "Was that me?"

Dr. Shedhorn gently put her hand on Dorothy's arm.

"They're all you."

Act II

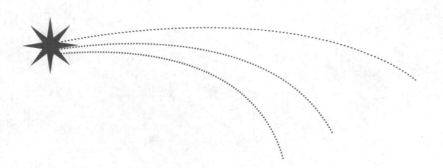

11
AFONG

(1836)

Afong woke in a boardinghouse.

She knew by the house rules posted on the back of her door.

She stared out the window, looking up at the crescent moon, remembering how her original managers, the Carnes cousins, always paid for an extra hotel room. Her life with the Hanningtons had been markedly different. Her first night in their care, Mrs. Hannington put her in what she described as a home for all-female boarders, which Afong later realized was a brothel. The strange place smelled like perfume, dried flowers, and vinegar. The women all wore thick layers of makeup and stared at her as though she were competition, and the men looked at her for other reasons altogether.

Since that evening she had seen her share of strange rented rooms. From the Irish boardinghouses where women often offered up their children as collateral. To the negro boardinghouses, which were not as bad as she had been led to believe. Other people described the houses as hotbeds of filth and of vile degradation, but Afong found them clean, the residents pleasant and courteous. She enjoyed their company because none of them judged her. Instead they marveled at her clothing. They offered sympathy and good humor toward her bound feet and queer predicament. Perhaps that was because there were negro guests who also had deformed feet and legs. Though Afong suspected that, like her, their deformities were caused by someone else.

As Afong heard people laughing in the hallway, carrying on in the room next door, she surmised that she was in a sociable boardinghouse. The type of place where residents could send out for beer. They could joke and fraternize. Afong preferred these places to the serious boardinghouses that favored *respectable boarders.* Afong learned that meant *white and preferably non-drinking.* At those establishments playing cards were not allowed, reading in bed was forbidden, and smoking was an evictable offense. The rooms were nicer, cleaner, and more decorous. But the last time Afong stayed at one she barely saw her room. Instead, after her performance, she was sent to the basement laundry, where she worked until sunrise.

Afong heard people closing their doors as she sat up and rubbed her eyes. She lit a candle and poured a cup of water from a pitcher on the nightstand. Her hands shook as she sipped. Her head reeled. She reached up and felt a swollen knot above her left ear as she vaguely remembered briefly waking up in a moving carriage with Mrs. Hannington, who said, "You were getting so restless, girl, one of the doctors gave you a few drops of Hoffman's Anodyne." Mrs. Hannington pantomimed pouring liquid on a handkerchief then placing it over her nose and mouth.

"You breathe it in."

"I . . . do not . . . understand?" Afong mumbled in Cantonese. She scrunched her nose at the acrid burning in her nostrils, in her mouth, the sour taste when she swallowed.

"Spirits of ether, dear. They gave you some medicine to help you relax. It's like sweet dreams in a bottle. I should be so lucky."

Afong closed her eyes and recalled bits and pieces of the backstage examination.

Doctors removing her footwear, tossing aside her red lotus shoes. They cut through the outer bandages. She remembered pleading, *"Ng hou,"* again and again, but the men did not understand, and even if they did she doubted they would have stopped, because they removed the inner wrapping along with her pantalets. She had vague memories of being surrounded by bearded men, of being scared, feeling cold metal and rough hands as they touched her body, her thighs, used calipers on her legs, her calves. They measured her head and her facial features. The men ignored the sour smell of dead skin, damp and decomposing, and poked and prodded her feet and toes, which now ached and were swollen, throbbing in pain. Afong realized that the doctors must have tried to straighten her feet. In the process, they broke bones that had already been fractured several times before. All while speaking in and out of a language she vaguely recognized as Latin, squabbling over whether she should be considered Mongolian or Ethiopian. The doctors argued, citing the Bible, and Adam and Eve, and how to most of them, Afong was obviously an inferior creature descended of neither.

She also had another memory, of being

hit upside the head.

She assumed that she had done something wrong and was punished by Mr. Hannington, though now as she tried to remember she realized the world turned sideways and it was her head hitting the stage floor. She must have stumbled, fainted, passed out from the ether. She remembered the cool, dusty wooden floor, looking up at the lights as though she were staring at the sun. Then hands reached out. The Chinese man in the golden waistcoat came into view as he picked her up, carried her away. She remembered how warm he felt. How he smelled like Burmese soap.

Was he real at all or am I addled from falling, hitting my head?

Did he say something about my family?

Am I still dreaming?

Her growling stomach answered and she knew she had missed supper.

She drained her cup, set it aside, and opened her leather valise, which she kept next to the bed in case there was a fire or she had to flee, or both. Inside she found scraps of surplus cloth that she could use to bind her broken toes and support her feet. She looked for her lotus shoes, grateful and relieved when she found them. During her first month on tour, Mr. Hannington took her footwear each night, making it harder, if not impossible, for her to get very far should she attempt to run away. But Mrs. Hannington put an end to that and brought them back one night. "Don't tell."

Where would I go?

Afong did not have an answer as she carefully rewrapped her feet by candlelight, feeling bones shift as she cinched the fabric tight, locking everything in place with a needle and thread as her ah-ma taught her. Afong winced with each knot.

"How much pain you can endure shows what kind of wife you will become," her ah-ma once said, pointing to her own lotus shoes. "It shows that you will be able to work hard, to cook, to give birth to many children, and take care of them. To a future husband, your ability to suffer only makes you more attractive."

As the moon disappeared and it began to rain, Afong thought she must be the most beautiful girl in the world by now.

When Afong's head began to clear, she changed into a button collar and a simple green dress, which was her favorite because the hem was long enough to hide her shriveled toes, her broken arches. She still felt strange in this upside-down world where

194

men wore trousers and women wore dresses, instead of back home where long gowns were reserved for men and women wore pants rolled up to the knee.

Too hungry to sleep, she blew out the candle, peeked outside her room, and surmised the hour must be quite late as everyone was already settled in for the evening. She limped down the hallway and descended the servants' stairs, wincing, gripping a railing to keep from falling. At the landing, she spied the dining room. Her stomach rumbled and she hoped that there might be a pot of soup or a plate of biscuits and jam left out for her, as some boarding-houses provided. If not, she would find a larder where she could at least find a piece of bread. When it came to meals, she had become accustomed to the boardinghouse diet, which consisted of hard tack and stews. She tried not to dwell on memories of her ah-ma's steamed dumplings dipped in vinegar, spicy turnip cake, and the sweet fried gao her family ate every Lunar New Year. She tried to be grateful for any food at all as she traveled, even if the only chicken she ever saw was little more than legs and pinfeathers, and the only fruit she had eaten in months had been prunes. Once she was served rice pudding, which she found confusing and disgusting, but the others practically licked their bowls clean.

As Afong touched the simple unvarnished furniture in the dining room and looked around, she realized this was one of those establishments where boarders rushed downstairs at the sound of the dinner bell. Where they ate quickly, eyeing each other warily, gulping their food like stray dogs until there was nothing left.

Her heart sank and her stomach grumbled again, as there were not even crumbs on the floor or beneath the table. The door to the kitchen had been locked and barred.

She heard the ruffle of a newspaper.

A man spoke in Cantonese, *"Sik zo fan mei?"*

Afong turned and saw him in the drawing room. Deprived of his golden waistcoat, he looked like an American dandy in his tightly fitted tailcoat, bespoke trousers, and linen cravat. He sat in an overstuffed chair that looked as though the upholstery had been ripped and resewn numerous times.

"Yes," she said in her native tongue. "I am quite hungry."

He wore spectacles, glinting in the lamplight, and was reading the *Baltimore Saturday Visitor.* He pointed to a plate on the table next to him.

"It's not much. Just bread and sausage. A few slices of apple."

"What are you doing here?"

"At the moment, reading a sad poem called 'Tamerlane,' about death and young love, written by a mysterious, anonymous Bostonian." The man set aside the newspaper. "But beyond that, I'm staying here." He smiled. "I suppose the Hanningtons would have put me elsewhere if there were more convenient vacancies that aligned with their thriftiness. But for now, we are sharing the same roof."

He stood and offered her a seat. "I'm Nanchoy Eu Tong. I've been hired as the Hanningtons' new interpreter and also as your English tutor. Won't you please join me?"

Afong felt overwhelmed, and not just because of hunger. Hearing someone speak to her kindly, sweetly, in her own language was like a lullaby.

Most of the boardinghouses she stayed at were regarded as promiscuous establishments — places where both men and women were allowed — though the women usually lived on a separate floor. She even stayed at a few houses where married couples lived, newlyweds without a home of their own.

Despite the abundant company, Afong always found boardinghouses to be lonely affairs. No one else spoke Chinese, of course, though they all seemed to recognize who she was. They gawked at her, gushed their curiosity. Laughed and nodded when she tried to speak English. But *befriend* was a term she had not employed in the two years since she arrived in this country.

Now Afong found herself beaming with happiness. The last time she felt this way, filled with such joy, was when she saw her first snowfall in New York City. The thought that something so magical could fall from the coal-smoke skies and land softly on the spit-tobacco-stained sidewalks gave her hope for something more. All was not lost. She felt that way again when she looked at Nanchoy. He returned the look, staring at her, but at the same time trying not to stare.

She sat down across from him in a rocking chair.

"You must be lonely," Nanchoy said. "Being the only Chinese woman."

He pushed the plate toward her.

Afong regarded him for a moment, then nodded.

She pulled the bread apart with her fingers. She had learned to appreciate the dark brown bread that everyone in New England seemed to favor, the kind sweetened with a kiss of molasses or honey. She chewed slowly, trying not to eat too quickly even as she smelled the savory garlic, fennel, and pepper in the sausage. She did not want to seem like a beggar at a feast, but she also knew that once she finished eating, the owner might appear and send her to her room, alone. Without Nanchoy explaining what he whispered to her at the theater.

"When was the last time you were in the Great Qing?" She tried not to talk with her mouth full, but she had to know more. "How did you come to hear about me? You said my family has not forgotten."

"My last time in China? Many years ago. I grew up in a Christian orphanage outside Canton. That's where I learned to speak English, to read and write. When I was ten, they sent me to a monastery, but it wasn't for me. *I didn't feel the calling,* as they say. So I ran away," he mused, "before they kicked me out."

Afong watched as he shrugged. As though escaping and going to an entirely different country was an easy thing to do. She realized that for a man, it was.

"I caught a ship to America. I was just a kitchen steward, loading crates of food, washing pans and cutlery. But when merchants found out that I spoke a bit of English, they spared me from those labors. I've been here ever since."

Afong thought about her ah-ma. *I knew that she would eventually find out I had been sent to America.* Afong imagined her ah-ma all alone, crying, her heart breaking. A daughter sent to America was a like a child given to the moon.

"I learned about you, my dear, like everyone else, in the newspaper. You've become quite a novelty," Nanchoy said. "I heard about your mother, however, through one of the Chinese traders. He was offering goods to sell after your performances. I was translating for him and he mentioned how your mother had gone to Canton and pleaded with merchants to find you, to bring you home."

Home.

Afong stopped chewing. She could not believe what she was hearing. Her ah-ma's words, even quoted by a stranger, made her feel weightless. Made her feel like she could run. She had been in so many newspapers and broadsheets, on so many stages, and in so many lecture halls. Despite the crowds, she always felt abandoned, alone. Now she seemed real again, valued, worthy of something other than this life of sorrow and servitude. She was not forgotten.

"Where is this trader?" Afong asked, wide-eyed. "I would leave right now. I could gather my things. Please tell me where this man is. I would do anything . . ."

Nanchoy did not say a word. He removed his glasses, put them away.

Afong could see the contentment leave his face. How his gaze, which a moment ago had been filled with such delight, was now laden with concern.

"I'm sorry." He leaned forward, their knees almost touching. "Even if Mr. Hannington released you, or if you slipped away, I'm afraid there is no way to return. You see, it's always been illegal for a woman to leave China."

"How can that be? I am right here."

"You are. You were brought by men who may have meant well, perhaps they planned to give your family money. Maybe they sought to hire you. It's possible that they didn't know, they just saw an opportunity. But I'm certain whoever let you go was well aware that if you ever returned, the punishment would be death."

Afong remembered Dei Yu's wives, smiling as men from America escorted her away during the first day of the Festival of the Hungry Ghosts. They walked her down the praya in the early morning, past large junks dressed with green and yellow signal flags, to a cargo lighter decorated with lanterns, red and black, bearing Chinese inscriptions that she could not read. She boarded the skiff and watched the sunrise as sailors rowed with the outgoing tide, past hundreds of floating paper lanterns set adrift the night before. When they came alongside a steamship, she was carried aboard and locked in a berth far belowdecks, where she remained for the entirety of the three-week journey. She would have cried, screamed, even pounded on the door, but she quickly became seasick and curled up on the floor, wishing the world would stop moving, rocking, heaving. In that time, she became so used to the smell of salted meat and an ever-ripe chamber pot that when they arrived in a strange city and she was finally taken topside, she thought someone had perfumed the air.

Afong took another bite, but the bread seemed to have lost its sweetness.

"I understand how you must feel. I was profoundly homesick when I arrived in this country." Nanchoy sighed. "In New York City, there are two hundred thousand people. Seventy thousand are foreigners, but the only Chinese I found were in a boardinghouse. The men who lived there were all seamen and laborers. Their mere appearance — being able to speak to them in our common tongue — was a gift. Though they regarded me warily, with suspicious eyes, because I cut my queue, grew my hair out like American men. I later realized they thought I was sent there as a spy."

"For a moment, I thought you were," Afong said. "That Mr. Hannington sent you to watch over me." She glanced up at her new acquaintance.

"They needn't pay me for that." Nanchoy loosened his tie ever so slightly. "I was quite happy to take this job. I traveled all the way from New York for very little pay and accepted this position, despite the Hanningtons being . . . *themselves.*"

Afong cocked her head, appraising his words. She was flattered by his company and ached for such kindness, but she remembered that her heart belonged to Yao Han. Though the chance of ever seeing him again was predicated on her freedom, which Americans talked about but she never experienced.

"Did you come all this way," she asked, "just to be with me?"

Nanchoy hesitated, then nodded.

"Why?"

"Because I'm afraid I have something in common with the Americans."

To Afong, his gaze felt warm, like summer.

"You're the first Chinese woman I've ever seen."

Afong stared at him in disbelief as a clock chimed 12:30 a.m.

She almost laughed.

Then she regarded his sincerity, his earnestness. She knew that back in China women were rarely, if ever, seen outside their homes, and then only on their wedding day. "You must have met at least *one*. Your ah-ma, someone in your home village, a peasant in the field . . ."

Nanchoy looked uncomfortable in his plush chair. "I didn't *have* a home village. My first memories were within the walls of a Jesuit orphanage. Even outside those walls, I was a day's journey from the nearest town." He shook his head, shrugged with embarrassment. "There were no women. From there I was given to a monastery in the mountains where the servants, like me, were all boys. When I left, I hid as I traveled, avoided markets and shops, people altogether. I made my way to a seaport where the only women I saw were British or American, merchant's wives, captain's spouses. Though of course, during my years here, I've seen many women, American, British, Irish, Spanish, Negro, hundreds . . ." He hesitated. "But they're not like you."

"Back home I am nothing special." Afong was not as tall as her sisters. She was not as beautiful as her cousins. Her feet were not as small as her ah-ma's. Afong always felt rather plain. She knew that being the youngest meant she would be the last to marry, but she still felt it was because she was painfully ordinary.

He leaned forward and put his hand on top of hers.

"But we're not back home," Nanchoy said. "I wish I could help you find your way back to your family, but I can't. But if there's any other way I might be of service . . ."

Afong looked down at his hand, which was warm, soft. She hesitated, excited, but also confused. She slowly pulled her hand away, pretending to adjust a collar button.

"Can you write a letter for me?"

Nanchoy paused, thinking.

"Even if I was allowed to leave, I do not have enough money for a passenger ticket home," Afong said. "But I can at least afford postage."

"I could write your letter." He nodded.

"A mailbag is sent on each ship."

Afong thought she might cry as she gushed, "Thank you." She could not believe what she was hearing. Like her ah-ma, she did not know how to read or write. But now, being able to communicate with her family was like praying at an altar for the dead and hearing a reply. She wondered how she could possibly get a letter to her mother without it going through her father. Maybe he would be away as he often traveled. Maybe he would welcome news of her well-being. Maybe he would burn the letter.

"There is also a young man . . . ," Afong blurted. "He can read and write. If you sent my letter to him, he could find a way to share it with my mother."

The man sitting across from her looked uncomfortable, frowning as though he had bitten into an unripe bayberry, swallowing the pit as well.

"Of course. I will do my best," he said as he put his glasses back on and stood up. He glanced at the clock. "It's late and I'm tired. Enjoy your supper."

He walked upstairs without looking back, leaving her in the drawing room hoping she had not offended him, and if so, wondering what she did wrong.

■ ■ ■ ■

The following night she sang like never before, the song of a dying swan for a sold-out crowd at Baltimore's Carroll Hall, while dreaming about going home. She envisioned her ah-ma's tears of joy, the warmth of her embrace, how she always smelled like rose-water. She imagined reaching out to her sisters. Perhaps she would even learn *nushu* — women's script — the secret language used in Hunan between lou tung. Afong wished she had a friendship like that, someone so close they were bonded for life. The closest she ever had outside her home was Yao Han, since they grew up together. She wondered what poems he must have created in her absence. If he finally took the Imperial Exam and became a Confucian apprentice, or whether he qualified for the more rigorous provincial tests, ascending the imperial ladder and moving far away. Selfishly, she hoped he had not left, though she felt guilty for imagining him leaving school and working in her father's orchard, waiting, hoping.

No, he said he would come back for me.

Afong closed her eyes as she sang and prayed the gods would allow Yao Han to hear her. That he could follow her voice and find her. That somehow, she would be able to leave this place and find her way home. She did not care that it was a crime for a woman to return to China. She could change her name. Cut her hair. Dress as a beggar.

When the song ended, she breathed in the applause, but it was not enough. She opened her eyes and nodded to the crowd. Then she glanced to the wings of the stage and saw Nanchoy in his golden waistcoat, his hair slicked back, clapping.

After weeks of sold-out shows, Afong began to weary of the perpetual spotlight. The endless routine. The thousands of faces who gawked at her, smiled at her, laughed at her, praised her, but none of them knew her, which only magnified her loneliness. To be so well known and yet so unknown at the same time, the madness of — as Yao Han might say it — being praised for having wings but kept in a cage.

In her mind, home was close enough to see, to smell, to hear, but she could not touch it. Those feelings, that longing, only made her want to retreat, to find a respite from the stage, to remember who she really was. Instead Mr. Hannington paraded her around the city in an open carriage as a form of advertising.

He would stand, waving his top hat, bellowing to the people on the avenues. He pointed with his cane and shouted, "Hear ye! Hear ye! This is your one free look at the Chinese Woman! Goddess of the Celestial Kingdom!" He put his hand on the back of her neck and whispered, "*Siu.*"

He knew a handful of words in Chinese, all of them commands.

Afong smiled as instructed.

When he let go, she would look back helplessly at Nanchoy, who always walked behind them, passing out leaflets to people on the sidewalks.

During these journeys, Afong paid special attention to landmarks. Not only did it make her feel less like a lost traveler in a strange city, but her observations allowed her to imagine possible escape routes. Where she would escape *to* was an unanswered question. Nevertheless, when they traveled the streets of Baltimore, she made note of the Peale Museum, the cemetery, parks, the great churches and rectories, the enormous roundhouse that Nanchoy said was where horsecars were made. She remembered the location of the towering Washington Monument, with a man on top made of stone. The column itself was impossible to miss and near the harbor, directly south of where she would be staying. But she also noticed something not seen in previous cities. Breadlines and soup kitchens, and police, breaking up protests and riots.

"It's the Hessian fly," Mr. Hannington said when he saw her puzzled look. He swatted at gnats and the occasional buzzing bluebottle. "It's not just Baltimore. It's killed wheat crops all over the damn country." He looked down at a newspaper through the quizzing glass he wore around his neck. Then up at the lines of men, hats in hand, waiting for food. "The price of King Cotton is plummeting as well."

Afong looked at Mr. Hannington. Despite his fancy, Beau Brummell frock, his elegant haberdashery, his exuberance, this was the first time she had seen him worried, chewing on an unlit cigar, rubbing his beard, grumbling to himself.

Nanchoy followed behind them, wary of the unhappy people.

Despite his concerns, Mr. Hannington said, "We need to hunker down and weather the storm," so he extended their run in Baltimore, adding more weeks, which became months. He referred to it as "Afong's going-away party."

During this time, she had been learning to read English and was increasingly grateful for Nanchoy, his English lessons, his friendship, his companionship, the times they shared meals together. She listened to the stories of his travels, which made her feel closer to home and yet more homesick than ever. Which is why her heart nearly burst the first time she arrived at the concert hall and saw a painted banner that read, *THE CHINESE LADY'S FINAL PERFORMANCE.*

But when the curtains were drawn and the lights dimmed, when she asked Mr. Hannington if this meant she could finally go back home, he laughed while counting the night's receipts. "Girl, you're as innocent as a lamb and twice as dumb."

Afong understood what he meant by her sixth *final* performance, though perhaps Mr. Hannington's ruse was wearing thin as crowds were getting smaller each night.

Onstage, Afong listened to the chatter of tonight's audience as they waited restlessly in their seats; she noticed Mrs. Hannington standing in the wings. She peeked through the side curtain, then sauntered to center stage with another woman at her side.

"Afong," Mrs. Hannington said as she

took Afong's elbow. "This is my sister, Trudy, she lives in Mount Vernon and I wanted her to be able to see you up close and maybe even talk to you. We have plenty of time. Mr. Hannington is out front hawking tickets as we speak. You wouldn't mind, now would you?" Afong barely understood. She smiled and nodded as though she had a choice.

"Look at you! Strange, yet so lovely. Such peculiar fashion — more elegant than the Esquimaux family that Captain Hadlock brought to the city last year — but still, so . . . primal," Trudy gushed, touching Afong's sleeve and her hair, petting her like an animal. "This all must be so thrilling for you! How do you like it here in America? How do you like your new home?"

Nanchoy translated her words.

Afong hesitated as she remembered a reporter asking the same question last year while she was in Buffalo for a performance. She tried her best to respond in English, but her answer came out awkwardly. "It is cold here. I am very sad to be so lonely."

When Mr. Hannington read her quote in the newspaper, he stormed into her room. Afong was half-dressed, wearing only a chemise and a stay. He grabbed a fistful of hair, jerked her out of her chair, and berated her, beating the back of her legs with a cane.

Afong blinked and saw Mrs. Hannington and her sister smiling, waiting.

"I like it here very much," Afong said in Cantonese. Since Buffalo, she learned to always say praiseworthy things about the Hanningtons. In the morning after that beating, the bruises were so purple and swollen she struggled to get out of bed and could barely stand, which confused Mrs. Hannington, who grumbled, "Chinese are so lazy."

"Mr. and Mrs. Hannington have been so good to me, so kind and generous."

Nanchoy translated and Mrs. Hannington excitedly clapped her hands.

The last month *had* been exciting, since every week Nanchoy wrote a letter on Afong's behalf and delivered it to a packet ship bound for China. The return address was the post office in Baltimore, where they expected to spend the winter.

Afong anxiously awaited any correspondence.

Now, while smiling at Mrs. Hannington, Afong said in Cantonese, "Has a letter arrived yet? Has there been any news of home, of my family?"

Nanchoy translated as the two women listened, then he spoke a bit more in his native tongue. "It's better that we discuss these things later." He patted his coat pocket.

Trudy seemed to swell with pride and excitement as though she were in the company of royalty instead of the sideshow attraction Afong knew she had become. "Tell me," Trudy asked, "what has been your favorite part of America? You've seen so much of it. I'm most curious what this great land of ours must be like to a girl like you."

Nanchoy repeated the questions in Cantonese.

Afong turned to Trudy but spoke to Nanchoy. "You can answer her any way you like. But if a letter has arrived, I must insist. I might not see you after the show and I cannot bear to wait." Afong knew that sometimes he was sent on errands for a day or two, or he would have to leave and accompany Mr. Hannington as a personal valet.

The first time she dictated a letter to send to her mother, Nanchoy took it to a ship and returned that afternoon. The second time, when she asked him to write a letter to Yao Han — expressing how much she missed him, how she wished he might become a merchant and come to America — Nanchoy disappeared for a week. She worried that he might never be coming back. That she upset him somehow. But he said he was sent to help secure another concert hall with Mr. Hannington.

Nanchoy nodded, then turned to Trudy. "Afong says her favorite part of America has been the music. Especially songs played on the piano, which seems like a magical invention." He then glanced at Afong. "There is good news, but there is also news that will upset you. Let's not talk about this now."

Afong's heart soared. Then she breathed in through her nose and held it for a moment as she braced herself for bad tidings. She worried for the safety of her older sisters. That one of them might have died in childbirth. She worried that her mother might have been cast aside in favor of a second wife.

She glanced at Nanchoy, who glanced at his pocket watch.

"Please," Afong said. "I am begging."

"Ooooh," Trudy squealed. "Ask her — if I may be so bold — what she thinks of American men. Not the Irish, but the natives, the white men who were born here."

Nanchoy nodded to Trudy as though they were sharing a secret, an inside joke. "A very good question." He turned to Afong and sighed wearily. "The letter is from your mother. She is well and misses you dearly. She shared that your oldest sister has a child, a son. Both are in good health. She's been able to visit them. Your father's business is doing well, but I'm afraid he has no desire to seek your return."

Afong knew her father had no use for her, this was no surprise. If Nanchoy had bad news, she hoped that was all of it. Telling her something she already suspected was a confirmation, not a condemnation. But as she watched him loosen his cravat, she could tell that was not the bad news.

"Your mother found someone to help her write this, which she hoped you would understand." Nanchoy hesitated, then he produced a slip of paper from his pocket. "Please, I think it would be much better to have this conversation in private."

"Tell me!" Afong snapped, then glanced at Mrs. Hannington and smiled again, though it now hurt her cheeks to do so. "Just read it."

Nanchoy unfolded the slip of paper as he cleared his throat, then looked at her as he spoke. "The thread in the hands of a fond-hearted mother makes clothing for the body of her wayward girl; Carefully she sews and thoroughly she mends, dreading the delays that will keep her far from home . . ."

As Afong recognized the words, a version of Ming Jao's classic poem about a mother's undying love, it seemed as though time stopped. All was silent, except for her breathing, her beating heart. Mrs. Hannington and her sister became statuary, mouths open, mid-conversation. The swirling dust particles illuminated by the gaslights seemed frozen in amber. The only thing that moved was Nanchoy as he spoke.

"I'm sorry, Afong. Your mother is deeply sorry as well, for not being able to help you, for not being able to bring you home, and for not being able to tell you in person that on the one-year anniversary of your departure . . ."

Afong stared at Nanchoy in fearful anticipation.

"Your friend, Yao Han, took his own life."

For a moment, she was transported to a grassy meadow back home. Afong was a little girl again, sitting beneath the willow with Yao Han as he recited the Bearer's Song. Now here, on this stage, she felt the lines of that tragic poem: *Even the Maker of All could not bring the life back to my limbs.*

"It rained for weeks and the Chu Kiang overflowed near your village. Witnesses saw him walk directly into the rushing river. Watched him get swept away." Nanchoy put

217

the note away. "His body was never found."

Mrs. Hannington tapped Nanchoy on the shoulder, clearing her throat.

He turned to the ladies and smiled.

"She says that she finds American men to be quite handsome. So much taller and . . ." He struggled to find the words. "She finds them strong and fearless. Able to conquer this great land. Though she hopes to someday find a suitable Chinese husband."

Nanchoy looked back at Afong as he switched to Cantonese. "I am sorry."

"Oh, you poor thing," Trudy said. "A heart is a flower that needs to bloom. Someday, perhaps, when you find your way home." She winked at Nanchoy. "Who knows? You might find what you're looking for right here in America."

Afong bit her lip and tried not to cry. She tried to think of something other than the flooded banks of the Pearl River. But when she thought of horses, she saw them pulling a hearse. When she thought of a rabbit, she remembered how they shrieked and screamed when her mother butchered them. When she thought about a ship, all she saw were sails and steam paddles leaving without her.

"Well, I suppose we should slip offstage," Mrs. Hannington said. "Come along, Trudy,

I have a bottle of sherry waiting for us."

Trudy waved goodbye as they walked back into the wings.

Afong stood alone in the darkness as the backstage lights began to fade. She thought about Yao Han, imagining him entering the cold water and disappearing. She dabbed at the corners of her eyes with her sleeve. Then she heard the audience fall silent, the footsteps of Mr. Hannington as he took his place on the other side of the curtain, center stage, in the spotlight that would soon be shining on her. Afong knew his words, his showman's routine, she could quote him in English if she tried, but now she heard nothing, just garbled sounds where a voice should be. A voice that spoke as though underwater. She heard muffled clapping from beneath the waves. The curtains were drawn and she moved to her mark in the spotlight, staring up from the cold, dark bottom of the ocean.

During the carriage ride back to the City Hotel on Fulton Street, Afong ignored Mrs. Hannington, who sat across from her. The elegantly dressed woman's cheeks were rosy, and she removed her shoes and stockings while happily humming a minstrel song.

This evening's performance at Carroll

219

Hall ended with a standing ovation despite a smaller crowd than usual (because Mr. Hannington hired shills to cheer and lead the audience to their feet). But as people applauded, Afong could not smile. She did not bow. All she saw as she looked out at the audience were the bars of her cage.

She thought about Yao Han and wondered if she would have felt this distraught in the Yu home. Would the constriction of her bound feet have spread to all her extremities, all her senses? Until she moved like the other married women she had known — her ah-ma included — as if they were ghosts in their own homes, ever present but unable to leave. Would she choose the path of a barren wife or dejected concubine and eat poison — British opium — dulling her pain until she felt nothing at all? Or would she decide all was lost, no matter where she was or who she was with, and choose the path taken by Yao Han, following his muddy footsteps into a river?

She stared out the open carriage window, her nostrils filled with the wet, grassy smell of horse manure as Mrs. Hannington put her shoes back on and began her usual retinue of warnings and admonitions. "Remember, you never, ever, want to be seen loitering alone on the street," she slurred.

"If the police see a single woman idling near some alley, they assume you're a woman of ill repute and we don't want that."

Afong had heard Mrs. Hannington's many cautionary tales, the things that might happen to her if she were to leave their custody.

But tonight, she did not care.

When she arrived at the boardinghouse, Nanchoy was there to escort her inside. With his hand on her arm, she understood now why Chinese folk tales about love always ended in tragedy. Maybe that is why she still cared about Yao Han. His stories were the hopeful opposite of poems like "Song of Everlasting Sorrow," where the highest-ranking concubine in the land is forced to hang herself while her beloved, the emperor, is made to watch. *The gods must be lonely in their heavens,* Afong thought.

"Would you like me to find you something to eat?" Nanchoy asked, walking slowly so she didn't have to hurry on her sore feet. "I'm sure I could find something . . ."

"Thank you. I am not hungry."

They walked in awkward silence.

"I'm sorry, Afong. I should not have told you."

She shook her head. "I insisted."

Afong had been in dozens of newspapers,

in more cities than she could remember. She had met the president of the United States in the White House. She performed beneath a spotlight, and people applauded her, but tonight she felt little more than a prop, a clotheshorse. She was whatever she was onstage, and that person diminished with the size of the audience. Offstage she was empty, hollow, unloved.

"Is there anything else I can do for you?" Nanchoy asked.

Afong did not answer.

She took his arm and let him help her up the servants' stairs and down the hallway to her room, which was across from his.

He said good night with a shrug.

As they closed their doors, Afong glanced over her shoulder, and for a moment she thought she saw him smiling.

That night Afong dreamt she was onstage in some nameless theater in a nameless city performing before nameless people. She stood beneath the spotlight in a smoke-filled auditorium and tried to sing but could not make a sound, could barely move. She was frozen in place, staring out at a packed audience, all of them faceless, except for a small Chinese woman in the middle. She had gray hair and wore a white funeral gown. Afong recognized her yin yin. She stared at her long-dead grandmother.

The old woman stood up slowly. She opened her mouth to speak, her lips moved, trembling, but Afong could not hear a sound as water exploded from the exits and came roaring down the aisles and the voms, torrents submerging the audience, swamping the stage, filling up the theater. As the cold water rose, roiling toward the ceiling, it snuffed out gas lamps and chandeliers that sizzled and popped in bursts of fire and showers of sparks. Afong's heart raced as she kicked and flailed beneath the surface. She felt the suffocating heaviness of her waterlogged clothing. She opened her eyes in a panic and saw a blur of people, audience members, men and women, bodies, floating, tumbling, sinking. She felt the current as though a watery hand grabbed her, pulling her deeper into the darkness.

She tried to scream.

Afong bolted upright in bed.

She heard polite knocking and looked around the moonlit room, confused. She heard knocking a second time. Then a third.

She suspected who it was and said, *"Jap loi."*

Nanchoy gently opened the door. He peeked inside and then stepped in. He

223

walked lightly, as though she were still asleep. "Are you okay? I heard you cry out. You were calling for help."

He closed the door behind him.

Afong slowly remembered where she was. Who she was.

She looked around the dimly lit room and remembered the home she lost, the family she would never see again, her mother, her grandmother, her sisters, Yao Han. She touched her blanket, her clothing, her hair, expecting everything to be sopping, but the only wetness she felt were tears running down her cheeks. She looked away, pulled her robe from the bedpost, and wrapped it around her as she tried not to cry, but she might as well have tried not to breathe. Light-headed, she flinched as she felt Nanchoy's hand on her shoulder. Then she surrendered to her grief and turned, gripping the front of his nightshirt with both fists, pulling him toward her, burying her face in his chest, anguished, openmouthed, crying until she was out of breath, voiceless, gulping the air between sobs. She felt his arms around her, holding her tight. He rocked her and was speaking, but she did not know what he was saying. All she could hear were her ears ringing, her heart pounding, her blood thick with anger and rejection and loss.

She looked up at him, tears still running down both cheeks.

He smiled in the dimly lit room.

And kissed her.

For a moment Afong splashed back beneath the surface of the water.

Sinking.

His lips felt warm, but his teeth smashed into hers and his breath reeked of tobacco. She felt his hand on the back of her head, pulling her hair as he kissed her again.

"Ng Hou," she said as she struggled to turn away.

He put his weight against her and pressed her down, her shoulders to the mattress, the back of her head into the pillow. He was on top of her, taller, older, twice her weight.

She felt his leg, his knee, slip between hers.

"It's okay," he said.

"No."

"Shhh . . ."

She opened her mouth to yell for help but could not make a sound. She was frozen, submerged, drowning. She wanted to shout, wanted to plead, wanted to run, but she did nothing as she felt his hand over her mouth and another on the brass buttons of her nightgown.

I am not here.

"I came all this way to be with you, Afong. I've waited as long as I could."

She turned her head, aching to be home again.

I am sorry, Ah-ma.

"I won't let anything bad happen to you," Nanchoy whispered.

Afong stared out the window as the moon disappeared and the stars went out.

She was her yin yin, lifeless, vacant, eyelids half-open.

She could smell his sweat, hear his labored breathing.

She closed her eyes.

When Afong opened them again, she was alone in the dark, gasping for air. The sheets wet against her back from perspiration. She sat up, moving without thought, a puppet on a string. She touched her feet to the cool floor. Looked down at her nightgown. Felt the spot where a button was missing. She found it on the floor and held it in her hand, staring at it like a lost penny in the dimly lit room. She heard thunder and noticed the rain. She saw flashes of lightning on the horizon as she lay down, staring into nothing for hours, gripping the button, squeezing it until its edges cut crescents into her palm.

Afong slept in the next day.

Followed by the rest of the week and the week after that.

She slept in every day, sometimes late into the afternoon, right up until she had to get dressed to go to Carroll Hall. Though the word *sleep* was an exaggeration, as she often just closed her eyes, curled up in her blanket. Other times she would sit at the window. Instead of working on her embroidery — which the Hanningtons regularly took from her and sold as souvenirs — she listened to the lonely chorus of the city, the policemen's whistles, the sound of carriages and coaches. Barking strays and braying pack animals. Afong envisioned standing in the middle of the avenue and being kicked in the head by a draft horse or trampled by a team, waking up back in her village — all of this a bad dream — or not waking up at all. Both outcomes seemed equally satisfying in her mind, because every night she remembered feelings of terror, helplessness, nothingness, then waking up alone, hoping it was only a nightmare. Then she would smell him on her, on her clothing, the sheets. Even on the nights when he did not appear in the dark at her bedside, hands on his belt buckle, she could no longer rest. She would hide beneath her blankets, fearful of sounds from the hallway, a creaking staircase, a door, footsteps, a man's cough. Or conversely, hiding from the many hobgoblins of her imagination. The dread that circled overhead like a black-eyed raven.

Nanchoy, however, was not so burdened, as each morning he acted as though nothing were amiss. In those confounding moments, filled with self-doubt, self-loathing, Afong found herself wondering if this was what love really was? Perhaps the poets were wrong, or deceptive, dressing up the ugly truth, putting a string of pearls on a fat pig, bringing flowers to a funeral, polishing an apple full of worms.

Afong was rubbing her eyes when Nanchoy opened the door and walked in, fully dressed for the day, bringing with him a tray with corn pone and a bowl of popcorn in sweet milk, which he relished but which turned her stomach. Also on the tray was a handful of purple flowers in an old, brown medicine bottle, and a folded newspaper. He set the tray down by her bed, then stared at her as she donned a robe.

As Afong sat up, she could make out a headline: *FINAL PERFORMANCE OF THE*

CHINESE LADY BEFORE SHE RETURNS TO HER HOMELAND.

Afong wanted to set fire to the paper, burn the theater to the ground.

"Every ticket for this weekend's grand finale performance has already been sold," Nanchoy said. "Old man Hannington has been out on street corners and in town squares, promoting you all day. He's even offering a drawing for a grand cash prize of one thousand dollars. I'd say it's been a successful week."

"For who?" she asked.

Nanchoy smiled. "Would you like to resume your English lessons?"

Afong stared out the window, then shook her head. "I am going to get dressed. I will meet you in the parlor as soon as I am ready."

"What are we doing?"

"I would like to go out."

Afong donned her green dress and wore a flowered silk bonnet that Mrs. Hannington had given her. "This is to spare you the indignity of being recognized on the street. I don't want people to think you're a mulatto, or mistaken for a free slave."

As Afong tied the long ribbon around her neck, she tried her best to look plain, like the American women who all appeared the same to her. The same pinched noses and powdered faces, rouged lips, and dangling, spiral curls.

She met Nanchoy in the parlor, who seemed overdressed in his tailcoat and hat, a white linen neck cloth tied around his neck. She ignored him when he offered his arm, and stepped out into the crisp spring morning. She appraised the busy street, which looked chaotic, long lines outside banks and offices. There were fewer carriages and delivery wagons. The people she was used to seeing, groups of men in stovepipe hats, smoking and talking, gaggles of women shopping, were all gone. The flower carts, bread stalls, and vegetable stands that were normally filled with cabbage, garlic, and root vegetables were now empty spaces beneath black awnings spattered with bird droppings.

"What happened?" Afong asked.

"I don't know," Nanchoy said. "But banks are closing early."

In her time in America, Afong rarely went out alone, even though her shoes were durable and she learned to tolerate the pain and discomfort that accompanied a two- or three-mile walk. Her curiosity and desire to get out was generally overshadowed by her fear of getting lost, or attracting too much attention, or as Mrs. Hannington put it, "The wrong kind of attention for a girl your age. You'll get there someday."

When Afong crossed the street, away from a breadline filled with men who looked hungry for food, a job, or simply a break in their string of misfortune, she felt sympathy. She did not see the men as nefarious or *the wrong sort,* the way Mrs. Hannington described them. They were just poor. The poetics of poverty, the expressions of servitude, the dialects of desperation, were all languages Afong was well versed in.

As they passed a negro man in a blue suit who had climbed atop a carriage to tie down a stack of steamer trunks, Afong recalled the few times she navigated the busy city streets without an escort. The first time was in New York, when she visited a ticket office for a steamship company near where she was staying. Afong could not read the sign but recognized a painted ship on the window. When she went inside and tried to speak, the confused man at the ticket counter tapped a board with prices, all of which were far beyond the meager collection of coins she had managed to hide. Another time she went exploring was when a cholera outbreak in the north compelled them to travel to the southern states. It was in Charleston that Afong walked in a straight line away from her boardinghouse toward the city center and saw broadsides for upcoming auctions. Afong knew enough English to read, *A girl about 17 or 18 years old. Has been used for house and garden work. She is sold for no fault. Strong back. Sound as a dollar.* Afong struggled to understand, then looked down the street to a town square and saw black women, black children, and black men in chains, stripped of their clothing, brought to a viewing stand, and sold to the highest bidder. White men and women went about their business, talking and laughing. Afong turned and walked away as fast as she could.

"Where are we going?" Nanchoy asked.

Afong pointed to the large monument that towered over the brick buildings nearby. The giant column was even taller than the church spires. "I am going to see the ocean," she said as they walked down the cobblestone street.

They passed through the enormous square of paved brick near the waterfront, and Afong began to smell salt in the air, fish, the odor of unwashed men who were busy loading and unloading tall ships that sat along each pier, great hemp ropes streaming like spider silk, wrapped around rusted metal capstans.

Along the waterfront they found a bench near a bandbox, looking out over the harbor where several ships sat at anchor in the middle of the bay. She reflected on how she had been prepared for an arranged marriage since she could walk. Like her siblings, she was given over to strangers. She wondered how her sisters must have felt, seeing their husbands for the first time on their wedding days.

Afong knew that in America it was not legal for a white man to marry her and her choice of suitors was limited. There were rarely more than a hundred Chinese men in any given city at one time, most of them seamen, without homes on land. If they had wives and if they fathered any children, they would rarely ever see them.

"You should know," Nanchoy spoke as though he could read her mind, "I asked the Hanningtons for permission to marry you."

Afong opened her mouth but could not find the words.

She wanted to scream.

"They didn't seem surprised," he said. "I guess it makes sense to them. In case you're wondering, they said they would have an

233

answer for me tonight at the theater. I think they're planning something special for us."

Afong stared at a wrecked ship that had foundered and been left to rot.

"Who knows," Nanchoy said. "Someday you might even be able to return to Canton as my wife. Perhaps the laws will change. Wouldn't you like that?"

She imagined the water draining away from the harbor, leaving a ruinous landscape, dotted with sunken vessels, half-buried, covered in seaweed. Fish unable to breathe, dying in the sun. She wondered how far she would have to walk before the mud swallowed her whole.

Nanchoy kept talking, but she was not in the mood to listen.

He stood, shoved his hands in his pockets, huffing, "I wish you would say something. I've gone to a great deal of trouble to be here with you. I've sacrificed . . ."

Afong looked away.

He grabbed her chin and turned her face toward him. He leaned in and she felt his breath, which smelled like spoiled tea, rotten like an abscessed tooth.

"*Gong waa,*" he snapped in Cantonese. "Say something!"

She stared up at him, unblinking. "I do not care what you wish for."

234

He slapped her.

Afong flared her nostrils and brushed her hair back to reveal a tear that slowly descended her throbbing cheek, down her neck.

"I'm sorry," Nanchoy spat out as he adjusted his jacket. "I'll be better. After all, in this country a man shouldn't hit a woman until they're married."

He took out his handkerchief, wiped his mouth, and then handed it to her.

The bit of cloth smelled like him. She let it drop to the ground and wiped her tear with the back of her hand as he stalked away, leaving her to find her way alone. She did not mind because as he left the clouds parted and she felt the sun come out. She sat there for an hour, content, bathed in warmth, listing to birdsongs. Then she quietly remembered that it was September once again, the time of the Ghost Festival. She watched the tide go out, imagining the waves littered with joss paper, a ghost ship launched from the quay. She wished she could join its offerings of oranges and sugared fruit, her life, provender for wayward spirits. Then she sighed and slowly walked back, taking her time, careful not to trip on the cobblestones.

No one noticed her. No one cared. They

were too busy watching angry crowds surround the Bank of Baltimore as more financial panic rippled through the city. Men shouted, tossed bottles and bricks as police arrived with wooden clubs in hand, blowing whistles. After so much time onstage, Afong appreciated being unknown, unnoticed, invisible as she took an oyster knife from a shellfish cart and hid it up her sleeve.

Afong climbed the servants' stairs back to her room, closing her door as quietly as possible. She sat on the bed and examined the knife. It was small but weighty, with a handle that fit the size of her fist. The blade was as long as her middle finger.

She looked outside and the sun was setting behind the buildings across the street. She lit a lamp, turned up the wick, and stared into the mirror, knowing she would have to get ready soon. With a deep breath, she loosened her collar buttons. She let her dress fall from her shoulders to the floor. She removed her petticoats and chemise. She stood before the mirror in her stay and pantalets. She touched the contours of her neck with her fingers, turning her head to the right, to the left. She remembered how she helped her mother slaughter chickens. She recalled the clucking and crowing of an animal that could not fathom that its life would soon be over. Afong put the point of the blade against the hollow of her neck, felt the metal against her skin. She envisioned plunging the knife into her throat, feeling warmth spread down her chest, soaking her dress. She wondered what would happen to her body. Chinese laborers who died in the US had their hearts cut out or their bones bleached so they could be returned to their families and properly buried.

Afong heard the door open behind her, watched a shadow cross the wall, saw Nanchoy's reflection staring at her, shaking his head.

"What are you doing?" His voice sounded more annoyed than surprised.

She turned, holding the knife in front of her.

"You're going to stab me?" Nanchoy asked. "After all I've done for you?"

Her voice cracked and her hand trembled as she said, "Get out."

He snatched her wrist, twisted her arm until the knife dropped, chiming on the floor. He picked it up then spun her around, pinning her arm behind her back. He put the blade to her throat. She could feel his heart pounding, his heavy breathing, his body pressed against hers. He pulled her head back and she closed her eyes.

Ah-ma.

He let go and she slumped to the floor.

"We're late." He stuck the knife into her headboard. "Get dressed. I'll deal with you later."

"There they are," Mrs. Hannington said, clapping with delight as she bounced on her toes outside the theater. Her husband stood next to her, staring down at his gold pocket watch. Nanchoy stepped out of the carriage. He let the driver help Afong.

"My girl, we've allowed you to be in the care of Nanchoy for all these weeks. Such a good boy to look after you. I told my husband, 'Have faith, dear, they've never once been late for a performance, not a single time,' and you didn't let me down."

Mr. Hannington put his watch away and huffed, "You nearly ruined our gala finale." He shoved an unlit cigar into his mouth. "We sold out the entire theater this time — packed them in cheek by jowl at twice the price — though I had to wag a lot of money at these rubes." He pulled a slip of paper from his pocket. "When the time comes for the drawing, I'm going to hand this to you so you can read the name and announce

238

the winner." He showed her the paper. On it was the name George Codhooker.

"Do you understand, girl?"

He glanced at Nanchoy. "I thought you said she could read this?"

"I can," Afong said, nodding. "I will."

"The winner," Mr. Hannington said, "is an actor that I hired. He will come forward, take the ticket from you, the show will end in celebration, and that will be that."

Afong nodded.

"Good." Mr. Hannington lit his cigar and puffed until the end flickered red. "Now. I suppose you're waiting on me for some kind of answer?"

Afong felt Nanchoy's sweaty palm, his fingers laced with hers. She looked down as though his hand were a growth, a massive wart, something she could not scrape off.

"This is going to be your last performance for a while. The world is going to hell right now with this financial panic and people are falling out of work. Mrs. Hannington and I will be traveling back to New Jersey. In our absence, I see no reason why the two of you shouldn't be together. After all" — he pointed at Afong but spoke to Nanchoy as though relieved of a great burden — "someone has to look after her now."

■ ■ ■ ■

When the show ended, Afong was light-headed, exhausted, grateful to have made it through the evening without breaking down. She stood next to Mr. Hannington as he worked the audience into a frenzy, shouting, "Now the time you've waited for is upon us. Ladies and gentlemen, who's ready to get rich here tonight?!"

He went on about all the things one could do with a thousand dollars. Meanwhile his wife and Nanchoy walked up and down the aisles passing out pencils and slips of paper, collecting the names and putting them into Mr. Hannington's top hat. Mrs. Hannington then giddily returned to the stage, enjoying the spotlight as she handed the hat to her husband. He dipped his hand into the crown and made a great show of mixing up the tickets as the audience fell silent and a pianist played a frenzied melody.

He drew out a slip of paper.

"It's pronounced Hepworth!" a man shouted from the back and the audience tittered. "How much for the China girl?" another man yelled. The audience laughed, growing restless and rowdy, their high hopes on display.

Mr. Hannington held the slip high and the audience quieted. "Now is the moment you waited for, a dream of riches galore. I will now ask the Chinese Lady to do the honor of reading the winning name." He handed her the slip of paper.

Afong took the paper and opened it.

She read the name Codhooker, then gazed out at the audience. She watched the swirls of cigar smoke, saw the eager, bearded faces, the stern men who were already spending the money in the storefronts of their imaginations. Smiling women clung to their husbands in eager anticipation. Afong looked to the back of the theater, beyond the standing-room-only crowd, beyond the glass ticket booth, beyond the city blocks, the brick buildings, smoking chimneys, the crowded harbor, out over the ocean, all the way to the shores of a home she knew she would never see again. Not in this lifetime. Then she looked down and saw Nanchoy on the steps leading up to the side stage, in his golden waistcoat, his hair slicked back, smiling. She looked toward Mr. Hannington, to Mrs. Hannington, who joined her husband on the apron of the stage. She was staring at her, mouthing something to Afong, motioning, admonishing her to read the slip of paper. They smiled, but their gaze, their intensity showed their impatience.

Afong looked down at the note in her hands.

She felt the eyes of everyone in the theater upon her.

"The winner . . ." Afong glanced up as everyone leaned forward in their seats. Many in the back rows stood up so they could hear.

"The winner . . ."

"Out with it, girl!" Mr. Hannington snapped.

"The winner is . . . Nanchoy Eu Tong."

Afong smiled as she pointed to him.

He looked stunned, confused.

"No, no, no," Mr. Hannington bellowed. "There's been a terrible misunderstanding. She's illiterate, she doesn't know a thing that she's saying."

Afong crumpled the paper and dropped it to the floor as a handful of audience members began shouting. Men rose to their feet.

"Draw another name!" a man in the front row demanded. Others joined in, insisting that the Hanningtons pull another name from the hat.

Afong stepped back as the audience turned into a mob.

"If you'll all just calm yourselves," Mr.

Hannington shouted back. "Is there a Mr. George Codhooker in the audience, he's the name she meant to read."

"It's rigged!" one man yelled. Another shouted, "I want my money back!" Their voices joined a chorus of men and women, roaring with anger.

"Ladies! Ladies! Ask your men to settle down," Mrs. Hannington hectored the audience as though scolding a group of misbehaving children. Her pleading was met with a ripe apple that bounced off her forehead. Her arms flailed as she toppled backward, falling like a tree, her head bouncing off the stage floor.

Afong backed away as she watched three men in the front row seize Nanchoy. Other men alighted the stage, demanding the money that was promised.

Like a ghost, Afong slipped behind the curtain and headed for the rear exit. She heard Mr. Hannington yelling, the rage in his voice ceasing, turning to fear, then to silence amid the sound of boots on the stage, the tumble of bodies, the smacking of fists on cheekbones. Afong left the theater and thought she heard Nanchoy pleading for help. She listened again for a moment, then closed the door behind her.

Afong hurried down the street, but all she

could manage was an awkward shuffle, tripping, stumbling, falling to the wet pavement. She climbed to her feet and kept going, trying to run. People stopped and stared, they pointed at her clothing, her face, her features that set her apart from everyone else. A drunken man shouted, calling out to her. A group of women looked offended as they gasped at her presence. Even a freeman regarded her with bewilderment, raising his eyebrows and scratching his beard.

When she finally reached the boardinghouse, sweating and out of breath, she caught her reflection in the window. Her hair clung to her face, which looked pale, like ivory, a mask of carved alabaster. Her skin felt cold, clammy, her stomach turning. She walked through the door, startling two other residents, young men who were smoking pipe tobacco in the drawing room. Afong ignored them but could not ignore the smoke that made her nauseous. Her mouth felt dry as she climbed the stairs, went to her room, stepped inside, and closed the door. Dizzy, shaking, her hands trembled as she reached for an empty brass spittoon and dropped to her knees. She struggled to breathe for a moment, holding back, then her body seized and she expelled what little she had in her stomach. Her eyes watered and she smelled the sour spew as it splattered on the inside of the cold brass vessel, a wet, hollow ringing in her ears.

Fifteen minutes later, Afong's head cleared and her stomach settled enough for her to sip water and begin quickly packing her belongings. She tried not to think of what would happen to her at the hands of Mr. Hannington, though a part of her hoped they would just leave town as planned, leaving her behind. She heard a commotion in the hallway, and a female boarder shrieked as Nanchoy stumbled into Afong's room. His face a swollen purple mess, dried blood caked beneath his nose, his ears, his mouth. He staggered in, one hand on his stomach where he pressed a silk handkerchief, now soaked with sanguine fluid. His hand was shaking as he collapsed on Afong's bed. He struggled to breathe as he tried to move. He grimaced in pain, wheezing. He stared down as a bloodstain on his shirt, a red flower, the size of a fist, grew even larger, wet and sticky and smelling like an abattoir.

"What happened?" Afong asked, though she already guessed.

"The mob . . ." Nanchoy coughed up a dram of dark liquid that dripped down his chin. "They stripped off Hannington's clothing, dragged him out to be tarred and feathered. He screamed that I cheated him. A white man, cheated by a Chinaman." Nanchoy sucked in a deep breath. "Someone shot me."

Afong shoved her remaining things into her bag. If they did this to Nanchoy, she worried what they might do to her.

"Please, Afong," Nanchoy wheezed. "No one else would help."

She opened her mouth to speak but felt a wave of nausea and rushed to the spittoon and threw up again, gagging, coughing.

Nanchoy tried to sit up but collapsed back on the bed, clutching his stomach and moaning, one leg dangling on the floor. "Don't leave me . . . Afong. Please, find a doctor."

Afong hesitated, catching her breath. Then she wiped her chin and stepped toward Nanchoy. She sat on the edge of the bed, reached as though she were about to caress his cheek, then she pulled the oyster knife free from the headboard.

She stood over him. Her hand shook as she gripped the knife.

He coughed again, looking up at her.

He spat blood on his shirt as he spoke. "You don't even know . . . do you?"

Know what?

He smiled.

Know what!?

"You're . . . pregnant, Afong," Nanchoy gurgled, then spit up more blood. "I knew it. Mrs. Hannington too. Now you have to help me. We have to get married. Do you know what happens to women who have a child out of wedlock? You're a foreigner. You won't even find work as a wet nurse. You need me."

She realized she was shaking. "I do not need you." She heard a commotion in the hallway, doors opening, slamming, voices asking what's the matter, others shouting for police or calling out for the woman who owned the boardinghouse.

Nanchoy closed his eyes as Afong raised the knife.

"Well then, you should know, that boy we wrote to, the one that you care so much about. He's alive, Afong," Nanchoy whispered, his breath becoming liquid. "It's true. He was going to come find you."

She froze, felt an ache in her chest.

"But" — Nanchoy struggled to swallow, struggled to breathe, struggled to laugh, as he fought to get the words out past his cracked lips — "I told him you were dead."

Nanchoy opened his eyes and grinned.

Afong hesitated for a moment as though his words were picks, poking, probing, before finally unlocking the door to a place inside her where she closeted her rage, her hopelessness, the sorrow that was too frightening to let loose. When she looked into that place, she screamed and drove the knife into his chest, feeling it scrape bone.

The light went out of his eyes as he exhaled, a long, slow hiss, but his face remained stuck in that hideous smile, a rictus of contempt.

She pulled the knife out, dropped it to the floor.

She wanted to undo her entire life. She wanted to shake Nanchoy and make him undo what he had done. Then she noticed blood on her shoes, her fingers. She looked up and caught herself in the mirror, saw the reflections of people in the doorway behind her. Other boarders, wide-eyed, horrified, gasping through mouths that hung open.

She heard a woman whisper, "What happened to that poor man?"

Yao Han. Forgive me.

Afong snatched her valise, the tin cup she used for drinking. She slipped through the stunned gathering in the hallway, who backed away as though her misfortune were contagious. She found her way down the stairs, through the parlor, out into the street where rain was pouring from the sky. She limped away, soaking wet, freezing, sinking beneath the waves, drowning again, extinguishing once and for all the flickering candle of hope. She stumbled away from who she was, who she once wanted to be, disappearing into the dark night, vanishing from the newspapers, the headlines, forever.

12
DOROTHY

(2045)

"How are you feeling?" Dr. Shedhorn asked as Dorothy was being awakened and reintroduced to her surroundings. She looked around, disoriented, the room spinning.

"I think I'm going to throw up."

She vomited what seemed like buckets of her childhood, turning her inside out, but instead of bile she expelled laughter and loneliness, joyful prose and faded obituaries, spotlight moments as the center of attention, and holidays spent alone, forgotten. Eventually the room stopped moving.

"You're taking to this treatment extraordinarily well," Dr. Shedhorn said as she scrolled through the data retrieved from an array of monitors.

"You're joking, right?" Dorothy asked, wiping her chin. "I haven't felt this way since . . ." She looked down and touched her stomach, then looked up, mortified.

"Since I was pregnant with my daughter, Annabel. I had terrible morning sickness." Dorothy held her head in her hands. "No. No. No. No . . ." *I can't be pregnant. Not now.*

"I'm not joking and you're not pregnant, Dorothy," Dr. Shedhorn reassured her. "I know this because we look at your blood-work each week before treatment to be certain. You're probably feeling this way because you're more receptive to this than any of my other patients. Far more receptive. I used to do studies where patients would take microdoses of MDMA, which, therapeutically, is like putting your psyche under a microscope. But this is much deeper and sustained. Your brain activity is off the charts."

"Why?" Dorothy asked, relieved, but also noting concern in the doctor's voice, as though she were a mechanic who'd tuned up a car only to find it could now go three hundred mph. The performance was as impressive as it was potentially dangerous.

"I'm not sure," Dr. Shedhorn said, hesitating. "Your right inferior parietal cortex, which is normally dormant during REM sleep, is fully active. In layman's terms, most people are passive in their dreams. Yours, for some reason, are quite active."

Active? Maybe that's because my reality is one of abject passivity, Dorothy thought as she looked at the time.

Standing in the rain, Dorothy felt a bit better. She felt unmoored, but adrift on a calm sea. Which felt better than her years in therapy, sorting through the bits of her adolescence as though she were reaching into a bag of broken glass. To Dorothy, epigenetic treatment was more like young Alice stepping through the looking glass and everything on the other side was not just raw emotion that needed to be processed, but emotions laden with portents and meaning, then scrambled as though by the Jabberwock. Everything was poetry that only made sense nehw daer drawkcab.

When thunder rumbled in the distance, she gave up on Louis coming to get her and drifted in the direction of the nearest subway stop. She walked, trying to figure out a way to describe to Louis what she'd just been through. She imagined standing soaking wet, yelling at him, but even in her own daydreams she was left mute. Her mouth moving, her angry words unable to reach Louis as he turned away, his back toward her, as always, invested in something else, usually himself.

As she passed an alley, the hairs on the back of her neck stood on end, and she felt a tingling down her shoulder blades. She felt a wave of sorrow and shuddered. Her eyes felt molten even before she stepped back and peered into the narrow, garbage-strewn passageway with overflowing dumpsters, boarded-up windows, broken, rusty remnants of fire escapes, and potholes that were now puddles, shimmering with gasoline rainbows. Amid the flotsam and jetsam of urban Seattle was a rag doll figure of a woman, legs out in front of her, bare feet splayed like the broken hands of a clock, her arms resting lifelessly on the filthy pavement, thumbs out, palms up. The pose reminded Dorothy of a photo she'd once seen taken in the locker room of a losing football team. The skinny placekicker crumpled on the floor, back against the wall, catatonic with defeat, having attempted to drive the winning kick through the uprights only to have the ball sail wide right, costing everyone on his team the championship game.

Dorothy felt the cold rain running down her cheeks, her neck, saw the woman's soiled dress, or what was left of it. Her hair a wet, matted carpet. Her tiny feet, having long since succumbed to a manmade shrivel. And there was blood and a foul odor, though neither deterred another homeless person who crouched over the woman, going through her belongings, or other figures who approached in the distance.

She felt her cell phone vibrate, glanced down, and read the text from Louis: *Work ran late. I'm on my way. Did you pick up Annabel?*

Dorothy groaned and ground her teeth. When she looked up, the woman in the alley had vanished. Everyone was gone, which Dorothy realized was an easy trick, considering none of them had been there in the first place.

"So, how was it?" Louis said in lieu of an apology for being late.

Dorothy closed the car door and grabbed a University of Washington sweatshirt that was lying in the back seat, something she could use as a towel to dry her face, her hair, as she sniffled. "Do you really want to know? Right now? Because we don't need to talk about it if you're just going to find something new to criticize."

Louis looked surprised, taken aback for a moment. Hurt even.

That was one of Louis's natural defense

mechanisms, Dorothy realized. Obliviousness. Because he was chronically obtuse to her concerns, and his own failings as a partner and parent, whenever Dorothy pushed back, or in this case, snapped back, he'd often retreat into a shell of nescience. Dorothy grumbled as she watched him pout, licking his imaginary wounds. She knew that he must be replaying whatever had just happened. But instead of him being chronically late, forgetting to pick up their daughter, leaving Dorothy in the rain (again), she envisioned the story he was telling himself. He was now the victim in this tragedy, the noble partner footing most of the bills, his financial support an expression of his unselfishness. In his mind, she didn't even appreciate him leaving his meeting and coming all the way to Ballard to pick her up.

Dorothy hated that in these moments she reacted emotionally and always immediately regretted it. She'd often wondered how simple life would be if she could be like others, feeling less, which seemed to afford those carefree people a respite from worry and the frustrating self-doubt that had plagued her for most of her life.

"The treatment was . . ." Dorothy searched for the words. "Exhausting."

"Did it help at all?" Louis asked, momentarily letting go of his aggrievement to place his hand on top of hers.

Dorothy drew a deep breath and slowly exhaled. "I feel different. Unburdened, lighter." As she said it, she realized she'd just thrown a softball pitch over home plate, giving Louis ample opportunity to drive one to centerfield. *That's your wallet that feels lighter.* She imagined him sniggering, *All for treating your unique combination of fatigue, depression, and gullibility.* She added, "I guess I just feel okay."

Louis shook his head as he drove through the rain in silence.

He never understood that to Dorothy, feeling okay after a lifetime of feeling everything — rage, grief, anxiety, sadness, confusion, disconnection, and longing — to just feel okay was as wonderful as it was unfamiliar. She felt intoxicated by normality. She tried her best to explain what happened while she'd been under, but the more she spoke, the more she shared, the more she realized she was singing a song with high notes that Louis was unable to hear. His frequencies were lower and he merely nodded, tuning the radio to the day's financial report. The news was grim as the stock market had taken another huge tumble, machinists were on strike at Boeing, and Amazon had its customer database hacked for the umpteenth time. Plus, there was speculation that this year's typhoon season could bankrupt insurance agencies in the Northwest whose actuarial tables had never been designed to account for 140 mph winds.

Dorothy looked out the window, peering down every alley and side street that they passed, searching, expecting to find the body of a woman with bound feet, but the back streets were empty. Dorothy searched for something positive as the rain increased and the streetlights flickered to life. The storms and flash flooding had snuffed out the eastern half of the state that had been on fire for months. Traffic was light because typhoon season kept tourists away, all but the most nihilist, the kind who enjoyed the violence of the storms and the windswept, sandblasted Washington coast, which had the rapturous, gothic appeal of a Wollstonecraft novel or a poem by Edgar Allan Poe. That's where Dorothy had come up with her daughter's name. Because in middle school, when Dorothy read the poem "Annabel Lee," she thought Annabel was Asian, like Bruce Lee.

"For the moon never beams, without

bringing me dreams, of the beautiful Annabel Lee," Dorothy would sing in Chinese as she rocked her daughter to sleep.

"You named her after a dead woman who's in a tomb," Louis complained with such frequency that it became a familial joke, though when he said it, neither of them laughed. Dorothy didn't like to remember that Louis — who hadn't been all that excited to have a child at the time — deferred to Dorothy when they were presented with forms from Swedish Hospital requiring them to officially name their daughter, who for a few days had merely existed in reality and on paper as Baby Girl Moy.

"Aren't we picking up Annabel?" Dorothy asked as they passed the street where their daughter would be waiting at the school along with unhappy teachers, eager to catch their trains home. Teachers who would pointedly restate their late-pickup policy.

"She's home already," Louis said. "My mom was in town, so I asked her to swing by and pick up Annabel when I realized you hadn't. You don't mind too much, do you?"

"Why would I mind?" Dorothy said, half-serious, half-sarcastic, all of her displeased. Louis was named after his mother. That's the kind of woman she was. A former Miss

Spokane, she graduated from Gonzaga Law School, summa cum laude, and passed the bar with flying colors. She quickly found her calling in corporate law, where modeling for a jury and carrying a caseload were more profitable than walking a runway and carrying a bouquet of roses. While many graduates of Gonzaga's Jesuit-led law program went on to be public defenders, or border lawyers, or argued against the criminalization of poverty before the US Supreme Court, her most notable case made it possible for corporations to anonymously donate to political campaigns and earned her the moniker "The Woman with the Sandpaper Heart."

Dorothy smiled and said, "You know I love it when your mom comes to visit."

When they stepped into their apartment, Dorothy saw her de facto mother-in-law sitting at their dinner table, going through a stack of mail.

Annabel sat next to her with a box of crayons, busily drawing.

"Ah-ma's home," Annabel called out, then she went back to her artwork.

"Hello, Louise," Dorothy said, even though the woman had often implored her to call her *Mom*. It had been a magnanimous

259

gesture, but Dorothy sensed it was less of an invitation to the family and more of a way to let her know that she was a child and Louise the stable, mature, venerated grown-up. Besides, since Dorothy had lost her mom at a young age, she was in no hurry to find a replacement or even a surrogate mother.

"I thought I'd clean up a bit for you, do some organizing around here, make myself useful," Louise said. "I don't know why you keep all of these rejection letters lying around? Who wants to be reminded of failure?"

Dorothy set her jaw as she realized the woman had gone through their mail, even casually opening today's, en route to sorting it. In the pile had been form-letter rejections from the many online job applications Dorothy had filled out. As well as letters from prestigious artist residencies, far away from typhoon season. Though Dorothy didn't know how she'd be able to attend even if she got into one of her top choices — Yaddo, Ragdale, or Ucross — since leaving Annabel with Louis for a month was out of the question. Dorothy glanced at her partner, who merely shrugged. She remembered him saying that his mother always opened his mail when he'd been younger, that it was an OCD thing. But then again, before they'd moved in together his mother had hired a cleaning service to attend to his dirty dishes, make his bed, and do his laundry once a week, so maybe it was, or maybe it wasn't.

"Really, you don't need to," Dorothy said.

"Oh, it's no trouble," Louise said, smiling innocently. "No trouble at all. You know me, I'm always happy to help out when I can."

Dorothy watched as she sorted their bills into two piles. Their apartment lease, power, and car payments, which she split with Louis, and the bills from her therapist, her prescriptions, and the bills from Epigenesis, which she alone paid, despite her income having been reduced to whatever she could manage from substitute teaching.

"Why even bother applying to these?" Louis asked, pointing at the rejection letters from the residency programs as he kissed his mother on the cheek.

The two of them stared at Dorothy, and she realized the question was more than rhetorical. "I don't know," she said with a shrug. She couldn't bear to tell them that she applied because an acceptance letter would at least feel like validation, that she was worthy of someone's time and consideration. Even that of a group of strangers.

■ ■ ■ ■

Dorothy sipped a cup of dragon pearl tea and lingered in the kitchen as Louise made dinner. She'd offered to help, but Louise had said, "I have all the help I need," as she nodded to Annabel, who was making a show of squeezing lemon halves into a bowl.

"Lemon artichoke pesto." Louise smiled. "My boy's favorite."

Dorothy smiled. "Great." She hated artichokes almost as much as the fact that Louise knew this and conveniently pretended not to remember.

"You know, I was thinking," Louise said. "Maybe Annabel would like to spend a few weeks with me in Spokane where the weather is better and she can actually see the sun once in a while. I'm only four hours away, after all."

"That's very generous," Dorothy said, glancing at Annabel, who had washed her hands and was now busy sharpening her crayons. "But her friends are here, her classes at preschool . . ."

"Along with tropical storms, blackouts, downed powerlines, emerald fever. Oh, and the perpetual smell of rotting fish, as a bonus," Louise said as she casually sprinkled a pinch of salt into a pot of boiling water. "It's a veritable Disneyland around here. I can understand why any mother would want her child to grow up in the middle of all this."

Dorothy looked around their lavish apartment, a place better suited to Louis's desire to impress others. The penthouse allowed him to sit with clients at the Canlis restaurant, where over a plate of winter crab with kani miso remoulade, he could casually point his fork to the Seattle skyline and say, "You see that tall building, the one reflecting the sunset. I have a place at the very top."

Louise hadn't stopped talking. "And there's a new Anglo heritage center in Lincoln Heights. It just opened. They even have a play group for children Annie's age."

Dorothy frowned and poured her tea, which was getting cold and bitter, down the sink. She wearied of how Louise insisted on calling her granddaughter Annie. Louise even took it so far as to order a baby blanket and ceramic dishes for Annabel's first and second birthdays, emblazoned with the name.

"An Anglo what?" Dorothy asked.

"An Anglo heritage club," Louise said. "With the way the world is changing, I thought it would be comforting for Annie to understand where she comes from. Louis said she's been acting up a bit. I even discussed it with her school and they said . . ."

"What? What did they say?" Dorothy felt on edge, especially since she hadn't found an opportunity to discuss Annabel's worrying behavior with Louis.

"Oh, they said she's wonderful," Louise said. "She's so creative, just like her mother. They just want her to learn to color between the lines, that's all, and I thought that some added structure might help. I mean, it's one thing for a child to act out or go through a phase, have a flight of fancy, as they say, but it stops being charming and adorable when those odd behaviors define who they are as an adult."

Here we go, Dorothy thought. *Another episode of* Passive Aggressive Theater. She'd learned to tolerate Louis's mother because she was family and Dorothy knew from painful experience that families are like a school of sharks: it's a miracle they don't eat each other or simply swim their separate ways. Something compels them to stay together.

"I don't understand what you're saying," Dorothy lied. A feeble attempt to keep the peace. "Annabel's doing just fine."

"Hey, that smells incredible," Louis said as he breezed into the kitchen for a bottle of sparkling water. "Nice to see the two women in my life getting on so well."

"I think you're forgetting somebody," Dorothy said, and Annabel waved from the dinner table, which was covered with her drawings of ships and airplanes.

"I know you're talking about me," she said, then began coloring.

"I was telling Dorothy about a special class," Louise said.

"An Anglo heritage club," Dorothy informed Louis, her eyes wide, her arms folded as if to signal, *You'd better catch up and be on my side of this discussion for once.* "Quick question. Does . . . Annabel look Caucasian to you?"

"Wellllll . . . ." Louis stretched out that single syllable as far as he could, and Dorothy knew that he was only waiting for his mother to come to his rescue. If she didn't, he might be elongating that word until his face turned blue for lack of oxygen.

"I know she's different," Louise said with an inflection best used for statements like *I know he's in prison* or *I know they're addicted to heroin.* Her statement was more of an accusation and not one aimed at Annabel.

Clearly Louise found fault with Dorothy.

"And she's special, of course," Louise continued. "I just thought that considering — and I don't know how to put this delicately, so I'll just say it — you don't know who your father was, Dorothy dear, and your mother has been gone for twice as long as Annabel's been alive. If anything, I'm being optimistic for her future. This could be a clean slate for Annie. A fresh opportunity for her to learn about the *other* side of her family. Our side. The one that's still here, still thinking about her potential, still looking out for her best interests in a world that might not always be so . . . understanding."

"She is who she is. A precocious little girl. There's nothing wrong with her," Dorothy said, with startling conviction. "And I'm fine with letting her be a normal kid, who will grow up and figure out her own definition of *who* she is and *what* that means."

"How's that worked for you, dear?" Louise said as she poured pasta into the pot of boiling water. Then she looked directly at Dorothy. "How did that work for your mother — what was her name — Greta? Did she figure out who she was? Because the one thing she wasn't, was a decent, responsible parent, or you wouldn't be the way you are, now would you? Don't you want your little girl to at least have a chance to be normal?"

Dorothy turned to Louis, who pretended not to hear, his attention turned to his phone. He glanced up absently. "What?"

Dorothy stormed off to their bedroom, which seemed fitting because as she looked outside all she saw were dark clouds. More rain. More hail. More howling wind lay in her future. As she looked out the window she noticed her reflection. *I look like my mother. No, I look like the woman who died in that alley. I look like a ghost.*

Dorothy tried to remember and felt an unusual craving — salty French fries with strawberry yogurt — what she'd craved when she was pregnant with Annabel.

"I'm not pregnant. I'm not pregnant." Even as she whispered those words to herself, a part of her wanted to run to the nearest pharmacy to pick up an in-home pregnancy test. *If I start having Braxton Hicks contractions, I'm going to scream.*

Dorothy remembered reading about a woman who showed up at the emergency room at Harborview Hospital in pain, screaming, certain she was in labor. But when the doctors examined her, they realized she didn't have a uterus. Her medical records confirmed the hysterectomy three years earlier. The poor woman ended up receiving the mental health treatment she badly needed, but lost custody of her children, a fact that haunted and terrified Dorothy as she touched her flat belly.

She sighed as she remembered a line of poetry from Andrea Gibson and wondered if, perhaps, Louis's mom was right: *Our insanity is not that we see people who aren't there, it's that we ignore the ones who are.*

Though in that moment Dorothy wished she could ignore certain people. Particularly Louise, who cheerfully proclaimed, "Dinner's ready!"

Dorothy suggested that Annabel get ready for bed early. A preemptive move in case Louise, who was busy doing the dishes by hand, tried to seize the opportunity to take over yet another one of Dorothy's motherly privileges.

"How long is Yin Yin staying?" Annabel asked as Dorothy helped her change into her favorite pair of footie pajamas. Which were green and made her look like a frog, though Dorothy called her a tadpole every time she wore them.

"Just a day or two," Dorothy said as she envisioned her daughter living with Louise in Spokane, where she'd probably tell Annabel to call her Grandma instead of speaking Chinese. "Do you like it when she comes to visit?"

Annabel shrugged.

"Would you like to go stay with her for a few days?"

Annabel shook her head and frowned.

Dorothy sighed. Then she kissed Annabel on both cheeks, her button nose, and then her forehead, twice. She still smelled like lemons. "That's my girl," Dorothy said with a conspiratorial wink. "Do you want me to read you a story?"

Annabel shook her head again and curled up beneath her blankets, oblivious to the storm winds and rain that pelted her night-blackened window.

"I want you to tell me about your ah-ma."

Dorothy smiled, but only on the outside. "Well, she was brilliant, just like you. She was very unique and saw the world differently, just like you. And she was beautiful, just like you." She brushed Annabel's bangs from her eyes and withheld the knowledge that Greta, like Dorothy, had always felt awkward, never able to fit in, to belong.

"Do you miss her?"

Dorothy hesitated, then nodded.

"What happened to her?"

Dorothy sighed. "She worked hard and was very successful at a very young age. All of this was before I was born, of course." Dorothy felt as though she were opening a book, but the chapters were cold and wet and fell apart as she turned each page. "But the ah-ma I knew had become very sad. She struggled. Always searching for what she'd lost and unfortunately, she never found it again. Then she finally went away."

"Why did she have to go away?" Annabel asked.

"Because she had a broken heart and needed to mend it."

Annabel contemplated this. "Did they make her all better?"

Dorothy smiled, but her eyes watered.

13
GRETA

(2014)

"There's our beautiful girl!" Anjalee said with arms wide open as Greta stepped off the elevator and into Syren's modest Belltown headquarters, where she was showered with adoration in the form of cheers, streamers, and fistfuls of confetti in the shape of tiny red and pink hearts that swirled in the air as though it were gently falling snow. The women on her development team, especially those who hadn't been invited to the awards dinner, wore T-shirts printed with the company's motto, *More Than Love®*. They were all wide-eyed smiles, jumping up and down — knowing that next week when the company went public, they'd all instantly become stock-option millionaires.

Greta hugged the members of her team and shook confetti from her hair. Paper hearts stuck to the soles of her shoes with each step. "You guys, you didn't have to do this. And this award doesn't make . . ." As the crowd parted, Greta noticed the giant real-time data stream monitors in the lobby that kept track of sign-ups. Yesterday Syren was just shy of six hundred thousand users. But now . . .

Anjalee took Greta's arm. "I think you'd better get used to having confetti in your hair. Because we just hit eight million users, overnight."

"Wait, wait, wait." *This isn't possible.* Greta looked at Anjalee as though she had just said the sky was purple paisley, or 4 + 7 = blue cats. "None of this makes sense. Are you sure there wasn't a breach?"

Anjalee brushed confetti from her shoulder. "Advertising you pay for, PR you pray for, and your prayers have been answered because we made CNN, the *Wall Street Journal,* the *New York Times, Wired,* and even *Scientific American* and *Psychology Today.* Plus — I'm not going to name names — we paid a few celebrities to post on their social platforms as well. Oh, and we've run your scrubbing algorithms to weed out spam bots and other fake accounts, and it still looks like we're easily at seven million and change. We're going to have to post about this today, and . . ."

Anjalee ran through her list of tasks, but Greta just tried to remain calm while quietly freaking out on the inside. She used her phone and took a video clip of the data stream as the numbers whirled by, as her coworkers laughed and took photos of her.

"I . . . still don't quite believe it," Greta said, her brows furrowed. "What's the demographic breakdown of all the new sign-ups?"

"That's my girl, always calculating," Anjalee said. "You'll be happy to know we're now the only dating app on the planet to have more women users than men, and also a growing percentage of users who identify as queer, trans, and nonbinary — and it just keeps growing."

Anjalee pointed to the monitor as numbers flew by. "That's how fast your world is going to change. Buckle up, you're not in Kansas anymore, Dorothy."

"I'm just a coder, I solve problems," Greta said, shaking her head. "Dating has always been such a riddle. I was really just trying to solve it. To improve my anemic track record with fellow humans of the opposite sex, or any sex, really. I guess I didn't realize I was . . ."

"Creating a cultural phenomenon?" Anjalee asked. "Positioning us as one of the most desirable start-ups to be acquired in a mega buyout? For someone who doesn't date, you've given Syren a dozen corporate suitors. Also, investment bankers will be lining up around the block for your hand in marriage, or merger, or some combination."

"I'm . . . just . . . ," Greta stammered. "I'm just stunned, I guess."

Anjalee led her down the hall, which was flanked by floor-to-ceiling portraits of Simone de Beauvoir, Betty Friedan, Angela Davis, and Yoko Ono. They breezed past the programmers' bullpen, where forty women stood and clapped, then up the stairs to the loft where the executives worked. She pointed toward a corner office. "That's yours now. We're setting you up with a publicist and we'll get you some media training so you're more comfortable doing on-camera interviews. Oh, and there's one other thing."

"There's more?"

"There's a handsome young man waiting for you in your office. He came early and has been here all morning." Anjalee smiled coyly, her eyes seeming to twinkle with mischief. "I'm going back to my corner, but I expect a full report."

Greta closed her eyes and suppressed a groan as she remembered her meddling, overeager, boundary-oblivious parents fixing her up with a total stranger and how she'd been tempted to go through his file, his résumé, his family history, but in the end, she left it unread. She shook her head as she took the papers out of her messenger bag and tossed them into a recycling bin.

There's no way I'm falling for this.

Even though the photo of Sam briefly carbonated her hormones, showing up early, hanging around her work, was inappropriate at best and creeptastic at worst.

Greta shook her head as she stood outside of her new office.

She liked the idea of a new space, even though it probably had a sweeping view of Puget Sound, the Olympic Mountains, and her ennui. She chewed her lip as she pictured opening the door, meeting Sam, someone she would be socially awkward with in two languages, two cultures. She readied her pretend smile, preparing to thank him for his interest and graciously show him the way out while saying, "See you later," when what she actually meant was *See you never and I'm going to murder my parents.*

Greta gathered her courage and politeness as the silhouette of someone in a dark blue suit, with dark hair, moved behind the frosted glass.

She opened the door and saw the man staring out her new window, appraising the view. She cleared her throat and said, "Hey, I know our parents mean well, but . . ."

He slowly turned around.

Instead of the man in the photo, it was the man she'd spent the last year avoiding. The silent partner who had been footing the bill for this view, this building, her salary, and all her hard work. Syren's mysterious angel investor. He looked boyish, with a precocious innocence, something the magazine articles celebrating his success were quick to build upon. He was shorter too.

"You must be Greta. I'm so sorry for intruding like this. I know this is your new office, but considering you haven't moved in yet, I hoped you wouldn't mind." He looked back out the window. "Sometimes sunrises demand to be seen and appreciated. Just like special people." He turned back to her. "I'm Carter Branson. I'm in your debt for turning my modest endowment into something, well, absolutely spectacular." He offered his hand, which was warm and soft, holding on for a beat too long as he smiled at her with knowing eyes. "I wanted to meet you so I could personally show my appreciation and pledge my continued support for your incredible . . ." He cocked his head and squinted as though solving a complicated math equation. "It's more of a social experiment, isn't it?"

Greta froze. She heard the rumors. The whisper campaign about Carter's executive assistant inviting new staffers — young, slender, and fit — to dinners, pool parties, or meetings that involved heels by Christian Louboutin, lingerie by Honey Birdette, and jets by Lear. There was also the hushed speculation about what happened to their CEO, who went on a trip to London with Carter and never came back. The gossip was that she was living in the San Juans, on some luxurious private island, or she was inpatient in Costa Rica, recovering — her silence bought off by lawyers and PR flacks. No one knew for sure, only that she'd been gone a long time.

"It's human algebra," Greta said. "People are abstractions."

They stared at each other as a police siren wailed in the distance, quickly fading.

"I'd like to hear more about your theories — how you think. Would you indulge my curiosity and let me take you to dinner tomorrow night?" He smiled innocently, with a hint of bashfulness, as though he were a nervous schoolboy, afraid of rejection. Instead of a man who had rung the opening bell of the New York Stock Exchange, hired Elton John to play his thirtieth-birthday party, and dined with two presidents.

"Dinner?"

"You know, a bit more formal than supper, and taken late in the day. Louis the Fourteenth ate dinner at noon, but with my schedule I'm more of a late-night-dinner kind of guy." Carter put his hand on her shoulder, then brushed off a bit of lint. "How do you feel about Dick's?"

Greta froze.

"Dick's Drive-In on Broadway."

"Oh." Greta felt herself blushing as she laughed nervously. "I'd say their burgers and fries are appetizing in direct proportion to how much you've been drinking."

"I wholeheartedly agree. It's basically American street food, and I'm a fan of that particular type of cuisine. Would you be up for pan-African street food?"

For a moment Greta worried that if she said yes, she might end up on a private plane bound for Mogadishu, Nairobi, Cape Town, or Addis Ababa.

"My chef is really into it these days. Grilled langoustine on a stick with pureed mint, all kinds of pickled vegetables, mogodu and ugali — which is more like African school food than street food — but he puts his own creative spin on things. With your interesting heritage, I'm sure you're up for the challenge. After all, you've probably partaken of some gastronomically questionable dishes in your time."

Growing up in a Chinese household, Greta's culinary adventures had taken her to the land of chicken feet, jellyfish, sea cucumber, and thousand-year-old eggs. She was mildly insulted and mildly intrigued.

"Sounds . . . weirdly appetizing."

Carter sighed with relief. "Okay. Great. Thank you. Why don't I have my driver pick you up here at around eight thirty tomorrow night? I know around here that's probably like sneaking out early, but I guarantee it'll be worth your time."

Before she could tell him that she hadn't actually said yes, he was gone.

Her colleagues watched him leave, then turned to Greta.

She saw the strange combination of confusion, worry, and envy in their faces. Then they all returned to their work, their conversations, their tasks, as though a master switch had been thrown. Greta closed her door. She sat in her new office chair, leaning back, eyes closed, trying to catch her breath.

■ ■ ■ ■

By noon, Greta had almost made it through her email, her voice mail, her regular mail, as well as the dozens of cards and notes that accompanied the bouquets of flowers, helium balloons, edible arrangements, arrangement of edibles, baskets of truffles, and bottles of champagne that had been sent by her peers and competitors alike.

As she collected her thoughts, she stared up at her task cloud, a disorderly collection of notes that she brought from her old office and that now covered an entire wall in her new space. In her cloud of notes there were already dozens of new reminders: Prioritize in-app features to monetize Syren. Find love matches that the PR department can use for testimonials. Find a firm to analyze all the new incoming data. Assemble teams to code the app in Japanese, French, German, Spanish, and Chinese. Have human resources figure out workspace for new hires, night shift workers. Call Mom and let her know how lunch went. Take a nap. Hire an assistant. Schedule a massage. Have a nervous breakdown. Find a way to get out of "dinner" with Carter Branson. She put the word *dinner* in quotes as a cautionary reminder.

Greta was intrigued by how nervous the mysterious boy billionaire had seemed, how approachable he was, a self-deprecating kind of confidence. She also knew that Carter's reputation was speculation. That the excuse men in his position used — whether they were sports stars, film celebrities, or plain-old wealthy men in positions of power — was that they were targets for opportunistic women. Greta shook her head. To her knowledge there were no formal charges of assault leveled against him, no lawsuits, just rumored settlements for inappropriate behavior, a storm cloud of conjecture. Many young, attractive female employees had been invited to special events at his home, his office, on business trips. Though recently his name had been anonymously added to an online list titled "Executives Behaving Badly." There were no other details.

As she weighed possible excuses to get out of, or at least postpone, dinner, her watch lit up with a message: *Sam is here for you. He says he's meeting you for lunch. Shall I send him back?*

Greta rubbed her tired eyes.

I can't believe this is my life.

Grudgingly she pressed yes.

Despite the terrible timing, a part of her

had to admit there was something sweet and charming about a blind date, embracing the unknown, tempting fate, flipping a coin. Even though Syren had been her brainchild, if anyone were to ask how she felt about relationships, she'd say, "I'm polynomial in a nonpolynomial world. I'm still searching for the right algorithm to bridge the uncanny valley of my heart."

When she opened her eyes, a man stood in her doorway in jeans and a jacket, open collar, no tie. He looked like his photo, though his hair was in a topknot, and he was taller than she imagined, and a bit less tan, thanks to Seattle's ever-darkening skies.

"I'm Sam." His introduction almost sounded like an apology. He looked in awe of the place, perhaps embarrassed. "Um, in case you're wondering, no, I've . . . never done this before. I'm afraid my parents got a little carried away . . ."

"I'd say both of our parents are at fault," Greta said as she stood and introduced herself, which felt strange considering he probably knew all her secrets, like how she'd been kicked out of prep school twice, how she didn't like the ocean because she always got seasick, and how she never wore sandals because she thought her feet were gross.

"They mean well. Yours, anyway. Mine —

I think they're just trying to save face — to not look like parental failures to their nosy neighbors." Sam smiled. "Either way it's quite generous of you to even consider lunch under such strange circumstances."

"What can I say, there's something in the blood."

Sam looked confused.

"Filial piety," Greta said. "I swear that's part of our DNA. Maybe the next Human Genome Project will locate our highly evolved guilt triggers and the overwhelming desire to never let our Asian parents down. It's like karma on steroids."

"Indeed." Sam smiled and nodded in agreement.

Greta closed her laptop. "So, knowing all of that, what do you think about dating apps?" she asked, folding her arms.

He smiled, as though to keep from wincing. He looked at her, then peeked his head out of her office, looked around, then turned his attention back to Greta. "Hmmm . . . at this point in my life, I've been stricken with what my friends call terminal honesty. So, if you ask, I'll always tell you the truth. I'm not really an app guy."

"Oh." Greta respected his candor. "What kind of guy are you then?"

Sam found Greta's coat on a hook behind

her office door and opened it, offering to help her with the garment. "I'm more of a share-an-umbrella-in-the-rain kind of guy."

She let him put her coat on for her. "Good answer."

Too bad it's not raining.

As they chatted and walked up the street toward the Space Needle, Sam listened with what Greta felt was genuine interest, instead of waiting for his turn to talk over her like so many other men had done on first dates, first lunches, even simple meetups for coffee. Nor did he treat the fact that she'd helped create a dating app as a sign that she was somehow more promiscuous or had slept with scores of men and possibly women, as research. She found herself relaxing in his company, even though she had a million things to do and a dinner tomorrow night to get through, or avoid.

"You know," Greta said, "I'm afraid you might have become the unwitting victim of my parents' irrational fear of me never getting married. It's because my *zou mou* was a rebel flower. My dad's mom got kicked out of some bohemian boarding school in England back in the twenties and remained single till the day she died, though she did manage somehow to get knocked up later in life."

Sam shrugged. "Some women want a child but not a husband."

"Not in my family. In my family that's either a scandal or a tragic failure. Some sort of character flaw. But she raised my dad and he turned out reasonably okay."

Greta brushed up next to him as they squeezed through a crowd of middle school children assembled on the sidewalk for a field trip. He felt strong but gentle. Solid but graceful. He seemed unhurried, unstressed. The opposite of what Greta saw whenever she looked in the mirror. "Where are we going for lunch?"

"Well, considering how busy you are and how you've probably eaten at every restaurant within walking distance of your office, and also considering how parking in this city is seemingly theoretical . . ." Sam led her around the corner and up onto the grass parkway of Seattle Center, walking in the direction of the towering sculpture of red cylinders known as Olympic Iliad. Near the sculpture, in the shade of a maple tree, a picnic blanket had been spread on a wide bed of grass. Standing next to it, looking bored and smoking a cigarette, was a young kid with a skateboard. Sam handed the boy

285

some money and thanked him. Greta looked on, somewhat bewildered as he left.

"I thought we'd do something a little different," Sam said, kneeling and gently removing her shoes. Then he removed his own and they sat down on cushions.

Next to the blanket was a large wicker basket and a round chafing dish, the kind Greta was used to seeing at catered office parties. Beneath it was a package of lit Sterno.

Sam smiled and then removed the silver lid. As steam wafted out Greta could smell rich bone broth with ginger and goji berries heated to full boil. She watched as he opened the basket and carefully lifted out several lacquered trays. He set them down and removed the plastic wrap to reveal elegantly arranged dipping items: noodles, dumplings, thinly sliced flank steak, pork belly, tofu, zucchini, squash, cabbage, bok choy, enoki mushrooms, and skewers with raw shrimp and scallops. He then set out two bowls and small bottles of chili oil and hoisin sauce.

"Is *fo wo* okay?" Sam said, looking up.

"You're kidding, right? I love Mongolian hot pot," Greta said. "How did you . . ." Then she realized her parents must have shared what her favorite foods were.

Sam smiled as he opened two bottles of sparkling mineral water. "I didn't bring any *baijiu,* but I figured you still have a busy day ahead of you, and sending you back to your office with a hangover is a bad first impression."

"This looks . . . amazing. I can't believe you went to all this trouble," Greta said, nervously looking around as tourists and businesspeople walked by, admiring their elegant lunch. A motorist honked and waved. "Are we allowed to do this?"

"I've been away from Seattle for a few years," Sam said. "But I'm pretty sure urban picnicking isn't a crime, though if the police come by we'll just tell them this is a mobile soup kitchen and invite them to join. I brought an extra bowl."

She watched Sam take out his phone. For a moment, she thought he might text a friend, or take a selfie with his food, or look for more viable dating options right there in front of her, as one disappointed dinner date had done. Instead he pressed play and Ol' Blue Eyes began singing "Both Sides Now" through a portable Bluetooth speaker.

Greta looked around, smiled, then got comfortable and unwrapped a set of chopsticks. She felt the heat, smelled the Szechuan peppercorns in the broth. She sipped sparkling water and their eyes met as she listened to the crooner sing, "It's love's illusions that I recall, I really don't know love, I really don't know love at all . . . ."

In that moment Greta realized she had such terrible luck at dating because she'd always imagined that there was someone out there looking for her, someone who'd understand just her, someone worth waiting for.

She stared at Sam, wishing she'd read his file. "Who *are* you?"

Greta left work early and went directly to her parents' house. She could smell her mother's cooking, hoisin sauce, five-spice powder, and sesame oil, even before she walked in the door. Inside, her father was in his favorite chair, chin tucked to his chest, fast asleep as the second game of a Mariners double-header was in progress. An untouched cup of tea sat cooling on the table next to him. Greta's mother waved and smiled from the kitchen, where she was chopping vegetables. She didn't look surprised.

Greta removed her coat and tossed it over a chair on the way to the kitchen. "Who is this guy?" She stared at her mother.

"Who, Sam?"

288

"Yes, Sam!"

"Lower your voice, I don't want to wake your father. He hasn't been sleeping well," her mother said as she chopped green peppers, onions, and smashed garlic. "I take it you went on your lunch date. How was it? Is he as nice as we'd hoped?"

"You tell me. He seems to know everything about me and I know nothing about him." Greta took a lid off a pot that was simmering on the stove. Brisket, ginger, and peppers, with a hint of sesame oil. She spied an empty can of San Marzano tomatoes. Her mother was making Chinese chili, another one of Greta's favorites.

She knew I'd come here.

Greta's mother slipped by her with the small cutting board and brushed the vegetables into the pot with the edge of a cleaver. "Would you stir that for me?"

Greta shook her head and stirred the pot while her mother washed her hands and then dried them on a kitchen towel. Greta thought about Sam and wondered if she could find his folder in the recycling bin at work. "He's *gwaa gong,* isn't he?"

"Oh, they're all leftover men, dear," her mother said.

Even before Greta went to work for Syren and became a specialist on dating culture,

289

she knew that China's one-child policy had successfully curbed the booming population. But it gave the country thirty million more baby boys than girls.

"So yes, in case you are wondering, he's a bare branch on his family's tree," her mother said as she rested a hand on her hip. "That's nothing so unusual."

"Then why did you choose him?"

"Do you not like him? Was he unkind to you?"

"No, that's not it. He's the opposite of that. He's kind and charming and conscientious and self-deprecating," Greta said. *And beautiful.*

"He's a widower," her mother said, and Greta fell silent. She stopped stirring the pot. "It's hard enough to get married in China these days, but somehow he managed it. He and his bride went to the Maldives for their honeymoon."

"Wait, he was married?"

Greta's mother nodded. "Then they came back and she fell ill at a family dinner. She was sick for weeks before they found out that she had ovarian cancer." Her mother shook her head. "She was gone in less than six months. That was three years ago. Sam hasn't dated anyone since. I suppose initially that was because he was in mourning, but in reality, no one will marry him now. He doesn't have a typical job. As you can see, he is mixed, which is not popular with traditional parents. And now he's seen as a beacon of bad luck. That's why his parents were desperately shopping him around. I'm sure he would have told you eventually. That's hardly something to discuss on a first date."

"But why me?" Greta asked. She thought about his smile, his sense of humor, his generosity of spirit. Being with him was like spending time with an old friend. She found herself genuinely interested. That's when she realized what she was really asking was *Why does he meet your approval?*

Greta's mother filled a pot with rice and began rinsing it. "It was at the Marriage Market that the matchmaker determined that Sam was perfect for you. I must confess, it was surprising, even to us. But your father and I would never doubt her."

"She's just some *mei po*," Greta snapped. "A superstitious octogenarian with a power trip and too much time to kill. How can you put my fate in the hands of some stranger?" Even as she said those words Greta knew how she must sound. After all, millions of people were now putting their romantic fates in the digital hands of Greta's algorithms. "I'm sorry, Ah-ma. I know that probably sounds hypocritical."

Her mother sighed. "The reason we never doubted her, *jyu dim,* is because she was the matchmaker who arranged for me to marry your father." She smiled and touched Greta's face. "You, my perfect raindrop, are proof that she was right."

At work the next day, Greta tried to think of a reason to back out of her dinner with Carter. But a part of her was surprised he was as approachable as he was, less ego-driven than she'd expected. He didn't seem like a misogynistic playboy. More of an awkward geek with newly developed social skills and the confidence that comes from having massive, generational wealth at his disposal. She was wary, but curious.

She'd emailed him: *Where are we going for dinner?*

She was astounded that he quickly replied: *Someplace you've been before.*

That made her feel better. She worried that his driver might take her directly to his home in Laurelhurst, or to a private yacht on Lake Union, or even to some penthouse hotel room where he would answer the door wearing only a plush bathrobe, coyly inviting her in for room service. She stopped worrying and accepted that there was something thrilling about the notion of going out to dinner with a billionaire. It felt like being strapped into a carnival ride. She could climb out, but that was dangerous. Instead she would hold on, bracing herself for an arranged marriage with gravity as she spun into the perilous unknown.

That's when Sam texted her: *I signed up for an account.*

She smiled. Then frowned.

Despite Sam's tragic history, her heart sank at the notion of him casually dating his way through Seattle's array of single women.

She responded: *Bored of me already?*

Quite the contrary. I just wanted to appreciate your work. Don't worry, I'm not looking for another picnic partner. Speaking of, would you like to get together again? Perhaps go for a walk around Green Lake?

Greta left him on read, stood up, and walked around her desk. She stared out at the calm waters of Puget Sound, the ribbon of traffic flowing through the Alaskan Way Viaduct. She hadn't dated anyone in almost a year. She hardly made time for coffee, let alone lunch or dinner, or anything beyond that, casual or otherwise. She'd thrown herself into her work, letting that be her excuse for going home to no one and waking up alone.

Anjalee knocked and popped her head in, smiling. "I hear you have big plans."

After work, Greta waited for her ride to dinner with Carter, and right on time, a silver Escalade glided to the curb. A driver stepped out, greeted her, and opened the rear passenger door. Greta half expected Carter would be in the back holding a near-empty bottle of Cristal, a girl draped on each arm. But the vehicle was empty.

Greta climbed in and took a seat.

There were today's newspapers, the *Seattle Times, San Francisco Chronicle, New York Times, Washington Post,* and a pair of magazines — tech journals — each with Greta's photo on the cover. Greta turned the magazines facedown.

"Where are we going?" she asked.

The driver smiled back in the rearview mirror. "Mr. Branson has instructed me to drop you off at the Space Needle. Sit tight, Ms. Moy, and I'll have you there in a few minutes. Would you like the radio on, news, some music, perhaps?"

"No thank you." Greta looked out the window and saw the iconic tower lighting up the night sky. She'd been there numerous times, for dinner, doing the tourist thing with friends on the observation deck, she'd even spent an afternoon on the lower level for a wedding. If Carter was trying to impress her, he'd have to try a bit harder. Then as the car pulled up, Greta noticed there were no other vehicles in the porte cochere.

She stepped out before the driver could assist her. She expected to find a hostess or a line of people queued up for the elevator, but there was no one else but her.

The doors of the golden elevator opened.

"Have a lovely dinner," the driver said as he wandered off, taking a pack of cigarettes from his pocket and lighting one as moths swarmed beneath a streetlight.

Greta drew a deep breath and stepped inside the elevator capsule. The doors closed and she watched the car, the driver, all of Seattle Center shrink from view. When the elevator slowed and she arrived at the top of the Space Needle, the doors parted and she stepped out into an empty restaurant, where some sort of lo-fi hip-hop was playing on the sound system, a gentle beat, the kind of music she liked to listen to while working late at night. She didn't see any staff or other patrons, not even a manager. She peeked around the corner and found

Carter sitting at the bar, on his phone. He looked up and smiled.

"Are we the only people here?" Greta asked.

"Oh no. My chef is in the kitchen with his sous chef and two assistants. The food here is a bit . . . pedestrian, but I've made generous donations to the Space Needle Foundation, so they indulge me once in a while. Besides, it gets quite noisy in here at times." He pointed to the empty dining room. "This way we don't have to shout."

Greta followed him to a table near the large, wraparound window. She'd been here enough times to know that the restaurant made a complete rotation every forty-five minutes and that diners sometimes put Post-it notes on the glass, drawings, messages, knowing they would appear to someone else later in the evening. Greta watched a note that read *I love Alyce* slowly drift by.

Greta looked around, searching for a waiter or a bartender. She felt uncomfortable in the emptiness of the restaurant. "What are we doing here?"

Carter glanced to the left, to the right, then whispered as though he were divulging a closely guarded secret, "We're . . . having dinner."

Greta gestured toward the window. "We

could have had dinner anywhere. I can't believe you went to all this trouble. I'm not exactly what you'd call high-maintenance."

"Well, how do I put this?" Carter asked as he looked around nervously, as though searching for the right words. "We're here because, honestly, this view is hard to beat. And I wanted to have dinner with you, because . . ."

He hesitated.

"We matched up on Syren."

Greta furrowed her brow and stared back. "That's impossible. I'm not on the app, and besides, that would be a conflict of interest. Also, just plain . . . weird."

Carter leaned forward. He cleared his throat and smiled. "You know, I didn't get to where I am in the tech industry without being able to decode a thing or two."

Greta noticed another note on the window, an *A* for anarchy. She sat back, her fingers drumming the table. She squinted at Carter. "You found Zoe, didn't you?"

"Would you be upset if I said yes?"

Greta felt equally impressed, embarrassed, and exposed. "That's my superuser account, in case you're wondering. I created Zoe as an identity for testing and debugging the app, not for actual dating or anything even remotely close to that."

297

Carter rubbed his chin, deep in thought. "But she's you. Isn't she?"

Greta tried not to wince. She named the account after her grandmother, Zou yi, who went by Zoe. She'd never married, never settled down in the traditional sense, and had gotten pregnant late in life because she wanted a child. But Greta *had* filled out the questionnaire honestly. Perhaps she'd been too honest.

She sighed and then nodded, reluctantly.

"What do you think that means?" Carter asked.

Greta thought of all the rumored things Carter had been accused of, the payoffs, the settlements, the ongoing whisper campaign. Was all of that conjecture, jealous speculation, emerald-colored rumors seen through a warped lens of jealously? Or were the stories all true and she was just as bad as he was? Maybe that's why she always failed to make lasting emotional connections outside her family, and even that had often been a struggle growing up.

"I'd say that some people's hearts are like the bottom of the ocean," Greta answered. "Largely unexplored."

After a bottle of Moroccan wine, the chef and his staff brought out an aromatic and elegantly presented dinner, featuring courses of freshly smoked samaki, something delightfully called *bunny chow,* which was chicken curry on a fresh half-loaf, couscous made of fermented cassava, stewed Senegalese sweet potatoes with black-eyed peas, Egyptian falafel, followed by Malva pudding and mini mandazi, still warm and covered in powdered sugar. All of which was accompanied by a pair of ice-cold Kenyan beers, which they drank straight from the can.

"What do you think?" Carter asked as he pushed away from the table.

"I think having a private chef is greatly underrated." Greta enjoyed trying new things, and the company, while awkward, wasn't as horrible as she imagined. In fact, he'd been a gentleman, and most of their dinner conversation was less of a date and more of a master class in software programming and database engineering, with deep questions about how Greta arrived at her array of mathematical formulas and the AI employed to harvest user data and assign matches.

"And what do you think about the future of Syren?" he asked.

Greta looked out the window as running lights from freighters and ferries glided across the dark waters of Puget Sound. Then she saw her reflection. She looked like her grandmother, Zoe, whom she'd seen only in old black-and-white photos.

"I'm guessing as our silent benefactor, you know more than I know."

"I know that you're about to change tax brackets," Carter said. "The investment bank that's underwriting next week's IPO has raised the estimated stock price from four dollars a share to twenty-three dollars. A lot of that has to do with your programming, your algorithms."

Greta tried not to think about what her net worth might be in a year, which was when she would be able to use her stock options to buy shares of Syren. She'd been given four hundred thousand options. At the projected price of $23 a share, that would be roughly $9,200,000. And the stock price might even be higher by then. What would Carter make — five hundred million? A billion?

What is that even like? Greta wondered. She didn't come from money, and with her student loans, she'd had a negative net worth since she was eighteen. Next week she'd potentially be worth millions, at least on paper. But she didn't get into this business for money. Relationships were just another problem to solve.

She asked, "Don't you suppose some of that has to do with the fact that people are realizing that a dating app run by women nets different, more sustainable results?"

"Oh, it's different all right." Carter smiled. "I noticed that right away when I came by the office. It's not every day that I'm the only Y chromosome in the building."

There was an awkward moment of silence as he refilled her water glass.

"Speaking of being the visiting rooster in the henhouse," Greta was just tipsy enough to ask. "I'm sure you're aware that there are a lot of unflattering rumors about you. How you belong to a certain club of bad boy billionaires. I appreciate dinner and am happy you've taken an interest in my work and all, but . . ."

"But you're worried that I'm a cad? A womanizer? A stalker, even?"

Greta didn't say anything, just raised an eyebrow.

"I can assure you that every one of those rumored instances has been false and/or strictly business. I mean it, Greta." He shrugged innocently and exhaled slowly, as though exhausted from the mere thought of impropriety. "Yes, some people see me as a very wealthy young man funding a feminist dating platform, and to them, that might seem hypocritical. But — to others — they see my financial involvement as benevolent, an ally putting his money behind a cause that he firmly believes in. I wrote a very big check. But you're the one making headlines. I have no position of power over anyone in the company — far from it — I've been completely hands-off. Yesterday was the first time I'd even set foot in the office. Does that sound like something a womanizer would do?"

Greta found herself wanting to give him the benefit of the doubt. Maybe the stories had all been gossip. Mean-spirited conjecture at the cost of an innocent man's reputation, who was just trying to help. She thought about how their profiles had matched. They both had one thing in common: loneliness. It must be isolating to be so wealthy, unsure of anyone's real motives because money always gets in the way.

"C'mon, it's getting late and I know you probably still have work to do. I'll walk you down and my driver will take you back to Syren."

He must have sensed her apprehension, her discomfort at bringing up such a sensitive subject, because he kept a polite distance as they walked to the elevator. Inside,

Greta thanked him, then held her breath for a moment, waiting for her stomach to rise as the capsule began its five-hundred-foot journey, a descent that would take forty-three seconds. Greta did have an enormous amount of work to do, and much of her staff would still be at their workstations. But she allowed herself a moment, a five-second vacation when she'd take in the gorgeous nighttime view, the solitude, being appreciated by someone successful and powerful. She'd stepped into his world and held her own. He respected her talent. There was a small victory in there somewhere.

She turned to thank him and he kissed her.

One hand on her waist, the other beneath her chin, his mouth over hers, lips parted. He tasted like saffron and beer. She felt like she was sinking faster than the elevator was dropping.

She froze. Stunned.

"Dinner was nice," he said. "Would you like to go someplace for dessert?"

Here he was, the golden child of the tech world, yet his words were so blatant, so comical — like the go-to move of a drunken frat boy — that she laughed out loud. But as the elevator settled and a bell chimed, she felt sickened, horrified, confused. The doors opened and she saw the driver standing next to the Escalade, the door open. But he wasn't a driver in that moment. He was another man, a collaborator. He was saying something but she didn't hear. When she felt Carter's hand on her lower back, she peeled away, wanting to slap him, stab him. She looked at him and he was smiling innocently, saying something, words, noise. She blocked out the sound of his voice and stormed off, her heels clicking on the cold, wet pavement.

"So, how was dinner with the one and only Carter Branson?" Anjalee asked the next day. She smiled as she sipped her latte. "I heard his personal chef used to own a three-star Michelin restaurant in the Bay Area, is that true? Or maybe it was two-star."

"I didn't ask," Greta said. Her heart raced as she remembered feeling trapped in that elevator, hundreds of feet up in the air, a billionaire's uninvited lips mashed on top of hers. It had begun raining as she'd walked back to Syren. She'd tried to think about work, but when she stepped off the elevator into the lobby and saw numbers on the data stream monitor zooming by as sign-ups passed fifteen million users, she felt ill and went home.

Anjalee kept talking, gesturing happily.

Greta sighed. She tried to relax. Tried to breathe normally as she asked herself, *Is this my fault? Did I put out some kind of signal that I was interested? Was he drunk? Was I drunk? Is this what he's done to other women? Did they fall for it? Or did he shackle them with golden handcuffs and then think he could do whatever he wanted? Can he?*

"So anyway," Anjalee said. "A writer with Bitch Media will be coming by a week after the IPO to do a piece about you. They're small and based out of Portland, but their content is sensational and they have six million readers that are the definition of our primary target demographic. It's going to be uh-mazing."

When Anjalee left, Greta sat back in her chair. She stared out the window and thought about the interview. She could tell the reporter what happened. She could out Branson as a world-class womanizer, a predator. But . . . it was just a kiss, right?

One he didn't ask for.

Maybe other women would speak out if she did. But what if they didn't? What if they were paid off, or had vested shares in something that compelled them to remain silent? Greta wondered about the many ways she could lose her job. Surely, she'd be terminated if she spoke out, and with her job she'd lose — she hated that money was a part of this — she'd literally lose millions. Carter hadn't explicitly connected her stock options to his advances; he didn't have to, it was implicit. While Greta personally didn't care about the money, she realized she could also help out entire generations of her family with that kind of wealth. Or she could give it all to charity — women's causes — like the Malala Fund, RAINN, or Girls Not Brides. There had to be a way to make this right.

Her phone lit up with a text message, from Sam.

Hmmm . . . you didn't reply to my invite to go walk around Green Lake. I know you're busy, so if I don't hear from you, no worries, I understand. Thinking of you, wishing you great love, abundant happiness, and most of all, parental approval.

Greta closed her eyes and grimaced. She was so busy, so angry, so confused. Then she remembered that Sam knew how to fight. Like, really fight.

She replied: *I'll meet you at the Green Lake Library. About six?*

She stared at her phone, impatiently waiting for a reply.

Then her phone lit up.

Sam: *Perfect* ☺

Greta sat on the steps of the Carnegie Library across from Green Lake Park, watching cyclists, joggers, dog-walkers, and teens who cruised by on longboards when she caught Sam's eyes as he emerged from a crowd with a beverage in each hand.

"I stopped at the Blank Space Café and grabbed us a couple of bubble teas." Sam held them up with a boyish grin. "Would you like mango or lychee?"

Greta thanked him and took the lychee tea, which smelled tart and sweet. She took his arm as they crossed the street to the walking path around Green Lake.

"Thank you for wanting to spend time with me again," Sam said. "For a moment there, I was worried that I'd somehow upset you, that urban picnicking was a little too . . . brazen, I guess. Or maybe you finally read my file . . ."

"I threw it away," Greta confessed as she sipped her tea through a fat straw, chewing on the mochi. "Sorry. That was more of an overreaction to my parents. Not your fault. I guess I'm like you, I'm not into dating apps, even though I helped create one."

Sam nodded and listened intently.

Greta shared how she took the job at

Syren because she needed to pay rent and student loans, not that she had any interest in playing digital Cupid. Though the idea of working in an all-female environment was intriguing. At first, Syren felt like a secret club — Wonder Woman's Paradise Island — where Amazons led a magical existence far from the affairs of mortal men. But she quickly realized they were all more scholar than warrior — mathematicians, coders, oddballs, and uber-geeks — whose super-powers were the ability to work twenty hours a day and debug software platforms without complaint.

As she talked, she led him past a flower garden overflowing with daffodils and found a nice bed of grass that hadn't been over-run by ducks. They sat and took in the view, listened to the sounds of the city, cars, buses, birds chirping, a group of grade-school violinists warming up before a lesson near the shore.

They shared a relaxing moment of silence and she realized she felt unusually comfort-able in Sam's company — more than com-fortable — she felt like her true self. Far from the money and machinations of Car-ter Branson, far from the stressful round-the-clock programming obligations of Syren, where she felt responsible for pairing up millions of users. She tried not to think of how many hearts would be broken if her algorithms failed. That's when she remembered what her mother had shared about Sam.

"I didn't read your folio," Greta said as she set her tea down and began pulling at blades of grass. "But my ah-ma did tell me you were married once. I'm sorry for your loss. I don't mean to bring up the past. I just wanted you to know that I knew, in case that was ever something you wanted to talk about. If so, I'm happy to listen."

Sam stared out at the lake as happy couples churned by in paddleboats. "That's very kind, very generous." He turned to her. "What would you like to know?"

Greta shrugged. "Whatever you feel like sharing."

Sam looked down at where a wedding band used to be. "We were both teaching English. Both expats, with families back in the states. She was . . ."

Sam looked away.

"I'm sorry, I shouldn't have brought it up."

He turned back toward her. "It's okay. I'm glad you did. What isn't in my file was that she cheated on me two weeks before our wedding."

Greta stopped drinking her tea mid-sip.

"It was a one-time thing, I guess. An impetuous moment with an old flame. I know I sound like I'm making excuses, probably because she's been gone for a while now, but at the time I didn't know. We got married. Everything seemed perfect. Our honeymoon was amazing. Those first few weeks as a married couple were the happiest moments of my entire life." Sam smiled but his eyes betrayed his sadness. "I never doubted that she cared for me."

Greta leaned toward him. "But then she got sick."

Sam nodded. "But then she got sick. It was during a hard week of radiation and chemo that she confessed, told me everything. I think she was feeling guilty, maybe thought that she didn't deserve someone looking after her. I suppose it was her way of trying to drive me away, so I wouldn't see her in so much . . ."

Greta looked in his eyes, which were glossy with emotion. "I'm sorry."

Sam shrugged. "I was hurt, of course. How could I not be? I was angry. But I realized that I loved her more than all of those other feelings combined. I guess that's what love is, and when someone is counting the time they have left in weeks instead of years, none of that other stuff seems to matter as much."

Sam looked at Greta and she took his hand, which was firm, rough, his knuckles calloused. But the way he spoke, the way he carried himself, was gentle, tender.

"I took care of her," he said. "I brushed her hair until it was all gone. I carried her to the bathroom when she was sick. I read to her when she was scared. I emptied her catheter each morning. I crushed tablets of morphine at night, mixed them with Ativan, and used an eyedropper to place the meds beneath her tongue to ease the pain. And I held her as she passed away in my arms. It still felt like a honeymoon, and she still looked wonderful to me. In the end, the whole thing was horrible and beautiful and I'm glad I was able to be there. But as you can imagine, having my heart broken two different ways in a short amount of time was a lot to contend with. A lot to carry around, let alone reconcile. Honestly, I had no intention of ever dating again. I felt so down, so unhappy. Hopelessly depressed, if we're being honest. I checked myself into a hospital for a while. I had given up on everything. On other people. On myself. On ever finding my way through the fog my life had become. It took me a while, but I got back on my feet. Started working again. Training again. Then one day my parents came for a visit. They showed me your file and I read about you, saw your photo, and I felt something I hadn't felt in a very long time."

"Love?" The word came out before Greta even thought about it.

Sam gazed at her. "Hope." He squeezed her hand and smiled gently. "Sometimes that's better than love."

"More than love," Greta whispered, parroting Syren's tagline.

Greta's heart beat in the exact opposite way it had with Carter. Here, in this moment, she didn't feel used or threatened or manipulated. She didn't feel on guard. She felt understood. She felt seen, even as she saw her own reflection in Sam's eyes.

"Is that what you're hoping for?" Sam asked. "Love?"

Yes. Maybe? I don't know. Greta had never been in love, more like adjacent to love, or spent a layover in love, but her final destination was always disappointment. She saw the way Sam memorialized his late wife, how his eyes lit up, and she wasn't even alive. Greta thought she saw a glimmer of that when he looked at her.

Is that what you want?

312

She wanted to answer Sam honestly, but didn't know how. There were other things she wanted. Practical things. She understood practical.

"I . . . want . . . you . . . ," Greta said. "To teach me how to fight."

Sam cocked his head and smiled again. "Excuse me?"

"Well." Greta felt herself blushing. "My parents said you teach boxing or tai chi or something like that? You know . . ." She made a fist the size of her heart.

"I teach Sanshou. Which is like Chinese boxing, but with kicks and takedowns. I used to compete — a little — nothing to get too excited about. I teach jujitsu as well."

"Can you teach me?"

"Right here?"

"Okay." Greta nodded as though his question had been an invitation.

"Okay then." Sam looked surprised but flexible in his plans, like he'd gone to get his oil changed and was told the next karaoke song was his and he'd better get ready.

They stood and he smiled as he helped her through a series of partner stretches to get warmed up. Then he showed her a few basic self-defense techniques that were especially useful for women, how to escape a wrist grab, how to turn and counter when grabbed from behind, how to check an attacker's arms while delivering a knee to the groin. They ended up tumbling to the grass, laughing, their arms and legs entangled.

"May I show you something a bit more advanced?" Sam asked. "It's a leg choke, so we're going to have to get kind of intimate here. But I don't want to do anything that makes you uncomfortable."

"It's okay," Greta said. "Thank you for asking."

Sam showed her how from her back, she could control an attacker's position by wrapping her legs around his waist, by pulling him close, controlling his arms so he couldn't hit her or choke her. Then he showed her how to throw one leg over his neck, while holding his arm, then bring her other leg over her ankle and clamp down, like the camber of a jar with a latch. Locking her legs around his neck and arm, cutting off the flow of blood to the brain, would effectively put an attacker to sleep.

Greta was astonished at how much she liked being in this position, in charge. She rotated her hips and flipped him over, her legs still locked around him until he patted her leg and she let go. Breathing hard from wrestling, she lay on the grass, happy, content.

"You did great," Sam said with a laugh. He seemed more impressed than surprised. "Seriously, you're a natural at this."

"You're just saying that because I almost choked you out with my thighs of steel." Greta laughed and then rolled back on top of him.

Now Sam seemed surprised.

"I wish I hadn't thrown away your file," Greta said.

"Why's that?"

"Because I want to know everything there is to know about you."

"You know the big stuff."

"What about the little stuff then. Like . . . is Sam short for Samuel?"

"My parents are Buddhists. It's short for Samsara. That's the Sanskrit word for *wander,* but what it really means is rebirth." He looked up at her and smiled. "Maybe it means that if I'm lucky, I get a do-over."

Greta gently touched his cheek. "Maybe."

"Samsara is also Dukkha," Sam lamented. "Which means suffering. It's a karma thing. Sometimes we just don't get it right at this turn at bat. But there's a lot to be learned along the way, especially by how we treat others. My parents always stressed that karma is transpersonal. It's not about doing good or bad, making wise or foolish choices, for our own karmic benefit. It's about how our choices can improve the quality of other people's journeys. Our family's, our children's, our partners', romantic and otherwise. That being stated, I'd be lying if I told you I wasn't nervous about dating again."

In that moment, Greta felt safe. No, she didn't just feel safe. She felt strong. She felt in control, something she realized she'd never had enough of. She also felt grateful. For Sam's complexity, his kindness, his gentleness, his tenderness, his patience, his honesty, his spirit. She leaned forward, raised an eyebrow, and he smiled and nodded as she gently, softly, felt his warm, full lips. Their heads tilted, their lips parted. He tasted like fresh mango. Then she sat up, kissed her fingertips, and touched them to his lips, as though that gesture could somehow update the firmware of her heart, overwrite the bad memories, upgrade her expectations of what was possible.

"Thank you," Sam said, amused. "Just don't do that to your assailant."

A week later Anjalee caught Greta in the hallway on the way to her office. "The reporter from Bitch Media is here. I sent her back. I hope you're ready."

"Ready for what?" Greta asked.

"Um . . ." Anjalee hesitated. "I guess we'll just find out, won't we?"

Aside from struggling to accept that there was a news outlet called Bitch Media, Greta was as ready as she'd ever be. The week had been surreal. From sitting in her parents' living room and watching the opening bell of the New York Stock Exchange on CNBC, to moments later seeing SYRN scroll by on the ticker, followed by an eye-popping stock price of $34 per share. Her parents smiled, but stoically didn't ask what all this meant. They were suitably impressed that a company she worked for was on TV. They even called some of their friends and told them to tune in. Greta watched the stock price gyrate up and down as she wondered how she was supposed to feel. Her stock options were worth millions, yet she felt the same. Nothing else had changed. She didn't feel happier. Her coffee didn't taste better. Traffic wasn't easier to navigate as she drove to work. Even as she walked into Syren that morning and everyone acted like they'd won the Powerball, the Nobel Prize, the Super Bowl, and were awarded the title of prom queen all at the same time. Amid the celebration, she found herself wondering what

Sam was doing and when she could see him again. They'd spent a part of every single day together: jujitsu lessons at Green Lake, Cambodian food at Phnom Penh Noodle House in the International District, wandering around the Seattle Central Library. She wondered what he would think of her interview. Had his feelings for her increased, diminished, or simply been distorted by the possibility of new wealth? She was struggling for an answer when she arrived at her office and found a tall woman with a guest badge waiting for her.

"Hi, I'm Sophia Blessing." She shook Greta's hand. "Thank you so much for making time to meet with me, I'm sure you're incredibly busy right now."

"That's my new normal, I'm afraid," Greta said. "Please, come on in."

Instead of sitting behind her desk, Greta sat at a small meeting table across from Sophia, who pulled out a digital recorder. "Do you mind?"

"Be my guest." Greta hoped her polite smile would hide how nervous she was.

"I guess I should begin with offering my congratulations," the reporter said. "It's a unique occasion that a tech company helmed by women has such a breakthrough moment. Let alone one that focuses on dating and relationships. How's that going?"

Greta relaxed. "Sign-ups continue to reach new highs on a daily basis. We've added some new back-end functionality that not only improves the app, but also allows us to add a whole suite of monetized features."

"And how is it going for you, personally?" Sophia asked. "I don't mean business success, that's pretty obvious. I guess I'm here because, like so many people, I'm wondering how, or why, the creator of this app has remained single for so long? Have you ever considered putting yourself out there on Syren?"

Greta thought about her secret account. "No, I need a bit of distance from my work, and my personal relationships are one area that I steer clear of the actual app."

"Really?" the reporter asked. She raised her eyebrows as she made a few notes. "It wouldn't be because you have someone special on the side, would it?"

Great, they know about Sam. That's all I need right now, my social life to become news.

Sophia looked around the office and at the photos on Greta's desk, which were of her parents. Then the reporter pushed the recorder closer to Greta and asked, "I'm going to be blunt, Ms. Moy, is it true that this company is primarily funded by Carter Branson, a man cloaked in rumors about malfeasance with women?"

Hearing his name made Greta feel ill all over again. She hadn't told anyone about what had happened that night. The only person who even knew about her dinner was Anjalee. Yet Greta had been ready for this question. She nodded. "It's true. One of his holding companies gave us our initial seed capital to get off the ground. I wasn't part of that deal, of course. I arrived after he'd taken a majority interest in the company. To my knowledge, we're one of dozens of investments in his tech portfolio. In fact, to my knowledge, he's only visited our offices one time, and that was more of a courtesy call."

Greta tried not to fidget as she watched the reporter make copious notes.

Sophia looked up. "Some would say it's incongruous at best and hypocritical at worst for a company created by women and led by women to have a silent partner who's rumored to have paid women in the past to be silent."

Greta waited for the question she knew would be coming.

"How does that strike you? Do you care to comment?"

Greta glanced at the recorder. "I can definitely understand that perspective. However, his relationship to this company and its operations are so remote — so distant and hands-off — I never really think about him, and that's probably why most people aren't aware. I don't really know him personally, so I can't speak for his reputation."

I'm lying. Why am I lying for this asshole?

The reporter stared back.

Greta chewed her lip and waited for the reporter to say something.

"Ms. Moy . . ."

"Please, call me Greta."

The reporter's phone vibrated and she read the message. Then she made a clicking noise with her tongue as she looked up. "Ms. Moy, I'd like to know how you would feel if Carter Branson decided to cash out his entire position in Syren."

Greta almost laughed. She tried not to roll her eyes. "Wow. I would say that's a highly unlikely scenario. He would have no reason . . ."

"I think he might." The reporter held up an envelope, then removed a group of black-and-white photos and placed them on the table. The images were from a security camera in the Space Needle's elevator. It showed Carter and Greta in what appeared to be a romantic moment.

"To be honest, Ms. Moy, I came here because these photos showed up anonymously at my office. I thought the story would be about your inappropriate relationship with your silent partner, about the feminist teaming up with a womanizer," the reporter said. "But I just learned that Carter Branson has begun selling his shares in Syren. I'm not an expert on investing, but I would guess that he became aware that these photos exist and wanted to jump ship before it affected the stock's value."

The reporter looked down at her phone. Then she turned the screen around and showed it to Greta. On it was SYRN's current stock price. "That kind of sell-off usually drives the share price down, and that's what appears to be happening right now."

Greta looked past the reporter. Through the glass walls of her office Greta saw executives and staffers running about frantically, yelling at one another. She saw someone change the channel on a TV monitor that hung from the ceiling. They switched to TMZ and there was the photo of Greta and Carter, with the headline *SYREN'S SONG-STRESS LURES NOTORIOUS ANGEL IN-VESTOR (TO HIS DOOM?)*.

"I'm going to kill him," Greta muttered.

"Okay." The reporter switched off her recorder. "I think I have what I need."

"No, wait, please. I can explain . . ."

"Ms. Moy" — the reporter stood up — "someone just scooped me, so right now I have a story to catch up to. But you can definitely expect a follow-up."

As the reporter left, Greta refreshed her laptop. She checked Syren's stock price and saw that it was in free fall. She looked up at the staffers, who glared back. She saw Anjalee at someone's desk, on their phone. Anjalee kept nodding, listening, glancing toward Greta, then nodding some more. She hung up and walked to Greta's office, grim-faced, as though she were a prison guard on death row.

Three days later, Greta drove to Sam's apartment in Ballard. She had his address but had never been there, though he'd planned to make ma po tofu for her that weekend, part of a belated celebration. As Greta pulled into an empty parking space, she caught a glimpse of her office belongings in cardboard boxes, still piled up in the back seat, and wondered if they'd still have dinner. Or coffee. Or . . . anything.

She turned off the car and rested her head

on the steering wheel.

The reporter hadn't made it to the front desk by the time Anjalee had walked into Greta's office and said the board of directors had called and demanded Greta's immediate resignation. They also locked up her stock options, not that they were worth much at the moment, as only a small percentage was vested. "Do not touch your computer," Anjalee had warned. "I'm going to wait right here until security arrives to escort you out."

"Oh, come on, you knew I was having dinner with Carter. People saw him come into my office uninvited," Greta said. "He approached *me,* not the other way around."

"I have no idea what you're talking about," Anjalee said with a straight face.

Greta shook her head as she packed her belongings and turned in her key card.

Leaving the building had been a long, slow, walk of undeserved shame and well-earned regret. A blur of shocked, angry, disappointed faces. Her former coworkers shouted threats — legal and physical — and one creative programmer shook Greta's hand and said, "Enjoy your thirty pieces of silver. Now go hang yourself."

Greta couldn't blame them. The photo of her and Carter had been sent to dozens of news outlets at the same time. That wasn't an accident or the move of some lurid paparazzi. She suspected that Carter himself had been responsible. He'd groomed Syren, used the company, and then dumped it, just like the company had done to her.

If she'd had any doubts about his involvement, those were erased when Greta got home that afternoon and found a dozen roses delivered to her doorstep. The note, which was unsigned, read: *Don't take it personally, Zoe. It's just business.*

She'd called Sam, hoping, praying he hadn't seen the news.

She called again and again.

When he finally answered he didn't say a word.

"Sam, I'm sorry," she said.

There was an awkward silence.

"Hello. Are you there? Please talk to me," she pleaded.

"I'm not going to put myself through this again. Not in this lifetime."

"But it's not what you think . . ."

He hung up.

She sent emails and text messages. None were read.

She tried to give him space, time to think, to reflect, hopefully time to miss her enough to listen to her apology, her explanation, but she couldn't wait any longer. Every hour without being able to talk to him, to see his face, was torture. She even thought she saw his reflection in the rearview mirror, but when she turned he wasn't there.

When she stepped out of her car and went up the stairs to Sam's apartment, she didn't know what to expect. Would he talk to her? Would he let her explain? Would he ignore her and wait her out, hoping she'd just give up and leave?

She knocked. She waited. She knocked again.

Finally, she tried the doorknob, which was unlocked, and when she walked in her heart sank, plummeting like Syren's stock price. From millions, to dollars, to pennies, to nothing but sadness and regret. She looked around and cursed herself for waiting too long. She had screwed up again. The place was empty. No furniture, just a few lonely coat hangers in the closet. She might have thought she had the wrong address, or that Sam had never been here at all, except in the kitchen she found a folder and a note. The folder was the one Sam had been given, with all of Greta's information, her history, her life.

She paged through it, saw her smiling face in a photo.

Sam had taken a highlighter to her favorite things: food, music, books, movies. He created a list of ten things they might do together. Things that weren't your typical dinner and a movie. He'd written: *spend a day with Greta volunteering at the King County Animal Shelter, go pick strawberries on Vashon Island and figure out how to make jam, take her to Third Place Books to buy a novel and then read it to her.*

The last thing he wrote was: *have dinner at the Space Needle on July 4 so we can watch the fireworks in both directions, over Elliott Bay and Lake Washington. Who cares about the crowds or if it's a little cliché. We should*

He stopped mid-sentence.

She closed the folder. It was too painful, like looking at a photograph of a friend who had died, a story left unfinished.

Then she saw a stack of books, volumes of poetry she'd recommended to him.

He had dog-eared a single page, a short poem.

I found you
And you fit me perfectly
like a bullet
in the barrel of a gun

14
DOROTHY

(2045)

Dorothy opened her eyes to the booming sound of thunder. The noise was intense, reverberant. She could have sworn she felt the heat. But as she sat up and the rumbling faded into the patter of rain and the chorus of wind, she realized she'd been dreaming.

Louis, who was lying next to her, snored into his pillow.

In the near darkness, Dorothy donned the old silk robe she'd bought in Myanmar and padded to Annabel's room. She half expected to find her daughter wide awake, either immersed in an art program on her computer or staring out the window into the heart of the night, but she too was fast asleep, lips pursed, breathing softly like a kitten.

As Dorothy's eyes adjusted to the darkness, she sat on the edge of the bed, gently pulling the covers up and over Annabel's shoulders. She thought of what she told Annabel about her grandmother. Dorothy stopped short of explaining how the mother she'd known as a young girl had been an enigma.

"My ah-ma was a brilliant woman. She made and lost a fortune." Growing up, Dorothy didn't know much beyond that. Like most children, she picked up on social cues and if her mother didn't talk about something, Dorothy learned not to ask. Though as an adult she understood that her mother's loss had been much deeper than money. Looking back, Dorothy realized that her mother had gone from dating no one to meeting and losing the love of her life, to then eventually dating everyone, as if there were enough strangers in the world to fill the bottomless void of her heart. One of those strangers was Dorothy's father, though he didn't stick around when Greta got pregnant, so Dorothy never knew him. She just knew his type, because that's who her mother continued to pursue, as though looks, the mere resemblance of someone she'd lost, might be enough of a facsimile to fool herself into happiness, or at least a measure of contentment. Her mother hadn't been looking for love, she'd been looking for a tourniquet.

It was during those terrible years, Dorothy's early teens, that she confronted her mother, calling her ah-ma horrible names, telling her that she deserved to be alone, tearing her down with the crowbars and wrecking balls that only angry teenagers know how to wield against the weak spots in their parents' load-bearing walls. Dorothy's rebellious nature, her bouts of self-destruction, had brought her mother to tears before, but this was the first time Dorothy had done so with malice — blaming her mother's failure, her depression, her hopeless desperation, for Dorothy's own unhappiness. Dorothy chewed her lip as she remembered how her ah-ma had cried that night and how she never seemed to stop. Not even when her mother had voluntarily committed herself to Western State Hospital. That was the last time Dorothy had seen her. When she finally found out her mother had died, Dorothy had been living in a group home for two months. The other girls stared at her side-eyed, envious of the small inheritance that they knew awaited Dorothy on her eighteenth birthday. But Dorothy hated that money. To her it represented her own failings. That if she'd loved her mother enough, or was a better daughter and snuck away to visit, perhaps her ah-ma would still be here. Maybe her ah-ma would be the one sitting on the edge of Dorothy's bed, telling her, "You're safe now. It's just a bad dream. Tomorrow will be better, I promise."

Dorothy woke late, in an empty bed, in a quiet apartment. She walked to the kitchen for a cup of coffee, half expecting Louise to have taken over and be in the throes of making breakfast — something elegant like eggs benedict with Dungeness crab — or at least tossing out near-expired food while reorganizing their pantry.

Instead the place seemed vacant, though as Dorothy looked out the windows the whirling clouds of typhoon season lent the space an air of uncertainty, as though they were on a ship at sea, far from their destination, darkness on the horizon.

She looked around, walking through her own home as if she were wandering through a minefield. Then she noticed Louise's coat and purse were gone. Dorothy relaxed. She felt oddly victorious, as though the absence of Louis's mother was worthy of celebration, until Dorothy walked down the hall and peeked into Annabel's room. Her bed was neatly made, her desk smartly organized, but Annabel was nowhere to be seen. Dorothy's heart raced. "Baby-bel?" she called out, a note of pretend hope in her voice when what she was really feeling was the seismic trembling of a mother's volcanic anger bubbling to the surface. *How dare she take my daughter without asking me? She didn't even let Annabel say goodbye. She had no right . . .*

The front door opened.

Dorothy stalked into the living room and saw Louis hanging up his coat, smiling.

"Where's my daughter?"

"Hey, calm down, what's the matter . . ."

"Where is she!?"

"She's with my mom. Jesus. We were letting you sleep in, so we all went to the Fat Hen for breakfast. Afterward she said she'd take Annabel shopping for a new raincoat, then go to the Woodland Park Zoo, and maybe get lunch at Pike Place Market. My mom thought she would give us the rest of the morning and the afternoon alone, before she heads back to Spokane. Why are you so worked up?" Louis held up a drink with a fat straw. "Look, I even brought you a bubble tea. Lychee, your favorite."

Dorothy felt confused, but calmer, almost fatigued from her anger. She thanked him for the tea, had a polite sip, then set it on the kitchen counter. She was relieved, comforted, yet also still worried. She didn't trust Louise with her daughter, especially alone. Dorothy felt paranoid, worried that somehow Louis's passive-aggressive mother was sowing seeds of discord the same way Louis had, even though he always said he was joking or that Dorothy was too uptight to understand. She stared out the window at the Space Needle, which peeked above the nearest buildings. Then she felt disoriented. She leaned on the counter as though the world were slowly swirling, not just the subtle movement of the building in the wind, but something akin to vertigo.

She felt his arms around her, holding her. She leaned back into him. He smelled good, which became an inside joke between Dorothy and Graham, that pheromones were the only reason Dorothy stayed in this relationship. That she'd given up on love and instead settled for physical affection, which she tried to convince herself was an acceptable surrogate. She drew a deep breath and slowly exhaled as she felt a firm hand on her waist as her robe was untied. She heard pounding rain somewhere above.

"Seeing how we have a few hours all to ourselves . . ."

Another hand brushed her hair aside; she felt his warm breath, his lips on the back of her neck. She closed her eyes and inhaled and for a moment, she felt flush with emotion, blood rushing through her body; she wanted to get lost in the deep forest of those feelings. "Are you sure we have time? What if . . ."

"Stop," he said softly.

He pressed his body against hers.

Slowly, the room began to spin and she felt an ache in her chest.

"Sam, why did you do it?" Dorothy whispered. "I never meant to . . ."

A moment of awkward silence fell between them.

Dorothy froze, unsure of what she just said.

She opened her eyes and realized where she was, who she was with, and she recoiled from his touch. "I'm sorry."

"Wait." Louis stared at her. "What did you just say?"

She struggled to remember as other images flashed through her mind, all the times petty jealousy had reared its head in their relationship. From a bearded barista who once asked for her number to the time she considered a male therapist and Louis had flatly forbidden it. "I said . . . I'm sorry?" Her words came out as a question.

"No." Louis's blithe hopefulness had turned to anger. "You said *Sam.*"

"I must be tired. Still dreaming," Dorothy said. "I don't know what I'm saying."

"Who the fuck is Sam?"

"You wouldn't understand," Dorothy said, shaking her head.

"Oh, I'm sure I wouldn't. What was it that you didn't mean to do *with Sam*?"

Louis gripped the front of her robe. His face was inches from hers, she could smell his breath. "Look at me when I'm talking to you."

Without thinking, Dorothy snatched his elbow, swept his front leg, and tripped him to the wooden floor. As he crashed, he grabbed the closest thing to him — her — and she fell on top of him. He grunted angrily and rolled her over to her back, pinning her down with his arm, pressing her shoulders to the floor. He was cursing, threatening, yelling at her as spittle formed in the corners of his mouth. When he leaned forward, she grabbed a handful of his sleeve, threw one leg over the back of his neck as her other leg cinched down across her ankle. She clenched her jaw and squeezed until she saw his eyes, filled with anger and confusion, roll back and his body go limp.

She let go and pushed him aside. She sat up and looked at her hands, her legs, not quite understanding what she'd done or how.

She noticed him stirring.

He slowly opened his eyes, blinking, staring up at the ceiling, confused, as though he were waking from a pleasant dream. "What are we doing on the kitchen floor?"

Dorothy hesitated. *You grabbed me. I reacted.* She wanted to try to explain. Instead she said, "I don't know. You fainted. Did you guys have drinks at breakfast?"

She helped him to his feet, then suggested he go lie down and rest as he wandered to the bedroom, in a daze, rubbing his sore neck.

"Please state your full name," Dr. Shedhorn asked.

"Dorothy Margaret Moy," she answered as she tried to relax at her latest treatment, to breathe normally. Which was quite difficult considering the assortment of wires and monitors attached to various parts of her body, along with an IV, and Dr. Shedhorn's assurance that this time Dorothy's treatment would be even deeper.

"Are you expecting me to forget who I am?" Dorothy asked.

"Would it stop you if I said yes?"

All the tubes and equipment made Dorothy feel uneasy, like she was fourteen again and running away from a temporary foster home after her mother was gone. Back then on a cloudy evening, the kind where everything seems to get dark an hour before it should, Dorothy walked to the International District and found the last surviving phone booth. The box of rusted metal and broken glass smelled like urine-soaked pine needles and pigeon droppings. She stepped inside, closed the door, sat down, wrote a letter of apology to herself, and consumed an entire bottle of Tylenol PM. She fell asleep to the sound of rain and woke up in the ER, where she overheard one of the doctors say, "It figures. Poor kid. Her mother was the one caught up in that local tech scandal. Her whole company imploded, billions lost, and then she went completely off the rails."

"I'm joking, Dorothy," Dr. Shedhorn said. "Though most of my patients do have residual memories for several weeks, fragments, which are to be expected. But it's piqued my curiosity enough that I've considered creating an app for my patients. It would let them keep track of their new memories, and then let them see if there are any correlations to the memories of others. I realize it must sound a bit far-fetched, but listening to my patients talk about their recollections makes me wonder if we're not all genetically interconnected in some larger way. It's a theory I'm excited to explore."

"Interconnected, how?" Dorothy asked. "You mean like parent to child?"

Dr. Shedhorn sat back. "I mean, have you ever met someone for the first time and felt like you've known them forever? I went into this thinking that if I'm able to help a patient change how they remember trauma, it will free them up to make different choices in the future. It's based on a theory called Hebb's Rule that says, 'Cells that fire together wire together.' An engram is thousands of cells in the brain firing all at once, which creates a neural network that can be passed down epigenetically. But what if we're passing down all high emotion memories — not just trauma? What if we're passing down a neural network that encompasses attraction, temperament, kindness, and familiarity, not just pain, anger, sadness, anxiety, and other things that can lead to suffering and sociopathy? If we pass along the bad, it stands to reason that we pass along the good."

Dorothy stared up at Dr. Shedhorn. She wanted to explain what had happened in the altercation with Louis, but she feared the doctor would halt her treatments, which were confusing but also gave her feelings of hope. They'd shown her a light at the end of a very long tunnel, and she felt compelled to keep moving in that direction.

"Our future is determined by choices we make in the present," Dr. Shedhorn said. "But if our present is a collection of routines that were created in the past, by changing how we remember, we will inevitably change future outcomes."

"Isn't that just a fancy way of saying we're creatures of habit?" Dorothy said with a shrug. "We're trying to break those habits by re-remembering."

Dr. Shedhorn's eyes widened. "But those patterns fall into the category of systems biology, which reduces all human behavior to information — raw data — that can be examined through the lens of physics, in a field that my colleagues call quantum biology. Because our habits are generally based on interactions with other people, if we change our memories, we're inevitably going to change who we interact with in the future and how we engage with them. A theoretical physicist might suggest that if we make different choices in those memories, we're literally altering the trajectory of a future reality. And if we're exploring *your* epigenetic past, who's to say your great-grandchildren aren't doing the same thing, and their epigenetic past is our present?"

Dorothy furrowed her brow. "I feel like you just sent me on an untethered spacewalk. You may have to explain that to me again, slower, and in plain English. I wouldn't be insulted if you resorted to stick-figure drawings."

"Don't worry. We'll talk more as we progress through your treatments. It'll make more sense as patterns emerge." Dr. Shedhorn touched Dorothy's arm. "You okay?

"I'm fine," Dorothy lied.

"Good." Dr. Shedhorn smiled. "Don't worry, I haven't lost anyone yet."

Residual memories? Dorothy wondered. Her recent dreams had been intense. All kinds of anxiety bubbling to the surface of the placid lake of remembrance. She dreamt about Greta. That was the kind of relationship they had in the end, the kind where you're on a first-name basis with your own parent. Dorothy had dreamt about Zou yi, the grandmother she'd barely known, who everyone called Zoe. And Zoe's long-lost mother, someone named Faye. Dorothy dreamt about her own precocious child as well. Dorothy knew that a part of her had wanted a baby so she could try to rewrite her own failed mother-daughter relationship. That it was an opportunity, a second chance. She would do things better. But what just happened with Louis was more than a dream, or a nightmare, it was a booming echo. She later tried to talk to Louis, to apologize, though she wasn't sure how much he remembered from their altercation.

"I can't deal with this right now, I'm late for work," he said the next day, which never made sense to Dorothy since he owned the company.

He guzzled a cup of lukewarm coffee, then checked his phone.

"Can't you even offer me a little support for what I'm going through?" she said.

He grabbed his raincoat. "Look around you. Look at our finances these days. I've been supporting you for years. You can't even hold down a teaching job."

Dorothy stared at him. Yes, he was supporting her, after she let him drain her bank account years ago. *But I let him. I did that, willingly.*

"Look, I don't know who you are anymore, who you're involved with, or what else you've gotten yourself into. I'm not sure I even want to know. If it weren't for Annabel . . ." He shook his head, walked out, and slammed the door.

That was the unspoken truth between them.

Dorothy had gotten pregnant early in their relationship, when they were fluent in each other's love languages. Back then anything seemed possible.

She should have known better when his first reaction was "Are you sure?"

"That I'm pregnant?"

"No, are you sure that it's mine."

He'd been looking for a way out then, and she should have let him go. She should have run far away. Instead she smashed her life into his, a strange mix of hubris and naïveté. Six years later, they functioned more like vaguely intimate roommates. The odd couple, redux. She wasn't sure if he even remembered the name Sam.

"Are you ready?" Dr. Shedhorn asked.

Dorothy felt as though she were strapped into the front seat of a roller coaster at night, with no lights, the cars inching closer to the precipice before plunging into total darkness. She nodded, but deep down, she wasn't sure anymore. She closed her eyes and drifted off to the sound of someone crying.

15
LAI KING

(1892)

Lai King woke in the middle of the night when she thought she heard sobbing somewhere in her building. She wrapped a threadbare blanket around her shoulders and padded across the cool wooden floor of her family's tiny apartment. She crept to where her parents' bed was and peeked behind the curtain. Her mother and father slept so soundly, so quietly, that she grew nervous under quarantine and felt the need to check on them. She appraised their darkened silhouettes in the moonlight, staring intently at the blankets and quilts, watching the covers gently rise and fall with their breathing.

Lai King sighed.

Her fears worsened a week earlier, when she looked out the window at sunrise and saw a creaking wagon roll by with the uncovered bodies of the Chun family —

mother, father, and their oldest son. They looked as though they were sleeping, but their skin was gray and mottled with bruises. Lai King didn't know where the Chuns' two daughters were. They were about her age. Maybe they weren't sick. Maybe they'd been given to another family. Lai King chewed her lip as she watched the wagon disappear.

Who would take such sick girls, with so much bad luck?

That's when Lai King wondered, who would take *her* if something awful happened to her parents? She went to bed every night, listening to other families in the nearby apartments, some fighting, arguing, a few crying, wailing.

No one laughed anymore. No one sang.

Become a ghost hero.

Lai King thought she heard the wheels of the wagon coming back. Her heart raced and she climbed into her parents' bed, squeezing between them. Her father barely moved, but her mother stirred, opened her eyes with a drowsy smile. She pulled the covers up just enough so Lai King could slip beneath them.

When Lai King woke, her mother was in the kitchen, but her father was gone.

"Where's Ah-ba?" Lai King asked as she looked around.

"He went downstairs." Her mother placed a bowl of congee in front of Lai King, topped with fried garlic and dried mushrooms. "Now eat."

Lai King stirred the mushrooms into her porridge to soften them up. As she ate, she couldn't help but notice the worried look on her mother's face, the troubling silence as she sipped her tea.

"When can I go back to school?" Lai King asked. "I swear I'll go this time."

"You'll go when it's safe," her ah-ma snapped. *"Sik fan."*

Lai King frowned. Then she heard a commotion outside; it was her father, not shouting, but certainly speaking in Chinese above his normal calm demeanor.

Her mother drifted to the window and parted the curtain. Lai King followed, peering outside. She saw the carriage from the Health Department, the men in white, with a pair of police officers. Her father said they were here to help during the quarantine, but whenever she saw them she felt more dread than relief, more fear than comfort.

Today the ghost men set up a table, and on it was a collection of bottles and brass instruments. Lai King spotted her father in front of a row of Chinese laborers. He was translating for the men in white, who instructed all the laborers to remove their shirts, which they did, albeit reluctantly and only with encouragement from her father. Lai King stared down at the men, their shoulders and arms tan and sinewy, their queues hung between their shoulder blades. One old man's braid was so long it hung down to the back of his knees. The men shifted nervously, shuddering in the cool morning breeze. Lai King watched as the ghost men began an inspection of the workers, poking and prodding their necks, their backs, their underarms, taking measurements with brass calipers.

"What are they doing?" Lai King asked.

Her mother didn't answer. She didn't blink. She seemed frozen, a matronly statue, a mother and wife in repose. She held on to the curtain, her knuckles turning white.

Lai King stared back out the window. She winced as one of the men in white picked up a brass instrument with a long, sharp needle.

She listened as her father translated the words of the ghost men.

"This is medicine," her father translated to Chinese. "A great man, named Sir Waldemar Haffkine, found a cure for cholera, and

346

when he did, the queen of England knighted him for this miracle. Now he has discovered a cure for this great pestilence, the blue sickness that has taken so many of our friends and neighbors."

The Chinese men muttered to each other as they stepped back.

Her mother let out a soft cry, and Lai King glanced over and wrapped her arms around her slender waist. Lai King felt her mother's heart beating.

When she looked again, Lai King saw that her father had removed his shirt as well. He spoke to the gathering of workers and then held out his arm. One of the ghost men approached, held up a long needle, and tapped it.

Lai King winced as one of the men in white held her father's arm and poked the sharp metal through his skin. Her father glanced up at their apartment. Then he turned his attention to a man in white, who wrapped his arm in a bandage. He put his shirt back on and motioned for the men to follow his lead, which they did, albeit slowly, hesitantly, until one by one they each received the injection.

Lai King watched as her father disappeared beneath an awning, then she heard him coming up the stairs. She hid behind her mother, worried that he was coming to bring them down to be stabbed by that long and frightful needle.

"*Gam sam mou!*" her mother exclaimed as her father walked in. Lai King was taken aback. She rarely heard her mother raise her voice to her father. She paced about their apartment, pointing to the window. "Why did you do that!? You're an interpreter, not a doctor. Let those white men test their cure on themselves if they think it works."

Lai King's father gently took her mother's hands. "I'm sorry." He spoke in Cantonese, softly, calmly, as though trying to tame a skittish, cornered animal. "I had to. They're not letting anyone leave." He looked into her eyes. His words were measured. "They paid me generously for my help. Enough so that if things get worse . . ."

Lai King's father glanced at her, then back to her mother, who seemed to understand. She nodded, then collapsed into her husband's arms.

Lai King didn't sleep at all that night.

Hours after her father received the cure, his arm swelled up to twice its normal size and he lay in bed, so fevered that his body soaked the sheets. She stoked the fire in their cooking stove, heating tea and soup made from honey dates and goji berries, as her mother sat in the auburn glow of an oil lamp, wiping his forehead with a damp cloth.

Lai King listened as her mother prayed. Watched as she lit sticks of incense, washing herself in sandalwood smoke. Then she placed small mirrors around her father to confuse and scare away demons who might come to try and lead his spirit away.

"Is Ah-ba going to die?" Lai King asked, her voice quavering.

She waited in the silence, unsure if she wanted an answer.

Her mother finally said, "He's been given a small amount of death — smaller than a single grain of rice. But it's powerful, this magic. He takes this grain of death inside. It sickens him. Causes him to cry out and wear this fever like a mask, so when death comes, it passes by thinking your father is already on his way to the spirit world."

Lai King crinkled her nose. This was the type of fable her father might tell her. Not an answer, but a story with a riddle inside.

"Why doesn't he turn into a sparrow and fly away from this place, far from the sickness," Lai King asked. "Like his ah-ma did when he was a baby?"

Her mother looked at her and drew a deep breath. She set aside the wet cloth, wiped her hands on her dress, and then parted Lai King's hair from her eyes. She gently kissed her forehead. Her ah-ma smiled ever so slightly, as though doing so took all the strength she had. "Your father doesn't have any magic of his own anymore. Neither do I." She got down on one knee and held Lai King's hands. "We used up all of our magic when we created you. Look how wise and beautiful you turned out."

Lai King tried to stay awake, leaning against a windowsill. But she woke beneath her blankets and realized her mother must have carried her to bed. All was quiet except for swallows and killdeer chirping outside on a telegraph wire. She enjoyed their birdsongs because they were affirmations of spring. Like a poem she'd learned in school about the scent of vanilla across a frozen valley. Beneath the birdsongs lay a comforting silence, a welcome absence compared to the sounds of her father in pain.

In the quiet of the morning, Lai King rose, walked to her parents' bed, and pulled back the curtain. They were both asleep. Though her father's skin looked pale, mottled with purple bruises the color of a ripe eggplant, and Lai King hated eggplant. She looked at her mother, whose eyes were puffy from crying. She searched for telltale signs, the swollen neck, the dark splotches. But as she looked at her mother's skin all she saw were a few fleabites, nothing out of the ordinary.

Lai King heard bells in the distance, the sound of weeping through the walls, the rumble of a wagon outside. She wanted to climb into bed with her parents, to curl up between them. Instead she restarted the cooking fire, opening the stove door as quietly as possible, loading the firebox with kindling. She filled a kettle with water for tea. Then she sat by the window again. She longed for the bustle of sailors and merchants. The noisy chaos of saloons and gambling parlors. She even missed school. Instead there were men pushing a cart filled with dead animals, cats, dogs, and rats. A few Chinese men and women moved about the quarantined neighborhood, but they walked far apart from each other, their faces covered. When she looked up she saw an elderly woman hanging laundry from her window. The white cloth looked like a flag of surrender.

Lai King turned as she heard her father talking in his delirium. He spoke in single words, unfinished sentences, truncated messages. *Start. Stop.* Like a telegram. *Stop.* She listened as he drifted in and out of Chinese and English.

"Ah-ma, where have you been? You frightened me. *Geng sei luh,*" her father said. *"Ngo gin dou nei.* Yes. I see you. Will give her *seon sik.*" Then he bolted upright, wide-eyed, struggling to catch his breath, as though waking from a nightmare.

Lai King's mother startled and sat up partway, her eyes scanning the apartment. She saw Lai King, then looked to her husband, slowly realizing this was not a dream, that he was sick, that they were still in quarantine. She struggled to swallow.

"He was talking," Lai King said.

"And I was dreaming," her mother said. "About your ancestors."

Her father moaned and Lai King watched as her mother tended to her father's sores and bruises with a tincture made from marigolds. For a moment it looked as though his spirit had returned, intact. He looked lucid. He looked at Lai King and then at his wife. He smiled and reached up, and Lai King watched as her parents embraced. She watched as he pulled her mother close and whispered in her ear.

"I will," her mother spoke softly.

Then what wakefulness he had fled his body and his eyes closed. He lay back down, shivering, and her mother found another blanket and piled it on top of him.

She turned to Lai King and said, "It's time for us to leave."

Lai King sat across the room from where her father slept, the curtain closed. "I'm going to find someone to help us," her mother said as she wrapped a scarf around her nose and mouth. "Stay in this room. Understand?"

"But what about Ah-ba?"

"This is what he asked me to do," her mother said. "This is what he wants."

That was four hours ago.

Lai King stared at her father's small suitcase, packed with all her clothing, a few books from school, her old pair of shoes that didn't even fit anymore. Her mother's suitcase remained unpacked. Though there was a canvas bag filled with pruned fruit, nuts, and chewy strands of dried cuttlefish — the last of their food. She stood at the window, her only access to the outside world. More windows had laundry draped beneath. She counted fifteen, twenty, maybe more. As she counted, Lai King realized these people weren't hanging their laundry.

They were hanging a sign, letting the neighborhood know when someone was infected. She looked down and realized her mother had hung a similar piece of cloth.

Lai King wanted desperately to ask her father about all of this. He always seemed to have a hopeful answer, or at least an interesting story, the kind that would puzzle her, charm her, keep her up late at night contemplating the possibilities, what was real and what was a tall tale, especially during the Lunar New Year.

"What's that one?" she'd asked as they walked down the crowded street to get sweet dumplings, months ago, eyeing slips of paper that dangled from colorful lanterns hung by shopkeepers to celebrate the holiday season.

Her father stopped to read the attached riddle out loud. "Hmmm . . . this is a good one. What belongs to you but others use it more than you do?" He looked at her with a smile and raised eyebrows. "I think I know . . ."

"Don't tell me!" Lai King struggled for an answer. Then she began to guess. "My hands? No, that's not it. Our house? Is it our house!?"

"Oh . . . so close." He smiled. "The answer, Lai King Moy, is your name."

Now he was silent.

She wished he would say her name again. She wished he would say anything, make any sound. She couldn't even hear his ragged breathing anymore. She crept to the sheet that separated them.

Her mother had strictly forbidden her from going near. "For your own safety."

"But you're not afraid," Lai King had said.

"A woman carries her fear inside of her," her mother replied as she scratched the fleabites on her arms. She'd cleared her throat, trying not to cough.

That's when Lai King began to fear the worst.

She paused, holding her breath so she could hear the slightest of sounds, but all she heard were bells ringing in the distance. She reached for the fabric, closing her eyes, bracing herself for what she might see.

"LAI KING!" her mother shouted, bursting through the door. "Step away from there right now! What did I tell you? Get your things and come with me."

Lai King's heart raced. She heard her neighbors, furious chatter, people shouting.

"We need to leave right now," her mother said. "Grab your things."

"Ah-ba's not coming?"

"This is what he asked us to do. This is

355

what we both saw in a dream. We must obey. You've been given a gift and now you must accept it with both hands."

She picked up the suitcase and followed her mother, down a crowded staircase and out into the street, where Lai King saw more people than she had in weeks. There was yelling, shouting, chaos in every direction. Chinese men carried their belongings, slung over their shoulders, in canvas bags made from sacks of rice. They ran down the alleys, past old men who staggered, lost and confused. The few families who lived in Chinatown, the ones who weren't sick, huddled together, searching, as though trying to decide what to do, where to go. Where *could* they go? The exits had all been roped off and guarded by policemen and now she saw soldiers, too, in tall boots and brown uniforms. They had red scarves around their faces and long rifles with fixed bayonets.

Lai King smelled fire.

She turned and saw thick black smoke billowing over rooftops in the distance. Tall orange flames licked the sky like forked tongues. Long sheets of tin, used as roofing material, floated up like joss paper, curling and drifting away from the heat. Then crashing down, clanging, crumpling on the street as ash and soot fell from the sky.

"Why is everyone running away?" Lai King asked as her mother gripped her hand so tight her fingers felt numb. "Why is no one trying to put out the fire? Where's the wagon with the pump? The engine that sprays water?"

Her mother dragged her in the direction of the pier.

"Ah-ma!" Lai King shouted to be heard. "Where are the firemen?"

Lai King noticed her mother was walking with a limp, and tears welled up in her eyes. "They were the ones who set everything on fire."

Lai King had been anxious, worried, but now her heart was racing.

She did her best to keep up as her mother said, "They're burning all of Chinatown to keep the disease from spreading to other parts of the city."

Her mother snatched the suitcase from Lai King's hands and led her down the steep hill toward the long pier of Chinatown's seaport. An ocean liner sat at anchor in deep water that looked black as ink beneath the smoke-filled sky.

Lai King squinted at the steam barkentine and saw an American flag.

"Where are we going?"

She wiped ash from her eyes and walked

briskly down the timbers of the pier as frantic seabirds cawed overhead. She followed her mother to where a group of Chinese men and women were clambering down a net, handing over their belongings and then climbing aboard a ship's boat. A half-dozen sailors sat at the oars.

Her mother knelt down and held Lai King's shoulders. "Look at me, Lai King. Listen to me. Are you listening? Your father earned enough money to buy passage to Canton. I have family there, which means you have family there." Her mother placed an envelope in Lai King's coat pocket. "Hold on to this."

Lai King didn't want to leave the city. She clung to her mother.

"What about Ah-ba?" she asked meekly.

She felt her mother's arms around her, squeezing her tight. Her ah-ma's body felt hot, but she was shivering. She rocked Lai King and let out a muffled sob.

"Let's go! We don't have all day!" a sailor yelled.

"You go first." Her mother smiled but tears framed her cheeks.

Lai King hesitated, then climbed down the net as her mother dropped her bag to one of the seamen. When Lai King looked back up to help her mother, the boat was already pushing away from the pier. She called for her ah-ma, who shook her head, grim-faced, crying as she took a step back.

"I love you, Lai King, my beautiful, brave daughter," her mother shouted.

Lai King screamed for her mother as the other passengers on board cried out, pointing to the firestorm that was swallowing up entire buildings. Even from far away, Lai King could feel the heat. She looked at her mother; she glanced at the others on board, then at the water. She threw a leg over the side of the boat, ready to dive in, but felt hands on her clothing, pulling her back inside the boat.

"Ah-ma!" Lai King screamed as someone held on to her, pinning her in place while the boat rocked with each stroke of the oars. She cried, watching her ah-ma grow smaller, a silhouette surrounded by the inferno. Lai King reached helplessly for her mother, who waved back until she was consumed by the flames.

When they reached the iron-hulled ship, Lai King heard the rumble and clank of the steam engines. She pictured a great locomotive trapped somewhere within. The kind that traveled the rails of the Southern

Pacific Line her ah-ma's family helped build.

Ah-ma . . .

She read the name on the side of the ship, SS *City of Rio,* as she climbed a rope ladder and was helped aboard. On deck, she was given her belongings by a steward and directed to the forecastle where new passengers gathered, mostly Chinese, who were weeping, or staring numbly, feeling the reprieve, the safety of the water amid such loss. A doctor looked in everyone's mouths, examined their eyes, touching their necks and underarms.

The ship's other passengers — those already on board and elegantly dressed, excited to travel to the Orient — stood back and watched, unsure what to make of this incursion of beleaguered refugees and the burning neighborhood they'd left behind.

Lai King ignored them and turned back toward the city, searching in vain for any sign of her ah-ma, but the place where her mother once stood was now a smoky ruin. Lai King bit her lip, trying not to cry as she thought about her father.

He's become a ghost hero.

In that moment, she hoped for the best, that her father stopped breathing before the fire arrived. She closed her eyes and tried to sear her parents' faces, their voices, their touch, into memory. She felt even more alone when she realized she had no photos of her parents, no keepsakes, nothing to place in an altar. She remembered her father's tale about her yin yin, how her grandmother had come to this country alone as a girl, not much older than Lai King. How her yin yin never saw her family again.

Then Lai King remembered her mother had stuffed something into her pocket. She reached in and pulled out a crumpled envelope. Inside was a letter, some money, and a small hand-drawn map to a village. The letter read:

My Lai King,
  If you are reading this my spirit can rest, knowing you are safe. Keep this money safe as well. Hide it. I am sorry there is not more. I used everything we had to get you aboard that ship which is bound for China. This is what your ah-ba wanted. This is what we wanted for you. It's going to be hard. But be brave.
  When you dock in Canton, show this map to a steward. Ask them to help you with directions to Ai Gong in the Hoisan District. It's not far. When you arrive at my

old village, go through the gates and shout our family name as loud as you can. People you are related to will come out to see you. Tell them who you are. You are family, they will help you. I promise you they will.

I am also including the words of a Chinese poem:

Sailing Homeward
Without a pause,
Trees that for twenty thousand years
Your vows have kept,
You have suddenly healed the pain of
    a traveler's heart,
And moved a brush to write a new
    song.

You are our new song,
Lai King.

She touched the Chinese characters on the note as though her ah-ma were right there, alive on the page, ink for blood. She wiped a tear and pondered the prospect of sailing home to a place she'd never been. Then she carefully folded the note as though it were a sacred text and slipped it into a rip on the inside of her coat. She worried that someone had seen her hide the envelope, but those around her stared at the horizon of fire and smoke, the burning buildings, the families and businesses they'd left behind, everyone in shock and mourning.

Lai King felt as though this were all a dream and if she closed her eyes she might wake up in bed, between her parents. But as she looked around the deck, saw the enormous masts and booms, the steam funnel, the faces of well-heeled strangers, their looks of contempt became knife edges, dismembering the life she'd known, gutting her faint hopes. She heard a whistle, and they were told to line up with their belongings in front of them. She looked at her small suitcase and wished she had packed some of her mother's clothing, that she might cover herself in the fabric, feel something familiar, smell her ah-ma's perfume.

A man in a black uniform with polished boots approached the gathering, heels clicking on the deck with each step. He wore a black cap with a gold ribbon that matched the piping on his sleeves. His chest was broad, and Lai King thought the two rows of shiny buttons running down the front of his jacket might give up trying and burst at any moment. He stroked his wide mustache, appraising her and the gathering of Chinese passengers — most of whom were rich merchants. Amid the white passengers staring back at them was a boy, about her age, with a brace on one leg.

He offered a polite wave but looked the way Lai King felt.

"Good afternoon and welcome aboard. I am Chief Officer Mark Cappis," the man bellowed. "You may call me Mr. Cappis. It is by the grace of God and the forbearance I have reached with you and your families that you are here."

Lai King listened as Mr. Cappis spoke like her teacher, elegantly, but with icicles dripping from his words. She caught the eye of the boy. When Lai King waved back, he looked down at the deck, teetering on his bad leg.

Mr. Cappis continued. Something about all the hardworking Chinese who had been transported to the United States aboard this vessel. How the merchants would be shown to their cabins in second class. The rest — meaning Lai King — would be escorted to steerage. She didn't know where that was, but the way Mr. Cappis spoke, it sounded like a place to be endured but not enjoyed. While the other passengers were told that they were allowed on deck anytime during daylight hours, those in steerage were allowed topside only for what Mr. Cappis called *sky liberty*. One hour each day, weather permitting.

"That is to mitigate any potential spread of the Great Mortality," Mr. Cappis said. "Anyone showing signs of illness will be thoroughly examined. But if our ship's doctor determines that they are fully in the grip of this particular disease of reckoning, those passengers will be quarantined belowdecks, in a small berth, for the entire duration of the voyage. If someone should succumb to this disease, they will be hastily buried at sea, without ceremony. In my career, I have served aboard ships stricken with cholera, typhus, and yellow fever. Hence my profound unwillingness to let the *City of Rio* become a floating coffin. These rules apply to anyone on this ship. As Walt Whitman might say: married men and single men, old men and pretty girls; milliners and masons; cobblers, colonels and counter-jumpers; tailors and teachers; lieutenants, loafers, ladies, lackbrains, and lawyers; printers and parsons; black spirits and white, blue spirits and gay, passenger or crew — myself included — all must be quarantined. Am I perfectly clear?"

Everyone nodded, except for two of the Chinese businessmen. Mr. Cappis waited as one of the other stewards who spoke rudimentary Chinese did his best to translate, which included gestures so pronounced they were almost comical and reminded Lai King of playing charades in school. She watched the Chinese men and saw the exact moment when they guessed right and gravely understood.

"If the winds are favorable," Mr. Cappis said, smiling for the first time, "we will be in the Orient in forty-five days, with a brief stop in the Hawaiian Islands."

A junior officer proceeded to escort the new passengers to their quarters. While the rich merchants and their wives went in one direction, Lai King descended a series of ladders, slipping through narrow hatches that took her deep into the belly of the ship. There she found a servant's pantry and an old woman polishing the wooden cabinetry.

"Oh, there you are," she said, wiping her hands on her apron when she saw Lai King. "I heard there was a China girl coming my way. I'm Miss Anna, the steerage matron, but the passengers down here all just call me Mama."

Lai King wasn't ready to call anyone Mama. "Can I call you Auntie Anna?"

"Auntie? Oh, that's fine too," the woman said as she tucked a thick wad of chewing tobacco inside her cheek and picked bits off her tongue.

Auntie noticed the look on Lai King's face. "No smoking down here."

She turned and led Lai King into a large barnlike space divided into doorless staterooms on either side, each with barely enough room for a skeletal set of double bunks and a small sink below an even smaller mirror. A dozen women in various stages of undress occupied the bunks, lolling about like alley cats. Others sat on the floor playing cards or reading. The only illumination came from a flicker of a gas lamp in each berth and what little sunlight found its way down through the shaft of the mainmast that jutted through the ceiling as though someone had planted a great, limbless conifer.

"Don't worry. Your eyes will adjust," Auntie Anna said. "This area here is for single women like us." She winked at Lai King. "Families are quartered behind me. Beyond them are the single men. And in between is a dining parlor. Food's not so bad. In fact, Captain Ward eats from the steerage kitchen once a week to make sure."

Lai King tried to listen as she was introduced to some of the ladies. The other passengers looked genial and kind. Some even offered her a cup of beef tea, but it had the steamy aroma of stale sweat. Auntie Anna continued on about what to do in case of bad weather, how the hatches would be sealed and it would become even darker. Lai King saw the privy, which smelled so bad it turned her stomach. Or perhaps that was the slow rocking of the ship, which seemed worse when she was deprived of a view of the ocean. She looked at the portholes on either side, which were so close to the waterline they were practically submerged. No fresh air would be coming through them.

It was still midday, but Lai King was exhausted. She thanked the matron and the ladies and curled up in her assigned bunk, the blanket stiff and scratchy. She felt queasy and closed her eyes, realizing she was getting seasick. Auntie Anna placed a bucket near Lai King's bunk. She spoke kindly, but Lai King was too overcome to say anything. She closed her eyes, tried to escape into her imagination, but all she saw were her parents in bed, in their night clothes, holding each other, safe beneath blankets that did not move.

Lai King woke in the middle of the night, her stomach churning. She immediately reached in the darkness for the wooden bucket and vomited. Her eyes watered from the smell and the loss of bodily control, and she vomited again. She wiped her chin and lay back, feeling the ship rock, rise and fall, the sound of the ocean against the hull, the groaning of the timbers reminding her that was all that stood between her and the unfathomable deep. She heard the ladies around her snoring, the occasional mumble, grateful that the bunk directly above her was unoccupied, though a part of her longed for company. She listened in the dark, the sounds reminding her of her final days with her parents. That's when she pulled the blanket over her head, curled into a ball, and finally broke down crying. She tried to be silent, but the more she tried, the more her shoulders shook as she sobbed into her pillow, the more the tears came, the more her blanket felt like a funeral shroud.

She cried until she felt a hand on her shoulder.

"Ah-ma?"

"Shhh, it's going to be okay."

Auntie Anna wrapped her arms around her, and Lai King sobbed into her bosom until she felt completely depleted, exhausted. Then fear replaced sorrow and she bit her lip. Her stomach still turning, her heart somewhere buried in the burned-out rubble of the home she'd left behind. Auntie Anna rocked her gently in the darkness, until Lai King could no longer determine if her eyes were open or closed, if she were awake or dreaming, if she were alive or had failed as a ghost hero.

Four days later, after subsisting on broth, tea, and ship's biscuits, which were as hard as rocks, Lai King's head cleared and her stomach settled. With little else to do but wallow, she dried her eyes and resigned herself to follow the rest of the passengers in steerage up the ladders for her first hour of sky liberty.

"I knew you'd come around," Auntie Anna said as she gave Lai King a hug that was as warm and soft as it was smothering. Then the woman helped her up the ladder. "That fresh air will do you good. You'll see."

Lai King squinted as she went higher and when she emerged, a seed in a fallow field, she stretched toward the afternoon sun, which seemed brighter than she remembered. The breeze felt cleansing, refreshing, the closest she'd had to a bath in a week. She heard crooning seabirds and dozens of gulls trailing the ship, swooping down as buckets of bones and offal were discarded from the galley. The birds reminded her of life, at least until she saw sharks and dogfish rise to the surface to contend with the birds for the chum that had spread out across the waves.

As Lai King's wobbly legs adjusted to the back-and-forth rhythm of the ocean, she fixed her gaze on the horizon. She tried to find her bearings, searching for any sign of land, then gave up, resigned to the fact that they were now somewhere in the middle of the Pacific. She held on to the taffrail and watched crewmen on their hands and knees holystoning the wooden deck and sprinkling sand on the whitened surface so passengers wouldn't slip. She heard deep, melodious singing among the sounds of the ocean and peered up at sailors — some of them as high as eighty feet in the air — who clung to the masts or stood on the booms and spars, barefoot, belting out a sea shanty, "Wives and sweethearts, don't you cry. Amelia, where you bound? Sons and daughters wave goodbye, across the Western oh-shun."

Lai King's heart raced when she saw men walking effortlessly across the swaying timbers. She imagined their view, then felt dizzy and looked away, trying to think of something else: her parents, the note inside her coat, the little boy whom she'd seen days earlier, who was now watching her from the starboard rail. He removed his cap and she saw his curls of dark hair. He regarded her with a gentle smile. Lai King smiled back, then heard a commotion as a man in a tie and morning coat was escorted to the quarterdeck.

"Found him, Mr. Cappis," a crewman said as two others, their faces covered in sack-cloth with holes for their eyes, held on to his arms. "He rabbit-punched the doctor, then he hid in a wardrobe."

The man fought against the sailors holding him. Then began hacking so hard they let go and he dropped to his knees, coughing into a rag. The men on deck, even the riggers in the foretop above, all covered their mouths with scarves and kerchiefs.

The crowd parted and Mr. Cappis appeared. He looked stern but weary. "Don't make us waste a bullet, sir," Mr. Cappis said, as though dying were a minor inconvenience. "After all, an aged man is but a paltry thing. W. B. Yeats."

"Please," the man pleaded, "I'm feeling better. You'll see." Then he coughed again as he struggled to speak. "I can pay." He spat blood.

Everyone on deck, on the masts, on the rigging froze like statues, watching the scene unfold, a one-act play, knowing this drama would end in tragedy. No one spoke in the poor man's defense. They knew what one sick person could do to all of them.

Lai King and the boy stared at each other, unwilling to watch, as the man was dragged belowdecks. His pleading diminished and all was quiet. The passengers on deck all stood like stone statues, no one wanting to cough or sniffle, or move an inch in the wrong way. Except Lai King, who crept to the railing. She peered down at the roiling ocean. Then she felt the boy next to her as the passengers slowly dispersed, grumbling, chatting, reciting prayers. The sailors and jacktars went back to work.

Lai King stared at the water. Then she glanced at the boy.

He glanced back and for a moment she marveled at his eyes, blue-silver, like Tahitian pearls, then they both continued gazing out at the water as though this were a wake and they were sitting vigil with the body of the deceased. They stood mesmerized by the sea, feeling the wind and the salty spray, until the boy said, "That man is my uncle. He became my guardian after my mother died six months ago and my father left."

Lai King listened, thinking about the man who would be locked away for the next forty days. She had little doubt that the man would suffer the same fate as her father.

"His name is Albert," the boy said, clearing his throat. "I'm named after him, even though most of my family considers it bad luck to be named after a living relative. I'm not sure why. He's a merchant of dry goods. He traveled to the Orient many times and would bring me stories about life at sea, like 'The Oblong Box' and 'MS Found in a Bottle.' He was taking me to learn his trade. Now he's dying and I don't know what's to become of me. I suppose they might auction me off as a bond servant when we arrive." He sighed. "You probably don't understand a word I'm saying, do you?"

Lai King watched the sun emerge from the clouds. Felt the warmth on her cheeks, saw the tops of the waves shimmer as though crested with diamonds.

She turned to the boy, "How do you do, Albert?"

The boy looked surprised, a bit embarrassed. Then he tried his best to stand up straight, which was challenging because of the lameness in his leg. He held out his hand, though it trembled. He looked down as he said, "Call me Alby."

While the lonely days at sea drifted into lonesome weeks, Lai King was grateful to have found her sea legs, and also a friend. Though as she lay in her bunk, waiting for the weather to relent, she grew restless and wondered what Alby was doing to pass the time.

"What's it like up there?" Lai King had asked.

"Sad, mostly," Alby said, an answer that surprised her. She found that he could be shy at times and wasn't sure if that was because of his withered leg or because she was a girl. Though on occasion he could be direct, even awkwardly blunt.

"My uncle died and was buried at sea last night. One of the sailors told me at breakfast. Passengers weren't allowed to watch," Alby said. "I didn't know him well, so I don't know how to feel, but I wish I'd at least been able to say goodbye."

Lai King didn't say anything. She understood.

Alby tried to change the subject. He talked about the food, the pipe organ, the formal dinners that he had no interest in attending.

"What happened to your parents?" he asked. "Why are you here by yourself?" Lai King told him and for a moment, her grief belonged to someone else. As though she were reciting someone else's story. One with an equally unhappy ending.

"I'm sorry," Alby said as he stared down at the brace on his leg. He fiddled with the buckles. "My mother died of polio. I guess I almost died as well, but I don't really remember. I was too sick with fever. Sometimes I think we just learn to forget bad things."

Lai King's heart ached for all the things she wished she could forget.

"After she died," Alby said, "when my father said goodbye, I could tell by the way he looked at me, I knew I'd never see him again. That was when I was sent to live with my uncle. He wasn't around much. But he was my only family, at least until . . ."

Both of them fell silent. They'd sat on the deck, two unlikely strangers, or long-lost friends, stepchildren from shotgun marriages of fate and tragedy. They stared out at the endless seascape, while a seven-piece Hungarian orchestra tuned up for first-class passengers in some elegant parlor with crimson carpets and velvet lambrequins.

In steerage, Lai King slept, mostly, or thought about Alby as she darned her stockings with a needle and thread her ah-ma had packed for her. Sometimes she listened — as though she had a choice — to the other passengers singing, or the old woman who played a violin that she called a fiddle as passengers in steerage danced barefoot, stomping, twirling, and wheeling. Their happiness felt tidal, it swelled and lifted Lai King with it. But when their joy receded, Lai King sank into an imaginary landscape of mudflats, dead fish, and rotting kelp. Other times she watched the ladies playing bridge, but their laughter, their hopeful smiles, only made her miss her parents.

"Don't worry," the steerage matron said as she hugged Lai King. "The weather is about to clear. I can feel rain in my bones and those aches are going away."

She'd learned to trust the older woman, and within an hour the rain had faded to a weepy drizzle and Lai King felt fresh air flowing down into the belly of the ship for the first time in days. While waiting to go up top, she filled her sink with soapy water. She washed her hair, her clothing. She tried not to stare at the others. Many stood naked as they washed every raiment, every garment.

When a whistle finally blew, Auntie Anna announced that it was time for the passengers in steerage to enjoy their one hour of daylight. Lai King slung her blanket over her shoulder and went up the ladder.

She emerged from belowdecks, the sky overcast and gray, the water an even darker shade than she remembered. It seemed as though the ship were floating in a cloud. But it was warm. The fresh air, though humid, was glorious.

Alby smiled when he saw her. He pointed to an area near a life-boat and Lai King joined him, spreading out the blanket on the polished deck. She curled her dress beneath her and sat down as he uncovered a wooden tray with two bowls of rice soup, flavored with lemon and sweet potatoes. There were also two dark pieces of roasted chicken, a half-loaf of sourdough, servings of marmalade, black currant jam, and butter that they'd both learned to ignore because it was always rancid.

Alby caught her up on the latest gossip in second class, like how a minister got drunk on rye and threw up on a woman. Lai King shared how in steerage, an old woman got drunk on gin and threw up on the same man when he came below to proselytize.

"God works in mysterious ways," Alby said.

Lai King noticed other passengers staring at them as they walked by.

"They're not staring at you," Alby said, "they're staring at me. Or you *with* me. Or me with you. Maybe both, I don't know." He shrugged.

Lai King took a careful bite of bread and jam. "I was born in California," she said. "But I'm still used to people staring, pointing, whispering." She looked at the brace on Alby's leg and suspected that he knew exactly how that felt.

Alby nodded in agreement. Then he scooped out the sweet potatoes from his soup, the best part, and gave them to her.

She smiled for a moment, thanked him, and then they ate in silence.

When they finished, one of the sailors shouted, "Ho! Womb fish!"

Lai King helped Alby to his feet and they peeked over the rail. A pod of dolphins flew beneath the surface of the water, fins skimming. They crisscrossed in front of the ship, zooming back and forth, dipping beneath the bow, then charging forward, leaping, spinning. It was the most incredible thing Lai King had ever seen. She felt free. A prisoner of misfortune, ransomed by the playful creatures.

"My father once told me a story about the Goddess of the Yangtze River," Lai King said. "A young girl was being taken out on a boat by a greedy man who intended to sell her to the highest bidder. But once he was alone with her, he became enraptured by her beauty. The only way for the girl to escape was to plunge into the river and drown."

Alby frowned. "That's a terrible story."

"But later" — Lai King smiled — "when fishermen saw a beautiful dolphin, leaping, they knew the girl had come back. She'd been reborn."

As they watched the joyful leaping, twirling, splashing, Alby leaned close, their arms touching, and she put her head on his shoulder.

"Is that her?" Alby asked.

"No." Lai King drew a deep breath, then whispered, "That's us."

That night Lai King dreaded going to sleep. Not the actual sleeping part, that was fine, in fact the rocking of the ship had become a comfort instead of a perpetual cause of nausea. What she dreaded about going to sleep was waking up. Because so many times she'd stir in the morning, expecting to see her ah-ba whistling his way out the door. She'd rub her eyes and stretch, looking around her berth, confused that she wasn't back in her apartment, that her mother wasn't in the kitchen making congee. Then the smells of the ship, the privy, the sounds of her fellow passengers would remind her of where she was.

Even her dreams offered little comfort, because the closer they got to China, the more she had nightmares that her feet had been bound, her toes and arches hideously broken. Other nights she was a bride given to an old man. Forced to kneel at a family altar, next to a husband she couldn't see. When she turned to the man she was forced to marry, he was always gone, and a rooster would be in his place.

"Rise and shine," Auntie Anna crowed.

Lai King looked around, wishing there really was a gamecock on board. Because her ah-ma always said that evil spirits are scared of a rooster's crow.

In the dining parlor, Lai King heard Auntie call her name. "Looks like someone has a special visitor." She looked up and saw Alby slowly coming down the ladder, taking his time, careful not to slip. A pail hung from the crook of his arm.

When he reached the bottom, he strained to see in the gloaming as his eyes slowly adjusted to the dimly lit room. He looked around the warren, appraising the tight quarters, then spotted Lai King. "Fancy place you have," he said. "I brought you breakfast."

She smiled and Auntie Anna winked as

she left the room.

"I hope you don't mind?" He took fabric that was draped around his neck and spread it on the floor of the pantry like a small picnic blanket. "One hour of sky liberty is hardly enough for anyone, so I thought I'd come visit." He pulled bread and apples out of the bucket, plus dried cherries and a small piece of cheese with holes in it. Lai King couldn't stand the smell or taste of the fermented — *whatever it was* — but she thanked him and politely took the tiniest of nibbles.

"You didn't have to come all the way down here," she said.

"Well, you're not allowed up in my quarters. But there's no rule forbidding me from coming down here. Besides, Mr. Cappis said we're nearly to Hawaii."

Lai King didn't want to think about what would happen when they arrived in Canton. She would go her own way, to her mother's village. Alby would go where — to an orphanage? Perhaps a work farm? Or he might become an indentured servant. Wherever he ended up, she doubted they would see each other again.

"I'm in no hurry," Lai King said as she took a bite of apple to hide her sadness.

Alby coughed, or choked on a bit of bread,

as he nodded. "Me neither."

They ate and spoke and laughed, and at times almost cried, as they talked about their families, and of their homesickness for places that no longer existed except somewhere on the faded maps of memory. With each bite, they seemed to be savoring the seconds, counting the days and their rationed hours of fresh air and sunshine.

After they ate they talked late into the afternoon. The other ladies in steerage passed through the pantry, first on their way to breakfast, and then later to lunch, and if anyone begrudged Lai King's visitor they kept that opinion to themselves. But most just smiled. That was the difference between first class and steerage, Lai King realized. Down here, no one cared about decorum or pretention. There was no need for fancy dresses, the putting on of airs, the ever-changing kaleidoscope of domestic rituals she never really understood and couldn't keep up with anyway. That's the one good thing about being poor, having nothing, Lai King thought. *Happiness is free.*

Lai King waited with Alby until it was time to go topside for sky liberty, which, for once, lived up to its name and more as they emerged from the darkened hold to an azure firmament devoid of even a single cloud. Not even a mist or a puff or a haze.

They found their favorite spot on the starboard quarter near the aft, watching the waves crest, their whitecaps looking as though they were pushing the vessel forward.

"My father used to say there's nothing like a clear blue sky out on the ocean," Lai King said. "He claimed that old sailors told him that on rare days like this, if you watch the sunset and don't blink, just before the sun disappears below the horizon, you'll see a green flash. He said masts and rigging will sometimes glow."

Alby looked at the horizon and furrowed his brow. "Do you believe him?"

"I used to," Lai King said. "I'm not sure what to believe anymore. He also told me that once before an earthquake in San Francisco, he saw glimmering lights in the sky and that the wings of birds and butterflies were covered in blue flame."

"Sounds like a ghost story."

Lai King shrugged. "Ghosts aren't always bad. Sometimes they're just our ancestors checking in on us." A seagull landed on the deck, and they both stared at the bird, half expecting it to glow, but it just looked at them.

Alby coughed and the startled bird took flight.

Lai King watched the bird disappear behind the small sail that, she had learned, the steamer used to stiffen the ship. Then Alby turned away, trying to clear his throat. When she touched his shoulder to see if he was okay, his cheeks were reddening. He removed his kerchief and she noticed a bruise on his neck for the first time.

"I'm sorry . . ." He apologized as he coughed until his eyes watered.

Lai King noticed that a few passengers who were grouped on the starboard side of the ship to look for dolphins had turned around and were looking for who might be coughing. She gently rubbed Alby's back, silently begging for him to stop as she noticed that more passengers halted what they'd been doing and were eyeing them warily.

Lai King smiled at them, hoping they couldn't see how scared she was.

When they turned away, she touched Alby's cheek as he caught his breath. In the cool breeze of the afternoon, she thought he felt too warm. "You should go below deck."

Alby shook his head, suppressing a cough. "Maybe I'm just tired . . ."

Lai King tried to remain calm, even though she noticed that his voice had become hoarse, and inside she was shouting, crying for him to not cough again. She noticed that one of the crewmen, shirtless with leathery skin and covered in scars and tattoos, was staring at them. She put her arm around Alby and helped him up. He wasn't coughing anymore, but his limp had become noticeably worse. She led him back to midship, where he could go down to his cabin and rest as long as needed. They were almost to the stairs when Lai King felt someone grab the back of her hair. The sailor turned her around, then squeezed her arm as he held Alby by his shirt collar.

He looked askance as he yelled, "Mr. Cappis, we may have a problem!"

Lai King felt a cool breeze and cold spray from the ocean as the chief officer shouted from the quarterdeck, "What have you, Mr. Fawcett?"

The sailor pruned his face as he regarded her, touched her neck, rolled up her sleeves, and examined her arms as though he were checking a slab of halibut to see if it was spoiled or still worth eating. He even sniffed her skin.

He did the same to Alby, who struggled, trying not to cough.

The sailor lifted his neckerchief and covered his face.

"He's fine," Lai King said, as she put herself between Alby and the seaman. "It's just a stomachache. I told him not to eat the butter but he wouldn't listen."

"Report, Mr. Fawcett," the chief officer shouted.

"Please," Lai King said, "please just let me take him belowdecks. I'll take him down to steerage. I'll keep him there with me. If he gets worse, I'll tell the matron."

The sailor looked at them, spat a glob of chewing tobacco over the railing, then shook his head and grumbled, "Take him below. I'll let Mr. Cappis decide."

"Thank you," Lai King said. "You won't even know we're there." She ushered Alby away. He stopped coughing but looked pale and tired, though with her help, he was able to manage the ladders.

When they reached steerage, Auntie Anna removed her bonnet and apron and looked at them, one hand on her wide hip. "It was okay for a visit, my dear, but you know he can't stay down here forever."

"He's not feeling well," Lai King confided because she had no one else to turn to. "I have an empty bunk. I thought that maybe . . ."

"So you thought that you'd play nurse-maid to that boy?" she asked, but the question was more of a statement. "Down here?"

Lai King looked at her, pleading with her eyes.

"Fine." Auntie Anna sighed as she led Lai King down a narrow hallway. "In here." She opened a small half-door into a storage room. "Take him inside. I'll go grab some bedding. You know it's not wise for him to be down here. Even worse of an idea for you to be so close to him. If he's really sick . . ."

"It's nothing. I'll be fine."

Auntie Anna opened her mouth as though she were about to lecture them, then softened, shaking her head. "You have my sympathies, child."

Lai King helped Alby inside. She took the blankets and a pillow from Auntie Anna and made a bed on the floor behind barrels of salt pork and flour. She tucked Alby in, and he didn't complain about the hard floor or the darkened closet that was probably a dungeon compared to his stateroom in second class.

"You're going to be okay," Lai King said, though she wondered if she was lying, and if so, whether it was to him or to herself. She touched his forehead, his cheek. "I think you have a fever. It may just be the croup. You need to sleep."

He nodded, then whispered, "Thank you," as he closed his eyes, shivering beneath the blankets. As her eyes adjusted to the darkness, she watched over him, thinking about how she'd watched her parents sleep. How they fell ill and she didn't.

He stirred and coughed again. "You should go."

"Shhh . . ."

His teeth began chattering. "You need to leave me, Lai King."

"And you need to rest."

"Please," Alby said.

"I won't leave you," she said, her heart still aching from the loss of her family. "I'm going to stay right here with you, all night if I have to. I'm not going anywhere." She curled up next to him on the floor. She covered her mouth with part of the blanket.

"I'm so glad I found you," he said. "I've never known anyone like you before."

"Someone like me?"

"A friend," Alby whispered. "I've never had a real friend before," his words slurring as he succumbed to fatigue or fever, the rocking of the ship. "I always . . . wondered what that would feel like." She could see him smile for a moment in the darkness. "It feels . . . good. I want you to know . . . how grateful . . ."

Lai King waited for him to finish his sentence, but he was already fast asleep.

Lai King woke in the early morning to the sound of cooking pans and realized Auntie Anna was up, making breakfast, kneading dough. The woman hummed as she worked, occasionally singing a happy tune, which sounded out of place in the darkened hold where Lai King had slept. In the pitch black of the room, she crawled across the floorboards to where Alby was. She had a vague memory of him coughing, waking up, and leaving the room to use the privy.

"Can you make it okay?" she'd whispered. "It's dark down here."

"Don't worry," he said with a slight wheeze. "I'll find my way back to you."

She fell asleep again, unsure of when he returned.

Now as she reached the blankets, they were cold and he was missing. "Alby," she called out, "Alby, where are you?"

She called out again as the door to the storage room creaked open and she squinted at the brightness. She shaded her eyes from the glow of the gas lamps that flooded the cramped space. Backlit was a tall, broad silhouette, spoon in hand.

"I thought I heard you awake in there," Auntie Anna said.

Lai King stood, rubbing her eyes as she asked, "Where is he?"

There was an awkward silence between them. Then a pot of boiling water bubbled over, hissing on the iron stove. "I thought he was in there with you," the woman said before she rescued whatever she was cooking. "Oh dear. Oh, my heavens . . ."

"Where did he go?" Lai King asked in desperation.

Auntie Anna said nothing.

"Where did he go!?" Lai King shouted, then pushed past the woman and climbed the ladder as fast as she could. She emerged on deck as the sun, a globe of radiant orange, peeked above the horizon. Her eyes adjusted to the light, and she saw there were no passengers anywhere, just a handful of sailors, tending watch.

"Alby!" Lai King shouted, painfully aware of how small and feeble her voice was, lost in the chorus of the ocean, the creaking of the ship's timbers that groaned like a slowly ticking clock.

Mr. Cappis spotted her from the forecastle, where he was talking to another officer. He donned his cap and descended a ramp. He walked soberly in her direction.

She shouted, "What did you do to him? He was away from everyone else, he wasn't going to hurt anyone. I was taking care of him. He was . . ." She scanned the deck.

Mr. Cappis straightened his black coat. He didn't smile, but he didn't frown either. "Miss, I would ask you to calm yourself if you're going to address me in this way."

Lai King fell silent, though inside she was screaming.

"I didn't do anything to anyone," he said. "If you're talking about the boy . . ."

"Where is he?"

"I have no idea," Mr. Cappis said. "But I can assure you I didn't do anything to your young friend."

Lai King felt quiet relief. "Then where is he?"

She stepped to the taffrail and stared down at the endless sea, which for once was unusually calm, like a sheet of glass. In the distance, she spotted a single dolphin skimming the surface of the water, leaping once before it plunged and disappeared.

16
DOROTHY

Dorothy sat on the main deck of the MV *Suquamish,* looking through the rain-streaked windows of the old ferry that served the thirty-five-minute route between downtown Seattle and Bainbridge Island. Annabel sat on the green, cushioned bench directly across from her mother, staring at the water as though searching for something and restlessly banging her tiny heels against the metal beneath her seat.

Dorothy gave her daughter a look and she stopped, though she kept fidgeting.

"Why can't I go outside?" Annabel asked, pointing to the bow of the ship.

"Because it's raining, Baby-bel," Dorothy said. "And it's windy and nasty out."

Annabel recently refused to go to pre-school because she said she had nightmares during nap time, so Dorothy suggested that the two of them take what she liked to refer

393

to as a *swimming lesson.* Dorothy took the idea from an old poem by Mary Oliver, about finding your way back to land after being tossed in the sea. It was Dorothy's idea to take a mental health day; Louis, however, called it a *lack of wealth day.* Because from his perspective, Dorothy being a frequently out-of-work teacher was already akin to a vacation. Why would she need any extra time away from that?

To Louis, the need for self-care was a sign of weakness, at best, and vocational failure at worst. He especially hated it when Dorothy included their daughter in this tradition, a holiday that he refused to observe. But all Annabel knew was that it was a special day away from school with her mother, without a designated nap time, and she could follow her own interests, which Dorothy encouraged. She offered to take Annabel to the Seattle Aquarium, or the Pacific Science Center, or even to the Seattle Art Museum, but to Annabel, those places felt like school in disguise. Instead, she wanted to don their raincoats and wander around Seattle's International District, where they could eat dim sum for lunch and go to Pink Gorilla, a Japanese toy store. They'd finish the day with a ferry ride over to Bainbridge Island and back, and if they were still hungry they'd order Ivar's clam chowder from the galley, followed by hot chocolate and apple pie.

Dorothy relished the thought of spending a day alone with her daughter, stealing away to do something spontaneous and joyful, if only to counteract whatever vaguely racist, critical, and self-loathing thoughts Louis's mother might have planted in Annabel's head. "You sure you don't want to go spend a few weeks in Spokane with Grandma Louise?" Dorothy checked during lunch.

Annabel had pruned her face and shaken her head, much to Dorothy's relief.

"How about you go to England instead," Dorothy half teased. "When you're older you could go to Summerhill, the boarding school where my great-grandmother went. It's artsy and creative, and full of children just like you. They come from all over the world and are allowed to study whatever they want."

Dorothy remembered a black-and-white photo of her great-grandmother, Zou yi, with a Summerhill teacher, a young English woman who had one of those intense looks you sometimes see in old photographs. Her cleft chin was up, her eyes staring down intently, a slight smile on her face, the kind of expression that men see as intimidating but women see as confidence. Dorothy always wanted to go to Summerhill. She didn't care about her education, she just wanted to come away with that kind of spirit, equal parts boldness, élan, and self-possession.

Especially after Greta was gone.

Annabel said, "Okay," much to Dorothy's surprise.

"You know England is another country, far away?"

Annabel looked out the window as though she were searching for where this mysterious land might be. Then she looked at Dorothy and shrugged.

As the ferry cleared Eagle Harbor and was under way back to Seattle, Dorothy gazed through the heavy glass doors and saw a boy outside, leaning against the rail, seemingly oblivious to the weather. He reminded Dorothy of herself at that age. How she could be utterly mesmerized by the sea. She'd loved going upstairs to the sundeck where passengers stretched out on yoga mats, went for leisurely strolls, or even walked their dogs, who strained against their leashes to bark at seagulls. When it was sunny the warm breeze had a fragrance of salt water and evergreen. But she especially loved going outside when it was stormy.

There was something romantic and intrepid about standing on the prow in the rain, alone, especially when there were high winds and the ferry would gently sway, listing to the right and left as it navigated the churning, whitecapped waters of Puget Sound. Greta had always bundled Dorothy up and gone out there with her. As a girl, Dorothy felt like a Victorian maiden; as a grown woman, those moments felt like a slice of Emily Dickinson: *No man moved me, till the tide went past my simple shoe, and past my apron, and my belt, and past my bodice, too.* Though even maidens have their limits, as Dorothy once turned green from seasickness and another time had windburned her eyes so badly they were bloodshot for days.

Dorothy chewed her lip as she wondered how long the ferries would be operating. There was a larger storm out there, Typhoon Tenjin, three hundred miles over the watery horizon. Dorothy's phone had been tracking the barometer, which was holding steady, but the tide had risen six feet with waves coming in every nine seconds, meaning that if the cyclone didn't slow down or change course, the Northwest could be hit within days.

Annabel pouted. "Are you sure I can't go

outside?"

"What did I say?" Dorothy tried her best to reason with a five-year-old.

"You used to go out there," Annabel argued the way preschoolers do, subtly planting seeds of logic in guilt-rich soil, hoping that they might eventually bear fruit.

"Well, I used to do a lot of things that I wouldn't recommend," Dorothy said. "I'd come in freezing and catch a cold. You don't want to get sick, do you? I feel sorry for that boy out there, he's probably going to catch pneumonia if he doesn't come in soon."

Annabel turned in her seat. "What boy?"

Dorothy looked up and the prow was empty.

"Never mind," Dorothy said. "His kind, loving, and incredibly wise mother must have come to her senses and made him come inside to warm up." She scanned the passengers in the bow, the business commuters, the retirees, the rebellious youth who had tattooed their faces with geometric patterns in bright colors to throw off the surveillance cameras that were everywhere. Dorothy didn't see the boy.

The ferry rocked and Dorothy felt a wave of vertigo. She gripped the bench and held her breath, addled, reeling as though she were a child stepping off a merry-go-round. Dizzy, gravity pulling at odd angles, stumbling to the grass, looking up at the sky as the earth slowly spun beneath her. Amid that loss of equilibrium were currents of sadness and melancholy. She felt disconnected, like whenever she woke from one of her treatments and struggled to reconcile her confounding landscape of emotions, her new memories, with the sterile, clinical environment of Dr. Shedhorn's facility.

I'm safe. I'm sitting down. Everyone else is okay. Dorothy exhaled slowly as she tried to calm herself. *It's just a bout of déjà vu. On steroids.*

Dorothy looked out the window and saw her reflection. She was shockingly pale. Her forehead was damp, her mouth filled with cotton. She carefully stood up, steadied herself against the bulkhead, made sure the room wasn't spinning, then removed her coat and hat and placed them on the seat. Then she found a small sketchbook and some crayons in her handbag and gave them to Annabel.

"Hey, Baby-bel." She drew a deep, calming breath. "Mommy has to go to the ladies' room." Dorothy pointed to the doorless entry directly across from their seats. She suppressed a moment of panic as she felt as though the air had been sucked from the passenger deck. She touched her chest, felt her racing heartbeat, heard a dull ringing in her ears. "I'll be right back. Stay here, okay?"

"I'll be right here," Annabel said, glumly pointing to the floor with a crayon. The way she elongated the word *here* made it sound like she was shackled to the bench.

"Sing 'Row, Row, Row Your Boat' so I can hear you," Dorothy said.

Annabel sighed and then began singing as she drew a sailboat.

Dorothy forced what she hoped was a reassuring smile, then hastened to the lavatory, trying not to stumble, bracing for a full-on panic attack. She walked into the restroom and grabbed a handful of paper towels, wet them in the sink with warm water, and wiped her brow, then her cheeks. She glanced up and was startled by the reflection. She had a complete disconnection from the face staring back. As though she were observing a different person altogether, someone who looked like her but had their own thoughts, feelings, autonomy. The disturbing sensation was reminiscent of when she'd taken psychedelic mushrooms with friends in college and then looked in the mirror. She held on to the sink as her doppelganger smiled back at her.

Annabel sang, *"Merrily, merrily, merrily, merrily. Life is but a dream . . ."*

Dorothy's vertigo turned to nausea as the rocking motion of the ferry grew in intensity. She hung her head, felt her stomach churn, then put her finger down her throat and vomited into the sink, painfully aware that the other women in the ladies' room were staring at her in concern, recoiling in disgust, or had left altogether.

I have to get back.

She spat into the basin, wiped her eyes, her hands shaking as she washed them, but the world had stopped spinning. She took one last look in the mirror, then went out to check on Annabel. When she walked out of the restroom, she smelled seafood and ginger and cigar smoke. She stepped back to make way for tuxedoed waiters who carried away enormous trays on their shoulders, piled with empty dishes and platters of discarded crab and oyster shells. She gazed around the elegant shipboard drawing room and saw Chinese men and women in evening finery — all speaking Cantonese — milling about, laughing and ordering rounds of cocktails and bottles of wine and liqueur. She smelled perfume as a slender woman in a yellow cheongsam dress glided by offering cigarettes and mints on a silver tray. Dorothy turned and squeezed her eyes shut, confused, worried that she was having a new kind of breakdown. A lucid, spectral, dissociative episode, but one more severe than anything she'd ever experienced or at least remembered. When she opened her eyes the rain was gone, and in its place she saw the sunset — a palette of crimson and burgundy — through ornate, leaded-glass windows. But she couldn't find land. Not Bainbridge Island in the vessel's wake or Seattle to the west or Kingston to the north. Just an endless horizon.

She heard a band playing swing jazz, something by Glenn Miller.

"Excuse me, miss," a familiar voice asked. "Are you okay?"

She turned, surprised that the man in front of her was Caucasian. He wore a dark suit with finely pressed creases and a tie of emerald green. He had thick, dark hair that curled in the front and he sported a look of wide-eyed innocence, as though he'd stepped off his mother's porch after helping her do the dishes on some dairy farm in Iowa or Kansas or Ohio, a contrast to the tall glass of champagne in his hand.

Dorothy looked about the strange room, took the glass, and drank half, hoping the crisp, sparkling liquid might clear her head or at least freshen her breath. She regarded the half-full glass as the fragrant carbonation tickled her nose.

She drained the rest.

The man's eyes widened. "Remind me not to get into a drinking contest with any women while I'm over here. I'd be punching above my weight."

She stared back, confused.

He furrowed his brow. *"Nei mou si maa?"* He pronounced the words slowly, carefully, as though he were walking out onto a frozen lake, unsteady steps on thin ice.

He sighed and gently took the empty glass from her hand and placed it on the tray of a passing waiter. "I'm sorry, my Cantonese is as graceful as a dog on a unicycle." He shrugged. "All I can do is keep trying, right?"

Dorothy realized he wasn't sure if she spoke English. He was talking to himself as much as to her. She touched his arm and asked, "Do I know you?"

He smiled and cocked his head. "I don't know. Do you? There are thirty of us on board. Now that I think about it, we probably all look alike, huh?"

"Us?" Dorothy asked. She scanned the room and spotted a handful of Caucasian faces in the crowd, a few gathered at the bar, a few more dancing, all of them men about her age, in suits, clean-shaven with slicked-back hair.

"Gwai lo," the man said, pointing to himself. Then he whispered, "Americans."

All of this felt familiar as Dorothy tried to remember.

"Would you care to dance?" He offered his arm with a curious look, as though he were unsure if he was in breach of some cultural norm. He pointed to the dance floor. "I can do the Jive, the Lindy Hop, and the Big Apple. I can kind of do the Samba and a slow Bolero, but I'm afraid if we do either of those I'll have to follow you. My big sister taught me those dances and she always insisted on leading. Gave me a new appreciation for that quote about Fred Astaire: *Sure, he was great, but Ginger Rogers did everything he did, backwards and in high heels."*

She hesitated, then took his arm, still trying to comprehend what was happening, as he led her to the middle of the room. The band began to play "Moonlight Serenade" and he turned, took her hand, and placed his other on the small of her back, holding her close in a gentleman's embrace. He was warm, like an afternoon lying in the sun, eyes closed, mesmerized by the summery heat.

"Is this okay?" he asked.

She nodded.

"It's a slow song." He leaned in so close she felt as though their eyelashes might touch. "Foxtrot?" She nodded again and he gently pressed his body to hers and smiled. "Here we go." He stepped forward, leading her back, then to the side, then twirling counterclockwise as the other couples did the same. Everyone swirling around the smoky room in the same direction, paired off like peach-faced lovebirds.

"Going home to Rangoon?" he asked as they stepped to the music.

She glanced up at him, slowly shaking her head as though she couldn't quite remember where home was. She held on and followed his movements, listening to the music, trying to recall why she was here. "I needed a change, I guess."

He nodded to the silver pin on her lapel. "A change from nursing?"

She glanced down, surprised to see a silver caduceus, two snakes around a staff with wings, the type of pin worn by doctors or nurses.

"You're quite brave to wear that in public, especially while we're on board. The Japs have a standing order to arrest all medical personnel fleeing China. If we were stopped by a Japanese warship . . ." He raised his eyebrows.

Dorothy didn't feel brave as she studied his handsome, familiar face, filled with curiosity and kindness. She felt delirious with happiness, but also deeply afraid.

"It's okay, we're almost there. Your secret is safe with me." He beamed, showing his dimples. "Your English is beautiful, by the way. Where did you go to school? My old teacher back home, Mrs. Hanson, she'd give you an A." Then he whispered conspiratorially, "She gave me a C-plus and she was my aunt."

Dorothy looked out the window, as though the answer to his question were hidden in the sunset. "I think it was my mother who taught me."

As they circled the dance floor he followed her gaze through the leaded glass, now lit up as though by fire. "Hung with the sunset's fringe of gold; now strangely clear thine image grows, and olden memories are startled from their long repose."

Memories.

Dorothy stared at him, searching, longing, hoping. "Like shadows on the silent snows, when suddenly the night wind blows."

Startled from their long repose.

"That's Poe," she said. "You surprise me."

He touched his cheek to hers, their feet moving together as they glided around the dance floor. "Not nearly as much as you astound me."

When the song ended, people clapped and she realized why she was afraid. It was the fear of losing someone you love. She held his hand as he led her from the dance floor.

"You know," he said, "I should introduce you to one of my companions. He's a surgeon. He's supposed to take care of us flyboys and grease monkeys, but I swear, from the looks of it, his team consists entirely of a medic and a bottle of iodine. He would fall all over himself if he found out there were a Chinese nurse on board who speaks English better than yours truly. That is, if you don't already have plans? Maybe wooing the baron of some teak plantation or going diving with the sea gypsies?"

"I didn't really make plans." Dorothy imagined the trade winds in Burma, filled with the fragrance of sweet plumeria and the intoxicating, buttery scent of almond blossoms. The warm tropical rain on her skin. The seductive prelude to typhoon season.

She wanted to spend every moment with him.

"If you wanted, you could come with us," he said. "We won't be based too close to the ground fighting, at least not at the moment. But we're going to see a lot of action in the air, and having you there could literally save our lives. And it sure would be nice to share a moment like this with you again. Might even be worth it to get shot down." He winked. "You'd be surprised at what these poor, lonely fools would do to get a girl's attention out here."

This time she was the one smiling, her head spinning.

"My name is John, by the way. Nice to meet you. And you are?"

He looked into her eyes, then past her shoulder, and she heard glass breaking, as though a waiter or a busboy had dropped something.

People were shouting, screaming.

An older woman yelled in English, "Someone grab that little girl!"

Dorothy turned and was on the ferry, her head reeling from the champagne and swirling about the dance floor. She stood frozen for a heartbeat, still confused, then instantly sobered as she saw Annabel on the other side of the glass doors, in the rain and howling wind, climbing up the metal railing. Passengers dropped their phones and coffees, others leapt to their feet. Dorothy shoved past them frantically, pushed through the heavy doors, felt the chill in the air as she ran, reaching Annabel just as she'd thrown a leg over the top rail. Dorothy pulled her down, wrapped her arms around her, the embrace of a terrified mother. Annabel was cold, soaking wet, confused.

"What are you doing out here, Baby-bel?" Dorothy tried to remain calm, but she was scared, shaking Annabel and shedding tears of relief. She tried not to think of her daughter plummeting into the dark, roiling waters below. Annabel didn't know how to swim and the water was frigid, deep, the storm currents deadly.

The ship's horn sounded, and the bow rose and fell as it eased through the waves. When the blaring faded Dorothy heard the thrum of electric vehicles on the car deck below. Other passengers queued up behind the glass doors to disembark as the ferry slowed. The downtown terminal flashed its lights in the distance. Dorothy saw the Smith Tower. Saw the lights at the top where their apartment was. She felt as though she'd been awakened from a dream and shoved face-first into a cold, cruel reality.

"I told you to stay put," Dorothy said, rocking Annabel, squeezing her, trying not to break down sobbing. "What if something happened? What if I lost you?"

"I'm sorry." Annabel looked crestfallen. "I saw the boy. The same one you saw. He was waiting for me to come play, but when I got out here he was gone."

Dorothy looked around. There was no boy. Just more rain.

She picked Annabel up and walked inside as the other passengers stepped back, regarding her with a mix of shock, relief, and disdain for the type of mother who would let a five-year-old wander out there all alone in this weather. They shook their heads at Dorothy as she passed. She recognized the angry expressions, the whispering. She'd experienced the same reaction more than a decade earlier when friends, strangers, and social workers had disapproved of her own mother's neglect and incapacitation. As an adult, it took Dorothy years to stop blaming herself for her mother's pain, her trauma, her death. Now, as a parent, Dorothy realized that during all those years it had been the other way around, and despite her best efforts, the cycle was repeating.

■ ■ ■ ■

When Dorothy and Annabel got home, Louis and his mother were sitting on the couch in the living room. They whispered, then stopped speaking and instead exchanged knowing looks and put on welcoming smiles. They looked like fraternal twins, one with more mileage than the other, but the same make and model.

"Um. Hello," Dorothy said as she helped Annabel out of her boots and new raincoat. "I thought you'd gone back to Spokane already. Did they close Snoqualmie Pass again? I heard there was another mudslide warning because of all the rain."

"You know me. I couldn't leave without giving my sweet girl another hug," Louise said to Annabel, arms outstretched.

The happy five-year-old walked into her grandmother's open arms, though when the older woman squeezed, Annabel said, "You're. Squishing. Me."

Dorothy didn't want to see Louise, not again, not tonight. She didn't appreciate how the older woman could make her feel like an unwanted guest in her own home. Or worse — a servant, someone whose presence was functional, nothing more.

411

"What's going on?" Dorothy asked as she removed her coat.

"Louis called me as I was leaving. He thought we should talk." Louise spoke in a manner that reminded Dorothy of an old boss, the department head at Seattle Central Community College who had fired her for too many absences. Louis wanted to sue the school for wrongful termination, but Dorothy talked him out of it. The thought of being stuck in a windowless conference room for days, having to give a deposition to strange men who could subpoena her therapist's notes and ask her humiliating questions, was worse than being temporarily unemployed.

Louise kissed Annabel on the cheek. "Why don't we let this wonderful girl of ours go to her room so we can let you in on our discussion."

"Well, that sounds ominous," Dorothy said, envisioning Louis spinning a wheel of misfortune and watching it land on *Mother Moves In* or *Let Me List Your Flaws,* or the dreaded *Spokane Getaway,* where Louise would insist on taking Annabel home with her until typhoon season had passed. It wasn't a terrible idea, on paper. It was eminently safer on the other side of the state, despite the rise of nationalist separatists the closer one got to the Rocky Mountains. Dorothy patted Annabel on the shoulder. "Baby-bel, why don't you go work on your drawings. I'll come read you a story later, okay?"

Annabel sighed and then trundled off to her room. "Grown-ups talk about the weirdest things."

Dorothy sat down across from Louis and his mother.

This is my home, not hers. But her mind became a zoetrope of emotion, with flickering images, lingering memories of a boy on the bow of the ferry, sitting on the grass of some lakeside park with someone named Sam, the hauntingly familiar smile of the man who had asked her to dance. Dorothy stared across at Louis, who for once wasn't staring at his phone. She remembered his eyes rolling back, his body going limp, him waking up on the floor confused and disoriented. *Is that what this is about?* she thought. *Great. This is going to be like one of those Hollywood tabloid cover stories, where the girlfriend is accused of physically abusing her loudmouthed boyfriend.*

"Is everything okay?" Dorothy asked, wishing she were somewhere else. Perhaps back on a ship somewhere in the Andaman or South China Seas.

Louise spoke first. "My son has been telling me about these special treatments you've been undergoing. Experimental treatments. Frankly, he's worried . . ."

"He shouldn't be," Dorothy said. "Believe it or not, they're helping."

"Obviously." Louise rolled her eyes.

"If this is about the cost," Dorothy countered, "I'm sure I can work out some sort of payment plan with the clinic. My doctor even joked that I'm such a good patient, she should be paying me. Besides, it's my health and my body and I'm working on it my way. I'm sure, I mean I hope, neither of you has a problem with that."

Neither Louis nor his mother smiled anymore.

"Look, dear," Louise continued. "I know things haven't been great between you two for some time. Sometimes that's normal. Other times there are — shall we say — unforeseen circumstances. But I can assure you, his concern for your well-being is . . ."

"Louise . . ."

"He said you've been acting erratically. I know some people have postpartem depression, but Annie is five years old now, so we're left to surmise that these treatments of yours are only making your already tenuous relationship with reality all that more

414

difficult and, well, what I'd like to discuss is . . ."

"Louise —" Dorothy insisted.

"He said you're having certain mood swings. Anger issues and —"

"Louise, if you're not going to fucking let me speak, then let him."

Both of them looked shocked and offended. Victimized. Dorothy hated losing her temper, but she was tired and emotionally drained from her day. Almost as much as she hated the wordless exchange she observed between mother and son. The nervous glances and the subtle, disapproving shakes of their heads to each other. Dorothy felt cornered, outgunned. She'd first felt that way in the second grade when two kids on the playground took her lunchbox and tossed it back and forth, playing keep-away until Dorothy punched one of them in the stomach. Then she immediately began crying. The vice principal called Dorothy's mother, who never picked up her phone or even bothered to show up. The vice principal handed Dorothy a note to be signed by her mother, but she threw it out the bus window on the way home and no one ever mentioned it again.

Louis cleared his throat. He held up his hand just as his mother was about to speak, again. "You're absolutely right. I should be the one leading this conversation. This affects me far more than —" He glanced sheepishly at his mother, who looked at him as if to say, *Fine, get on with it.* "Dorothy, I've tried to be patient with your . . ." He searched for a polite word for what he really wanted to say. "Your artistic eccentricities. But I'm legitimately concerned that your attention has been occupied elsewhere. You don't have to explain yourself. I'm not accusing you of anything, though I suppose I could. Look — I'll be the first one to admit that I haven't been the most supportive partner . . ."

"You think?" Dorothy crossed her arms.

"But that's not the issue," he said. "If we can't work things out, I get that. That's comprehensible. We gave it a shot. But what I'm more worried about is a certain kind of behavior, which isn't acceptable if you're going to remain Annabel's mother."

Remain?

He took out his mobile phone, glanced at Louise, who nodded, then pressed a button on the screen. He turned the phone around so she could see a video of Annabel on the ferry, standing alone, then walking away. He turned the volume up, and Dorothy imagined the room swaying as though she were

416

back on board. She felt fearful, tearful again as she heard the passengers yelling, screaming. Then she saw herself in a moment of panic push through and grab their daughter just as she swung her leg over the top railing. She saw herself angrily shaking Annabel, then hugging her, squeezing her.

Dorothy's eyes welled with tears. She took a deep breath, rubbed her temple as though she could erase those memories. "You don't understand . . ."

"Oh, I think we do," Louise huffed. "You're simply unfit to be a mother. It's not your fault, dear. Our parenting skills are based on modeled behavior."

"Wait." Dorothy looked up. "Why do you have a video of me? It was a terrible, hysterical moment, but certainly not enough to go viral."

Both of them stared back.

Dorothy crossed her arms, her mouth hanging open in disbelief. "Did you actually hire someone to follow me?"

"It wasn't him, dear," Louise said. "It was me."

"It was my idea," Louis added, with a hint of regret.

"Yes, but I'm the one who paid for it." She patted her son's knee, then looked back at Dorothy. "I'm the one who just filed a protective injunction for Annie. And I'm the one who's going to be taking my granddaughter with me to Spokane in the morning. It's either that or we're going to be showing this video to a judge and arguing for full custody of Annie as well as a restraining order against you."

Dorothy said, "Wait a minute . . ."

"Louis thought you were running around, seeing someone else. But endangering your own daughter is far worse than some passing fancy. Please don't take this personally, dear. Don't make it harder than it already is. We're doing this for you and for her. It's the best thing for everyone. I'm not saying this needs to be permanent. If and when you can pass a basic test for mental fitness and competency, and with the proper parenting classes, I'm sure you could be given visitation rights."

Dorothy could not believe the audacity of what she was hearing. She turned to Louis. "You actually agree with this?" As he opened his mouth, struggling to find the words, she already knew the answer. With Annabel in another city, being taken care of by someone else, he'd be free again. He could go out with clients late into the evening, he could sleep in on weekends, he could become a parent in name only, not that he was the most attentive parent to begin with. She listened to him vacillate between excuses and explanations. He might as well have been a weathervane spinning in the wind.

"I honestly think it's better for Annabel right now. Safer, especially with the bad weather and all, the typhoon," he said. "And it would even give you and me the opportunity to work on us. If that's what we decide to do, together."

Now you care about me, now you care about the weather?

Dorothy stood up, shaking.

"Where are you going?" Louise asked. "You can't run from this, Dorothy."

Dorothy walked away. "I'm not running from anything. I'm going to read my daughter a story, one with a happy ending."

Hours later Dorothy sat in the dark, in the chair where she'd spent countless hours nursing Annabel, long nights gently rocking her beautiful girl to sleep. Dorothy had kept watch until Louise finally left, but not before she made a great, noisy show of her departure, making sure that Dorothy could hear her promising to return for Annabel in the morning. Afterward, Louis bumbled about the living room for a while, turning the television on and off before finally going to their bedroom.

Dorothy tried to wrap her head around the idea of Annabel going off to Spokane. She knew that it was a practical thing to do, the same way it was practical for an army to surrender. Waving a white flag was a guaranteed way to bring a swift end to hostilities, which was fine as long as you didn't care who wins or loses, or what happens after.

She tried to think of calmer things.

"What's the most peaceful, relaxing, centering thing you can imagine?" Dr. Shedhorn asked after Dorothy's last treatment. The answer came tumbling out as Dorothy pictured Annabel in her favorite green pajamas, eyes closed, lips slightly parted, long dark hair splayed across her pillow. Her little arms and legs akimbo as though she'd been dropped from a great height and crash-landed atop her downy comforter, protected by a menagerie of stuffed animals. Dorothy could hear Annabel's soft, gentle breathing when the furnace shut off and the room was so still it felt as though time had stopped.

"It has to be the look on my little girl's face when she's sleeping. I would give anything to be able to sleep like that again," Dorothy had said. "A close second would be the exact opposite of that, whenever she puts music on in her bedroom and dances around. She's so perfectly wild and happy — she seems so free."

"What does she dance to?" Dr. Shedhorn began taking notes. "You could add those songs to a playlist and take that slice of happiness with you. Enjoy those songs whenever you're having a bad day, or feeling a bit low, or just need a boost."

"I have those songs already," Dorothy said. She knew the encouragement was a suggestion to help tide her over until her next treatment, which would have to wait until the storm had passed to be rescheduled.

"So you're way ahead of me, then," Dr. Shedhorn said.

"I guess so."

Dorothy had assumed that Annabel's similar musical taste was a coincidence. She reasoned that her daughter played a few songs on the lesson computer in her bedroom — whatever sounded good to her little ears — and an algorithm created a playlist that mirrored what Dorothy listened to, classic bands like Queen, or the Vaccines, or Origami Button, or vintage performers like Frank Sinatra and Billie Holiday. Now as she watched her daughter, twitching while dreaming as though touched by something unseen, Dorothy contemplated something else. *I never played any of those songs for her. Not in the car. Or at home. I don't even remember playing them for her when I was pregnant.* She furrowed her brow. *Those songs are on an old workout playlist.*

Dorothy remembered what Dr. Shedhorn had said about scorecards and echoes. How each generation is built upon the genetic ruins of the past. That our lives are merely biological waypoints. We're not individual flowers, annuals that bloom and then die. We're perennials. A part of us comes back each new season, carrying a bit of the genus of the previous floret. If true, then Dorothy feared for what Annabel's life might become without her, but also — as hard as it was to admit — with her.

Like most parents, Dorothy hoped that Annabel would feel more love in her life, more security, have greater opportunities. But what if her mother was born encumbered with the weight of past generations? What if that was Annabel's epigenetic inheritance?

Dorothy imagined herself as a copy of a copy of a copy. Each version less sharp, less clear, more muddy, blurry around the edges of happiness and contentment. If so, then what did that make her daughter? What chances would Annabel have for a life better than her own? Dorothy grew up feeling disconnected and anxious. She still felt out of place. Out of sorts. Out of her mind half the time. Her modicum of success as a poet only made her feel more isolated. Words of praise from her peers made her feel more unworthy, left her searching. Feeling dread in the happiest moments, because when the door was open to let in joy something else came in and took up residence. Meanwhile, Louis would say, "Why can't you just be happy?"

Annabel rolled over, snoring lightly, almost imperceptibly.

Dorothy smiled. Then saw that it was 12:37 a.m. and frowned. She'd sat down hours ago and couldn't remember what she'd done for most of that time. *Was that how it was when I was on the ferry? Was I staring into space, daydreaming?*

She closed her eyes and felt the reverberations of her treatment sessions. The sounds, the smells, the tastes, and the touch of the people she'd known, longed for, and lost, how she felt inside the memory of the bleeding woman in the alley, so alone, unremembered, unloved, so homesick and so heartbroken.

Dorothy heard footsteps and opened her

eyes, expecting — hoping — to see someone other than Louis, who stood in the dimly lit doorway. With only the glow of a nightlight, Dorothy saw that his hair was a mess. He had a glass in his hand, a handle of whiskey or scotch. He didn't drink much, if at all, a token restraint that stood in place of other, better personality traits.

"I thought you went to bed?" she said.

"I did. I tried. Too restless to sleep. How are you?" Polite small talk between strangers. "You've been in here a while. I thought you'd just tucked in with Annabel."

Dorothy brushed a lock of hair from her sleeping daughter's cheek. "I couldn't sleep either. Too worried, I guess. Plus, your mother always gets me spun up, and there's no way I can ever explain anything to her. Especially after . . ."

Dorothy watched him nod and sip his drink, ice clinking in his glass.

"What happened on the ferry?" he said. "That was bad."

"I'm sorry."

"Your treatments . . ."

"They're helping."

"Helping who?"

Dorothy held her head in her hands.

"Look," he said. "I'm sorry about having you followed. It was my bad idea and she

424

ran with it. I know my mother can be stubborn and willful and full of her own conceits and agendas, but she really does just want what's best for all of us. Especially . . ."

"If you think I'm about to let her take Annabel —"

"That's actually not what I came to talk to you about," Louis said quietly. "Though I'm sure we can sort out some kind of parenting plan in the morning. I guess I just couldn't rest without knowing, without talking, without asking at least — about us — and whether you think we should even . . ."

Dorothy waited, but he didn't have the conviction to finish his sentence. He stared down into his glass, too afraid to look her in the eyes as he waited for her answer.

"I don't love you," Dorothy said, turning to the window. She surprised herself at how easy the words came out. She was comforted by the finality of that statement, like a bell that couldn't be unrung. "I'm sorry, Louis. This wasn't the answer I was expecting to discover during my treatments, but this is what I have figured out along the way."

She saw his reflection, nodding in the awkward silence that filled the room.

He finished his drink. "Who *do* you love? Is it this Sam? Is he your doctor?"

Dorothy didn't answer. She stood, walked

to the window, and placed her palms on the cold glass. She stared up into the darkness. The sky was cloudless, filled with stars and possibility, the calm before the storm.

Dorothy didn't sleep at all that night. After Louis finally went to bed, she stayed awake, worried that if she dozed off she might oversleep and wake up with Louis gazing down at her, informing her that his mother had already left with Annabel. Instead, Dorothy walked about, haunting their apartment like a barefoot apparition, listening to the wind and welcoming the nighttime view, the quiet, the solace of being alone. Something that her abandonment issues always prevented her from appreciating. *Is this what peace feels like?* she wondered. She didn't need an answer.

When she could see the faint silhouette of the Cascade Mountains to the east and the horizon purpling with the first glimmers of morning, Dorothy quietly stuffed a backpack with Annabel's clothes, her mittens, and hat. She added her daughter's favorite toys and a few books. She donned the backpack and then picked up the sleeping child, who woke for a moment as she was wrapped in her raincoat, then drifted off again as she was carried to the elevator, her head on her mother's shoulder.

Dorothy's heart sped up as she waited, though she wasn't panicked, even as she heard Louis stop snoring. She didn't look back when the elevator opened. She turned as the doors were closing, bidding farewell to her old life.

She felt a joyful weightlessness as the elevator descended, then heard it say, "Good morning, Ms. Moy. You're up awfully early. Might I offer you directions to a nice coffee shop or patisserie? Perhaps I could summon a car for you?"

"That won't be necessary. Thank you, though."

When they neared the ground floor, the elevator spoke again. "I normally offer the daily weather forecast, but as I'm sure you know, Typhoon Tenjin is now predicted to make landfall in the Northwest within forty-eight hours. Could I make you a hotel reservation someplace away from the flood zone?"

"I'll be fine, thank you." Dorothy looked up at the security camera in the elevator that she knew was recording her. Then she said, "On second thought, please summon a car and make a weeklong reservation in Boise. No hotel preference. Surprise me."

The elevator buttons pulsed for a moment.

"You're all set. Your car will be here in approximately twelve minutes, and I made you a lovely reservation at the Owyhee Plaza Hotel in downtown Boise, Idaho. An itinerary with recommended dining and entertainment possibilities has been sent to your mobile device. Please drive safely, Ms. Moy, and enjoy your trip."

Outside, Dorothy didn't wait for the car. She hastened toward the nearest subway stop, took one last look at the horizon, which had become a wall of cirrus clouds, then descended the concrete stairs. While waiting, she whispered words of comfort and assurance to Annabel, who began to stir. "Shhh . . . just close your eyes, Babybel. Everything's going to be okay." Dorothy expected questions about where they were going and why Louis wasn't coming with them. Instead she felt Annabel squeeze tightly, then relax as she exhaled. Dorothy felt her daughter's breath on her neck.

On the speeding train, Dorothy slowed down long enough for fatigue to catch up to her. She sat in a rear car, her back to a window where she could rest her head against the cool glass, Annabel asleep in her arms. She regarded the other passengers, a sparse mixture of early risers heading away from the storm, suitcases and backpacks tucked between their legs, and those heading home far too late, from night jobs or Typhoon parties, looking like hangovers in human form. Dorothy avoided eye contact and stared out the opposite window, past the empty seats across from her, watching the flicker of advertisements and graffiti on the station walls as the train sped by, those images interrupted by semidarkness as the train slipped through sections of the subway where the lights were out. She appreciated each respite of shadow, then each refulgent return, imagining the back-and-forth moments as larger passages of time, tidal echoes of days and nights, years and lifetimes. Then in the long tunnel beneath Beacon Hill, she saw a woman about her age sit down across from her. She had dark hair, cut short with Medusa-like curls that framed her face. On her lap was a violin case. Dorothy felt oddly at home in her company. *Maybe she's running away as well.* Growing up in a coarse carnival of group homes, Dorothy learned to trust her intuition when it came to the plight of strangers, runaways, and the discarded.

The woman smiled warmly as though in greeting, and then spoke with a British accent. "You have a beautiful girl there, that little lass of yours."

"Thank you," Dorothy heard herself say. She looked at the woman, trying not to stare, but there was something oddly familiar about her.

"Promise me you'll look out for her when the time comes."

Before Dorothy could reply the train emerged from the tunnel.

The woman was gone.

"I promise," Dorothy said to the empty seat where the woman had just been.

Dorothy held on to Annabel and finally surrendered to the rhythm of the train, the motion, the white noise, the flicker of lights, which all conspired to bring Dorothy closer to the destination she'd been avoiding: sleep.

17
ZOE

(1927)

When Zoe finally slept, she dreamed of lying beneath a great, fruited tree on a sunny afternoon, her head in Mrs. Bidwell's lap as her teacher brushed the hair from Zoe's eyes. She looked up and her teacher was everything to her. She was warm. Her clothing smelled like summer. Her eyes were oases of contentment, blue-green and shimmering, too good to be true and too inviting to be believed. She leaned down, her lips drawing closer. Zoe's heart was pounding.

That's when Zoe opened her eyes and realized someone was banging on the door to the bedroom she shared with two other girls, Lily and Mildred. An orange glow peeked through the trees outside their window. She sat up as Mildred shouted, "Go away, we're dead. Have some respect." The knocking continued until Lily groaned

431

and padded across the room in her pajamas and socks to open the door.

Three senior girls stood in the hallway, fully dressed.

"Step aside, we're here for her."

Zoe saw them pointing in her direction and froze, panicked that she'd been caught, seen last night in a moment of impropriety with her teacher. *But we didn't do anything.* Zoe tried to calm herself long enough to formulate a defense.

The girls in the doorway smiled. "She's been reassigned."

"What?" Zoe sat up. "This is my room."

"Not anymore. Get your things. You have five minutes."

"Says who?"

"The new school marshal."

Zoe groaned and rolled her eyes as she remembered last night's meeting where teachers and student body had collectively decided to run the school as a fascist state, a weeklong object lesson in government. Her roommates shook their heads. Mildred pulled a blanket over her face, trying to go back to sleep.

"Are you seriously going to let them do this?" she said to her roommates.

Lily went back to bed and put a pillow over her head.

"Just do as they say and leave us out of it." Then Mildred mumbled, "You'll be fine, Z. Just play along. Besides, better you than us."

Zoe pulled her suitcase out from beneath her bed. She sat it on the mattress and began piling her clothing and personal effects inside.

"No books," the older girl said.

"What are you talking about?" Zoe asked. "These are my textbooks! I need these for my classes. How am I supposed to do my homework?"

The older girl grabbed a waste basket and stepped forward. She began tossing Zoe's books into the trash. "You won't need any of these where you are going. You're not allowed to attend class anymore until further notice. You've been given work detail. And this." She held up the book of poetry that had been given to her by Mrs. Bidwell, whom Zoe still felt uncomfortable calling by her first name, Alyce.

"All poetry and fiction have been declared contraband. The school marshal has determined they will only weaken your mind and confuse you." The girl threw it in the trash.

Zoe snatched the book of poetry from the waste bin and returned it to her now-empty bookshelf. "Can I at least get dressed?"

The girls stared at her, and for a moment Zoe was astonished that she'd actually asked permission. She got dressed, shaking her head at how quickly people changed.

Zoe was escorted to a large shed and told to wait inside with a handful of students. The other children — none older than twelve — who'd been rousted from their sleep and brought to this field at sunrise were Karan and Neysa, a brother and sister from India, Koji from Japan, Zofia from Poland, and Ethan, Samuel, and Naomi, who were all Jewish. Much to Zoe's surprise, there was also Theo, the handsome lad whose tongue-in-cheek suggestion that they operate the school as an authoritarian regime had been taken seriously and started this Sisyphean ball rolling. He'd arrived under escort as well and looked dejected, resigned to be among them.

"Are you here to supervise us personally?" Zoe asked. Her voice was a cannon loaded with accusation, her fuse of anger lit and burning.

"No. I'm here living with my regret, mainly," Theo said. "I was elected to be the leader for the duration of this exercise. We spent a few hours drafting a constitution. We even planned rules for class attendance,

434

work, and chores, and how meals would be prepared and served. But it didn't take long before members of our group began pointing out their concerns. That they didn't like how some of us chose not to attend class, the ones who liked to lie about all day. Then someone complained about the students with no interest in math and science. So, music, art, and literature were banned. French and Spanish would no longer be taught, only the Queen's English, for efficiency. And no one likes chores, of course, so we created one group to do them exclusively. You all come from a class of people subjugated by British rule, so by extension, that group is you."

"Then what are you doing here?" Zoe asked.

"Oh, that," Theo said as he looked about. "I thought I had a plan for organized, benevolent rule. It didn't seem that terrible of an idea, until I was set upon at five a.m. by a group of boys, who bound and gagged me. Apparently, someone else had another meeting after I went to bed. While I slept, they gathered another group, within the whole. I should have seen it coming." He sat down and scratched his head. "The maiden voyage of our new government hadn't even set sail and there was already a mutiny."

"Led by who?" Zoe asked, though she suspected she already knew.

"Good morning."

Zoe turned and saw Guto standing in the light. He wore a crisp white shirt and a black tie, tucked between his breast buttons. He was flanked by other boys and a few of the younger girls, who all wore white shirts and black ties.

Guto held up a fistful of black ribbons. He tossed them on the ground. "These are for you. Each of you needs to wear one around your neck, day and night. A collar, so to speak, so we know who is in charge and who is not."

"Oh, this is nonsense," Zoe said. "I don't have to go along with any of this. I'm not playing your silly game." As she spoke she wondered where the grown-ups were. Where their schoolmaster was? "The teachers will put a stop to this."

"Most of the teachers and staff are in town," Guto said. "I've given them a forty-eight-hour holiday. Those who didn't take me up on my magnanimous offer are confined to the faculty residences, including the headmaster. It's just us for now."

"Fine, you can do what you want, but I'm leaving."

"You could leave." Guto held up the book of poetry that had been given to her by Mrs. Bidwell. "But since you left this behind . . ." He opened the cover. "Look, there's even an inscription from one of the teachers."

Zoe froze.

"May you be released from grueling anxiety and be my ally in love's battle."

"That's a gift! It belongs to me!"

"And you wrote something quite interesting beneath, shall I read it to everyone?"

Zoe fell silent as she remembered what she'd written. The words were almost like a prayer, an ablution that she recited in her mind in the morning, all day, and into the night. *Dear Lady, don't crush my heart with pain and sorrows. But come here, if ever before, when you heard my far-off cry.*

"I'll take care of your possessions *and* your secrets," Guto said, closing the book. "All I ask is that you show your allegiance by doing as you are told."

Zoe stared him down until he looked away, then she tied the ribbon around her neck. As did Theo. As did their younger classmates, all following suit, all falling in line.

Zoe, Theo, and the others were led to the school garden, a fenced acre of squash, zucchini, cabbage, endive, carrots, Brussels sprouts, turnips, parsnips, and onions. There were also rows of tomatoes and strawberries. Guto knelt down, plucked a ripe berry, and took a bite. Then he wiped his chin and threw the rest away.

"You will be called the Extraneis," Guto explained.

Zoe and the Theo groaned. *Outsiders.* They remembered the word from their Latin class. Though Zoe wasn't sure if the name was meant literally — as she looked at the field — or figuratively as she touched the ribbon around her neck, loosening it a tad.

Guto told them to remove their shoes and hand them over.

Zoe looked at him, confused.

"It's so you don't run away," one of Guto's girls said with mock sympathy as the shoes were taken from the younger children. "We'll give them back at supper."

Zoe hesitated, then remembered that Guto had her book. She unlaced her leather shoes, removed her socks, and felt the cool earth, pebbles between her toes. She told herself that if she had to, she'd go wherever she needed to barefoot.

Guto pointed them to a wheelbarrow that was filled with hand trowels, shovels, hoes, and rakes. "You will report here at this hour each morning for garden duty. At noon, you will be escorted to the back of the kitchen where you will take your meals, outside. You will be given fifteen minutes to rest. Then you will come back here to continue your work. You are not allowed to go anywhere else on campus. Zoe and Theo will be your supervisors while you are in the field. They are to follow my instructions and you are to follow theirs. Understand?"

Zoe heard one of the girls say, "This is stupid." It was Zofia.

"I don't want to do this," she said in a Polish accent as she started to walk away. "I'm telling the headmaster and the teachers that you're making us be your slaves."

Zoe looked at Guto, expecting him to do something, but he merely stared back at her, raising one eyebrow and smiling. She thought about her book. The love letter she wrote was still inside, with Mrs. Bidwell's name on it.

Zoe hung her head. "Zofia," she said with a sigh as the younger girl turned around. "This is what the headmaster decided we should do. It's just a lesson, okay. He wanted us to learn and appreciate other systems of government."

Zofia stopped, still seeming unconvinced.

"Look," Zoe said. "You can eat strawberries all day if you want."

Zofia said, "Fine." She followed Zoe to the garden tools and grabbed a rake.

That evening, at supper, Zoe, Theo, and the rest were told that once again they would have to eat outside while the other students had use of the dining hall.

"It's fine, everyone," Zoe told the younger kids with a grim smile. "We'll pretend we're having a picnic."

They found a soft bed of grass and everyone spread out.

"I'm not hungry. I'm going to go jump in the pool," Zofia said. She began to undress, when Zoe remembered her note in the hands of Guto and stopped her.

"We shouldn't," she tried to reason with the girl. "We're all so muddy, we might make the water dirty for everyone else, and you wouldn't want that, would you?"

Zofia shook her head. "I don't care."

"But you just ate." Zoe switched to plan B. "Teachers always say we should avoid swimming after we eat, and by the time we wait it will be dark already."

Zoe was grateful that her reasoning was enough to convince the younger girl. Though Zoe did feel bad considering how many times she and the older kids had gone skinny-dipping in the pool well after dark.

After dinner, a messenger told them that their shoes could be found in the now-defunct art studio. Inside they discovered that all the easels and painting supplies had been stuffed into supply closets. Now it was just an empty room, a wooden hollow, like the cargo hold of a ship but with paint on the floor and on the walls. In the middle of the studio they found their suitcases and enough blankets and pillows for all of them.

Zoe curled up on the floor, dirty and exhausted. As did the others.

The teachers and headmaster will be back in charge in a week.

Zofia sat up, rubbing her eyes as she turned to Zoe. "I can't sleep without a story." Karan and Neysa both chimed in, pouting, "We can't either."

Zoe looked around for something to read, then shrugged at Theo and gathered the littles around her as she spoke softly. "There once was a girl who lived in a kingdom by the sea, who was in love with a very special person. A person smarter than her, stronger than her, braver than her. But this person was cursed by a maleficent mapmaker — an evil, wicked, cruel, and callous man — who knew every corner of the world, but could

441

never read the map of someone's heart."

"Hearts don't have maps," Zofia said.

Zoe smiled. "Oh, but they do. They're written inside you, and only a very special person can read it and follow its directions to a buried treasure." Zoe touched the place above her heart. "We all have a buried treasure and it's right here."

Zoe told the story, making up each moment as she went, about a girl who followed her heart map across a great ocean made of purple flowers. About following tigers that roared through the sky. She spun her tale until the children began to drift off, happy and content in a made-up world where the stars rise in their true love's eyes.

Zoe touched the black ribbon around her neck and looked toward the windows and light wells, wondering if Mrs. Bidwell was nearby or had gone home. Wherever she was, Zoe could endure whatever nonsense Guto presented. *This was not permanent and in the end, he's only alienating himself from students and staffers alike. It's hard to be dismissed from Summerhill for poor behavior, but this might do it,* Zoe thought. She might be giving Guto just enough ribbon to strangle himself.

When she heard the younger students snoring, Zoe closed her eyes to try to sleep.

She smelled the stale wool of the blankets, paint and solvent that had become a permanent fixture of the room, and, much to her surprise, the faint hint of something lovely, something floral and fragrant. She looked up and noticed a wreath of violets hanging from the ceiling by a bit of twine.

She sat up, looked around, and found a small stepladder.

"What are you doing?" Theo whispered in the fading light.

She ignored him, positioned the stepladder, climbed up, and untied the wreath, which felt soft and cool in her hands. She held the circle of green and purple to her nose and inhaled the happiness, the hope in that circlet of flowers.

"I guess they didn't dispose of all the art," Theo said, rolling over and pulling up his blanket. "What are you going to do with that, wear it to bed?"

She looked at him, then at the door. "I'm going out for a walk."

Zoe crept through the shadows, wary that Guto and his lot might have monitors watching them, creeping about, up to no good. But the evening was peaceful, quiet but for a symphony of crickets as she walked back to her favorite glade, which was empty, except for a woman sitting at a picnic table, reading a book by lamplight.

Zoe carried the wreath, her heart speeding up with each step.

Mrs. Bidwell looked up from her book. "My mother used to say that flowers have a language all their own. They're Victorian symbols that say something about the giver and the receiver." She smiled. "I see you got my message."

Zoe sat next to her teacher, waited a moment, then threw her arms around her. She hugged Mrs. Bidwell, who hesitated, then hugged her back.

"I'm so glad you're here," Zoe said.

Zoe thought about what Mrs. Bidwell's life at home must be like. How lonely it must be to want to hang out on the school grounds while it was still in the grip of Guto's cruel social experiment. "What are you reading?"

"It's a study of Edgar Allan Poe," Mrs. Bidwell said, closing the book. "About how Poe writes about women who are mentally strong and have moral fibers more powerful than their male counterparts. Like Ligeia, who is fierce, but eventually she dies. It seems that all of Poe's women are fated to tragic ends. Madeline Usher, Berenice, Annabel Lee. They're the ideal feminine, and yet they all die in mysterious ways."

The sun disappeared and Zoe felt a cool breeze. She sat closer. "Maybe they put their fates in the hands of the wrong people?" Zoe spoke, thinking about Mrs. Bidwell's husband. She watched her nod in agreement. Then Mrs. Bidwell held Zoe's hand, causing her heart to race. She felt warm and head-spinningly happy. She held on, not wanting to let go as her teacher stood in front of her, taking both of Zoe's hands, letting an unspoken moment pass like a warm breeze, then she let go and took the wreath from Zoe's lap.

Mrs. Bidwell smiled as she placed the ring of laurels atop Zoe's head.

"Be mindful of whose hands you place your fate in, Zou yi," Mrs. Bidwell said.

"I will, Alyce." Zoe inhaled the fragrance of the wreath.

"That would make me very happy." Mrs. Bidwell kissed her fingertips, then touched them to Zoe's cheek. Her teacher was smiling, but her eyes betrayed a certain sadness. She sighed and climbed atop the picnic table, sitting behind Zoe, one leg on either side. She felt Mrs. Bidwell's slender fingers running through her long dark hair and leaned back as her teacher moved it aside. Zoe's arms turned to gooseflesh. She felt the gentle exhalation of breath on the back of her neck. She trembled, heart racing, and closed her eyes in anticipation. Then Zoe realized her teacher was untying the black ribbon from around her neck, freeing her.

"The most important lesson I can teach you," she spoke softly as she used the strip of fabric to tie Zoe's hair, "is to never settle for what others want you to be. Find a way to be the person you need to be to truly be happy. Don't give in to convention. Don't make the same mistake I did. Marriage to the wrong person is like stepping in quicksand, you lose yourself, bit by bit, slowly suffocating until you disappear completely."

In that moment, Zoe's heart didn't just long for her teacher, it broke for the young woman Mrs. Bidwell must have once wanted to become. The woman named Alyce was stuck in the only life available to her. In that life, Alyce had been replaced with a shadow bearing a man's last name. Despite all that, Mrs. Bidwell was still the most strident, intelligent, and bravehearted woman Zoe had ever known. A maverick teacher at a maverick school, yet trapped in an unhappy marriage to conformity.

"Why can't you leave?" Zoe asked as she looked back at her teacher, whose fair skin appeared spectral in the lamplight.

Zoe tried to interpret the wordless reaction of her teacher. A sad smile. A pitying look, but also perhaps a yearning for the innocence of youth.

"You're so dear," Mrs. Bidwell said. "Unfortunately, the state can only grant me a divorce if I prove cruelty, or insanity, or adultery. I can't even prove desertion, since he comes home at least once or twice a year. Who knows where he really is or what he's up to when he's so far from home? But as long as he comes back once in a while — like he did this week — I have to play the role of dutiful wife. Even though he always accuses *me* of being unfaithful. I'm like a toy on a shelf that he rarely plays with or even remembers. Yet if his toy goes missing . . ." She sighed and looked up at the stars, as though waiting for a wish to come true. "Some prisons have armed guards, bars, and iron gates, and some have a white picket fence and a garden."

Zoe listened, but what echoed in her mind were the words *this week.*

He's home. That's why she's here. Avoiding the fate of domestic subjugation.

"I'm so sorry. I must apologize," Mrs. Bidwell said, flustered with emotions bordering on despair. "Please forgive me. I shouldn't be discussing these things, burdening you with my problems. It serves no useful purpose. I need to try again, to spend more time loving who my husband is instead of hating who he isn't."

"You never need to apologize," Zoe said. "I feel gifted whenever you share anything with me, especially the books."

Zoe danced around her own truthful moment. She offered consolation to her young teacher when what she wanted to do was ask, *Who do you wish he was?*

"I wish," Mrs. Bidwell said. "I wish I didn't have to leave you, but it's getting late. I told Stanley I had work to do, but I can't be gone so long or he'll have a fit."

They regarded each other, and for a moment Zoe felt as though they were trying to read each other's minds as easily as they could read each other's hearts.

Mrs. Bidwell interrupted their brief reverie to kiss Zoe on the cheek. "Good night, Zou yi." She hastened away, leaving the oil lamp behind.

Zoe sat lingering in the moment as the lamp flickered. "Good night, Alyce." She sighed, then watched as her teacher became one with the shadows.

After a full week of Zoe and the rest of the Extraneis laboring in the garden, Guto showed up midmorning with a wooden folding chair. He claimed he was there to supervise their progress and offer suggestions. Instead, he sat with his feet on a stump and read Zoe's book. "Hey, you know what? This is really good," he taunted.

Zoe tried her best to ignore him, to focus on the work.

She and Theo led the younger ones to a cabbage patch on the far side of the garden, framed by two rows of lavender. The woody, balsamic fragrance was soothing, and reminded her of Alyce, whom she hadn't seen the rest of the week. There had been no more floral surprises, no readings in the glade. Zoe was left counting the days, not only until this Sunday when they'd be free from this odious assignment, but because at their all-school meeting she'd finally be able to see her teacher again. The thought made her feel lighter, made the birds' melodic chirping in her ears sound filled with hopeful purpose, a gentle reminder that this place could be a paradise at times.

But every time Zoe felt a fractional moment of peace, a tiny respite, Guto would pipe up. "Who knew poetry could be so interesting?" He slowly licked his finger and turned the page. "Would you like me to read some to you?"

Zoe knelt in the dirt, pulling weeds, wiping the sweat from her brow.

Only a few more days of this.

She squinted back and saw Zofia as the younger girl dropped her rake and stomped barefoot toward Guto, muttering more loudly with each step.

Theo saw her too and leaned on his shovel. "Zofia, come back . . ."

Guto looked up from his book and smiled.

"I'm not playing your stupid game anymore," Zofia shouted, venting her anger and frustration to Guto and anyone else who was listening. "You can't make me!"

Zoe stood, stretching her back. She sighed and walked toward them as Zofia was yelling at the larger boy, who closed the book. He looked annoyed, as though she were interrupting a moment of deep thought. Then he stood, sneered, and shoved the girl, who stumbled and fell to the ground, stunned for a moment, mouth open.

She began crying.

"Hey!" Zoe shouted. "That's enough."

She walked toward Guto, removing the scarf she wore around her neck to prevent sunburn and wrapping it around her fist, as the other kids looked on.

"You're not wearing your ribbon?" Guto said. "There will be consequences. Put it on now or I'll tell the kitchen to serve you nothing but bread and water."

Zoe kept coming.

"Fine," Guto said, nervously tossing the book at the ground near Zoe's feet. "Take it. But now I'm going to starve all of you."

He looked at her with shark eyes as she bent down and picked up the book. She tried to flatten the cover, which was now bent. She brushed off the dirt, flipping through the pages. No pages had been torn out, but something was missing. "Where is it?"

"Where's what?"

"Give it back."

"Give what back?"

"I mean it."

"Or what . . ."

Guto barely got the words out as Zoe ran headlong and tackled him.

She landed heavily upon him as they tumbled to the dirt. She heard the wind knocked out of him as he hit the ground with a heavy thud. Her heart raced, anger in her veins, her knees skinned, bloody. He felt soft and doughy, struggling against her, reeking of boy sweat and cigarette smoke. He fought back and grabbed her wrist, digging in his fingernails. The other hand pushed frantically against her face, scratching her, pulling her hair. She heard yelling, cheering from the other students. Theo's voice floated above the din, pleading for calm. She remembered how Guto's lips felt, his hand on the back of her head, gripping her hair, how he tried to shove his tongue down her throat, how he tasted, how sick it made her feel, how weak and helpless. She knocked his hand away and punched him hard in the face until he let go. Then she hit him, again and again and again, until her knuckles were bloody. Still he squirmed beneath her, laughing hysterically.

"Where is it!?" she shouted.

She punched him again and felt her knuckles ache.

"I don't have it." He smiled, gasping for breath.

"Where's the letter I wrote!?" Zoe's hand was on his collar. She ripped a button as he tried to pull away. "What did you do with my letter?"

"Do?" Guto asked with a giggle as though the answer were obvious, inevitable, like how the sun rises in the east, how storm clouds bring rain. He touched his swollen upper lip. "I mailed it, you daft twat. You stupid chink."

Zoe froze, her arm in midair, her hand a swollen fist.

"Oh, no?" he said with a mocking pout. "Did you not want me to?"

She felt a tightness in her jaw as he kept laughing, even as blood ran from his nose. He smiled, dirt on his face, blood on his teeth and gums.

He wiped his mouth with the back of his hand. "You should thank me."

What have I done?

She looked around at the others, who went from cheering to bewilderment.

"I did you a favor," Guto said. "You and your special friend."

Zoe stood up, trying to catch her breath, seething, horrified, embarrassed, scared, knowing that Mr. Bidwell — Stanley — was home and had likely received the mail. This was why Alyce stayed away all week. This was why her goodbye felt final.

Guto was playing a sick, twisted game, and Zoe thought she was always one move ahead of him, that she could run out the clock. But while she'd been playing by the rules, he had literally gone and sacrificed her queen.

Zoe ran to Mrs. Bidwell's office, swimming in apologies, rehearsing the words she would say. Hoping that her teacher would be there and would somehow understand.

I'm so sorry. I love the book you gave me. I got carried away. I didn't mean to . . .

When she opened the door, the headmaster was there, pipe in hand, looking scholarly in a tweed jacket, a rolled-up newspaper beneath his arm. He was with two other students, who looked at Zoe and shrugged apologetically.

Zoe felt heartsick when she saw them taking down Mrs. Bidwell's poster calendar for the Royal Scot, the train between London and Glasgow. Zoe wished she could board that steam locomotive and escape to the Highlands. Instead she stood and watched helplessly as her peers removed framed pictures and certificates from the walls. Photos of Mrs. Bidwell's parents, her family, who smiled earnestly for the camera, and her husband, who did not. The headmaster sat down in Mrs. Bidwell's wooden chair, which creaked beneath his weight.

Zoe felt his eyes upon her. When she met his gaze, she saw that his expression was filled with pity, compassion, but not surprise. He nodded soberly, his countenance beleaguered with grudging acceptance, if not surrender.

"Thank you, that will be all," the headmaster said to the other students. "Please take what you've packed and leave the boxes by the gatehouse at the school entrance. Mr. Bidwell will be coming to collect them this afternoon."

Zoe felt as though she were sinking in a sea of regret, drowning in anger, caught in an undertow of jealousy at the thought of Mrs. Bidwell's husband finally coming home to be with his neglected wife. She pictured him reading the letter. The argument that must have ensued. The rage. She pictured Alyce in an infirmary, beaten, her face bruised and swollen.

"Where is she, Mrs. Bidwell? Is she all right?"

It's all my fault.

The headmaster sighed and chewed on the end of his pipe. He looked sad and weary. He gazed out the window, but Zoe could see that he was really just staring at his own reflection. "I don't like this any more than you do, my dear."

"What happened?" Zoe asked, but part of her already knew.

"Mrs. Bidwell was a fine teacher. One of the best we've ever had. She had a certain . . . vitality. She also had a well of strength, fortitude beyond her years."

"What do you mean, *had*?"

The headmaster took the rolled-up newspaper from beneath his arm and set it on

455

the desk as though it were a telegram informing him of the death of a loved one, a biopsy report, an obituary. The day's headline on the *Leiston Observer* read: *SCHOOLMISTRESS EMBROILED IN TAW-DRY AFFAIR WITH FEMALE STUDENT, AGE SIXTEEN, CLAIMS HUSBAND.*

Zoe grew pale skimming the article. Much of it featured Mr. Bidwell's accolades in the Royal Cartographic Society, his travels to Burma and Siam to help map new lines for the British Colonial Railroad, his lofty, worldly status in their humble community. The résumé of his wife, however, was absent. Instead the newspaper listed her supposed improprieties as a teacher, speculated on her corrupting influence, her perversions and wantonness. Concluding with her ultimate failure as a woman and wife, her unwillingness to quit teaching and bear children.

The headmaster looked at Zoe. "You know I would do nearly anything for my students, my teachers, for the workers and staff."

"But we didn't do anything! We discussed poetry."

The headmaster's hair seemed grayer. The lines on his face deeper. "Zoe, I was prepared to go down with the ship. To let them try. Let them come for us. This place is everything to me, and yet I was ready to risk it all to do what's right."

"Then why didn't you?"

The headmaster drummed his fingers on Mrs. Bidwell's desk.

"Because she resigned first."

Zoe remembered a line from the book of poetry Mrs. Bidwell gave her. She felt the words: *It is as if my tongue is broken, a subtle fire has run over my skin, I cannot see anything with my eyes, my ears, buzzing.*

The headmaster stood up, looking about the near-empty office. "She loved this place, the students, the teachers, the ideals we aspired to live by." He turned to Zoe. "But she wasn't going to allow herself to be the reason we fail."

Zoe didn't know what was worse, Mrs. Bidwell being forced to resign, embroiled in scandal, or knowing she was the cause. "Can I see her?"

The headmaster rubbed the stubble on his chin. "Someday, perhaps."

"Her husband is not going to punish the school. For that I am grateful. I've managed to convince him that you're young and impressionable and that none of this was your doing, so you're not in any trouble. The newspaper didn't even name you."

457

"Let them!" Zoe argued. "I'm not ashamed." Yet even as she spoke, she realized that Guto would tell and soon the entire school would know. The town, eventually.

"It's too late, she's already left Leiston." The headmaster looked as though a part of him was breaking inside. He shook his head. "It's done."

Zoe hung on, hoping that she'd heard the worst of it, that she lost her teacher, that Mrs. Bidwell had lost her job, lost whatever had transpired between them. But she would be okay, elsewhere, that she would recover from this. The damage wasn't permanent. But the look on the headmaster's face revealed something else.

"He's had her committed to Broadmoor," the headmaster said. "He is her husband, after all, and unfortunately it is fully within his legal power to do so. I'm afraid there's nothing anyone can do. This world is not deserving of people like Mrs. Bidwell. Yet for all of us, and that means you, my dear, she went willingly."

The words found purchase in Zoe's mind, and she felt as though the room were spinning. She blinked and heard the hissing of a radiator.

"I'm very sorry," the headmaster said.

She shook her head, unable to speak.

"I don't know why he doesn't divorce her if he's so displeased," the headmaster said. "I believe it would be the right thing for both of them, and certainly the best thing for Mrs. Bidwell. To send someone to Broadmoor — an asylum for the criminally insane — why would anyone do such a dreadful thing? She's not insane and she's certainly not a common criminal."

The headmaster noticed how pale Zoe looked. "Are you all right, my dear?"

Zoe struggled to hold back tears as she bolted from the office.

Zoe became the talk of the school.

She thought that the weeks would ease the gossip, but everywhere she went, the other students continued to stare. Some laughed. Though after seeing Guto walk around with a broken nose and two black eyes, no one dared confront her or tease her. Instead they laid siege to her heart, catapulting volleys of silence. Firing trebuchets of piercing glances that always managed to find their target even if she was seeking refuge in the garden, or in the library, or like today, holding her breath at the bottom of the swimming pool.

Zoe shivered underwater. She looked up

and the blue sky looked welcoming through her watery lens. She sat on the bottom for as long as she could, thinking of Mrs. Bidwell until her heart, like her burning lungs, felt ready to burst. She pushed from the bottom, kicking until she broke the surface, gasping for air.

She was completely alone. No one else, not even the littles, cared to swim this late in the year, which was fine by Zoe, who toweled off and turned to the empty tree branch where Mrs. Bidwell used to sit and play her violin, her feet dangling a few feet above the tall grass. Zoe couldn't remember the names of the songs her teacher used to play but hummed the melodies as she quickly got dressed. Then she climbed up and sat in her teacher's favorite spot in the shade. Zoe took comfort in her book of poetry. On those well-worn pages, she read narratives and pastorals, elegies and villanelles, the voices of women who shared their secrets, their love, their pain, their sacrifice. All so that Zoe's generation and those who follow might find the buried meaning through their shared codex of silence and longing, of suffering and splendor.

In the evenings, Zoe took long walks, gathering violets and wisteria, touching the velvet flowers, inhaling their perfume. Then she'd go to bed after her roommates, who had been more understanding, had settled in for the night.

"It's okay, Z, we all have crushes," Mildred said. "I once thought I was in love with my dentist. I had been dreading it for months, and then when I finally met him, he was younger than I imagined and so handsome. The pain was worth it just to lie there, almost in his arms. He was so close I could feel his breath. I think I might have said some embarrassing things as I was waking up from the ether. I'm not certain, but when I sat up he was blushing and my mum never let me go back."

Lily had a different perspective. "All you have to do, Z, is lean the other way in an overly dramatic fashion. Just shag one of the older boys and let him brag about you, and all of this bollocks about Mrs. Bidwell will be forgotten."

Zoe appreciated their honesty but was unconvinced that replacing one scandal with a lesser one was an effective solution. Besides, she'd gained a reputation, but Mrs. Bidwell had lost her job and quite possibly her entire career. Without being able to financially sustain herself, the possibility of leaving her husband was now nil.

That's when Zoe decided to leave Summerhill and go find her teacher. If she could only speak with Mrs. Bidwell face-to-face, perhaps she could tell Zoe what to do to untangle this skein of romantic misadventure.

Zoe went to bed and, after a restless night, got up the next morning, waited for Lily and Mildred to get dressed and leave for breakfast, then quietly packed a small valise with a change of clothes. She stepped out into a gray, dewy morning, but instead of following the other students in the direction of the dining hall she walked to the gatehouse. She surreptitiously left school property and headed toward town without declaring her absence to her roommates or notifying the school office.

She walked five miles, past the ancient tower of St. Margaret's church, past the steam works that made portable engines, until she reached the town square in Leiston.

There she waited for a postbus to Crowthorne.

Outside the Royal Mail office, she sat on a bench in the shade of the old brick building, next to an old man who smelled of whiskey, who edged a little too close to her for comfort as he slurringly introduced himself again and again.

"You're a pretty lass, aren't you? Shouldn't a bird like you be in school?"

She didn't feel like talking and looked away.

He kept pestering her in a way she was certain would never happen if she were a boy. She cleared her throat and shook her head, hoping he'd take the hint.

"Where are you going?"

Zoe finally turned and stared at him. "Crowthorne." Her tone of voice said, *Leave me alone.* "I'm going to Broadmoor."

The man's eyes widened. Even drunk, he recognized the name of the asylum and found a place farther down the bench. He didn't speak to her again.

When a horsebus finally arrived, the carriage was packed. Even the garden seat on top was completely occupied, so Zoe paid the postie and stood on the knifeboard, where she held on tight as they bumped along the pitted country road.

They passed a pear orchard, and she smelled burning tar from the smudge pots beneath each tree. Zoe's nose itched and her eyes watered as she thought about what she would say to her teacher. She'd written several new poems, all of them for Mrs. Bidwell. Most were about her, though one cursed the villainy of her husband. But Zoe had kept them hidden at school, guarded, fearful that if discovered they would only make Mrs. Bidwell's predicament worse.

Could it get any worse?

When she finally arrived in Crowthorne, Zoe followed wooden signs in the village to Broadmoor, which was hard to miss because the building looked more like a penitentiary than a hospital, with tall curtains of red brick and enormous twin towers flanking a gated entry. Everywhere she looked, the windows had been barred. Zoe heard laughing in the distance, somewhere inside, followed by hysterical wailing. She shuddered at the thought of Alyce locked away somewhere therein.

I'm so sorry.

Girding her courage and her conviction, Zoe strolled through the heavy iron doors, walked through the waiting area, and found an administrative desk. She signed in as a visitor for Mrs. Bidwell, keeping her eyes down, worried that the clerk might recognize her as the mysterious girl alluded to in the scandal-ridden newspapers. But the woman merely stamped the time on a visitor's pass, handed it to Zoe, and barked, "Next!" to the person standing behind her in line.

With pass in hand, Zoe was directed to a

small courtyard used for visitation. She sat at a picnic table, wary of the staff who wore the uniforms of prison officers instead of the capes of the Royal College of Nursing. Broadmoor was supposed to be a hospital, but when the patients are all deemed criminally insane, the bedside care evoked severity and punishment, instead of looking out for the health and well-being of the residents.

Zoe spent forty restless minutes watching visitors and patients come and go. She tried not to stare, casually observing how some of the visitors shared tears, some shared letters, while some consoled their loved ones as they keened and quaked with madness.

A door on the other side of the courtyard finally creaked open and a man in a dark blue uniform pointed toward her. Her heart raced when she saw the woman she'd known as Mrs. Bidwell step out of the shadows, squinting up at the overcast sky. The woman who once looked so strong, so confident, yet always softened by her wry sense of humor now looked like a beleaguered doppelganger, a wilted flower, a funhouse mirror reflection of the person Zoe hoped to find. She stood and tried to smile, but fought back tears when her teacher removed her hat. Alyce's head was shaved and bandaged. She looked wan and pale, in a tattered gray dress that Zoe realized had once been white in a previous lifetime. There were stains and soil marks, rips that had been patched and repaired by hands better suited to meat-cutting than sewing. She wondered how many women had worn that frock. Had they worn it until their departure? She feared that the previous occupant of that dress had likely worn it until their demise. The horrible image of male orderlies flashed through Zoe's imagination. She envisioned men with thick forearms tasked with undressing corpses before cremation, quietly disrobing the men in workmanlike fashion, but ghoulishly leering and touching the bodies of the women. She could almost hear their laughter. Zoe chewed her lip and hoped they laundered the dresses before doling them out to the next patient.

Patient? They're inmates.

Mrs. Bidwell walked across the pebbled courtyard in her bare feet, stepping gingerly, flinching each time she stepped on a sharp rock. Zoe held her breath in anticipation. The bald woman looked around, confused, at the guards, the high windows. She finally sat but stared down at the table.

Zoe tried to make eye contact. "Mrs. Bidwell?"

She said nothing and looked at her hands, which were shaking. She had ligature marks around her wrists, bracelets of purple bruising. Her fingernails were worn down to nubs, bloody and swollen from some self-inflicted abrasion.

"Mrs. Bidwell. It's me, Zoe from school."

She didn't say anything, swatting at imaginary gnats.

What did they do? What did I do?

"Alyce? It's me, Zou yi."

Her chin raised, trembling, as though her neck were being ratcheted by an unseen wrench. She met Zoe's gaze, and for a moment the noble spirit of Mrs. Bidwell returned like a mysterious voice unleashed by some cult mystic, a theosophist, an automatic writer in the throes of a trance.

She smiled through cracked lips and whispered, "Zoe."

Zoe watched as the glimmer of joy and resiliency of Mrs. Bidwell's former self faded. She glanced around and her smile quickly retreated into a place of fear, not just in the shadows of the tall brick walls that loomed above, but back into the dark hollows of her mind. She began to pick at a sore near the corner of her mouth.

"What are you doing here?" Mrs. Bidwell asked as she glanced behind her, as though someone might set upon them and drag them away, screaming. "They might see you. See us." She grit her teeth and her eyes widened. "Oh no, no, no, no, no. They caught you too, didn't they?" Tears formed at the corners of her eyes. "I was afraid of this." She let out a soft cry. "It's all my fault. It's all me. I'm so sorry for what I've done to you. I'm so sorry. I'm so sorry. I'm so sorry . . ."

"You didn't do anything." Zoe placed her hand on Mrs. Bidwell's arm, trying to reassure her, but her former teacher recoiled from Zoe's touch as if her fingers burned.

"I wish we'd never found each other," Mrs. Bidwell said. "I wish . . . I wish . . ."

"It's okay, Alyce," Zoe said, whispering gently, the way you'd coax a dog that had been beaten so much it was afraid to take table scraps when offered. "It's just me, Zoe. I left school and came to see you. I even wrote some poems for you. Would you like me to read one? Or I could just give them to you." She held up a small notebook and began to turn the pages. "I'm sure they're terrible, but . . ."

"You can't." Mrs. Bidwell snatched the book, closed the cover, and placed it on the table. She kept her hand on top as though something horrible and demonic might escape, as if it were a bomb that might explode. "Whatever you've written, burn it." Her voice quavered. "Burn it all. Get rid of everything."

"But . . ."

"Destroy it. Or they'll do to you what they've done to me."

"Alyce . . ."

"Don't let them . . ."

"I won't."

Mrs. Bidwell swallowed. She blinked and looked around again as though waking from a bad dream, more lucid than she'd been just moments before. Then she regarded Zoe again for the first time. "You're my only visitor. The only person I wanted to see. But it's not safe for you." She began to mutter and her voice trailed off.

Zoe thought about Mrs. Bidwell's husband, Stanley, and how he must have abandoned her here. She wondered if he'd grant her a divorce now.

"I'm going to wait for you, Alyce. I'm going to be there for you when you get out, when you come home. I won't let anything bad happen to you again. I don't care what anyone says. I don't care if I have to leave school."

Both of them refrained from talking as a guard walked by, eyeing them.

When he had passed, they held hands across the table. Zoe felt her teacher's warmth, as well as the tremors that racked her body. Zoe felt hopeful as long as they were touching. They seemed stronger together. As though 1 + 1 now equaled 10.

They shared a moment in silence as the words from a favorite poem echoed in Zoe's mind: *We loved with a love that was more than love.*

"I'm going to find a way to take you home," Zoe said.

Her teacher smiled as though enraptured. Then her eyes turned to glass and she slowly let go, as though she were on a boat being pulled out to sea. She stared up at the sky as a formation of geese flew by, struggling against the wind.

Through cracked lips Mrs. Bidwell said, "This *is* my home."

Zoe watched helplessly as Mrs. Bidwell, her teacher, her crush, her love, her shame, her loss, her heart's ruin — her beloved Alyce — touched the bandages around her temple as though she suddenly remembered they were there. She touched the empty space where her hair used to be. She sat in silence for a moment, as though trying to remember something, and when she did it horrified her. She stood up and looked down at Zoe with surrender in her eyes. "Don't be like me, Zou yi."

Zoe opened her mouth as if to speak, but she couldn't find the words.

"Promise me."

■ ■ ■ ■

Aᴄᴛ III

■ ■ ■ ■

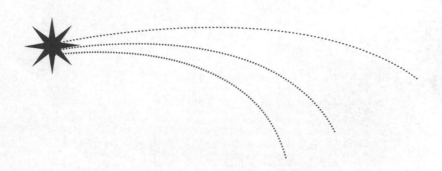

18
FAYE

(1942)

Faye said her goodbyes to the body of John Garland and stepped outside into the light rain and humidity of Kunming. The sun was setting behind the clouds, the sky turning a deeper shade of gray, occasionally illuminated by explosions from the Japanese bombers that had begun targeting the steel and cement plants on the far side of the city. Faye was used to the bright flashes and the booming sounds that followed a few seconds later, like counting time between a bolt of lightning and the thunder rolling in. She felt caught, suspended in that moment in between. That's where she'd met and lost the stranger whom she couldn't stop thinking about, dreaming about; he came and went between blinding light and the resounding darkness.

She glanced up as night fighters, P-40s with Chinese pilots who joined the ranks of the American Volunteer Group, roared overhead. In their wake, cinders from distant fires began to rain from the sky. Faye remembered how last month a textile plant had been hit and the subsequent inferno sent pieces of burning silk into the heavens, where they floated on the heat before drifting down, gently settling upon the muddy streets like brightly colored snow. *Everything here falls apart.*

She heard footsteps and noticed the monk she'd met before.

Like the other townspeople, he too had become inured to the bombing on the horizon. He hastened down the street, walking briskly, but not panicked, not yet.

Faye ran after him, barely avoiding a honking Willys jeep as she wove her way through a small parade of handcarts pulled by merchants who had been selling their wares in an open-air market. The men and women, and in some cases entire families, packed up and were now heading home or to destinations away from the bombing.

The monk was heading in the other direction, swimming upstream against the current of humanity. As Faye followed him, she caught a faint breeze that smelled like camellia and plum blossoms, so light she wondered if she was imagining it. The fragrance was a welcome respite from the harsh odor of benzene and petrol smoke.

When she saw him go inside a small Buddhist temple, she hesitated. She hadn't been to a temple, or any shrine for that matter, since she was a girl in Canton. For years her mother, Lai King, had implored her to at least go during the Lunar New Year.

But Faye never felt as though she belonged in a place so reverent. Because in her teens, she had brought shame to her family, something she never spoke about, never allowed herself to think about. In that absence of thought, the memory faded away, like a god whose existence depends on someone remembering them. Since then she had moved forward. Becoming a nurse, living her life, traveling and helping others, and with each of those actions, those efforts, she sought redemption.

"Why don't you come with me this year?" her ah-ma asked the last time they'd been together. "Just once before you leave for wherever it is you're going this time. You don't have to stay long, you could simply light prayer sticks as an offering. You create good karma that way. It will help you when you travel."

Karma.

"You know why I don't go," Faye said.

477

She looked at her mother and the two exchanged knowing glances, replaying old records, sad lullabies. "Please don't make me speak of it," Faye said as a painful memory washed over her, and when it did she felt as though she were drowning.

The memory was of when she was fourteen.

That was when she didn't leave the confines of her home — not once — for an entire year. The year her father couldn't look her in the eye. The year her mother took care of her but struggled to hide her disappointment. Because that was the year Faye carried a child that belonged to an older boy who had charmed her, lied to her, and then abandoned her. He lived elsewhere and vowed to return, but when he learned that she had given birth to a baby girl, she never heard from him again.

In the days that followed, Faye remained silent as her parents said they'd found a new home for the baby. Faye didn't argue. She didn't fight for her daughter. She felt unworthy of being a mother, because no one of worth wanted her.

In the aftermath, Faye's parents acted as if that entire year had never happened. Though she eventually realized they weren't ashamed, they were just worried. That they cared enough to send her to a university so she could become a nurse. They were so proud of her, yet they avoided the subject whenever someone mentioned the possibility of an arranged marriage, leaving her to hold out for a love marriage that never came. There were widowed men who wanted a caretaker for their children. There were boys from unlucky homes who were deemed unfit for a traditional marriage. Then there were outright scoundrels, men who seemed charming and generous and showered her with conditional affection. But Faye swore to never again be so naïve. She would avoid infatuation and the trouble and heartache that came with it. She refused to settle for just anyone, which sounded brave and noble to some, proud and stubborn to others. But she knew it was merely a way to reframe her perpetual spinsterhood.

Faye stared at the ornate temple door and sighed. When women bled they were discouraged from visiting sacred places, because their prayers would fall on deaf ears. Surely the prayers of a woman who gave away her newborn daughter would always be wasted. Despite her apprehension, she wanted to talk to the monk. If only so she could speak to someone who wouldn't think she was completely mad.

She knocked softly, timidly, then opened the door as small bells announced her presence. She stepped inside, saw a warm glow down the hall, felt the warmth of a fire. She could smell gardenias and the minty, pine scent of eucalyptus.

Faye heard footsteps, then the monk appeared, mildly surprised.

"Oh, hello. It's nice to see you again. If you're seeking shelter, I don't think the bombers can reach this part of the city, which is well defended. Though you're more than welcome to join me for tea. Is something amiss at the morgue?"

I think. I wish. I don't know anymore.

"Everything is fine," Faye said.

She thanked him for his offer, but her tone was laced with apology. She felt like an interloper, an uninvited guest at someone else's holiday feast. She felt shame.

What am I doing?

"Please, come in. All are welcome here," he said. "My name is Shi."

"Fei-jin." For some reason her Chinese name seemed more appropriate here. Not just in its formality, but in its honesty. Then she relaxed and said, "Call me Faye."

She removed her shoes and followed the monk to a small zendo, where a cast-iron stove heated the open space. Faye stepped gently on the wooden floor, tiled with large white and magenta squares in a checkerboard fashion. The floor was adorned with well-worn rugs and cushions. On the far side of the room, illuminated by candles and hanging lanterns, was a wide wooden altar with a golden statue of the seated Buddha, a sun behind it, like a flower, with eight petals radiating from the center. Around the statue were more figures of beings in various states of enlightenment and repose, surrounded by offerings of fruit and flowers, cups of tea and water, and prayer sticks, always in groups of three. Smoke from the burning incense swirled, caressing the statuary as it floated to the ceiling. Faye thought the wisps of smoke looked like butterflies caught in a jar, trying to escape.

She followed the monk up a flight of wooden stairs to a landing with a dozen potted orchids in different stages of growth, beneath a closed window, streaked with rain. The dark sky flashed with bolts of electricity or bomb explosions — from inside it was hard to tell. He led her to a simple kitchen where a kettle was beginning to boil.

"Please, sit," he said.

She sat as he placed two cups on the table.

"Do you live here by yourself?" Faye asked.

The monk thought for a moment, as if this were a question with many possible answers. "I suppose I do. I've never really thought of it that way."

He carefully poured tea for both of them. Found some flower cakes — Dian-style mooncakes — which smelled like the roses that grew nearby in the hills.

"I don't get many visitors these days," he said. "What brings you here? You seemed a bit lost back there, grieving, yet at the same time curious."

Faye thought about her ah-ma, who had come from America as a little girl, fleeing a plague. She rarely talked about her childhood, but when she did she spoke in fables. How her mother was made of fire. How her father had become a ghost hero. Faye wanted to know more, but as a child she never asked. Now she felt like asking.

"I have some odd questions. I'm hoping you might be able to help me?"

Shi nodded and sipped his tea.

"The man back there, the pilot," Faye said. "He was searching for me. Yet I just met him and now he's gone. But I can't help feeling like I've known him. That we've spent time together or will spend time together." Faye thought about the photo with her handwriting on it. She wished she still had it. *Was it real?* The more she thought about the photo, the more she worried the monk must have thought she was a drunkard. Or a poor soul who has seen so much violence, hardship, and death that her mind had found relief in some fictional world in the far corners of her imagination.

"Maybe you have." He smiled. "Maybe you did know him?"

That wasn't the answer Faye was expecting.

"If you're asking me about some sort of past life, or rebirth, I'm afraid I will be of little help at best, and at worst, somewhat disappointing. My Buddhist teaching encourages me not to dwell on those conceptions. Because this thing we might call a past life insinuates that we had a primary one to begin with. It implies the existence of a soul that transmigrates from body to body. That alone can be motivating, almost intoxicating, but that idea is also a myth. The Buddhist view of the nonself rejects the existence of an essential soul. It's my belief that we are just an ever-changing collection of memories that, when added up, create the illusion of self. Does that make sense?"

Faye hesitated, then shook her head.

Shi thought for a moment, then took a sip of tea.

"If you plant an acorn," he said, "it may grow to become an oak tree. Yet there is no acorn within that wooden body. Has the acorn been reborn as a tree? Or does the acorn grow to be something else entirely? It's my belief that the acorn and the tree are an idea, spread out over an abstraction of time. And if that new tree, when fully grown, drops one acorn or one hundred, or a thousand, or ten thousand, that idea keeps progressing as this thing we call *life.*"

Faye listened and tried to comprehend what he was saying, but her thoughts wandered. She remembered how John Garland had tried to smile through his pain and injuries when he saw her on the runway. How natural it felt to hold his hand while she read to him. How when he'd died in her arms it felt as though the sun had gone down in winter, leaving her hoping, longing for spring.

"How does this explain how I felt about the stranger in the morgue?" she asked. "I see people die every day. I care for them. At times, I become quite fond of them. But this one . . ." Faye hesitated, sighed, and then sipped her tea.

"Perhaps he is a part of you," the monk said. "But instead of trees and acorns, you're both waves on the same ocean. Of course, you are separate, you crest and you fall as individual waves, but fundamentally you come from the same place, and when the ocean is calm, it is impossible to tell where he ends and you begin."

Faye furrowed her brow, trying to process what the monk was saying. "I just wish I could remember him the way he remembered me."

The monk began refilling her cup. "When you were sixteen years old, what did you have for lunch the first Thursday after your birthday?"

Faye almost laughed out loud. "I have no idea. How could I possibly remember?"

"You can't." Shi spoke as though he were giving her bad news as gently as possible. "And it's no fault of your own. We're consumed with the here and now, the death and destruction around us, our hopes and dreams, our longings and aspirations, our failings and our regrets. We're too occupied with the abundance of the present and our hopes for the future to remember all the details of the past."

Faye rubbed her forehead. "Is there ever a way to remember?"

"You have to calm your ocean," Shi said warmly. Then the ground shook from distant explosions. The tea rippled in their cups. "You are welcome to go downstairs and meditate on this for a while. The less you seek your answer, the better your chances of finding it." He stood up and smiled, extending his arm to show her the way.

Faye understood. She thanked him for his advice and for the tea. Then she walked back downstairs to the zendo. She sighed as she regarded the venerated space. She thought about the baby she'd given away, and the brief glimpse of her perfect face. The last she heard, the family who adopted her moved to England. Faye consoled herself, as she had done many times over the years, with the notion that her daughter was given a better life than what she might have been able to provide. It was little consolation, but all she had. She never stopped seeing her face.

Faye approached the altar, cleansing herself with smoke from the incense, then lit three sticks with one of the candles. She looked around, then found a seat on the floor. She crossed her legs, tried to get comfortable, and closed her eyes.

I don't know what I'm doing here.

She tried to quiet her mind, but guilty

486

thoughts appeared, interrupting her search for serenity. Married to those thoughts were the condescending stares from strangers that she'd endured as a young girl. The women who looked at her as though she were defective. How they made her feel unwanted. The lecherous smiles from men who hoped to prey upon those insecurities. She chased those thoughts away with memories of her parents. But even their unspoken expressions made her feel unworthy.

Calm your ocean.

She tried to think of . . . nothing. Which was harder than she thought it would be. She gave up on solving a mystery. Abandoned the idea of reconciling her past. Stopped trying to rewrite her mistakes. Instead she closed her eyes. She focused on the moment between inhalation and exhalation. The dot on a unicorn's horn. A liminal place — a bardo — where we go between this life and whatever comes next.

Find me.

In the silence she heard the rain, the wind, the crackle of the fire. She heard her own breathing, the dull ringing in her ears. She felt her legs begin to fall asleep; her neck and back grew weary. She felt the hardness of the floor. Then the ground began to shake again and she heard vehicles outside, the low rumble of diesel engines, a driver honking. People were on the move, but she hadn't heard the all-clear signal.

She opened her eyes.

The room was the same. She felt like a less tired, more restful version of herself. She stretched out her legs and then stood and walked to the front door. She put on her shoes and stepped outside as a small caravan of ambulances, trucks, and jeeps with medics were heading in the direction of the bombing.

"Faye?" a familiar voice called out. "Faye!"

She looked up and saw Lois in the back of a jeep, waving frantically. The new recruit told the driver to stop, and he pulled over. Faye ran toward them.

"What happened?" she yelled over the sound of more air raid sirens.

"The bombers," Lois yelled back. "They missed their target because of all the smoke and hit an orphanage." Then she looked up.

Faye heard them too. Another wave of bombers and more pilots from the AVG were soaring high above them, engaging the Japanese aircraft. She heard the whistling of ordnance falling through the sky, the thunder of explosions so close she could feel the concussive blast of air with each impact. In that moment, she thought about what her mother had once said. That the literal meaning of karma is action.

"You need to get out," Faye said. "Go back to the hospital, you'll be better off there, especially if the bombs get closer and the injured need to be evacuated."

"But they need us . . ."

"I need you," Faye said as calmly as possible, "to do as I say. Please. Go back and take care of your patients." *Take care of yourself.*

Faye helped Lois out of the jeep and took her place. The driver barked at them to hurry up, and Faye patted him on the shoulder as she sat down and said, "Go."

She watched Lois wave goodbye as a torrent of people, civilians and refugees, merchants and beggars, individuals and entire families, began running in the other direction. Faye knew that she would never see Lois again. She felt okay, with whatever happened next, with whatever danger and mystery lay ahead. She wasn't fearful, or worried, or even scared. Instead she felt oddly at peace. Perhaps because the death and horror and mayhem around her couldn't get through the emotional scar tissue that had built up over time. Or maybe it was something else. Someone else.

My ocean is calm.

As Lois disappeared and Faye turned to face the black smoke, the burning unknown, she felt comforted knowing that John Garland found her. She didn't know how or why, but for a brief moment she was able to hold him. She was able to feel what she'd spent most of her adult life believing she never would. The fleeting glimmer of love: it wasn't a mirage, it was real. Love was real. The way she'd felt — the way she still felt — was a confirmation. There was something and someone out there. There was more. That her lifetime of restless wandering hadn't been in vain. That her mistakes, her heartaches, her regrets, all led her here, to the place where he could find her.

19
DOROTHY

(2045)

Dorothy climbed the steps of the Beacon Hill brownstone that Graham shared with his husband, Clarke, and felt the eerie calm in the air swallowed up by the first gusts of Typhoon Tenjin. With Annabel in her arms, she knocked on the front door as rows of cherry trees that lined the street, planted by a previous generation, began bending in the storm. The surfaces of puddles, filled with algae, rippled as though the pools of standing water were alive. The windows of the stately building had all been covered with plywood. From a season of construction to one of destruction, apparently Mother Nature had little patience for gentrification.

"Why are we here?" Annabel asked, her hair blowing in the wind as Dorothy rested her on a hip and knocked again.

"You're going to stay with Uncle Graham for a tiny bit, Baby-bel. You remember

Uncle Graham and Uncle Clarke? It's safe here, the water can't get us, and Mommy will go buy some groceries for a nice, big dinner."

Dorothy tried to smile. "Okay?"

Annabel hesitated, then nodded.

Dorothy was about to knock again when the door opened.

"There they are!" Graham said as he stood in the doorway. "I can't tell you how happy Clarke was when I shared your text with him. We're so excited to have you over, even with the dreadful weather and all that's going on."

"Are you excited to see me or Annabel?" Dorothy asked as she stepped inside, trying to remain calm even though her mind was clouded by the thought of having to fight Louis and his mother for custody. That and Dorothy wearied for lack of sleep.

Annabel reached for Graham.

"Both," Graham said. "You're both dolls, but I can only carry one of you." He took Annabel in his arms and gave her a nuzzle and a bounce. "How's my little Toto?"

Annabel laughed and hugged him.

"You might have to fight to get this one back," Graham said.

Dorothy allowed herself to relax, to enjoy a moment of acceptance. She smiled as she spotted Clarke in the kitchen making breakfast, bacon from the smell of it.

"There they are!" Clarke grinned. "The weather girls." He wiped his hands on a kitchen towel and stepped away from the stove to hug Dorothy and kiss her cheek. "Graham said you have to run off for a bit, but won't you at least stay for breakfast? I made bagels with bacon cream cheese, red onion, and cilantro. I'm also making polenta lasagna and a Tuscan salad. Might even try my hand at homemade soup dumplings. Trying to cook all I can and get everything in containers in case the power goes out."

"You mean *when* the power goes out," Graham shouted from the living room.

"I'm being an optimist." Clarke shrugged.

"I'd love to, but I don't have time," Dorothy apologized as she noticed the fireplace, felt the comforting warmth. "I'll take a rain check, no pun intended."

"Well, I'll save you some in case you change your mind later," Clarke said, lowering his voice. "Speaking of changing your mind, Graham tells me you're taking a little break. A much-needed respite. That the weather report is just cover for the real storm at home." Clarke's smile changed to a look of solemnity. "I'm so sorry, Dot. You deserve better. You and Toto are both welcome to stay here with us — we have a guest bedroom, you'll have your own bath — stay as long as you need."

Dorothy thanked him, almost moved to tears by the compassion of friends whom she'd neglected for far too long. "I'm okay. I just need to do something before the storm gets worse. Are you sure it's not a burden to take Annabel for a while?"

"Are you kidding me?" Graham said, rejoining the conversation while still carrying Annabel. He made faces until she was giggling. "Any excuse to eat pizza rolls and hang out in our pajamas all day watching Disney movies is like a slice of heaven. The way I see it, having a kid is the next best thing to being a kid, and as you can tell, I'm not getting any younger despite the latest anti-aging treatments and skin rejuvenations. This will be my fountain of youth right here." He spun around with Annabel in his arms. "Okay, now I'm dizzy." He set her down and helped her off with her coat and shoes.

"More like the fountain of immaturity," Clarke teased. He handed Dorothy a mug of coffee. "Splash of cream and some cinnamon, just the way you like it."

Dorothy noticed the graphic on the mug, an armadillo sitting in the lotus position like the Buddha. Beneath the artwork was the word *KARMADILLO.*

"At least warm yourself up a bit before you head out again," Clarke said. "It's crazy out there and it's only getting worse. I heard they've closed the floating bridges and people have twenty-four hours to evacuate the waterfront. The subway will be shut down as well, as soon as all the city dwellers are done heading for the hills."

Dorothy remembered the storms in Burma. The lightning, the wind, the horizontal rain.

"Are you okay, Dot?" Clarke asked. "You look like you've seen a ghost."

Dorothy sat down at their breakfast counter. She watched Annabel play with Graham. As she sipped her coffee she didn't know where to begin.

Clarke noticed the awkward silence and whispered, "Did you finally realize you're way too good for that man? I mean, it's been obvious from where Graham and I are that you're the runner and Louis has been the chaser, and for too long you pretended you couldn't go any faster. But Dottie, dear, you could run laps around that man, laps."

Dorothy chewed her lip and fought to control waves of emotion. Grief and regret. Sadness and loss. She looked at Graham then back at Clarke. She wanted to melt into their kindness, their validation, their generosity. She sighed as she wished she was the person they saw. That she was that confident in her future, alone. In many ways, with her many problems and maladies, Louis had been a life raft in a sea of despair. He wasn't a cruise ship, a yacht, or even a sailboat, but he'd been buoyant enough to keep her from drowning. Now she was floating free, but in an ocean of uncertainty. The words of John Clare echoed in her mind. *I am the self-consumer of my woes. They rise and vanish in oblivious host. Like shadows in love's frenzied, stifled throes.*

I can get through this.

Graham got Annabel set up with some crayons and paper for drawing. Then he joined them in the kitchen. "You sure you need to go out right now?" he asked as he took Dorothy's hand. "Seriously, Dot, the storm might not make it this far inland, or it could travel right over the city. No one knows for sure. Why don't you just lie down for a bit? Play it safe, have some breakfast, then take a nice long nap."

Dorothy rubbed her forehead. She rubbed her tired eyes, patted her cheek to try to focus. *I need to see Dr. Shedhorn. Then I'll figure out what to do after that.*

Dorothy thanked them and respectfully declined.

She was tempted to stay, to hide from the storm and from life in general. She hugged them and felt in that moment more understanding, more kindness, and more tenderness than she'd received from Louis in months. Then she thought about her daughter. The woman on the train who had asked her to promise to take care of Annabel.

"I have to do something," Dorothy said as she stood up and walked to the living room. "I can't explain right now, but . . ." She left the sentence unfinished as she turned her attention to Annabel. Dorothy dropped to her knees and hugged her little girl. Squeezing her. She felt her hair. Inhaled every part of her. Dorothy wanted to care for her the way she always wished her own mother had. She'd grown up watching friends have normal relationships with their parents. Together they lived lives of solace and happiness, understanding and acceptance. All the things that were forever out of reach.

Dorothy recalled an old saying: *death by misadventure.*

The colorful phrasing seemed romantic and brave, like someone had perished while searching for a lost temple in the jungles of the Amazon, or on a sailing ship in winter, trying to discover the fabled Northern Passage, or high in the sky in a colorful dirigible, attempting to circumnavigate the globe. Dorothy remembered being disappointed upon learning that the phrase was a gentler way that Victorian newspapers described mental illness, madness, even suicide.

My whole life, an echo of so many generations, so close to love, to acceptance, to happiness, to joy, but always ending with so much . . . misadventure.

Dorothy held on as she wished to spare Annabel such a fate. She wanted her daughter to have a life with the love Dorothy had always felt was out there, just over the horizon, looking for her. She just didn't know how or where to find it.

Dorothy looked into her daughter's eyes.

"You're my brave girl. You're clever and creative and independent, and best of all you're safe right here. Okay? I'd never let something bad happen to you. I love you, Baby-bel. I'll always love you. And I'll be back as soon as I can."

In that moment, Dorothy realized that she wasn't her mother, Greta. She was stronger. She was choosing rather than existing. Acting instead of being acted upon. Helping and hoping instead of sinking further into despair. She would make things right, for herself, which she realized was the only way to make things right for Annabel.

Dorothy held her daughter, and her tears, all through her goodbye.

She thanked Graham and Clarke once again. She sighed as she watched her daughter, crayons in her tiny hands, drawing sky tigers as the door closed.

She walked to the subway with her hood up, her face down, in case facial-recognition cameras might see her and report her location. It was in the protective shell of her raincoat, hidden from the world, that the tears finally came, like the rain.

When Dorothy arrived in Ballard the veil of storm clouds that appeared earlier had coalesced into a high, gray overcast. But despite the cold rain that blanketed the city, people were still out on the streets in droves. Packing their cars, or queued up at grocery stores, hardware stores, liquor stores, and weed dispensaries.

Dorothy watched as locals passed the windowless office of Epigenesis without a glance. The small, nondescript, and un-adorned building, so out of step with the urban Botox that transformed the face of the city, now looked beautiful, sublime, and practical, the way constancy is comfort when surrounded by chaos. Plus, there were no windows to board up and nothing of pedestrian value to loot. The offices of Epigenesis looked like a silent observer, all-seeing but invisible.

A metaphor for their treatment, Dorothy mused as she tried the door, then cursed when she realized it was locked. She kicked it. Pounded on it furiously, screaming in frustration until her fist hurt and passing strangers looked at her pityingly, shaking their heads, whispering to one another as they hastened by.

With her hand aching, Dorothy immediately regretted coming here. She didn't have an appointment until well after the storm, but she was desperate and didn't know where else to go for help. She'd turned her phone off for fear of being tracked by the GPS. Then used an old phone card and left a series of messages for Dr. Shedhorn that she was now embarrassed by, as each one was a bit more frantic than the last. She came to the office hoping that someone would be here, prepping for the storm, moving things, or at least that there might be an *IN CASE OF AN EMERGENCY* sign with an after-hours number she could call, less frantically.

Dorothy rested her forehead against the

door's cold metal, admitting to herself that in addition to wanting to help Annabel, she came here looking for someone, for the familiar strangers whom she saw during her treatments, the people who kept appearing as residual memories, the neurological ghosts who haunted her, spoke to her. Danced with her. She came here because she missed them and she didn't know where else to turn.

She kicked the door one last time, then jumped when she heard it unlock from the inside. She stepped back as it opened, feeling as hopeful as she felt ashamed when she saw Dr. Shedhorn. Her hair was down, almost to her waist, and she wore a cable-knit sweater instead of her usual lab coat.

"Please, come in. I was expecting you," Dr. Shedhorn said.

"You were?" Dorothy hesitated, then stepped inside as the doctor closed the door behind her and locked it. "I didn't think anyone got my messages, I'm . . ." Dorothy felt a wave of anger. Louis and his mother — one of them must have called, maybe both — they could be on their way. Or they might even be here, waiting.

She turned to leave.

"It's okay." Dr. Shedhorn touched Dorothy's arm. "You're safe. It's just us. We're

501

alone. You have my complete and undivided attention. I'm here for you."

The doctor led Dorothy to a couch and asked her to sit down, which she did, though she kept her raincoat on. The doctor pulled up a chair next to her.

"I did get your messages," Dr. Shedhorn said. "And your partner, Louis, called."

Dorothy went to stand up.

"It's okay, Dorothy. Please, try to relax. Breathe," Dr. Shedhorn said gently. "I told him that I don't treat couples, and when there's an outside partner, my obligation, my confidentiality, my priority, is with my patient. He doesn't know you're here."

Dorothy covered her face with her hands. *Louis's mother wants custody of Annabel and they both think I'm losing my mind.* "What if he tries to take my daughter?" Dorothy asked, looking up. "What if he subpoenas my records here as part of a custody fight? Uses them to try to prove that I'm unstable, that I'm an unfit parent?"

"If anyone wants to look at your records, then they can get in line, because we'll be in Tribal Court. Even if he manages to get a county judge involved, I would go to jail for contempt before I ever surrendered my patients' records. Okay?"

Dorothy relaxed enough to take a deep breath.

"Before we talk about you, is your daughter safe?"

Dorothy explained that Annabel was with friends, she was safe, well away from the flood zone. Dorothy also shared that the memories from her treatments were becoming more dramatic, more real. She wasn't sure if she was having a psychotic break, or a therapeutic break*through.* She felt at peace but restless, confused but liberated, happy but longing. She never felt more alive than when she was someone else. But whatever was happening, it was happening to Annabel as well. Dorothy worried that it would only get worse. What would happen if Annabel followed these memories into oncoming traffic or over the railing of a bridge? What would happen if she dissociated so much she couldn't function in school anymore, in social settings, in life?

Is that what happened to my own mother?

"What you're feeling is normal," Dr. Shedhorn said. "Though I'm sure it's quite confusing at times. There was a famous mathematician named Norbert Wiener, the founder of cybernetics. He used to say that 'We are not stuff that abides, but patterns that perpetuate themselves.' That's what people are and that's what epigenetics is all about. That's what I'm trying to do here. Recognize a pattern of behavior, of repeated cycles of trauma and loss, and then rewrite the script by reconciling those memories that are floating around your limbic system. Your condition, however, is the most acute I've ever seen. In retrospect, this might be a situation where we'd only continue your treatments on an inpatient basis, over several weeks or even months."

"And my daughter?" Dorothy was too ashamed to share what had happened on the ferry. But too concerned — too scared — to ignore that horrible moment.

"Believe it or not," Dr. Shedhorn said as she rubbed her chin, "children usually outgrow this behavior. They forget. They give up their imaginary friends. Their stories are relegated to childhood fictions as their minds become occupied with making memories, not remembering them. The present becomes more interesting than echoes of an epigenetic past, though these things typically manifest in other ways later in life. But she's not the only reason why you're here now, is it?"

Dorothy closed her eyes. She listened to the sound of the rain and then looked around as though waking from a dream. "I haven't been able to sleep. I can't eat. I'm getting lost in memories. Every part of me wants to keep going, my treatments . . ."

"And I wholeheartedly agree," Dr. Shedhorn said. "But there's a typhoon bearing down on the city as we speak. I'm sure you can understand how it would be wildly irresponsible to resume your treatment right now, under these conditions, even if we were staffed up, which we aren't, even if I could, which I can't. There's just no way I can safely put you under while people are literally evacuating the lower-lying areas. We could lose power midstream. If things get really bad, we could be hit with a storm surge, any number of things. I have a solar-powered backup system, but honestly, it wasn't designed for catastrophic weather. I don't have any data on what would happen if the batteries failed before your session was complete, before I could bring you out gently, safely. I can't imagine it would be a pleasant experience."

"Please," Dorothy pleaded. "I need to finish what we've started."

Dr. Shedhorn shook her head as she took Dorothy's hands. "There's something you need to know. Even if I could treat you right now, even if the weather was all blue skies and rainbows, I can't. Or at least I shouldn't. Because your partner, Louis, sent over a court order halting your medical care, pending an investigation and an audit. How he got it done so quickly, I'll never know, but he must have a very good lawyer."

Louise. Dorothy angered.

"Can't you do anything? We're not even married."

"I'm afraid I can't risk it. While that court order is most likely meaningless and it's laughable that he's trying to stop you from receiving private medical care because that's entirely your business, if something were to go wrong while you were in my care, especially if I were to be reckless and treat you on a night like this." Dr. Shedhorn inhaled through clenched teeth. "Dorothy, as you know, the work I'm doing is still in the early, experimental, data-gathering stages. Becoming part of a drawn-out legal battle would slow down the progress I'm making with my other patients. And that's not even factoring in the bad PR, or the scrutiny that might follow. I fly under the radar on purpose so I can be free to help people. I have agency here and I have to protect that."

Dorothy pulled her hands away.

"But what I can do is this," Dr. Shedhorn said as she walked to her office and returned with a plastic prescription bottle. "These are very low doses of the light-reactive protein and neurostimulant that we use during treatment. It's an analog of what we give you intravenously. This is not a substitute by any means, okay? But it should keep your progress from backsliding. The neurons in your brain will be mildly stimulated, but relaxed, and without optic stimulation to fire latent engrams you shouldn't be troubled by new memories. It won't be anything like a real treatment. This is just a stopgap, a placeholder if you will. Think of it as tapering off a mood stabilizer by taking a smaller dose. Take these once a day, twice if things get worse. They'll keep you from losing the progress we've made, and it should flatten any residual mnemonic atavisms."

Dorothy regarded the pills, then the doctor. "I have no idea what you just said."

Dr. Shedhorn smiled. "Let's just say it'll keep the loose ends from fraying until we can weave them back together in a full session, okay?"

Dorothy was disappointed but nodded out of politeness.

The bottle might as well have been filled with placebos, sugar pills, wishes and kisses goodbye. The bottle looked weak and insubstantial compared to the advanced technology used in an actual session, wired in, monitored, connected to an IV, beneath an array of optics, under the doctor's direct care. The small capsules were like finger-sized Band-Aids for her gaping chest wound.

"Thank you," Dorothy said, even though inside she felt like screaming. Even with the weight of her disappointment she was grateful for all that Dr. Shedhorn had done for her. She hoped the doctor's research would continue after the typhoon, unabated. She hoped she'd be able to return to Epigenesis, to resume her treatments, with or without the legal challenges of Louis and his mother. But a part of her knew that idea was folly. The treatments gave her strength of will, clarity, but in that clarity Dorothy understood that hope was less easy to sustain. Louise would fight for Annabel. She'd use Greta, the tumultuous childhood Dorothy endured, her lack of employment, and the treatments, which were so far removed from traditional medicine — she'd turn those things into weapons — she'd use Dorothy's own history against her, and in all likelihood, Louise would win. That's when Dorothy heard the drumbeat of the rain on the roof turn into waves of hammering as a squall had reached the city.

She didn't blink. For once she felt at

peace, at home in the storm.

Sometimes bad weather is a good thing, Dorothy thought. *It tears down what's weak and forces you to rebuild something stronger, with a lasting permanence.*

She stood and went to shake the doctor's hand.

Dr. Shedhorn gave her a hug instead. She smelled like wool and wildflowers. "It's going to be okay, Dorothy. Now go take care of your daughter."

Outside, Dorothy stood clutching the pills in her coat pocket as gusts of wind shredded umbrellas and tipped over garbage cans. Their contents of recycled coffee cups and fast-food wrappers swirled like angry bees from a smashed hive. Street signs and billboards wobbled. She hung on to the plastic bottle as if it were a steel railing atop the rim of a bottomless canyon and she was staring down into the void. She twitched, wanting to take the meds now, even if their efficacy was only palliative.

Dorothy walked to the nearest subway station and heard sirens wailing in the distance, cars honking impatiently in the bumper-to-bumper traffic as people fled for higher ground. Amid the chaos, Dorothy didn't just wish for shelter, she wished for a quiet place where she could be alone. Free from worry or distraction or the possibility of interruption. A place where she could collect her scattered thoughts, gather her kaleidoscope of memories, and take the prescribed medicine without the risk of burdening those around her, or being completely vulnerable. She couldn't go home, that was certain. She didn't have an office anymore. While Graham and Clarke were dear to her, she felt guilty asking for more hospitality than she'd already been given, and if she lost her mind completely like her mother, Dorothy preferred to do so without company and definitely not in the presence of Annabel. She walked, holding the hood of her raincoat in place, weighing the possibility of going to a shelter for the night, or a hotel if one was available, or simply taking a train as far away as she could go. But she knew the trains would stop running soon and the power, in all likelihood, would fail. Being stranded somewhere underground, in the darkness — surrounded by strangers with only her thoughts and echoes to keep her company — seemed like a recipe for madness.

As the sirens faded and the congested streets slowly began to move, she saw an old military vehicle slosh by. Not a typical

Humvee used by riot police or the National Guard, but an old, noisy, open-top jeep, the type urban hipsters restored, like vintage Volkswagen Beetles or old Ford Broncos. Dorothy thought the jeep looked like a set piece from an old war movie, an olive drab relic of another time, another place, another generation. In the rear of the jeep, a Chinese woman in a nurse's uniform stared back as though she recognized Dorothy. The woman brushed her rain-soaked hair aside and smiled gently, waving as the jeep disappeared.

On board the last subway train, Dorothy stood elbow to elbow in a packed car that smelled of brake dust and wet denim. Everyone smiling in quiet relief with each mile.

"*Zhe shi jinji qingkuang,*" a woman's recorded voice chimed through the speakers. Her tone was calm, pleasant, as though she were saying, *This is an emergency,* the way someone might say, *Thank you and have a nice day.*

The voice switched from Mandarin to English and the woman said, "The storm is expected to make landfall in twenty-four hours. If you are not already leaving the flood zone, please be advised that the following bridges are closed . . ." Dorothy's thoughts turned back to her daughter. Annabel was safe. She was with people she trusted. She'd be okay. As the subway rattled its way around a corner, Dorothy remembered the woman she'd seen earlier, who implored her to protect Annabel. *The only way I can do that,* Dorothy reasoned, *is to finish this. To clear the slate once and for all.* That's when Dorothy felt something else in her pocket. She let go of the meds and touched something smooth and metallic. She pulled out the wafer-thin, gold-colored medallion with the likeness of the Buddha. The figure smiled serenely in a commercial, mass-produced way. She'd been given the trinket weeks ago by panhandlers in saffron robes. She should have tossed it, but as the train pulled into King Street Station, she was now grateful for the gift.

As passengers disembarked, Dorothy zipped up her coat and followed them off the train, through the crowded subway terminal that was teeming with Red Cross volunteers helping people evacuate. Dorothy walked outside into the heart of the International District, where despite the torrent of rain, she felt at ease. Not just because she was Chinese, but because the district had been perpetually left behind in the wake of Seattle's economic booms, and facial-recognition cameras were scarce. The few that had been installed years ago were often damaged or vandalized and rarely repaired. This was the one part of the city where Dorothy felt unjudged, free to be herself. Though the lack of street cameras also meant that whenever there was a rally downtown, the city would use barricades to funnel angry protesters away from banking centers, elegant restaurants, and retail finery, unleashing them in a neighborhood mainly populated with migrants and the elderly who subsisted on fixed incomes.

Dorothy wiped the rain from her eyes and looked to the west, where she saw rows of illuminated roadblocks that kept stubborn or foolhardy people from traveling back into dangerous areas near the waterfront. But to the east, directly uphill, there were flashing lights, red and blue, as police were helping load homeless people onto the city's light rail system, presumably bound for destinations away from the flood zones. Dorothy hastened in that direction, five, six, seven blocks, past the departing railcars and an officer who called out to her. She couldn't make out what he was saying above the thrum of the rain, the howling wind. She pretended not to hear and kept going, her heart racing, afraid Louise had already put out an Amber Alert for her and Annabel, though with fading cell service that possibility was diminishing by the minute.

Dorothy kept going, to the one place she suspected would be relatively unaffected if the power went out. A place of refuge that she had visited a few times as a homeless teen. Someplace she'd turned to when she needed to get warm, to sober up or come down. She felt a comforting familiarity as she reached the ornate wooden doors of the Gotami Buddhist Temple. She glanced up at the sky that had turned black, then she tossed the medallion into a garbage bin and walked inside.

Dorothy stood in the foyer and inhaled the familiar, woody aroma of incense powder along with the pleasant fragrance of fresh gardenias and drying citrus. The sweet scents tried in vain to mask the musty odors of soiled clothing, well-worn shoes, and unwashed hair. To Dorothy, the pleasant scents mixed with the aromas of poverty, addiction, loneliness, and desperation were like an olfactory déjà vu as she remembered coming here in her youth, often after having lived outdoors for days — sometimes weeks — at a time. She quietly cringed as she recalled the polite, sympathetic smiles of other temple-goers, grown-ups and monks, who noticed her dull affect, the sadness in her eyes. They always offered kindness and generosity of spirit as they pretended not to notice her obvious lack of supervision and hygiene.

Now as an adult, Dorothy couldn't help but feel compassion and kinship for the handful of people bedding down in corners and along one side of a grand hallway, stretching out on cushioned mats with their meager belongings as a young female monastic in an amber robe passed out woolen blankets.

An old woman, a *bhikkhuni,* with an identical sash, her head shaved to gray stubble, carrying an armload of white candles, noticed Dorothy. "Please, come in," she said. "I'm afraid the last bus of evacuees from the tent city in Wisteria Park just left, but you're welcome to spend the night here. We're above the flood zone and should be able to ride out the worst of the storm." As if to reinforce her point, thunder boomed overhead and the ceiling joists of the old brick building creaked and groaned defiantly in the wind.

Dorothy looked around. *This is where I'm meant to be.*

She was about to thank the old woman when the power went out.

Instead of worried cries and frightened voices seeking comfort in the lightlessness, Dorothy heard gentle laughter, pleasant cheering, as if someone had switched on a lighted Christmas tree in a darkened room. The absence of electricity made the glow of dozens of candles and hanging oil lamps even more beautiful, serene, and natural. She felt a deep and primal comfort in the warmth of open flames.

"There are towels over there if you'd like to dry off," the bhikkhuni suggested, pointing with her chin. "After, you can come with me and get warm."

Dorothy realized she was dripping on the tiled floor. She removed her raincoat, dried off as best she could, wiping her face and squeezing the moisture from her hair with an old bath sheet. She removed her shoes and left them on a shelf near the entrance.

She followed the old woman down the corridor, bowing as she entered the temple hondo, the main hall dedicated to objects of veneration. Once inside, Dorothy felt small, insignificant, dwarfed by two rows of red and gold pillars that reached up to the vaulted ceiling like trees in an orderly forest, holding up the sky. From the back of the hall, Dorothy could feel the ambient heat on her cold cheeks from the hundreds, if not thousands of lit candles that adorned the massive wooden altar at the front of the room. There, amid a slowly swirling fog of incense smoke, a statue of the seated Buddha rested, surrounded by a small army of golden statuary. Purple hydrangea and blood-red syabu deckled the elegantly carved shrine. Multicolored tapestries hung on either side, adorned with mandalas, painted in earthy tones of umber and ocher on a sea of cobalt blue. A handful of people sat on the floor, occupying cushions, as other female monks were busy unfolding cots between the pillars where people could sleep for the night.

Dorothy loitered in the back of the room, not wanting to leave the comfort of the sanctuary, but too nervous to step farther inside, even though she'd been casually invited. Dorothy recalled her travels, visiting temples in Burma. She was drawn to them but also always felt as though she didn't belong, a crass tourist gawking at someone else's place of sacred repose. A weed in someone else's garden. She wished for the ability to believe, to belong. *Life must be easier that way,* she thought, watching the old woman arrange the candles she'd carried to the altar, carefully lighting them one by one.

Belonging. That's all I've ever wanted. Not a father, though I wish I'd known mine. My mother tried, but she left too soon. My daughter, my beautiful girl, my tether to the world. If I could only give you what I've never had, always longed for. Home.

On her way out, the bhikkhuni stopped and asked, "Are you okay? You look a bit lost. Has someone offered you a place to rest?"

Dorothy scanned the hall. "I'd like to rest in here, if that's okay?"

"Well, I can't blame you," the old woman said. "The best room in the house, as well as the safest. Have you been here before?"

"A long time ago." Dorothy hoped she wouldn't be asked to elaborate.

"Then it's nice to have you back. I'm Xi. Are you a Buddhist?"

Dorothy shook her head. "In college, whenever someone asked if I was religious, I'd say I was a deist, agnostic, Shinto Jesuit. I'm nothing but a little bit of everything."

The older woman chuckled, wide-eyed. "I think that means you're a Buddhist, dear, and you just don't know it yet. Give it a lifetime."

"Just a spiritual refugee for now."

"Aren't we all?" Xi smiled warmly. "Welcome."

"Thank you for having me, again," Dorothy said with as much relief as gratitude. "You seem so calm, so relaxed amid the mayhem. Aren't you scared of the typhoon?"

"Of course," Xi said. "But as the saying goes: *pain is inevitable, suffering is optional.* Whatever happens, I look forward to the karma that accompanies it. Karma, after all, is the great teacher."

"I can only imagine. Nights like this must earn you a spiritual get-out-of-jail-free card," she joked, a reaction to awkward situations.

The woman smiled. "That's not exactly how karma works."

"Sorry." Dorothy hesitated, then said, "How does it work?"

"It's likely that I will spend the rest of my life trying to figure that out," Xi said. "But that's the point, isn't it, to keep learning, to grow, to do more good than harm, to create compassion, to understand that every person you encounter is not there by coincidence? All of us play a role in another person's life."

"What goes around comes around."

The older woman nodded as though she were a parent explaining basic math to a toddler. "You're thinking in terms of crime and punishment, which I'm afraid is a bit reductive. Karma is more like a suitcase. You have to be unafraid to open it up and look at what's inside, to unpack the things you don't need. Karma is the climate of the past, which shapes how much leeway we have in the future."

Dorothy looked at old woman. "You sound like a certain doctor I know."

The bhikkhuni stared up at the ceiling as though measuring the intensity of the wind. "It's going to be a very long night. If you'll forgive me for saying so, you look tired. I want to make sure you have a bed." She pointed Dorothy to a cushion near the center of the room. Atop the cushion sat a blanket and a water bottle. "Why don't you get comfortable and try to rest. Calm your ocean." Xi smiled again.

Dorothy bowed awkwardly as the woman walked away. Then she appraised the others in the room, a young couple with dreadlocks and matching backpacks, an elderly man with dark, wrinkled skin, whose mouth puckered inward for lack of teeth, a woman who rocked back and forth, eyes closed as though enraptured by something real or imagined, or merely lost in the desert of prayer. No one here would pay her much notice, but she still felt like a lonely person dining out solo, conspicuously seated at a table for one in a restaurant crowded with laughter.

Despite her apprehension, Dorothy found her way and sat on the cushion, her coat in her lap. The pose, the posture, reminded her of how she was never able to loosen up properly in a yoga class, let alone sit on the floor of her home and meditate, as many therapists and friends often suggested. The simple exercise of trying not to think had never been simple for Dorothy and always felt like a trick, an inside joke with a punch line that only other people understood. Or pretended to understand, the way people would talk about a classic novel at a cocktail party, in a florid, roundabout way, hiding the fact that they'd never actually read the thing let alone understood the metaphoric meaning, real or imagined.

She stared at the water bottle, remembering the medication Dr. Shedhorn gave her. She looked around, fished out the prescription bottle, opened the cap, and took out a capsule. Holding it up to the flickering candlelight, she examined the liquid inside, translucent, like a piece of amber with something unknown trapped within.

Calm your ocean.

She swallowed the capsule with a swig of water, unsure of what to expect, but expecting something eventually. She sat in the warmth of the hondo and contemplated what the bhikkhuni had said as she waited for the medication to kick in or at least grant her the ability to stretch out and fall asleep amid the ominous roaring of the gale-force winds outside and the deluge of horizontal rain lashing the building.

Instead she felt nothing.

She tried to remember a Buddhist poem, but all she could recall was one line: *Impermanence embraces the new-born, like a midwife, first, and the mother, afterward.* It was from an old Sanskrit story about a mother, filled with sorrow, sacrificing herself for her child. Dorothy thought of Annabel as she looked at the open pill bottle.

This is for you, Baby-bel.

Dorothy placed another capsule on her tongue and swallowed it.

She hesitated, her pulse racing.

This is for you, Ah-ma. I'm so sorry for the hurt I caused.

Dorothy swallowed another.

She felt hot and her hands were shaking as she stared down at the rest of the capsules. She pictured Dr. Shedhorn somewhere outside of the city by now, looking at her calendar, shaking her head and trying to figure out what to do with Dorothy.

Then all fell silent, peaceful, as though she were sitting in the eye of the storm.

This is for all of us.

Dorothy looked around to make sure no one was watching, then emptied the bottle into her mouth. She tasted the plasticky cellulose of the capsules. Felt the gelatin stick to the roof of her mouth as she chugged the rest of the water and struggled to swallow. She tried not to wretch or cough or gag as she felt a bitter gobbet stuck in her throat, the capsules collecting in her esophagus, slowly dissolving, burning into her gut. She quietly sobbed as though she'd consumed a lifetime of sadness and loss.

There's no going forward without going back.

Dorothy sat on the cushion and tried to collect herself, even as the building shook and she could hear rain pounding the roof, the hollow banging of unknown objects flying through the air outside. Tumbling mailboxes? Street signs? Sheets of plywood? Uprooted trees and broken limbs? A symphony of catastrophe, careening off the brick walls.

It had to be done.

She could hear metal bending, glass breaking. She expected to hear laughter or crying or music, strange smells, new tastes, anything to indicate that the past was within reach. But instead her stomach churned and ached, she felt sick, dizzy, nauseous; her head felt heavy, throbbing as though lit up with a cluster of jagged migraines. She squinted, raised her hand to block the blinding light, then realized her eyes had dilated, and looking at the array of warm candles was now like gazing into the sun.

I'm sorry.

She felt something heavy hit the back of her head, then discerned through the sharp pain that she'd blacked out and was now lying on the cool, hard floor, her ears ringing as she stared up at the gilded ceiling. The ornate, decorative patterns, leafed with gold, moved in the candlelight as though they were alive, reflecting, flickering, changing before her eyes — if they were still open — it was hard to tell, because when she shut them she still saw things, shapes, figures swimming in the darkness.

Dorothy came here to find peace for herself and provide a better future, a better mother, for her daughter. She hoped to embrace the familiar, tidal pull of memory, to be sustained, to embrace her newfound hopes with open arms. Instead she found herself paralyzed, unable to move, as though someone were sitting on her chest, forcing the air from her lungs in explosive exhalations. She wheezed, gasped, without the ability to inhale, to breathe. She wanted to cry out, to scream for help, as her body jerked, convulsed. She shuddered uncontrollably, for minutes, then hours, then lifetimes. Until she let out a long, slow gurgle as a bubble of saliva burst on her lips. As her cold skin turned a mottled hue of bluish purple. As her eyes teared up then glazed over. As the clockwork of her life began winding down until her heart finally stopped beating.

Find me.

20
ECHOES

Dorothy opened her eyes.

She was on the floor, seated on a cushion in the hondo of the Gotami Buddhist Temple, which wasn't as dark as she remembered. There were more prayer sticks burning than candles and light streamed into the hall through windows, painted gold and red, that were previously boarded up and hidden from view by tapestries.

She looked about, marveling at the sandalwood smoke swirling in the daylight. To Dorothy it appeared as though she were seated at the bottom of the ocean, looking up as motes of dust were carried by the currents of smoke like plankton in the sea.

When she saw that she was alone, she called out, but her voice merely echoed in the hollows of the building. She stood, noticing sounds from the street — car engines, the rumble of electric buses, the beeping of a delivery truck backing up —

noises that didn't make sense in the wake of a natural disaster. She remembered how after previous tropical storms, all she heard was an eerie silence, occasionally interrupted by the sound of supply drones, the cawing of returning seabirds, or the gurgle of overflowing storm drains.

Dorothy touched her hair, which was dry, touched her stomach, which was devoid of the nausea and the sickness she'd felt. When she peeked into the grand hallway, the sleeping mats were gone and those who came seeking shelter from the storm were nowhere to be found. The building even smelled different, like fresh paint or cleanser. The floors appeared recently mopped and the wall sconces held newly lit cones of incense. Down the hall she retrieved her shoes and reached for the door. When she opened it, she squinted at the brightness of the morning sun. She felt the chill of dawn surrender to the warmth of a summer day, a gentle breeze caressing her skin, the sky clear with nary a cloud, just a passenger jet high in the sky, leaving behind a billowing contrail. Japanese tourists clustered on a street corner, throwing up peace signs as they took photos using selfie sticks. Behind them, painted on the side of a building, was a mural of the Seattle Seahawks, proclaiming them *The Defending Super Bowl Champs.* Dorothy's nose itched with the strange, vaguely familiar smell of exhaust smoke and she realized the cars were all running on noisy, outdated, combustion engines. She felt her hip vibrating, reached into her pocket, and pulled out an antique smartphone. A text arrived from someone name Anjalee. *Where R U? A guy is here to see you.* Dorothy looked up and down South Jackson Street. She spotted a billboard with a large queen on a chessboard. The headline read: *YOUR MOVE.* In the corner was the logo for Syren and beneath it the familiar tagline: *More Than Love*®.

Dorothy put the phone away and looked around for a cab or an Uber, then patted her pockets as she realized she didn't have money, credit cards, or any form of ID whatsoever. It was a clear day, though, perfect for walking.

"There's our beautiful girl!" Anjalee said, arms wide open as Dorothy stepped off the elevator and into Syren's Belltown headquarters, where she was showered with adoration in the form of cheers, streamers, and fistfuls of confetti in the shape of tiny red and pink hearts. The women on her team, especially those who hadn't been invited to the awards dinner, wore T-shirts printed with the company's motto. They were all wide-eyed smiles, jumping up and down. Dorothy understood that when the company went public, they'd all become stock-option millionaires, for a while.

Dorothy shook confetti from her hair. Paper hearts stuck to the soles of her shoes with each step. "You didn't have to do all this . . ." Then as the crowd parted, Dorothy saw, once again, the real-time data stream monitors in the lobby.

Anjalee took Dorothy's arm. "I think you'd better get used to having confetti in your hair. Because we just hit eight million users, overnight." Anjalee brushed confetti from her shoulder. "We made CNN, the *Wall Street Journal*, the *New York Times*, *Wired*, and even *Scientific American* and *Psychology Today*. Plus — I'm not going to name names — but we paid a few celebrities to go social . . ."

"You're running my scrubbing algorithms to weed out spam bots."

"Of course." Anjalee pointed to the monitor as numbers flew by. "That's how fast your world is going to change. Buckle up, you're not in Kansas anymore, Dorothy."

Anjalee led her down the hall, which was flanked by floor-to-ceiling portraits of powerful, iconic women. They breezed past the programmers' bullpen, past staffers who were clapping and cheering in slow motion, then up the stairs to the loft, where Anjalee pointed to a corner office. "That's yours now. We're setting you up with a publicist and we'll get you some media training so you're more comfortable doing on-camera interviews. Oh, and there's one other thing."

"Oh?" Dorothy feigned surprise.

"There's a handsome young man waiting for you inside. He's been here all morning. I swear we didn't arrange it!" Anjalee smiled coyly, her eyes seeming to twinkle with mischief. "I'm going back to my corner, but I expect a full report."

Dorothy suppressed her anger as she watched her leave, then noticed the silhouette of the man in a dark blue suit who moved behind the frosted glass.

She opened the door and saw that he was staring out her new window, appraising the view. She cleared her throat and said, "Hey."

He slowly turned. The silent partner who had been footing the bill for this view, this building, her salary, and all her hard work. Syren's mysterious angel investor.

"You must be Dorothy," the man said. "I'm so sorry for intruding . . ."

After Dorothy agreed to meet Carter Branson for dinner, he finally left. Then she found the email address for Sophia Blessing at Bitch Media. Dorothy sat down and began to type, each keystroke like a nudge, a change in vector, pushing the ship she was on toward a new course. She wrote:

Dear Ms. Blessing,
I heard that you'd like a face-to-face interview. If you'll indulge me, I have something better.
As you well know, Carter Branson, through a holding company, is the majority owner of the company I work for. It's my belief that the rumors about his malfeasance toward women, his unwanted advances, his sexual assaults, and his cover-ups, are all true.
He's asked to meet me for dinner tonight. A car is scheduled to pick me up and whisk me away to a private meeting atop the Space Needle. If you can get here in time, I'd like you to go in my stead — to confront him about his misdeeds.
Also, after Syren's initial public offering, Carter Branson will dump his shares in this company. He's either shorted it himself, or

through a third party. You're excellent at what you do. I have no doubt that if you dig into Branson's ownership of Syren you'll find evidence of stock manipulation and insider trading.

I'm sure that right now you're wondering why I'm doing this, sharing this with you, which in all likelihood will cost me my job and millions in stock options.

All I can say is that I created an app to help others find love, but as the poet Nikki Giovanni once said, *Love is responsibility.* A dear friend once said, *Karma is action.*

Here is my act.

Dorothy sent the email, then sat in her office, oblivious to the dozens of bouquets of flowers, helium balloons, edible arrangements of fruit and truffles, and bottles of champagne sent by her peers and competitors alike.

Within minutes she received a response from Sophia, who was as alarmed at Dorothy's frankness as she was intrigued by the opportunity to put an end to the notorious behavior of an entitled, serial abuser.

Dorothy replied cordially and gratefully, with instructions on when and where the reporter was to be picked up and what to expect. She also strongly suggested that

Sophia record her encounter with Branson, since all his misdeeds boiled down to situations where it was his word and his copious wealth against that of his accusers.

She smiled and imagined the look on Branson's face when Sophia stepped off the elevator. Dorothy looked at her watch, a split second before it lit up with a message: *Sam is here for you. He says he's meeting you for lunch. Shall I send him back?*

Dorothy's heart raced as she pressed yes.

She closed her eyes, and when she opened them, he stood in her doorway.

"I'm Sam." His introduction almost sounded like an apology. He looked in awe of the place, perhaps embarrassed. "Um, in case you're wondering, no, I've . . . never done this before. I'm afraid my parents got a little carried away . . ."

Dorothy stood up and threw her arms about him. He felt so warm, the fragrance of his being so familiar, his touch strong but gentle. She didn't want to let go.

"I'm so sorry," Dorothy kept repeating as she held on to him. "I'm so sorry . . ."

"It's okay. It's all right. No worries. I'd say both of our parents are at fault," Sam said as he held her. "They mean well. Yours, anyway. Mine — I think they're just trying to save face with their nosy neighbors."

She finally let go of the embrace but hung on to his arms as she looked up at him.

"Well, it's so nice to finally meet you, too." Sam smiled. "Suddenly I feel like I owe that matchmaker a nice tip or at least a thank-you note. I don't normally make this kind of first impression. I was just happy you said yes to lunch under such strange . . ."

"Circumstances? What can I say, there's something in the blood."

Sam looked confused.

"Filial piety. It's in our genes," she said. "Among a lot of other things."

"Indeed." Sam nodded. He found her coat on a hook behind her door, offering to help her with the garment. And when he walked her down the stairs and past the reception desk, everyone's heads turned to see who Dorothy was with. Sam held the door and she stepped outside. When she looked over her shoulder, he was standing in the door-way. He looked happier than she remembered.

"What?" she asked.

He smiled as he pointed with his chin. "Keep going."

Dorothy hesitated, then turned, catching her balance, knees bent, arms outstretched as she stood perilously at the edge of the diving platform high above the new swimming pool at Summerhill. She looked down at her teacher, Mrs. Bidwell, who kept playing her violin. Dorothy surveyed the school grounds as the song reached its crescendo. Then she looked up at the pillowy clouds that adorned the August sky, drew a deep breath, pinched her nose, and jumped. She plunged into the cool water and felt as though she were being shocked awake. She opened her eyes, staring through the aqueous lens, appreciating the rays of light that illuminated the churning legs of the boys and girls above her in the middle of the pool. Dorothy heard a muffled tone as she pushed off from the bottom. When she surfaced she realized the sound was the sharp, clamorous ringing of the school bell. She climbed out of the pool and toweled off as her classmates were getting dressed, though a few ignored the bell and continued playing.

Dorothy felt goose bumps on her arms and legs as a breeze moved through the trees. She squeezed water from her hair and wrapped a towel around her shoulders, then walked barefoot to where Mrs. Bidwell was packing her violin.

"That was a brave leap," the woman said as she closed her case. "Even some of the older boys are afraid of jumping from such a height."

Dorothy turned her tan body toward her teacher, feeling comfort in the moment, as though life were starting over again in a familiar place the way the sun rises every day over the same spot on the horizon. "You really think I'm brave, don't you?"

"Fearless as they come," Mrs. Bidwell said. She smiled and Dorothy marveled at her dimples, the mischief in her eyes. She watched, spellbound, as Mrs. Bidwell brushed a dark finger curl of hair from her brow. The way she carried herself reminded Dorothy of Greek statues. To her, Mrs. Bidwell was regal, like Athena in twill trousers. She was confident, like Demeter, the daughter of Titans.

"Going to class today?" Mrs. Bidwell asked. "I wish you were still in mine."

They walked arm in arm as her teacher talked about women's suffrage, of marriage, of independence. Her deep thoughts and strongly held opinions interwoven with poems of the Enlightenment, the Romantics, the classics before them that had weathered the revenge-driven literary trends and the minor-key musicality of the Parnassians. To Dorothy, Mrs. Bidwell's words created doors that were previously unseen and opened avenues of possibility leading to places she always wished to go.

"But let my journey be a cautionary tale," Mrs. Bidwell said. "In the meantime, you should be so kind as to call me Alyce from now on."

Dorothy swooned.

"Well then, Alyce, I should be getting on to the library."

"When you're there you should look into a poem called 'Ode to Aphrodite.' It's in a book of Greek poetry that I ordered from the new bookstore in Brighton and Hove, just for you. I left it at the desk. You have a poet's heart, like mine, for better or worse."

"I wouldn't want to be any other way."

"And what way would that be, dear girl?"

"Mysterious," Dorothy said. "Let someone else be tragic."

When Dorothy arrived at the library, Augustus Moss was at the front desk.

"Hello, Augustus," Dorothy said with as little emotion as possible. "Mrs. Bidwell left a book here for me. I'd like to pick it up."

"You know I hate that name," he said, without looking up from the book he was reading. "Why don't you call me Guto, like everyone else?"

"You just seem more like an Augustus to me," Dorothy said. "My book, please?"

Guto frowned as he closed the book and set it aside. Beneath it was a smaller hardback, which he opened and pretended to read. He nonchalantly licked his thumb and turned the page. "Oh, this one?"

"That's the one. Please give it to me."

Guto scratched the inside of his right nostril and then used that finger to turn another page. "This is quite humorous, this book, I took a hard look at it. Did you know this Sappho woman was married to a man named Kerkos?"

"I know," Dorothy said, looking at the wall clock. "The name Kerkos translates to Dick Allcock and he lived on the Isle of Man. It's a pun, I get it. But what's funnier is that if she were married to someone like you, his name would be Rasputin Thimbleprick and he'd be banished to the Island of the Purple Parsnip."

Guto looked up, dumbfounded, as though he'd been tormenting a stray and realized the mutt had teeth and claws and could fight back. He slowly closed the book and rested it on the counter, his hands crossed atop of it. He smiled, but his brow was furrowed with concern. "How about I give it to you for a kiss?"

"I dare you to try," Dorothy said, staring back.

The bully in him seemed to shrink, his arrogance collapsing like a fallen soufflé, bitter chocolate turning into impotent mush. She reached over and pulled the book out from under his hands. "I'll take that."

The entire student body gathered in the dining hall — kids of all ages — from the littles, with their bare feet, restless energy, and uncombed hair, to those who would graduate this year. The faculty gathered as well, along with the janitor, the school cook, and the groundskeeper. Dorothy waved at Mrs. Bidwell. Her teacher bowed in return before taking a seat. Lastly the headmaster sat and everyone quieted.

"As you know, our weekly general meeting is more important to me than all the textbooks in the world combined," he spoke softly. "This is where we set rules, address grievances, and come together. Each of you has one vote, a simple yet precious and powerful thing, as do I. Together we will make collective decisions, and for a time, live with those decisions, because the best way to learn in this lifetime, in my opinion, is trial and error. Now, this quarter we will be studying one of my favorite topics of discussion." The headmaster removed his pipe and coughed. "Government."

Dorothy smiled as she heard booing.

The headmaster continued, "I don't necessarily disagree with you lads. As a school, we try to be a democracy. But a few of the faculty members have suggested that we operate the school with a different form of governance. An object lesson writ large. We will do so for one week." The headmaster bit down on his pipe. "And we shall see how we do. Now what form of government shall we explore?"

Dorothy looked on as one of the older girls suggested Trotskyism. One of the little boys waved his hand in the air and asked if he could be a king. One of the older boys, a lad named Theo, was about to speak when Dorothy stood up first. "We should try a matriarchy," she said. "Some primitive societies operated that way, and even the ancient Celts had rulers along matrilineal lines. We could be like the Padaung in Burma, where women have social privilege and authority . . ."

Before she could finish Dorothy was nearly drowned out by groans and snide comments from many of the boys. Some of the male teachers looked away, waiting, hoping the suggestion would go away so they wouldn't have to take a side.

Dorothy glanced at Mrs. Bidwell, who offered an approving nod.

"What about that?" the headmaster said. "Did you see how all of you — especially the boys — had a visceral reaction to the idea of a government led by women? Because of that I think we owe it to ourselves to seriously consider that option."

Ultimately, the school as a collective group selected three ideologies to choose from. Dorothy looked on as the headmaster called for a vote by a simple show of hands. Teachers would tally the votes. But since there were more girls than boys, more women than men, Dorothy had already been able to predict the outcome.

"Matriarchy, it is," the headmaster said as he stood up. "Outstanding. Those of the majority party — or those newly willing supplicants — you may gather elsewhere to select your leaders and your rules by which the rest of us will live for a week." The class waited as the girls and young women left the room along with nearly half of the boys.

Dorothy, holding the door, was the last to leave. When she stepped into the hallway, Mrs. Bidwell was waiting. "Well, now that was a deft move," she said. "I didn't see it coming. Now I'm not a religious person, but I daresay that was a revelation."

"I did it for you," Dorothy said.

Mrs. Bidwell was about to speak when they were interrupted by a man who stepped up to shake Dorothy's hand.

"That was quite a thing in there," he said. "I'm with the *Leiston Observer.* I'm on campus for an article about the school, and these meetings are rather peculiar but also quite noteworthy. That was a bold idea you had in there, miss. If you would permit me, I'd like to take a photograph of you for the paper." He held up a small box, dark blue, with a silver crank on one side and a leather handle on the top. "I never go anywhere without my trusty Ensign. Why don't we go outside while there's still daylight?"

Dorothy looked at Mrs. Bidwell, who winked and followed the man out to the front of the main school building. As he set up his camera and sprinkled flash powder in the trough of a metal lamp, Dorothy saw her teacher standing behind him, her hands on her hips. She looked amused, positively delighted.

"Okay, there we are," the photographer said as he looked down into the camera and held up the flash lamp. "Smile please and then hold."

She tried not to laugh as Mrs. Bidwell made faces. Then Dorothy relaxed, brushed the hair from her eyes, and smiled as she stared at her teacher in the setting sun.

The flash powder sparked, then exploded like a firework, a burst of white light leaving colored stars in its wake. Dorothy smelled the burning potassium nitrate and magnesium and heard Mrs. Bidwell's voice echo in her ears, "Well done."

When Dorothy's eyes readjusted to the daylight, she was in her room, standing over her bed. Her roommates were gone, and on her pillow sat a copy of the *Observer*. Beneath the newspaper, Dorothy found a sealed envelope that smelled like violets. She looked over her shoulder, then opened it and read the note inside:

Dearest —

I apologize for not telling you this in person, but I absolutely dread goodbyes. Which of course is my excuse for why I've packed a suitcase and left for Hamstead, without leaving a letter for my dear husband, wherever he is.

I'm meeting with a wonderful poet, Eva Gore-Booth, who has asked if I'd like to become a writer and editor for *Urania,* a secret journal that has, in many ways, taken up the mantle of *The Freewoman,* which ceased publication some years ago. I initially declined her offer, but — you've inspired me.

The opportunity doesn't pay well and I'll be forced to write under a pseudonym, but I will be allowed to be myself on the page and therein is a certain freedom, one without price. I'll take that freedom and feel rich for the rest of my days.

I will think of you, my dear, fondly and with great admiration. Life has its way and I know it will circle me back to you. I just don't know when. Until then, know that as a teacher, I've never learned so much from a student.

Truly,
Alyce

PS. Don't change. Instead change the world.

Dorothy sat down on the bed and held the note to her heart. She opened the newspaper, turning to a half-page article that featured a large illustration of the school and a small printed photograph of Dorothy, smiling as though she knew a secret.

She carefully folded the page and tucked it in her pocket. Then she hid the note beneath one of the drawers in her desk. She heard pleasant music playing somewhere far away, an orchestra. She walked to the door, stepped outside, and was surrounded by finely dressed people, most of them Chinese, paired off, circling a dance floor as the bandleader sang, "Each time I see a crowd of people, just like a fool I stop and stare, it's really not the proper thing to do, but maybe you'll be there."

Dorothy felt the gentle rocking of a cruise ship. Smelled a course of tobacco. She stepped out of the way as tuxedoed waiters and busboys breezed past, carrying arm-loads of empty wine bottles and trays of stemware and napkins.

"Could I trouble you for another dance?" a man's familiar voice said.

Dorothy turned and saw John Garland in his finely pressed suit and emerald-green tie. He offered his arm with a hopeful smile and a raised eyebrow.

She let him lead her back to the center of the crowded dance floor as the band began to play the first wistful strains of "The Way You Look Tonight."

"I'm afraid I wasn't completely honest with you earlier," he said.

She looked up at him, confused. "How so?"

"I actually know one more dance." He smiled and twirled her away, her hand still resting in his as he brought her back with an underarm turn before returning her to his warm embrace. He placed his hand on her waist as they moved together, stepping forward, then around, hips swaying to the staccato beat of a rumba.

They danced and she recalled how her mother had once given her a set of watercolors. She was a little girl at the time and didn't know what to paint, or how, so her mother simply said, "Paint the colors of happiness." As Dorothy glided about the room, she marveled at the ornate leaded-glass windows exploding with the red-orange splendor of the setting sun melting into the sea. The horizon a ribbon of burgundy. The purple underbelly of the clouds cast their reflections in the ocean below.

Dorothy held on to him, not wanting to let go as they orbited the dance floor again and again and again. She looked up at him and at times wasn't sure if they were moving or if they were frozen in the moment as the other elegant couples, the blurring lights, the crystal chandeliers, became a dreamlike carousel, whirling around them.

"I don't want tonight to end," she said.

"Who says it has to?"

I wish it were that simple.

More complete than strangers, she danced with him until they were the last ones on the floor. Then, as the song ended, the house lights flickered to life, brightening the room. A lone piano player took over. A lit cigarette hung from his mouth, his bowtie draped around his neck. Eyes closed, he began playing a soft, tinkling melody as members of the orchestra put their instruments away. Valets gathered coats and scarves left behind while servants collected drinking glasses and swept the dance floor.

"I suppose we should let these kind, hardworking folks have the room," he said. "It's getting late. I'd invite you to my stateroom, but I have three unruly roommates I'd have to kick out first. Besides . . ." He looked at her, searching. "I like the way you look at me — I'm not sure you'd look at me the same way in the morning."

Dorothy rested her head on his chest. *Don't be so certain.*

She closed her eyes and he held her. She couldn't bear to let go, though she finally relented when she heard one of the servants clearing his throat. She opened her eyes, glanced about, and spotted a sign through the glass doors of the adjacent room.

"I have an idea," she said as she took his hand and guided him into the drawing room, an elegant parlor adorned with porcelain statuary, Chinese vases filled with dried flowers, and silk paintings that hung from every wall. On the starboard side of the room was a door with a sign above it, painted with Chinese characters.

"What's in there?" he asked.

"You'll see."

He let her lead him into the other room, where hardback books filled the shelves built into every wall, divided by Ionic columns that stretched to the ceiling of pressed copper, inlaid with a motif of flowers and the words *Zi sik.*

"It means knowledge," Dorothy said, pointing to the characters.

"You brought me to the ship's library." He smiled.

"They call it a study." She surveyed the rosewood furniture, a polished desk, tables and high-backed chairs upholstered in sea-green fabric. A matching chaise lounge with white silk brocade sat in front of a fireplace, embers still burning. Dorothy felt the warmth, inhaled the woodsy aroma of pipe tobacco, the essence of dried flora.

"It's so peaceful in here," he said as he walked along a bookcase, tracing his fingers across the spines of a collection of leather-bound volumes. "And so many books."

"My people created paper, invented the printing press, we produced the first books six hundred years before Gutenberg printed his Bible," Dorothy said. "The oldest known manuscript on Earth is the *Diamond Sutra.*"

He turned his attention to her. "You've read it?"

She shook her head. "Just a few verses in school, some lines of poetry about stages of enlightenment and the nature of reality. How we don't have a stationary soul. That our existence is fluid and relational."

His brow furrowed and he nodded as she spoke. He tried his best to understand what she was saying. "It sounds deep. Complicated. What else does it say?"

"I don't remember very much," she said. "Just a phrase written by some unknown, long-lost poet — that we're all bubbles in a stream."

He smiled again. "That reminds me, you owe me a glass of champagne."

"Tomorrow?"

He held her hands. "I'm looking forward to it."

Dorothy marveled at him, so relaxed, so comfortable here, on a ship bound for a place he'd never been, to embrace a fate that was still unknown. Being with him, she felt as though all the clocks in the world had stopped. There was a beautiful stillness, like the soundlessness of falling snow. The peace of an ocean made of glass beneath a clear blue sky. In the silence she found herself hoping, wishing.

The fire crackled and popped, and she blinked as her senses reacquainted themselves with the steady rocking of the ship. She pointed to another sign. "That says we should be quiet, respectful of others, and that this place is open all night."

He looked at the chaise, then back at her.

She nodded, then blushed as she watched him remove his coat and slowly loosen his tie. They both removed their shoes. Then he lay back and she curled up next to him. He wrapped his jacket around her, holding her close.

"Is this okay?" he asked.

"That we're in here?"

"That we're together like this."

Dorothy held on to him again for the first time. She imagined letting him go and thought she could detect the faint hint of oil, diesel, ether. She felt a tinge of worry, of regret, an iota of sadness, a seed of hopelessness planted in an abandoned garden, destined to grow wild like pennyroyal, bearing thorns and poison.

He sat up as though he'd forgotten something.

He began to put his shoes back on.

"What are you doing?" Dorothy asked, not wanting to hear the answer, not wanting the night to end. "What's wrong?"

"Don't worry," he said. "I'm just going to fetch something."

"But . . ."

"I'll be back shortly. Stay warm. Enjoy the fire."

She wrapped his woolen suit coat around her, watching in disbelief. He left the room, and she wondered where he was going at this late hour.

He has to come back. His coat is here.

She stared into the fire, seeking answers as though beseeching the Oracle of Delphi, searching for meaning in the flames. But all she found was a sense of emptiness filling the room, even as she was surrounded by books filled with the imaginings of poets, scholars, and storytellers. Then she closed her eyes and cringed as she remembered posters with headlines like *Pvt. Caution Says, "Don't Take Chances"* and a training film that exhorted military personnel, "Don't forget — put it on before you put it in."

Had she given him the wrong message? Insinuated things she didn't mean to? She respected that he was trying to be careful, but it all felt so awkward now, and this wasn't exactly what she planned. His presumption reminded her of her teenage years, fateful moments when she was reckless and gullible. She chewed her lip, worried about his return, but more worried that perhaps he suffered a change of heart and might never return at all. She felt misfortune with each passing minute, knowing that her disappointment would eventually step aside for its progeny of grief and acceptance.

She glanced about the room, saw Chinese newspapers on a wooden rack, and remembered the folded page with her photograph. She retrieved it from her pocket, unfolded it, stared at her own portrait. She tore the photo from the paper and threw the rest into the fire, watching it go up in flame. She searched the library until she found a pencil in one of the desks. She examined the photo once again, now doubting that the man she met would ever return, but if so, she wanted to leave something behind.

She wrote *FIND ME* on the back.

With a weary sigh, she tucked the photo inside his coat pocket, then touched the fabric one last time like the tender caress of a coffin lid before it's closed and lowered into the cold, hard ground. She heard the door open, expecting to hear the voice of an annoyed custodian asking her to leave. Or a restless insomniac joining her sad tranquility.

"I'm so sorry that took so long."

He walked back in carrying something in his hand.

"Where'd you go?" Dorothy's frozen heart melted with relief. "I thought maybe you decided a good night's sleep is better than my company."

"I'm sorry I worried you," he apologized again. "Since you're a nurse, I went downstairs to the purser's deck to find something in the suitcase of one of my traveling companions. Took me a moment to find it. But if you'll indulge me."

Dorothy stood up. "I'm sorry you went to all that trouble. And I'm sorry this is so awkward, I just don't think we should."

"Should what?"

He looked confused for a moment, then his eyes grew wide and he blushed with embarrassment. He laughed, covering his mouth with his hand as he remembered he was in a library. "Oh . . . my . . . I feel so terrible. You must have thought . . ."

She raised her eyebrows.

"Of course you did, I dashed out of the room to go get something. How could you not think that I was running off to get . . ." He smiled as he shook his head. "And honestly, I would love to, but that's not exactly what I had in mind. I went to get something else."

She tilted her head. "What is that?"

He held up a stethoscope.

"Wait, is something wrong?" She began to worry all over again, for different reasons. She touched his cheek, checking for signs of fever. "Are you feeling all right?"

"I've honestly never felt better in my life. There's just something about you. If you'll allow me . . ." He gently put the eartips in her ears, then slipped the metal chest piece between the buttons of his shirt, directly above his heart.

"What are you doing?"

He smiled again and leaned closer.

"I wanted you to hear my heartbeat when I kiss you for the first time."

In the darkness, Dorothy felt the warmth of his body leave her side. In the void left behind, she felt coolness and the heavy rocking of the ship. She heard waves breaking against the hull, the creaking and groaning of timbers. The air smelled mustier, danker, a murky bouquet of fermenting barley, savory cooking spices, and straw, along with the smoky essence of pine tar, redolent of oil and freshly sawn wood. Her shoulders ached and her back was stiff as she sat up, realizing she'd been sleeping on the floor beneath a pile of tattered blankets. She looked around the darkened hold and could make out the faint outlines of a pantry: well-stocked shelves, barrels and casks, hogsheads and rundlets. She turned toward the sound of shuffled footsteps and saw a sliver of light as someone tried their best to slowly, quietly open the creaking door. Flickering lamplight from the galley spilled into the room where she'd been sleeping, and she saw the silhouette of a young boy with a limp, teetering on his good leg.

"Alby?"

"Go back to sleep," he said.

"What are you doing?"

He put a hand on the wall to steady himself as the ship swayed.

"I can't stay."

"Please," Dorothy said. "You need to rest."

Alby tried to speak but coughed instead, covering his mouth with his scarf.

Dorothy stood and gently closed the door. She found his hand in the near darkness. With her other, she touched his forehead, his cheeks, which were hot, damp with perspiration. He was shaking with chills, burning up with fever.

"Lie back down," she said tenderly. "Let me help you."

He hesitated, then squeezed her hand and with her assistance nestled down amid the pile of blankets. His teeth chattered as she knelt beside him, straightening the covers of their makeshift bed. She propped his head with a straw pillow and began unbuttoning his coat, careful of his swollen neck and the parts of his body that, like her parents, had been racked with purple sores.

He inhaled and then let out a soft, anguished cry, the unspoken language of someone without much time. He struggled to swallow, wincing.

"You shouldn't be this close to me."

"You're burning up," she said.

"I'm freezing."

"I know," she said. "Let me take care of you."

He tried to push her hands away.

"Just go," Alby said, his voice hoarse and raspy. "There's nothing you can do but get sick, and I don't want that. Not you, not anyone."

"I'm not leaving you."

She suspected that if he had the energy, he would put up a good fight, push his way out the door, but he had nothing left, no one left. He struggled to breathe.

She leaned him forward then slipped behind him, his back toward her, her legs on either side of his. Gently, she reclined him, holding him close. She hoped he could breathe easier by sitting upright — at least partially — to let gravity ease the gurgling in his lungs. She pulled the covers up to his chin and rested her cheek alongside the top of his head, running her fingers through his hair. "How's this?"

He didn't answer, but in her arms his teeth stopped chattering, she felt his shivering subside. Though even as he relaxed in her embrace he began to quake anew, like the panic of a stray animal in a thunderstorm, heart racing, on guard against an ever-present yet unseen menace.

"I miss . . . my mother," he said.

"It's okay to miss someone. It means you loved them. Grief is unexpressed love." She tried not to think of a certain woman, waving at her from a pier, a silhouette, swallowed by flame.

"I don't want to be here anymore."

"I know, Alby," Dorothy said, though she was unsure if he meant on the ship. Or in this life, this tragic moment, hanging on. "I wish I could take you someplace better."

He didn't say anything for moment, then he rested his hand atop of hers. "This is close enough to better," he said.

She held on to him, letting the ship rock them both in the cradle of the ocean.

"I'm scared," he whispered, his breath liquid.

"You're safe with me. I've got you right here."

She wanted to tell him everything was going to be all right. That she wouldn't let anything bad happen to him. That he would feel better in a few days. A few weeks, a few months. But she didn't want to lie. All she could give him was honesty. All she could do was hold him close even as she was letting him go.

"It's so dark." He tried to turn toward her. "Can I see your face?"

She slipped around him and eased his ragdoll body into the blankets. She tucked him in again, then lay next to him, holding his hand.

He looked at her, struggling to speak. "Will you . . . miss me?"

She wiped a tear from his cheek, nodding. "But I'll see you again."

He smiled, nodding, almost imperceptibly.

He drew a labored breath and exhaled, so long and slow she feared he was leaving her. Then he stirred. He patted her arm as though he wanted to share something.

She leaned in close, brushing her hair back.

His mouth moved, silently.

She turned an ear to him as he whispered. "Tomorrow, Dorothy."

He closed his eyes and didn't cough anymore. He didn't struggle. He slept, his breathing ragged, more uneven. She lost all sense of time as she held him for what must have been hours, singing, whispering to him in the darkness, until he was gone.

Dorothy stood near the taffrail while the other passengers slept, dreaming. She watched as Chief Officer Cappis nodded solemnly to a pair of sailors, who lowered Alby's body, shrouded in sackcloth, until he became one with the sea. Dorothy didn't hear the finality of a splash, just the wind and the constant churn of the ocean.

While most of the crew went belowdecks or retired to the afterhouse to keep warm, Dorothy found a seat in a gamming chair. She settled in with a heavy blanket around her shoulders. The wicker basket swayed as she listened to the snapping of sails and the rhythmic creaking of timbers that resembled the slow ticktock of a metronome.

She stayed on deck watching stars sink into the ocean, keeping vigil for her friend until the first orange blooms of morning began to unfold, and within minutes it looked as though someone had lit the sky on fire. She heard crewmen shouting from high above and herring gulls crooning as they swooped across the bow. The horizon turned into a purple silhouette of land, smokestacks revealing the jagged serration of a city. Dorothy grew more excited with each mile as sailors barked commands and confirmations to one another with a jovial, eager lilt in their voices. An officer declared that the tide was perfect, and she watched as the sails were finally taken down in sight of the harbor and the rigging was secured. Without the billowing of the mainsail all was quiet, and as the ship began to slow Dorothy heard the gleeful chatter of passengers hugging one another as much in relief as celebration. Together they watched as hawsers were cast to smaller boats that used the great hemp ropes to tow them closer to their destination. Once in range, crewmen heaved lines to the dockworkers, who tied them around stout bollards the size of tree stumps. On board, a half-dozen seamen wound their ends of the lines around an enormous capstan. Then they shoved bars into the barrel like spokes on a bicycle wheel and sang as they pushed, turning the great iron gear, slowly pulling the vessel alongside the dock, beneath a blue sky smudged with coal smoke.

Dorothy waited as wealthy passengers who had gathered near the bow disembarked down a private gangway festooned with laurels of black-eyed Susans. The rest of the passengers gathered toward the aft. Most ignored her, though some stared at her, pointed, and whispered among themselves. Others regarded her with a scorn and hostility she didn't understand. She stepped back as they walked down a creaky wooden plank with ropes for railings, their arms loaded with their belongings. Finally, a seaman nodded to Dorothy, and she took her turn down the plank. She was the last to disembark, but joyfully received the gift of steady land beneath her feet.

She followed the crowds of people down the dock and stepped off at Fells Point, where a malmsey-nosed handler noticed her, eyeing her appraisingly, and she remembered she was different — Chinese — an oddity in this country.

"Oy!" he called out, spitting on the ground.

She ducked her head and kept walking.

"Someone grab that yellow wagtail."

Dorothy disappeared into the crowd of

departing passengers and servants, eager to be as far away from the ship as possible, and porters, workingmen, day laborers coming and going from nearby warehouses, canneries, and gristmills, reeking of tobacco and sweat. Two of the men bumped into each other and began shouting, arguing. One man with a thick, Irish brogue yelled, while the other spoke in Italian and cursed in broken English. As the first punches were thrown and a scrum broke out, onlookers cheered, while some fled. Others, drunk and hoary-eyed, staggered by without noticing. In the mayhem, Dorothy snuck in with a group of young girls in tatters who were being led away by a pair of gib-faced nuns. One said, "Come along now, dears, the streets are no place for a lady." The sister had a sign that read: *Magdalene Society.*

Dorothy trailed behind, staring ahead, keeping to herself as two of the girls took notice, crossed themselves, and kept walking.

When her group reached the corner of Eastern Avenue, the crowds began to thin and Dorothy slipped away, crossing to the other side of the street where she felt heat radiating through the red brick walls of the Baltimore Union Stoneware Manufactory. She covered her nose and mouth as she smelled soot, tasted ash, and kept walking as bottle ovens and lime kilns spewed black smoke that bled into the sky like ink on paper.

She made her way down Broadway. Startled at the snap of a buggy whip, she skipped to the flagstone sidewalk, stumbling as a horse clip-clopped by pulling a phaeton carriage down the wood-block pavement. The bearded man at the reins tipped his coachman's hat as he passed, saying, "Mind your step." She looked down at a rivulet of fetid water streaming down the gutter, rank enough to attract mayflies, but not flowing heavily enough to carry the bloated body of a dead cat and the contents of last night's chamber pots down to the harbor.

Dorothy held her breath and kept walking until the foul odors abated and were replaced with the warm, sweet smell of wheat paste. She glanced about for the source of the aroma — a pastry shop or a confectionery — and bumped into a wooden ladder.

"Careful," a young voice said from above.

She looked up and saw a teenager with a long-handled brush, a paste-pot dangling from the ladder, and a satchel slung across his back with wide sheets of rolled-up paper. He was busy spreading a new poster for the American Temperance Union atop a faded, peeling broadsheet that read: *COME SEE THE CHINESE LADY.*

"Do you know what happened to her?" Dorothy asked.

"To who?" the boy said as he spread paste across the old poster.

"Her." Dorothy pointed at what was left of the previous advertisement.

"Back home to the Orient is what most say. Though some will tell you she signed up with a circus in New York City." The boy's eyes widened when he looked down and saw Dorothy. "You looking to join her act?"

I'm already part of it.

He shrugged, then went back to his work. "I swear I saw her once, in poor condition, I'm afraid. She was the talk of the town for a while, that lady." As he spoke, he covered up what was left of the poster for the Chinese Woman. "If I were you, I'd ask at the local almshouses. Though . . . don't discount the circus."

Dorothy thanked him and kept walking, slowing to peer down each alley that she came upon. Most were occupied by draft animals attending to bins of hay and troughs of water. Others were where horse-drawn carts and drays stood idle as stout men unloaded barrels of oatmeal, molasses, and crates of tea. Some of the narrow brick canyons were filled with mountains of festering manure and clouds of black flies so thick they looked like smoke. One arched alleyway was a depository for the putrefying carcasses of dead horses that lay rotting, the stench so foul it made her eyes water.

With each step, Dorothy understood why the streets were deemed *no place for a lady.* There were only a handful of women about, and those who did traverse the avenues did so with a retinue of servants carrying their belongings, their purchases, shading them with parasols and holding their gloved hands as they stepped off each curb. All of which made Dorothy's presence more re-markable, not just to bearded laborers in stained shirts in need of laundering, but also to businessmen in tailored suits sporting elegant haberdashery. Dorothy even en-countered — much to her surprise — a half-dozen Chinese workers who spoke to one another in a heavy Toisanese dialect as she passed. The men seemed confused, unsure if she was real. That's when Dorothy felt a tingle run up the back of her spine, looked back, and saw a policeman one block away who took notice of her. He followed, push-ing his way through a crowd that gathered on a street corner.

Dorothy hastened down the street, then began running, slipping by pedestrians as she sprinted past saloons and tobacco shops, bakers and coffee roasters, chandlers and fishmongers. She struggled to catch her breath, trying not to trip on the uneven sidewalk. She heard a shrill whistle, followed by a voice of authority shouting, "Come back!"

Her heart raced as she dashed down the nearest side street. She didn't look back, darting across the crowded avenue, down the block, then ducking into a darkened alley, looking for someplace to hide. Amid the filth and garbage, rats scurried out of her way. She caught her breath as church bells began ringing in all directions, marking the time, but to Dorothy it felt as though someone had sounded an alarm.

Then Dorothy saw her.

She sat against the wall, in the dirt, legs splayed like a marionette whose strings were cut. Her pregnant belly bulged beneath her frock, the bottom of her dress dark, soaked with mud and blood. Dorothy froze as she saw a homeless man kneeling next to her, reaching into her bag, knocking over the tin cup the woman used for begging.

Somewhere far away, Dorothy still heard the policeman's voice calling out to her, but she didn't care anymore. Because the clouds were moving and shards of light found their way into the darkness, where she could clearly see the woman's face, in so much pain and agony she seemed to be frozen. She broke the silence with a horrible wailing, the sound of a wounded animal, crying, birthing, dying.

The homeless man touched the woman's face.

"Leave her alone!" Dorothy screamed.

She stepped closer, saw that the woman sat in a pool of her own blood, bearing down, pushing. The stranger wasn't a beggar, or a thief, or a monster preying on a helpless woman. He was Chinese. He held her hand. He spoke to the woman gently as he tenderly wiped her forehead with a damp cloth and attended to her tears.

"It's okay," he said. "It's Yao Han. I've finally found you."

Dorothy felt as though she were in a speeding car and someone had slammed on the brakes. A sense of forward motion interrupted by the sound of wreckage, breaking glass, twisted metal, flying debris, the wind so loud she thought a train was bearing down on her. Amid the clamor she heard a man's voice as dark blurs around her coalesced into shapes, figures. She saw a face directly above hers, blocking what little light there was to be had. His hand on her forehead, his fingers pinching her nose, his other was on her chin, tilting her head back. She felt the stubble on his face, the strange, intrusive intimacy of his lips on hers as he blew air into her mouth, once, twice, filling her lungs. Her chest expanding, swelling with warmth, aching as though bruised. Lying there, she couldn't move, couldn't close her eyes, couldn't blink. She could only stare at the ornate ceiling, aware of her helplessness as she felt the warmth of tears running down her cheeks.

He let go, then placed the heel of his hand into the center of her chest. "Come back to me," he pleaded, pressing down hard, again and again and again.

I am back.

Dorothy heard him ask someone, "What did she take?"

"I don't know what this is," an older woman answered, holding an empty prescription bottle. "It's not a narcotic. At least not one that I know of."

I'm right here.

The pressing stopped. He pinched her nose again and she jerked, gasped, reflexively slapping his hand away, eyes wide. She wanted to sit up, to gain her bearings, sort out the confusion, but her chest hurt, her throat was on fire.

"Welcome back," he said as the wind began to subside, just enough for him to be heard without yelling. He glanced at his watch. "That was the longest ten minutes of my life. I thought I lost you." He sat back for a moment, exhausted.

She noticed his dark clothing — a policeman's uniform — damp. His raincoat discarded in a pile, his cap tossed aside. His dark hair disheveled.

He relaxed into a familiar smile. He looked happy.

Or was it just relief?

Dorothy saw that the temple was crowded now, packed with people caught out in the weather. But the candles and lamps continued to burn, the statues of the Buddha seated at the altar smiled with blissful contentment even as the typhoon raged.

"You sure know how to miss a party! I think you slept through the worst part of the storm," the officer said. "We couldn't wake you."

She opened her mouth to thank him but couldn't speak.

Then she began to gag. Began to choke.

"You're okay." He snapped to attention.

"I'm going to roll you onto your side."

Wait.

She felt a hand lift her head, another on her back.

"One . . . two . . ." He eased her sidelong, kept her hair out of the way as she felt her shoulders stiffen. Her spine seized up as the bitter contents of her stomach spewed from her mouth and out her nostrils. Her sadness, her regret, her rash decisions pouring out. When she finally caught a full breath, she was shaking, hands trembling.

"That's it," the officer said, his hand on her shoulder. "Breathe. You're okay."

"I'm so sorry," Dorothy mumbled as she dried her mouth and cheek on her sleeve. She sat up cautiously and looked down at her soiled clothing. A woman in a saffron robe was already helping her clean up. Another was wiping the floor with a towel. Dorothy saw that the other people in the hondo had moved even farther away.

"Where's my daughter?" Dorothy asked.

"Oh dear," the bhikkhuni said as she brought a bottle of water to Dorothy's lips. "When you got here, you arrived by yourself. Do you have a child out there somewhere?"

Dorothy sipped the water and remembered that Annabel was safe, though she

wouldn't be completely relieved until Dorothy had her arms around her. "It's okay. I
forgot," Dorothy said, rubbing her temple.
"She's with friends outside the flood zone."

I love you, Baby-bel.

"Then you should probably lie back down,
okay?" the officer said, still kneeling next to
her. "No one can go out until the storm has
passed and the winds have slowed. Plus,
there could be downed powerlines and
broken gas mains, flash flooding. The best
thing you can do for your daughter is stay
put, stay warm, and get some rest, until I
hear that it's clear. Then you can go home
and make her all the tofu and pumpernickel
sandwiches you want."

She recognized him, his affable nature.

He touched the radio on his vest, then
sighed when he heard static.

Dorothy nodded, then lay back down on
the floor in the center of the hondo. She
rested her head on the cushion. Felt a soft
blanket cover her. She knew some people
were still looking at her with concern,
wondering what had happened. She didn't
care. The typhoon was the star of tonight's
show, center ring. She was just a sidelight.

"Thank you," she said to the officer. "For
what you did."

"I'd say anytime, but . . . I'd really rather

not do that again if I can help it." His words
— his bedside manner — were cheerful, but
she saw the worry in his eyes.

"I'll be okay," she said.

"You sure?"

Dorothy nodded.

"Okay."

"You didn't give up on me."

"You didn't give up either."

He smiled approvingly, then left to check
on other people.

Dorothy let his words sink in.

The howling wind portended ruin and
devastation for the city. But she was reminded of another stormy night. When she
woke up in the ER at Harborview Hospital
as a teen, delirious, gagging as a tube was
pushed down her throat, awash in fear,
confusion, shame, anger — all of it mired in
despair.

Now as she examined her many shapes,
her myriad reflections in the gold leafing of
the temple ceiling, she felt palpable relief.
She relaxed, oddly at peace as her countless
images moved to the rhythm of the flickering candlelight. She felt safe, content —
beyond content — she felt hope. Hope for
her future and for her daughter.

"Looks like everyone's settled in," the officer said as he returned.

Dorothy appraised the two of them, tired but at peace amid the chaos.

"Would you like to lie down and rest?" she said to the officer. "There's another cushion and there's plenty of room. I seem to have scared everyone else away."

He glanced down at her, then scanned the room as he ran his fingers through his hair. "That's very kind. It's been a long day and I suspect it's going to be an even longer night." He smiled at her but slowly shook his head. "I really shouldn't. Though I want to, especially considering how we keep bumping into each other like old friends."

Dorothy wasn't sure if she admired him more for saving her life, for not judging her, or for respecting her in this odd moment. The one thing she was sure of, however — she loved the way he held her gaze. "It's okay. I understand."

"But if there's anything else I can do, if there's anything you need, just ask."

Dorothy thought for a moment.

"There is one thing," she said. "Someday when this is all over, I'd like my daughter to meet the person who saved her ah-ma."

"Done," he said. "And you saved yourself, remember."

Dorothy winced.

"Are you all right? I'm sorry, did I say

something wrong?"

"I just realized," she said, chagrined. "It's a bit embarrassing, but . . . I'm between addresses at the moment. Not just this — tonight — but out there, in the real world. I'll be fine, you don't need to worry about any of that. I'm just thinking out loud. I'm better off than most. I have options. It's just . . ." She looked around for her phone.

"Don't worry about it."

She looked at him, certain that she'd said too much.

He knelt down and held her hand. "I'll find you."

EPILOGUE

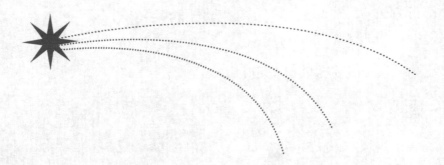

21
ANNABEL

(2086)
When Annabel opened her eyes, she saw her mother's face. Her ah-ma was young, the way she'd recalled seeing her in old photographs. The way Annabel's father had once seen her. The way Annabel remembered her from when she was a little girl.

Her Baby-bel.

Seeing her mother again, if only in memory, made Annabel both happy and sad. Happy to feel so near to her ah-ma again, so close she could almost touch her. In that mnemonic proximity, that lucid dream, that unsealed envelope of consciousness, she knew, without a doubt, how much her ah-ma loved her. But Annabel felt sad as well, disheartened as she slowly realized where she was and that her ah-ma had been gone now for almost three years. Every Mother's Day since became a day of mourning but also an observance — a celebration

577

— that she'd been so close to her dear mother for nearly four decades. How fortunate Annabel felt, knowing that when she was five years old, she could have lost her ah-ma, lost everything, on one fateful day.

But she didn't.

During the subsequent years, which Annabel now considers a gift, her ah-ma's life became less . . . stormy. The epigenetic clouds that her mother inherited, that muddled her thoughts, finally parted, making way for sunnier days with bluer skies.

"Goodbye, for now," Annabel whispered as she closed her eyes, drew a deep breath, and let it all go, feeling her mother's warm presence recede.

When she opened her eyes again, Annabel was seated beneath an array of lights that had stopped spinning and were fading to black. The aromas of rain-soaked clothing, sweat, and sandalwood were replaced by the smell of antiseptic and dried flowers.

"I can't believe how close I came to losing her," Annabel said to Dr. Shedhorn, whose hair was long and thinning and as white as her old lab coat. She looked at the doctor with admiration, knowing that she could have made millions with her medical breakthroughs, but instead had open-sourced all her methods. Rather than licensing what she created or selling it outright, she let others build upon her work so she could care for the families that had endured her earlier, more experimental treatments.

"We both came close to losing her that night," Dr. Shedhorn said, her tone filled with apology. "At least I was able to ease her distress in the years that followed."

You weren't the only one, Annabel mused as she thought about her stepfather, who was reunited with her ah-ma a few years after he saved her life. Annabel was seven or eight at the time, holding her mother's hand and leaving one of her poetry readings, and there he was, waiting. Her ah-ma recognized him immediately even though he was out of uniform. He came to listen to her, to know her better, to see her again. Annabel remembered walking with him that evening to the International District for lychee ice cream, her ah-ma's favorite, and after that they never spent more than a day or two apart. Even when her ah-ma went into the hospital and eventually to hospice care. He'd slept in a reclining chair right next to her, holding her hand.

For Annabel, those days were filled with so much sadness and grief, but her ah-ma never felt sorry for herself, never saw her life as one of loss.

She said, "It's okay, Baby-bel. You know, the best thing anyone can ever hope for in life is a good third act. And I've had a great third act."

She called me Baby-bel even though I was in my forties.

Annabel wished for more time. But she was comforted knowing that her mother was still a part of her, literally and figuratively. Her ah-ma had been the seed and Annabel the flower, and she was growing in a field with fewer weeds and thistles.

"It's been a while since I've seen you," Dr. Shedhorn said as the transdermal cuffs on each of Annabel's arms deflated. "How are you feeling these days?"

Annabel sat up.

She felt a beautiful mix of joy and melancholy, like a warm tropical rain, or the happy exhaustion you feel when you've worked so hard for something and finally, after a great struggle, achieved it.

There was so much to say.

So much more to do.

The word that escaped her lips was "Grateful."

A week later Annabel found her window seat on the New Empire Builder, the flagship bullet train from Seattle to Chicago.

She placed her phone in the slot on the side of her headrest so that when the conductor strolled by in his retro vintage uniform and cap, his counter would show that she had paid for an eTicket.

As the doors closed and the train safety video began to play in English, then Mandarin, Annabel pressed the button to recline her seat, but nothing happened. Her footrest was inoperative as well.

"Those things never work properly, do they?"

Annabel turned to see an elderly Chinese woman hefting a large carry-on bag into the overhead luggage compartment. The short, frail woman struggled to get it above her shoulders, let alone fit it into the small space that was nearly full.

Annabel stood up. "Please, let me help you with that."

The woman smiled as Annabel hefted the bag, rocking it until it squeezed in, then she closed the compartment door with a gentle click and a sigh of relief.

"Thank you," the woman said. "Just took a little teamwork, that's all."

Annabel went back to her seat as the elderly woman sat down across from her.

"Where are you off to?" the woman asked.

"I'm headed to a place north of Chicago

— an artists' residency. It's a place for writers, visual artists, musicians, composers, dancers, filmmakers — basically a herd of unicorns. I've been applying for years and finally got in," Annabel explained, fully prepared to be regarded as a life-waster, someone who majored in the arts while engineering, medicine, biochem were the more respected class of jobs.

The woman beamed. "That's so exciting. What kind of art do you do?"

Annabel hesitated and felt the train begin to move.

"I'm a poet."

"Good for you," the woman said pleasantly, much to Annabel's surprise. "You are giving the world something it truly needs. Look around." She waved her hand to the other passengers — business travelers, families, college students. Everyone on their phones or tablets or asleep from medication that would make them drift off for the duration of the journey, designed to wear off just as they arrived at their destination. "I think people have forgotten how to be human. Do you know what I mean?"

Annabel found herself nodding in agreement. "I do."

The woman looked at her with a sparkle of wonder in her eyes. "What kind of poetry do you write? I mean — what do you like to write about?"

Annabel thought for a moment. "I write about my family, mostly. Their stories." Annabel touched her temple and then her heart. "They're all in here."

"That sounds lovely," the woman said with a sniffle. "Do you know what? I have a favorite line from a poem, would you like to hear it?"

Annabel leaned forward, wide-eyed. "Yes. Of course. Please."

"Strangers are the people we forgot we needed in this life," the woman said reverently. "That line has stuck with me for years; I've never forgotten it."

"I love that."

"Oh, good," the woman said. "I wish I could remember who wrote it."

Annabel gazed out the window as the sun was setting, a cotton-candy swirl of orange and pink and red. The trees an evergreen blur. She turned back to the old woman, smiling. "I know who the author was."

"You do?"

"I do," Annabel said proudly. "It was my mother."

Annabel sat in the back of the driverless car that took her from Chicago's Union Station to the country estate in Lake Forest that would be her home for the next two months. She thought about the woman on the train. After they shared a meal together she'd asked, "Have you found your special someone?"

Annabel explained that unlike most of those in her generation, she didn't carry a genetic locator. After Dr. Shedhorn released her work, dozens of other companies sprang up, finding creative ways to monetize what she started. One particularly audacious corporation created an app that combined the aggregate data from the genetic screening of millions of people, along with a geolocator that would ping a user's phone when they were near someone whom their algorithms deemed they were compatible with. The idea was that if everyone carried the app, they would be able to appraise others who were, biologically and psychologically, a good match. Annabel, though, resisted the idea, preferring to do things the old-fashioned way. Though now that she was in her forties, she was often questioning that decision.

There is a price for being old-fashioned, she thought as she arrived at the estate and quickly discovered that there was no elevator to her third-floor room. Normally, she enjoyed stairs — saw them as a noble adversary — but she was already road weary and in need of a shower. *Here we go,* she told herself as she ambled up the three flights, carrying her copious luggage, hoping to avoid meeting other residents until she had time to freshen up a bit. Unfortunately, as she turned down the hall to her room she spotted a handsome man with brown skin coming from the opposite direction. As she walked toward her room, he seemed to get more attractive with each step, with long dark hair and a bright, energetic smile. She suspected he was having the opposite experience, watching this bumbling, disheveled stranger shed what loveliness she had as they got closer.

When they met in the middle of the hallway, Annabel realized he was assigned the room directly across from hers.

"Hello," she said, then she waited a heartbeat for him to look at his phone, a sign — a tell — that he was checking the app to see if she was a genetic match, someone worth spending time with, a shallow habit that she'd come to expect.

Instead he smiled and said, "Hi, I guess we're going to be neighbors. Looks like you're in the Blue Room. Past residents say it's haunted, if you believe in that kind of thing. They say the founder actually died in that room."

Annabel furrowed her brow.

"I'm sorry, I don't mean to be so weird. They also say that it's the lucky room. That good things happen to whoever stays there. I'm kind of jealous, actually."

"Lucky me." Annabel smiled ironically.

"I'm Pasha by the way. You look awfully familiar. Have we met? Like maybe at a conference or something, a workshop of some kind? I'm a fiction writer."

"I'm Annabel. I'm a poet," she said. "But my friends call me Echo."

He nodded his head appraisingly. "Wow, I love that name."

"It's a little . . . esoteric, I guess."

"No, your real name."

"Annabel?"

"Yeah, it's like — you know — the old poem."

He opened his door as Annabel opened hers.

Then he looked back at her and smiled. "We loved with a love . . ."

They stared at each other for a moment they both let linger, that neither knew how to end or extend, so they said good night and closed the doors to their separate rooms.

Once inside, Annabel collapsed on the bed. She felt the softness of the downy comforter. She wrapped herself in its warmth as she stared up at the ceiling and whispered, ". . . that was more than love."

ACKNOWLEDGMENTS

I've described this book as my *big box of crayons.*

I'm talking about the sixty-four-count carton with the built-in sharpener. That box was my weapon of choice as a weird, creative child. My wax-based arsenal from which I created alien spaceships, dinosaur-filled zoos, and caped superheroes who flew across the page and occasionally the walls of my bedroom. My wall art would inevitably be followed by a drawing of my angry mother, pulling out her hair. (A drawing that she would still put on the fridge next to my other, more celebrated eight-year-old scribblings.)

Speaking of crayons, the colors have changed since we were children. Sure, there's still the red, green, orange, and blue that you remember. But there's also —

brace yourself — Macaroni and Cheese, Wisteria, Tickle Me Pink, Pet Shop, Outer Space, Neon Carrot, Koala Tree, Unmellow Yellow, Timberwolf, and Grandma's Perfume.

Yes, there's actually a crayon called Grandma's Perfume. I have no idea what color it is in real life, but the name certainly brightens your imagination, doesn't it?

That's what I set out to do with this book. I wanted to use all of my colors to draw a story, with the old and the new, the familiar and the unfamiliar. To create a word-picture with as much wonder and possibility as history and remembrance.

In the process of writing, I broke a lot of crayons. But there were countless people who encouraged me, inspired me, educated me, tolerated me, and otherwise cheered me on, or left me alone as I stared into space, daydreaming.

I owe so much to so many.

There's Megan Stielstra, whose essays have aptly been described as lifelines. Megan's work cuts so deep it was unsurprising how she was able to diagnose my writer's block with surgical precision. She said, "It's okay to divorce yourself from the expectations of others. Let go of all that and get back to writing what *you* want to write about." That's what she may have said, but all I heard was, "Stop eating your crayons."

Then there are the artist residency programs that provided shelter from the storm:

Ragdale in Lake Forest, Illinois. I stayed in the room where the founder, poet Alice Judson Hayes, passed away in 2006. People call it the *lucky room.* It certainly was for me, because that's where a twelve-page synopsis poured out of my head and my heart and became the book you're now holding.

Also, for not laughing too much when I accidentally set off a smoke alarm and the fire department showed up, I'm grateful for my delightful cohorts: Robin Ha, Megan Stielstra (there she is again), Katherine Weissman, Christina Askounis, Rita Dragonette, Meredith Leich, Lily Hawkings, and Sophia Lin.

UCROSS in Sheridan County, Wyoming. UCROSS isn't a town, it's a bucolic unincorporated community with a burgeoning population of twenty-five. When I arrived, I had a bottle of Scotch, a handful of pages, but no publisher. When I left I had a two-book deal, half a novel, and a new home for my imaginary friends.

For their support and for trekking with me to the Occidental Saloon in Buffalo, I'm missing my dance partners right now: Noah Green, Shannon Stewart, Jamie Harrison, Christina McPhee, Tallmadge Doyle, Lee Running, Theresa Booth Brown, Hannah Novak, Jody Kuehner, and Marlys West.

Yaddo in Saratoga Springs, New York. I lived many lifetimes in the two months that I stayed at this venerated art colony. I occupied the room where the founder, writer Katrina Trask, passed away in 1922. Out of respect, I kept a stack of books she had authored on my desk. I don't believe in ghosts, but I *believe* in believing in ghosts, and while I didn't see any wandering spirits, I did hear the laughter.

For sneaking into the mansion late at night, for breaking out the Ouija board, for dashing to the liquor store (and once to the ER), for surviving the nor'easter that snapped trees and cut power for days, for the hike by moonlight, for the karaoke night, for the candlelight vigil at Katrina's grave, and for the all-you-can-eat feast of creative spirit, I will never forget: Beena Kamlani (Head Nut), Maeve D'Arcy, CJ Hauser, Erick Hernandez, Joshua Riedel, Karan Kandhari, Kylie Heidenheimer, Ru Freeman, Tatyana Tennenbaum, Krish Raghav (who also heard the laughter), Luba Drozd, Karen Tepaz, Mike Albo, Toni Ross, Sheila O'Connor, Steve Bellin-Oka, Spencer Reece, McCallum Smith, Steve Snowden, Mmgkosi Anita Tau, Carrie Fertig, Sigrid Rausing, and "the twins" Ryan Pfeiffer and Rebecca Walz.

Then there's the research.

For their work, their articles, their books, their experiments, and their examples, I am beholden to the following individuals and organizations regarding:

Epigenetics
Brian Dias and Kerry Ressler for their groundbreaking work at Emory University that showed how mice inherit fear from their parents, to which Marcus Pembry, emeritus professor of pediatric genetics at University College London, said, "It is high time public health researchers took human

transgenerational responses seriously." Laura Hercher, the director of research, Human Genetics at Sarah Lawrence College, put it more succinctly, calling it, "Crazy Lamarckian shit." (Lamarckism is a theory explored in the 1800s that suggests that organisms pass on to their offspring physical characteristics that the parent organism acquired during its lifetime.)

Dora L. Costa, Noelle Yetter, and Heather DeSomer, whose work on intergenerational transmission added more evidence suggesting that our parents' and grandparents' experiences affect our DNA. Their studies explored how trauma among US Civil War prisoners was passed down to their children and how a father's stress, nutrition, and mental health can affect his son's lifespan. (Thanks, Dad.)

Rachel Yehuda, who led a research team at New York's Mount Sinai Hospital regarding genetic changes stemming from the traumas suffered by Holocaust survivors and how one person's life experiences can affect subsequent generations. Yehuda also did research that showed how pregnant 9/11 survivors transmitted trauma to their children.

Adding fuel to this fire is the pioneering work of neuroscientists Steve Ramirez (The Ramirez Group) and the late Xu Liu. While at MIT they used optogenetics to implant a false memory into a lab animal. (You may want to read that sentence again.) Their work suggests that instead of using cognitive-behavioral therapy or drugs to treat depression, dementia, and PTSDs, in the not-so-distant future, scientists may be manipulating memories or performing memory surgery. Their work is literally mind-altering.

For further exploration (until neuroscientists can implant memories of these books into your brain) I suggest reading *The Body Keeps the Score* by Dr. Bessel van der Kolk, *It Didn't Start with You* by Mark Wolynn, and watching NOVA's *Memory Hackers* episode about engrams, editing memories, and deleting fears. As a fun adjunct, you can also explore *How to Change Your Mind* by Michael Pollan, with or without psychedelics.

If that wasn't enough to break your brain or at least give you a headache, listen to the presentations of Lee Bitsoi, Navajo, PhD Research Associate in Genetics at Harvard, who discusses how epigenetics is uncovering proof of intergenerational trauma. When speaking about how trauma is woven into the DNA of Indigenous peoples, Bitsoi said, "Native healers, medicine people and elders have always known this and it is common knowledge in Native oral traditions."

That's just the tip of the epigenetic iceberg.

When it comes to the study of heritable phenotypes, there's so much more to explore and learn. But if transgenerational epigenetic inheritance works as described in *Scientific American,* perhaps the DNA methylation of one of my grandchildren will be affected by my choices and life experiences and they'll grow up with preprogrammed inclinations to write fiction, or study genetics. Or just sing really bad karaoke songs.

ARkStorms

A century ago, Seattleites could go ice-skating on Green Lake. Now as I write this, they're recovering from their hottest summer on record. You can argue the root causes of climate change all you want, but as the philosopher Robert Zimmerman once said, "You better start swimming or you'll sink like a stone, for the times they are a-changing."

With that song ringing in my ears, I'm grateful for the United States Geological Survey (USGS) and their Multi Hazards Demonstration Project, which was as inspiring as it was distressing. Their study explored the atmospheric phenomenon of ARkStorms — typhoons that are carried across the Pacific Ocean to the Western Coast of the US.

It's believed that California's Great Flood of 1862 was caused by an ARkStorm. Whatever you want to call it, that tempest generated as much as 120 inches of rain over a ten-day period. Then there's the Columbus Day Windstorm of 1962, when Typhoon Freda crossed the Pacific and became an extratropical cyclone that lashed the coasts of Oregon, Washington, and British Columbia with sustained winds of 110 miles per hour. More recently, in 2016, Typhoon Songda took a ride on the jet stream and moved perilously close to the Pacific Northwest, prompting the cancelation of ferries, the closure of airports, and the opening of 325 emergency shelters.

Do you know the difference between hurricanes, typhoons, and cyclones? If you live in the Pacific Northwest, don't worry, I suspect you'll eventually find out.

Buddhism

Years ago, I ran into a young man named Timber Hawkeye at The Bookworm in Camarillo, California. At the time, I didn't know he was the author of *Faithfully Religionless* and had 500,000 fans on social media. He just had a peaceful, thoughtful affect, and a cool T-shirt that read: BUDDHIST BOOTCAMP. NON-JUDGMENT DAY IS NEAR. Suddenly he had 500,001 fans.

Timber once said, "By no longer identifying as victims of the past, we are empowered to change the future." I pondered that along with my own understanding of epigenetics and wondered how inherited trauma might be reconciled by rerembering the past. I also wondered how changing the past would affect the philosophical concept of karma.

I took my questions about the confluence of karma and intergenerational trauma to Jason Wirth, doctor of philosophy at Seattle University, and Soto Zen priest.

When I first met Jason, it was at Seattle's Kubota Garden. He asked about my faith and I cheekily said, "I'm a deist, agnostic, Shinto, Jesuit — a little bit of everything, with the option to change my beliefs as I discover new things along the way." To which Jason smiled gently and said, "I think that means you're a Buddhist." He may be right.

Jason and Timber were both incredibly patient with my coarse, unenlightened questions about Buddhism, karma, fate, and both entertained my abstract thoughts about epigenetics. My discussions with them were educational, enlightening, and edifying. I'm grateful for their kindness and the avenues of thought they opened up for me.

The Nonfiction Beneath the Fiction

In the process of writing this novel I consumed countless books, articles, and interviews for research, and there were some that I'm particularly appreciative of. These are the books that were not only educational, but were an absolute pleasure to read. Books that I thoroughly enjoyed while getting to pretend that I was "working" were:

The Chinese Lady: Afong Moy in Early America by Nancy E. Davis and Lloyd Suh's stage play, *The Chinese Lady*. One is nonfiction, the other fiction. Both were completely absorbing. Afong, you have not been forgotten!

The Flying Tigers: The Untold Story of the American Pilots Who Waged a Secret War Against Japan by Sam Kleiner. This was a fascinating encapsulation of a less understood, less appreciated, chapter of WWII. My great-uncles, both Chinese Americans, worked with the AVG. Perhaps someday their story will be known as well.

Summerhill: A Radical Approach to Child Rearing by A. S. Neill. Before there were alternative high schools, there was the audacious idea of Summerhill. Founded in the twenties, this maverick school in England is still going strong today — a democratic community celebrating nonauthoritarianism and genuine freedom. Oh, how I wish I had gone there as a child.

Plague, Fear, and Politics in San Francisco's Chinatown by Guenter B. Risse, and *The Barbary Plague: The Black Death in Victorian San Francisco* by Marilyn Chase. It was an eerie, head-shaking experience to write about a highly politicized epidemic in the past, in the middle of a highly politicized global pandemic in the present. As the saying goes, the more things change, the more they stay the same, and tragically, the more people die.

Then there are these bits of nonfiction that were inspiring. One deserves its own book (and a box of Kleenex for the accompanying tears), the other needs some venture capital.

First is the true story of Huang Huanxio. When young Chinese women of her age were getting married, Huanxio went to college, became a nurse, and was working in Hong Kong when the British colony fell to the Japanese in 1941. Because she spoke English, she was assigned to work with the Flying Tigers at Yunnanyi, where she became known as Rita Wong. The only Chinese nurse working at the hospital near the airfield, she fell in love with an American aviator who vowed to come back for her after the war. Tragically, because she spoke English, Rita was singled out for harsh punishment in the Cultural Revolution and was beaten so badly her back was broken. She survived, married, and spent the next six decades in Kunming before passing away in 2007 at age 95. A cousin later produced a cache of love letters from the pilot, postmarked 1946. The letters had been hidden from Rita. Not only had the pilot returned to China, he went to Rita's hometown in search of her, but was unable to locate the nurse who had captured his heart.

The other bit of inspiration was Siren, a real-life feminist dating app launched in Seattle in 2015 by artist and entrepreneur Susie Lee and Katrina Hess. Upon its debut, their unique creation was named GeekWire's App of the Year. What's more impressive, after one year of operation, Siren was the only dating app to report zero online harassers. No misogynistic creeps. No unsolicited photos of strangers' penises. But by 2017, having run out of future funding, Lee and Hess were forced to close their digital doors for good, and apps with deeper pockets, like Bumble, took over the marketplace.

While Siren had no real-life, misogynistic investor lurking in the wings as depicted in the chapters about Greta and Syren, a 2021 report on "Diversity in U.S. Startups" showed that venture capitalists are still funding entrepreneurs who are mostly white, mostly male. VC-backed startups, as of this writing, are 89.3% male and 71.6% white. And that's an *improvement* over previous years. Why do I mention this?

Because Susie Lee and Katrina Hess are Asian American women at the top of their game and still struggled to sustain enough funds to keep their successful company afloat. But hey, if you're an altruistic billionaire and you're reading this, I can put you in touch.

Poetry

In the film *Pretty Woman,* Richard Gere says, "People's reaction to opera the first time they see it is very dramatic. They love it or hate it. If they love it, they will always love it. If they don't, they may learn to appreciate it, but it will never become part of their soul."

That's how I feel about poetry and why I couldn't help but give shoutouts to Wendell Berry, Samuel Taylor Coleridge, Edgar Allan Poe, Nikki Giovanni, Rupi Kaur, Yukio Mishima, Eva Gore-Booth, Felicia Hemans, Ezra Pound, Anne Sexton, Gertrude Stein, Oscar Wilde, Sylvia Plath, Li Bai, Andrea Gibson, and Anis Mojgani.

Those last two are most dear to me.

I did a gig one summer in Oregon with Anis and fellow poet Cameron Scott. We trekked to town, in search of donuts, if I remember correctly. Then we raced back along Wallowa Lake and in a moment of spontaneity, pulled the car over, stripped down, jumped in the water, swam around, then got dressed and arrived at our event just in time. I stood at the podium, my hair dripping wet, feeling so present and so alive. Though I suppose those feelings could have been a by-product of jumping into an ice-cold lake in your underwear.

But that's what the spoken word magic of Anis and Andrea Gibson does for me.

In fact, the stethoscope scene in this novel between Faye and John Garland was inspired by one of Andrea Gibson's incredible performances. I saw them live in Green Bay and they recounted this hilarious and heartmelting tale:

"So, we're about to kiss for the very first time. And right before our lips touch, she jumps from the bed, runs to the closet and grabs a stethoscope, puts the ear thingies in my ears and slides the knob down her shirt onto her heart and says, 'I want you to listen to my heart speed up when you kiss me.' And I kissed her! And her heart got faster and faster y'all. Moral of the story, buy a stethoscope."

Seriously, go see Anis and Andrea perform live. Read their work. It's like a system upgrade for your heart.

While we're talking about racing heartbeats, you might notice that this book was published by Atria, which I'm told is plural for "a place where things grow and flourish." But the word *atria* itself also refers to chambers of the heart. I suspect that's why this particular division of Simon & Schuster is such an ideal fit for yours truly, and why I'm so happy to be working with Libby McGuire once again.

Finally, there is the triumvirate of my writing life.

My über-agent, Kristin Nelson, whom I have been with since day one and whom I will be with at day zero, when all books are James Patterson novels written by computers.

My amazing new editor, Lindsay Sagnette. When I was looking for a new home for this book I reached out to my original editor, Jane von Mehren, for advice. She had become an agent and while visiting with Jane in New York City she said, "I know this fantastic editor. Her name is Lindsay Sagnette and I think she would be a perfect match." Months later there was an auction for this book and the winner was none other than Lindsay. But let's be honest, *I'm the real winner here.* Thank you, Lindsay, for believing in me.

My marvelous wife, Leesha, with her Red Pen of Destiny. I once posted photos of manuscript pages that she had read and marked up. The response on social media was, "OMG! JAMIE'S WIFE TOOK HIM TO THE WOODSHED!" But it's always been love. Tough love, when I needed it most.

Okay, time to sharpen some more crayons.

Jamie Ford
Montana
September 2021

ABOUT THE AUTHOR

Jamie Ford is the great-grandson of Nevada mining pioneer Min Chung, who emigrated from Hoiping, China to San Francisco in 1865, where he adopted the western name Ford, thus confusing countless generations. His debut novel, *Hotel on the Corner of Bitter and Sweet,* spent two years on the *New York Times* bestseller list and went on to win the 2010 Asian/Pacific American Award for Literature. His work has been translated into thirty-five languages. Having grown up in Seattle, he now lives in Montana with his wife and a one-eyed pug.